PRAISE FOR *TURNED*

"If you're looking for a hot, sexy, emotional read, Virna DePaul delivers!"
—J. KENNER, *New York Times* and *USA Today* bestselling author of *Release Me*

"With *Turned*, Virna DePaul delivers a sexy and exciting new take on the vampire novel, one that comes complete with a kick-ass heroine and a to-die-for hero. I can't wait for the sequel!"
—Tracy Wolff, *New York Times* bestselling author of *Ruined*

"A captivating start to a fascinating new series with a hero who's to die for!"
—Nationally bestselling author RHYANNON BYRD

"Virna DePaul creates yummy alpha heroes, relatable heroines, and supercharged emotional plots. Run, don't walk, to snatch up one of her stories."
—*New York Times* bestselling author TINA FOLSOM

"*Turned* is intense, intricate, and insomnia-inducing (plan to stay up way too late!). Virna DePaul puts the awesome in the awesomesauce of paranormal romance."
—Joyce Lamb, curator, *USA Today*'s *Happy Ever After*

PRAISE FOR THE NOVELS OF VIRNA DEPAUL

"Seducer and protector—this vampire has it all."
—*Fresh Fiction,* on *A Vampire's Salvation*

"Virna DePaul is amazing!"
—*New York Times* bestselling author LORI FOSTER

"Incredibly well written, different, and hot."
—*New York Times* bestselling author LARISSA IONE

"A gripping tale! DePaul creates the perfect blend of danger, intrigue, and romance. You won't be able to put this book down!"
—*New York Times*
bestselling author BRENDA NOVAK

"If you have not yet started this [Para-Ops] series . . . you are really missing out."
—*The Book Reading Gals*

"This is my first book by Virna DePaul and it will definitely not be my last. *Deadly Charade* is a suspenseful story full of love, betrayal, and forgiveness."
—*Fresh Fiction,* on *Deadly Charade*

"Intense, emotionally charged, and thrilling."
—*Fresh Fiction,* on *Shades of Desire*

"DePaul's romantic suspense has shades of a thriller inside the pages, with damaged characters, love scenes that make the pages almost too hot to handle and hair-raising villains."
—*RT Book Reviews,* on *Shades of Desire*

"Plenty of chemistry between the leads—along with edge-of-your-seat suspense—will keep you riveted."
—*RT Book Reviews,* on *Shades of Passion*

"DePaul offers up an intriguing world rife with moral dilemmas and mistrust."
—*Publishers Weekly,* on *Chosen by Blood*

"Seriously sensual! The sexual tension leaps off the page. DePaul has made a name for herself with paranormal fans who aren't shy when it comes to titillating dialogue and interaction."
—*RT Book Reviews,* on *Chosen by Blood*

AWAKENED

BY VIRNA DEPAUL

Turned
Awakened

A Vampire's Salvation
Arrested by Love

AWAKENED

THE BELLADONNA AGENCY SERIES

VIRNA DEPAUL

BANTAM BOOKS
NEW YORK

A Bantam Books Mass Market Original

Copyright © 2014 by Virna DePaul
Excerpt from *Turned* by Virna DePaul copyright © 2014 by Virna DePaul

Published in the United States by Bantam Books, an imprint of Random House, a division of Random House LLC, a Penguin Random House Company, New York.

BANTAM BOOKS and the HOUSE colophon are registered trademarks of Random House LLC.

ISBN 978-0-345-54247-2
eBook ISBN 978-0-345-54248-9

Cover design: Lynn Andreozzi
Cover photograph: Claudio Marinesco

Printed in the United States of America

www.bantamdell.com

9 8 7 6 5 4 3 2 1

Bantam Books mass market edition: July 2014

For Craig. Love you, baby. For always and forever.

PROLOGUE

"Do it." Gary Maltese winced at how animalistic his voice sounded, but forced himself to continue. "Please."

"I can't!" Nick grated out. "Damn it, don't ask me to. We can find another way. We can find a cure—"

"No cure," he snapped, then, because that made his head hurt, he whispered, "No cure for me. No cure—" His body jerked as he was overcome by racking coughs. The blisters on his lips cracked and oozed. "It's too late for that," he managed to choke out. "Do it before the rage takes me again. Do it now!"

Silence. Struggle. Grief. It swirled around him, as heavy and suffocating as a humid North Carolina summer.

Home.

He longed to be back there. He should never have left. Not after he'd returned from the war.

But he'd wanted purpose again. He'd wanted to prove he was still a man. Still strong. Still capable of serving his country.

Like Nick . . .

Nick.

He stared into the face as familiar as his own. On some level, he knew what he was asking wasn't fair. Not fair.

But he didn't care.

He *hurt*. He hungered.

Not for food but for human blood.

His flesh was literally rotting away and the same was happening to his mind.

With each episode, fit, delusion, it became harder and harder to remember his own name, let alone who he'd once been. He wanted to die while some part of him was still intact.

Gary Maltese. Soldier. Son.

Brother.

He lifted a hand and reached out. For a moment, his flesh hung there, ignored. His fingers shook and he cursed his weakness. Cursed the fact he couldn't even hold up his fucking hand anymore. Not until the rage overcame him again and adrenaline pumped through his blood along with insanity. Then he'd regain his strength. Then even Nick might not be able to help him.

It was coming. He could feel it . . .

He was still himself, but he was someone else, too. Someone who'd killed, and not just to protect his country. He'd *seen* what he'd done. The women. God, *the kids*. The blood. The memories lingered in his mind, tormenting him further. Driving out all traces of the honorable man he'd been.

All traces . . . all traces . . . all traces . . .

But for the here and now.

Strong, warm fingers wrapped around his own and he knew this was it. His last chance.

"Please, brother. Look into my eyes. See what I've done. See what I *need*. Do it for me, just like you always promised. Take care of me."

He and Nick locked gazes.

He heard the whimper that melded with his own.

He felt the rod pierce his heart.

He saw his life flash before his eyes, years of pleasure and pain, hope and despair, brotherhood and loneliness.

These final moments, however, were bliss. He was going home . . .

But before he got there, he spoke his final words.

"Thank you."

CHAPTER ONE

San Diego, California

The lurid caption under the live video said it all: Runaway Virgin.

Unlike the other women on the SexFlash site, this one was scrubbed clean of makeup. With an odd beauty and youthful innocence, she'd attract clients with money to burn and a lot to hide. The kind of clients who'd get off on the fact that the girl's lips were parted with fear and shock, the same emotions currently ricocheting through Barrett Miles's body.

She'd been searching for Jane Small for almost a week, but to actually succeed in finding her . . . to actually confirm she'd been taken by sex traffickers, never mind sex traffickers that catered to vampires or were vampires themselves . . .

After everything Barrett had been through in the past decade—her brother Noah's death, what she'd seen overseas, what she'd discovered since she'd been recruited by Belladonna—well, she'd have thought she'd be immune to horror by now. Apparently not.

Before she could stop herself, Barrett pressed her fingertips against the monitor screen, as if she could actually reach in and pull Jane out to safety. Help her. Kill her captors. But how?

The only information she'd had up to now was that

Jane had disappeared, and her aunt, her legal guardian, believed she'd run away with a young man Jane had recently befriended. A young man named Dante who wore a vial filled with Jane's blood around his neck and liked to leave marks on her that were closer to bites than to hickeys. A young man who had disappeared around the same time as Jane, only he'd been found days later with his neck torn out and "wannabe" penned on his forehead with a red Sharpie. Of course, given Dante's predilections and knowing what she did, Barrett had instantly suspected a vampire had murdered the boy and taken Jane.

Unfortunately, Jane could be anywhere. Teenagers were sold for sex on sites like this all over the world. Virgins went for premium prices.

Purity mattered. That went double as far as vampires were concerned. According to Joseph Powell, the blood of a virgin was the best there was. It tasted like nirvana. It provided a euphoric high no controlled substance could come close to duplicating.

Apparently, despite her association with the dead fang banger and true to her ideals when she'd been fourteen, Jane was still a virgin, though Barrett hated to think how her captors had confirmed that fact. It was why Jane was probably going to be some vampire junkie's fix for the rest of her life unless Barrett could save her. Unfortunately, it was Barrett's fault the girl was in this predicament in the first place.

All because this girl's mother had trusted Barrett to keep her daughter safe.

The last time Barrett had seen her, Jane had been fourteen.

Though she'd kept intermittent contact with Jane's legal guardians, the aunt and her husband, Barrett hadn't seen Jane's face again until she'd gone missing and her aunt had given her an updated picture.

Jane's eyes flickered on the clear screen and seemed to round with recognition. "Miley?"

Barrett jerked and instinctively opened her mouth to respond.

Instead, she snapped it shut, forcing herself to remain silent so she wouldn't give herself away even as Jane was roughly jerked out of the camera's range.

Barrett Miles. *Miley.* It was the nickname Jane had given her years ago thanks to a popular Disney show actress. That meant she could see her. But why would her captors allow that? They had to believe there was absolutely no chance allowing Jane to see her potential buyers could hurt them. That had to mean those potential buyers were trusted. Vetted.

Barrett didn't fall into that category.

A woman in an overflowing bustier took Jane's place on the monitor screen.

This one knew the drill. Sultry pout. Thick black hair teased high. Hard eyes. She frowned at Barrett for a moment. "Powell, who the hell is this?" she snapped. "The girl called her Miley."

"No, no. This is my trusted friend, Barrett Klein. Don't worry about her. We are looking for someone special and I think we've found her."

Powell's deep voice came from just behind Barrett, causing her to stiffen slightly. She'd almost forgotten he was there, looking over her shoulder. Waiting, with a born vampire's patience, for her to choose a girl she liked enough to bring into the bedroom with them.

The image of his gnarled hands on Jane made Barrett sick to her stomach. It was a feeling she was intimately acquainted with. It was how she felt every time Powell put his hands on her.

"Yes." Aware the woman on the screen still looked suspicious but also slightly mollified by the thought of a potential sale, Barrett pasted a smile on her face. "Let's go with the . . . virgin. I think she'll be perfect and you said you haven't tasted virgin blood in quite some time."

"Hmm. It won't make you jealous? Knowing how incomparably delicious I'll find her?"

More delicious than me, he meant. And the fact he could joke with her meant he didn't understand how displeased Jane's captor was that he'd signed on to the site then allowed Barrett in to see Jane. Then again, as a born vampire he'd be very difficult to hurt or kill so he probably wouldn't be worried anyway.

Barrett looked up at the silver-haired man behind her; unlike most vampires, he didn't bother dyeing his hair, although he did wear contacts that disguised his silver pupils. His tall frame was slightly stooped and his large head hung forward. He reminded her of a vulture.

"She can give you better blood. I think we've already established that I, on the other hand, give the best . . ." She smiled suggestively.

Powell studied Barrett for a moment, assessing her. His eyes glowed briefly, an unearthly gleam in their unnaturally dark depths, making her wonder if he was trying to read her mind. But she felt none of the mental probing she'd been warned to watch out for. Maybe he wasn't trying. Or maybe he couldn't read her mind because he wasn't powerful enough or because the heavy gold bracelet on her wrist was doing its job. Concealed, of course, inside a designer cuff of glass-beaded silk.

That was just one of the nifty secrets Belladonna had uncovered about vampires: wearing pure high-quality gold blocked a vampire from reading not only a human's mind, but that of another vampire. Neither Barrett nor her fellow Belladonna agents, each covertly employed by the FBI to hunt down vampire criminals in a world where most humans didn't even know vampires were real, left home without it.

Not all vampires knew about the gold trick, but since

some humans had a natural resistance to being read, they often didn't make the connection. In Powell's case, it was entirely possible he suspected she was deliberately blocking his mind-reading powers and was only biding his time until he strip-searched her and killed her.

She sincerely hoped that wasn't the case.

He *did* seem to trust her, which meant he had no clue Belladonna existed, or that Barrett's team members, Ty Duncan and Ana Martin, had been responsible for shutting down Salvation's Crossing, a vampire blood slave operation in Northern California, two months ago. That could change at any moment, however, and Barrett's best chance of getting Jane home safe was by getting Powell to buy her.

"Powell," she prompted, keeping her voice soft. Cajoling. "I want her."

He smiled. Kissed the top of Barrett's head and reached down from behind her, sliding his hand down between her breasts and then in between her thighs. It was about as intimately as he ever touched her. She'd never actually had sex with him—a small distinction, considering the other things she had to do, but an important one for her. Her salvation—his inability to keep it up for anyone who was older than a teen—was also a curse for what was undoubtedly a long list of young victims.

He whispered, "We'll see."

Then, even as Barrett wanted to shout out and stop him, he tapped a key and the monitor went black.

"Now," he said, "show me how much you want her. Maybe then I'll buy her for you." As a vampire, he couldn't lie, which meant there was a chance he actually might buy Jane for her, even if it was only a small one. She tilted her head, offering herself to him. He kissed her neck, licked it, and Barrett instinctively braced herself for his bite.

She still jumped when it came. She had no fear Powell

would take enough blood from her to turn her into one
of his own kind. From what Belladonna had learned before Ty and Ana's infiltration of Salvation's Crossing,
doing so would result in his own death. Even so, she still
felt the swirling nausea that always overtook her when
she let him drink her blood. The nausea that signaled
her disgust for him and herself.

Closing her eyes, she forced herself to remain calm.
She even managed to moan with what sounded like a
decent imitation of pleasure.

Inside, however, Barrett's nausea was swiftly morph-
ing into hatred. Hatred for the vampire who still drank
from her throat. Hatred for the brunette helping to pimp
Jane out. Hatred for the unnamed, faceless others out in
the world who were doing the very same thing to hundreds of girls just like Jane.

Hatred for herself.

Jane Small was about to be sold.

Barrett needed to convince Powell to buy her before
anyone else did. At the very least, to tell her how to find
the girl.

She had to. Nothing else mattered.

Belladonna Headquarters
Washington, D.C.

The morning after seeing Jane Small's face on Powell's
computer screen, Barrett caught a flight to Dulles. Hours
later, weary and frazzled, she slammed her palms onto
the table inside Belladonna's library. Special Agent Peter
Lancaster's expression remained impassive, although he
had to be surprised by Barrett's rare show of emotion.

Desperation crackled inside her like electricity trapped
inside a bulb, straining for release.

Several months ago, she'd been just like every other

human on the planet—with no clue that vampires really existed and lived among them. That had changed soon after Peter had recruited her for Belladonna. Now Barrett was only one of a select few who knew that the FBI was engaged in the experimental turning of human military veterans into vampires. As far as the FBI was concerned, vampires were a potential threat despite their queen's claim that they wanted to exist peacefully with humans. According to FBI Director Rick Hallifax, the best way to counter that threat was by fighting fire with fire, or in this case, vampire with vampire. In theory, his strategy made sense, but creating vampire soldiers that would be loyal to the U.S. government was proving to be a challenging task for several reasons.

First, turning humans was against vampire law and morality; thus, the only vampires that were willing to turn humans into vampires were thugs and criminals. Second, the fact the turner might die as a result of the turning process made it highly probable that vampires were victimizing other vampires to do what the FBI wanted. Hallifax claimed there was no proof of such machinations and that even if there was, it would amount to collateral damage. Third, even as the Turning Program continued, the FBI needed to track down and eliminate the subset of vampire criminals that were exceeding the FBI's authority and preying on humans. The FBI had labeled these vampires Rogues and formed Belladonna to deal with them. Fourth, as Ty and Ana had learned on their mission into Salvation's Crossing, someone knew about Belladonna and had enough insider information to set up Ty and Ana, resulting in Ana being forcibly turned herself. Now she and Ty were in hiding; their betrayer was still out there and it was always possible that person could be an FBI mole.

No one at Belladonna knew whom to trust, but they'd had no choice but to keep moving forward, keeping their suspicions a secret, taking advantage of whatever resources and intel the FBI did provide, and following up leads on Rogue criminal activity. Barrett was taking the lead on the sex ring intel, while Collette and Justine worked on a variety of new developments in other areas of vampire crime. Collette had begun a complex investigation into the billion-dollar business of fake pharmaceuticals, focusing on blood products. Justine was staying with the field she knew: women who were in the business of voluntarily selling their bodies, figuratively or literally. Peter, the only other turned vampire in the group, stayed at Belladonna headquarters as their point person and direct link to Carly, Belladonna's mysterious CEO.

Unfortunately, Peter wasn't giving her anything at the moment that could help her, and that was making Barrett's panic rise. Despite her reiterating her request that he buy Jane for her, Powell had refused, saying the asking price was far beyond his means. Which, given how rich Powell was, meant Jane was a valuable commodity indeed. He'd also refused to reveal anything about the people who ran SexFlash or how he'd met them. She'd been afraid to push for more lest she drew Powell's suspicions and lost her ability to gather any information at all on vampire sex rings, but . . .

"Don't tell me you've come up with nothing, Peter! We work for the FBI and you're telling me no one can track down a sex ring site when I've given them the freaking URL?"

Despite his turned vampire status, Peter was tall and slim with light brown hair, chiseled features, and a smile that was potent when he chose to use it. He didn't try to charm her now so much as calm her.

"You gave us the URL Powell let you see, Barrett, and clearly someone has swept that trail clean. Without more . . ."

A flash of anger blotted out her other thoughts. What did he mean by "more"? More than what?

More than befriending a blood-sucking pedophile like Powell? More than letting him drink from her? More than doing sneak searches of his place on multiple occasions, risking discovery and death, only to come up empty time and again?

How much more did she have to give before she caught a break?

Anything and everything, she reminded herself. She'd been willing to put her life on the line numerous times to rescue victims she didn't know. She'd damn well do the same for Jane.

"I'll go back to Powell's," she choked out. "Convince him to buy Jane."

"Powell is gone. Might be dead, for all we know," Peter said. "His house has been cleared out."

Barrett's body jerked, not in surprise but in despair. She'd known Powell had pissed off the brunette. She'd suspected they might retaliate. But not so fast. Not before Barrett could get something—*anything*—out of him that might help her rescue Jane. "How?" she choked out.

He shrugged. "We have no idea. All we know is that a moving company showed up a few hours after you left yesterday and took his belongings to the flea market."

She put a hand to her forehead. "Powell made a mistake by letting Jane's captor see me. Whoever runs Sex-Flash took care of the problem, rerouting the site and 'relocating' Powell. If they got to him so soon after I was with him . . ."

Peter said nothing but he didn't have to. It was there in his eyes. The brunette had seen Barrett through the webcam. What if she'd had her trailed after she left Powell's? Granted, Barrett always followed the evasive techniques Peter and Ty had taught them to ensure no one followed her, but she was still new at all the secret-agent bullshit.

"He was my only lead to Jane," she choked out.

Her gaze focused on the intercom placed strategically near Barrett's leather armchair. Carly, Belladonna's leader, usually ran the show, so why hadn't she spoken yet? None of Belladonna's recruited female agents—Barrett, Ana, Justine, and Collette—had ever spotted a hidden cam in this room. But that didn't mean there wasn't one. When Carly still didn't speak and Barrett again failed to find any sign of a hidden cam, she rubbed her eyes in frustration.

Maybe she'd been followed. Maybe not. In the end it didn't really matter. And even if the brunette's accomplices had rerouted the SexFlash site, they had to have left some bread crumbs behind. Tracing their steps couldn't be that hard. Not with the might of the U.S. government behind them. Unless . . .

Her head snapped up. "The possibility of an FBI mole. Do you think—"

"Until we know for sure, we keep our eyes open, and we do what we need to do. We're sworn to protect the citizens of this country. No sacrifice is too great."

"Some of us sacrifice more than others, Peter," she said in a low voice.

"Perhaps," he answered evenly. His dark eyes, which she knew were actually black with silver pupils underneath the contacts he wore, blazed for a moment, reminding her that he hadn't *sacrificed* his humanity—it had been viciously taken from him. He never whined or complained about it, and that fact suddenly made Barrett's cheeks flush with shame.

She sure as hell didn't like the feeling.

They all had their crosses to bear. She wasn't up to keeping score right now. Rallying, she lifted her chin.

"Do you mind telling me how we're supposed to keep

going if someone in the FBI is truly conspiring against us? The seven of us alone—five with Ty still helping Ana through her turning—with a traitor in our midst? What can we possibly accomplish?"

"We don't know there's a traitor. Not yet. For now, we use the resources we have, limited as they are."

His tone suggested they might be limited but that they also might surprise her. "Care to enlighten me?"

The intercom crackled as Carly finally decided to speak. "Nick Maltese is one such resource."

Shock made Barrett's eyes widen. Memories made her skin tingle and her heart clench with longing and regret. She and Nick Maltese had crossed paths just over two years ago in Eastern Europe, after Barrett joined the army. Barrett had been working as a liaison to women and children forced into refugee camps as a result of ongoing conflicts.

Her mind immediately zoomed back to the moment she'd first seen him.

Tall enough to make her feel short—and at five feet eight inches she wasn't—with broad shoulders that stretched his army-issue T-shirt to the max. Dark hair, regulation short, which he'd scrunched into spikes somehow. Dark eyes that just fucking did her in. And that smile. Blazing white and wide when he looked at her.

He'd turned toward her, as if alerted by some sixth sense that he was being watched. Before that, she'd had just enough time to let her gaze roam up and down, from his dusty boots to cargo-pocketed camo pants that hugged narrow hips she'd instantly wanted—*really* wanted—to get a grip on.

Later, she'd learned Nick was in the region as a high-ranking noncombatant—a flexible term that basically meant *you're whatever we want you to be, soldier*. Offi-cially in charge of clandestine tech operations. Not black ops. More like gray. But he'd trained as a sniper and he ranked as one of the best. Unofficially, that was also what he did. Undercover and under the radar.

One of his inventions was a computer-tracking system to help locate trafficked children and teenagers in war-torn countries. There had been no way to save all of them, but Nick had put his own life on the line to get into the worst brothels, once rescuing two young girls who were barely alive. He'd pulled strings at the highest level and personally flown the girls and their mother to asylum and safety.

When not heading up humanitarian rescues, he some-times took out the worst of the bad guys. Sanctioned kills, every one, never reported on either side of the con-flict, accomplished with terrifying precision. His as-signed targets were shadow killers themselves.

He was tenacious to a fault. Unbelievably intelligent. Arrogant as hell.

And so damn sexy, so damn *tender* when he'd wanted to be. He'd had the power to make Barrett forget her grief and her duty and simply want to be a woman, one who could take shelter in his arms. Of course, it because of those very feelings that she'd ended things between them. She'd *always* intended to end things. Being booted out of the army for failure to obey orders had simply speeded her decision along.

"How—how do you know that name?" she forced out, praying her shaky voice didn't give her away.

Instead of answering her, Carly said, "Peter, Ty's on line two. I'll talk to Barrett about Mr. Maltese."

"Of course," Peter said quietly. He left, but not before placing an encouraging hand on Barrett's shoulder. The gesture did nothing to reassure her.

"I apologize for joining the party late," Carly said. "Ty called just as you walked in, then so did Mahone."

"Is Ana all right?" Barrett asked, thinking of Ty's

lover, the woman she'd barely gotten to know before Ana had infiltrated the Crossing and been forced to kill her own sister, a turned vampire gone wrong.

God, sometimes Barrett couldn't believe this was actually her life.

"She's doing well. Ty says another month and they should be ready to join us again."

That was good, Barrett thought. She was glad Ana had Ty to help her through whatever hell she was going through.

The four female agents of Belladonna—Ana, Barrett, Justine, and Collette—had been strangers before their recruitment, linked unknowingly to each other by a single tragic day and the vagaries of fate.

Seven years ago, Barrett had lost her older brother, Noah, when a gang shoot-out had started outside the ice cream shop they'd been visiting. He'd wanted to go straight home after the movie they'd seen, but no, Barrett had insisted on stopping for dessert. He'd suffered a heart attack and because of the gang activity outside, the ambulance hadn't gotten to Noah in time to save him. Logically, Barrett knew Noah's death wasn't her fault any more than what had happened to Jane was. But emotionally . . .

Barrett rarely let herself care too much about others. Whenever she had, she'd suffered. Noah. Sarah. Nick. Now Jane.

No, it was far better to keep herself distant, because when she failed, when she couldn't protect what was hers to protect . . .

An unseen vise gripped her heart and Barrett automatically winced even as she laid her palm against her chest.

The pain of losing Noah had never gone away. She'd just gotten good at pretending it wasn't there. If she failed to save Jane, how much harder would the pain be to bear? What would stop her from collapsing under its weight completely?

But she wasn't the only one who'd suffered tragedy, she reminded herself. In fact, it was for that very reason that Carly had brought Barrett and the other female agents together. Justine's mother had died. Collette was dealing with some mysterious illness that could very well kill her. And Ana? Ana's bad luck had started the day she'd been born to a prostitute mother and had continued well after she'd been forced to join a gang to survive. Ana had been smack dab in the middle of the gang shoot-out that had contributed to Noah's death, and afterward she'd spent two years in prison only to subsequently lose her sister, the last close relative she had. She deserved some happiness and, despite the violent event that had turned Ana into a vampire, Barrett had no doubt Ty Duncan would provide it. Who knew, maybe the rest of them would find some happiness, as well. As for her? Barrett thought once again of Nick . . .

Of everyone who had brought her joy in her life only to leave her far too soon.

Then she remembered Jane and instantly stopped feeling sorry for herself.

"Nick," Barrett prompted. "How—?"

"You told us about him," Carly reminded her. "In your intake interview. You were lovers as well as fellow soldiers. And, I believe you parted on good terms after you were discharged?"

Good terms? On the surface, yes. They'd been fuck buddies. She'd encouraged the term even though she'd known he was far more than that to her—and they'd moved on after Barrett had returned to the States. Farewell and no hard feelings. At least, she'd played her part to make it seem so. But it had taken everything she'd had to walk away from him, and afterward, when she'd allowed herself to think of him, she'd *missed* him more than she'd ever thought possible. So much so that her heart ached just at the sound of his name.

"Yes, you could say that. So?" she forced herself to respond.

"Mahone remembered seeing his name when he reviewed your files. When Peter's attempts to track down the SexFlash URL got nowhere, Mahone figured you having a special relationship with a techno wiz might come in handy. He went searching for him . . . and unwittingly found a gold mine."

"What do you mean?" Barrett asked. She'd never actually met Special Agent Kyle Mahone before, but she knew the guy had spectacular contacts, including an "in" with Bianca Devereaux, the infamous Vampire Queen. That link had enabled him to obtain useful intel about vampires—like wearing gold to protect one's thoughts, and the fact that one could kill a turned vampire by stabbing him or her in the heart with a blade coated in liquid nitrogen.

It was because of that intel that they continued to fully trust Mahone even if the same couldn't be said for his superior, Director Rick Hallifax, or any other employee of the FBI.

"The details are sketchy. Mahone said he encountered security blocks he had a hard time bypassing, even with his clearance. But because Mahone's familiar with the Turning Program, and the lingo and the way the Bureau gets things done, he's put several pieces of information together. Looks like Maltese is doing contract work for the FBI right now."

"You mean software development? Some kind of vampire tracking program?" If anyone could do it, he could. The only things Nick had been better at than computers had been hot sex. And cold killing. She couldn't forget about that.

"That's not something Mahone was able to uncover

yet. But he's still digging," Carly replied, her voice tight. "Bottom line, it's very possible Nick Maltese has information you can use. If not, maybe he'll be motivated to help you find it."

Barrett could take a hint. And it wasn't lost on her that even as pimps and Rogue vampires were selling the bodies of girls like Jane to the highest bidder, Barrett had been, if not technically, at least essentially whoring herself for her country. But no regrets. Sex was just . . . sex. She'd learned long ago that men were willing to be led around by their dicks, and that she could take advantage of that to get what she needed.

Nick hadn't been her first or last lover, but he'd been her best. It would be no hardship to give herself to him again if it meant convincing him to help her. Hell, she'd jump at the opportunity if only to wash away the memory of Powell's touch. Only, Nick was a *good* man. She didn't think it would come to that.

Even as her body mourned that thought, her brain rejoiced. It had been hard enough barricading her heart against him the first time. Now that she was reeling from the events of the past few months and the guilt of failing Jane, she had to be especially on guard.

"Is Nick here in D.C.?" Barrett asked. Had they been living in the same city? Not likely that they'd have met by chance, but the way she'd felt when she'd been with him . . . some part of her should have known.

"Mahone's attempting to access the information even as we speak, Barrett. One moment."

Barrett sank back into the plush armchair. The furnishings of the house were meant to impress. Not her taste, but awfully familiar.

Her great-grandfather's fortune had multiplied many times over, but he and his descendants disliked show and put family first; a close second was service to one's country. Her mother had different ideas. She would have adored this old house.

Expensive carpets muffled every step. Dark velvet curtains framed mullioned windows. A gilt mirror across the room over an antique side table added a discreet touch of sparkle. Posh and somehow suffocating, the decor never failed to remind her of similar mansions on Philadelphia's exclusive Main Line. She'd grown up in one before her father died and her mother had remarried and moved with her stepfather to Palm Beach.

She picked up an *Architectural Digest* and flipped through it, half expecting to see them on the pages showing off their Florida ocean view or their pied-à-terre in Paris or their twenty-one-room Newport "cottage." No mentions in this issue, thankfully. She set the magazine back on the side table.

Now that Belladonna agents were past their initial training, they no longer lived at the Belladonna compound full time. Barrett "made do"—her mother's condescending term—with a sublet apartment in Crystal City, across the Potomac from Washington proper. It was all she needed. She rarely set foot in it and had chosen it because it was near the airport. Home had always been an abstract concept to her.

Standing, Barrett walked over to the mirror and straightened the jacket of her cream linen suit. Her blond, shoulder-length hair held the crisp straightness of its classic cut, a look that required minimal styling. Her throat was pale and unmarked by Powell's recent bite marks since she always insisted he lick the wounds closed before she left him. She looked subdued. Classy. Nothing like a woman who would fool around with a loathsome pedophile (vampire or not) in order to wheedle information out of him. Nothing like the passionate, uninhibited woman she'd been in Nick Maltese's arms.

Carly's voice crackled on the intercom again, prompting Barrett to return to her seat.

"I just texted you the info, including email and phone numbers. Nick's living on a mountaintop in Tennessee."

Barrett smiled. The mountains of Tennessee. Yes, that sounded like Nick. Smart and strong and sophisticated, but at heart a good ol' boy. A man's man.

As for emailing or calling him? No. Ascertaining whether he knew about vampires and what he was doing for the FBI? That was definitely something that had to be done in person. Assuming he'd even let her within twenty feet of him, that is. But why wouldn't he? They'd fucked. They'd parted ways. There should be no reason he wouldn't want to help her.

Even so, the thought of having to see Nick face-to-face was a double-edged sword. It would be a lot harder for Nick to refuse her if she was standing right in front of him. At the same time, she'd undoubtedly be swamped by ever-intensifying memories of what she and Nick had once shared.

Sex, yes, but more than that.

For her . . . affection. And intimacy.

For him . . . he'd been protective of her, no doubt. Too protective. It had been one of the major things they'd fought about. He'd encouraged her to give up military life and pursue something else she'd been passionate about before Noah had died—art. But even so, once he'd put on his camo pants and returned to being big bad Nick, he hadn't seemed interested in affection or intimacy. And she hadn't missed how easy it had been to compartmentalize her in his mind.

Didn't change the fact that their connection had been intense, for as long as it lasted. She didn't want to get close again no matter how much she needed him now. Back then she'd merely been vulnerable. Today, though she'd never admit it to anyone but herself, it sometimes took everything she had not to curl up into a ball and hide from the knowledge of what her life had become. That she was part of a world where the bad guys weren't just teenage gang members or fanatical dictators with vast armies to do their dirty work. A world where the FBI had authorized the turning of humans into vampires even as it kept that fact a secret. A world where Rogues, some of them the FBI's former allies, were exploiting humans for blood and sex and she was one of the people responsible for stopping them.

She was tired down to her bones and so badly needed to share her burden with someone. Why not with Nick?

She knew why.

Breaking up with Nick would hurt far worse if she had to do it again.

Finding Jane might be her first priority, but protecting her heart was a damn close second.

CHAPTER TWO

The road up Nick Maltese's mountain was clearly meant to keep people out, but right now there were two red dots moving on the surveillance scanner he'd patched into a satellite mapping feed. Nick studied them carefully. He wasn't expecting company, which meant at this very moment he could have two harmless humans, two dangerous humans, two vampires, two *supremely* dangerous vampires, or any combination heading his way.

That's what came from accepting a kill contract with the government, limited as it was. Especially given his targets were vampires.

In exchange, he had plenty of downtime between jobs and some much-needed privacy. Coming up here to develop and test new gear had been a sweet deal. Nick had been given the run of the mountain, which was all government property and still a source of some rare mineral Uncle Sam didn't want to privatize. The feds had been nice enough to slap some fresh concrete over the crumbling bunker at the summit, an abandoned World War II lookout for enemy planes. The slot windows didn't let in much light, but no one could use them to get in. He liked it fine. Per his request, some other improvements had been made.

Home sweet home. Fairly cozy for a fortress. Nick didn't much care where he lived as long as he had something challenging to occupy his time. Right now, he was developing specialized equipment for the FBI, supervising the training of search dogs by soldier Kevin Day, and most important, dealing with the things those dogs were being trained to find.

The list of turned vampires he was supposed to kill wouldn't take him that long to checkmark, especially because someone else was helping him track them.

Vampires. Not the kind in movies. Real ones. What a learning experience.

After he'd left the army, Nick's former commanding officer had set up a meeting between him and the FBI. Little did he know then that his record number of long-distance kills was only one of the reasons. Sworn to secrecy, he'd been briefed about vampires—both the born and the turned variety. Hardly anyone knew about them—anyone human, at least. But that could change, and soon.

At first, Nick hadn't wanted to believe it. But the thorough documentation he'd been repeatedly drilled on—and his required attendance at an autopsy of the ghastly remains of vampire victims, drained of every drop of blood—had been enough to convince him. The secret operation was critically important.

There were other ex-ops on similar missions throughout the United States. He didn't know any of them. He doubted that the name on his orders was any more real than the signature. If he went down, the FBI would protect itself, which probably meant denying any knowledge of the half-assed vampire-turning operation it had lost control of some time ago.

But the story hadn't ended there. Far from it. It had taken Nick months to learn the real story. That the bastards in Washington had worked with what were essentially vampire criminals to turn humans. And not just any humans, but military vets who'd been incapacitated, either physically or mentally, by war, but who still wanted to serve their country. Military vets like his brother, Gary, who in the end had begged Nick to kill him.

And Nick had done it. Now the FBI's Turning Program had been shut down, but the FBI still had *three* vampire enemies to worry about: 1) the born vampires who said they wanted to live in peace and remain hidden but refused to give up their secrets; 2) Rogue vampires, plenty of whom had once worked for the Bureau but were now becoming bolder in their criminal activity against humans; and 3) the turned vampires that the FBI had itself created and were now the victims of some kind of neuron-rage and had to be put down like sick, useless animals. This last classification of vampires had become so violent and mentally imbalanced—in official lingo, a clear and present danger to innocent citizens—that they were named on The List.

It was a document that didn't officially exist, one that had been drafted when some freak club called Salvation's Crossing had been busted up out in California. Reliable intel, which had been shared with him, had it that the vampires would swiftly move east, to be closer to Europe, the part of it where he'd been stationed, anyway. Some of the major players apparently liked to commute from Nick's former stomping grounds.

He could manage a passable conversation in several Slavic languages. Basic shit.

No, I'm not looking for a hot time. Yes, this is a gun. Now get the fuck out of my way.

Which summed up the remainder of his tour of duty after Barrett had left him. Correction: after he'd made sure she would have to leave. For her own safety. He hadn't touched on the subject during their final, passion-crazed bedroom debriefing. She'd kill him if she ever found out what he'd done.

He missed her so much he'd like to give her the chance. Only shit had happened soon after she'd left him, shit that had changed him forever. Shit she didn't need to be exposed to given she was, last he checked, finally living life safe.

Would she despise him if she knew what he was doing now? How low he'd sunk? That he was in essence assassinating former human citizens who'd only wanted to be useful to their country again?

So far, Nick had taken care of numbers one, three through five, eight, and fifteen on The List. Number three, of course, had been the hardest . . .

Memories of Gary swamped him. Grief. Horrific images.

Pressing his palms into his eyes, he pushed it all back.

He couldn't go there.

He wouldn't.

As always, he had more pressing shit to deal with. And he was going to keep it that way.

Lowering his hands and blinking rapidly, he once more focused on his surveillance equipment. Right now, it looked like things were about to get interesting.

The scanner screen lit up. Nick and Kevin wore gizmos that identified them differently on their equipment. Nick assumed the two individuals represented by the dots were together, with one leading and the other following as a precautionary measure. The tree cover made it hard to determine exactly what was going on. The ultra-high-resolution scanner was one he'd designed but it was still in beta stage, prone to glitches.

The dots stopped. Dot two didn't catch up to dot one. Nick pulled up a topo grid that placed the dots in different positions at the bottom of a dangerously steep, narrow canyon leading directly to the top of the mountain. Staying put would give him a certain advantage. He waited.

The second dot moved sideways. Someone didn't want to tumble down the steep slopes of the canyon. Nick had done it himself once, when he'd first moved to the mountain. Not fun.

The first dot continued upward, slowly.

In terms of cover, the separation of the two dots didn't make sense. Maybe their goal was to cover as much territory as possible. But for what?

His military-bred instincts kicked in. Time to act. Nick went for his current weapon of choice: a crossbow he had designed to his own specifications. In the right hands—his—it was deadly and virtually silent. The new project he'd started on the isolated mountain might be discovered if gunfire startled the animals. It was a safe enough bet that he wasn't dealing with a couple of lost birdwatchers. He'd get a good look at the intruders first. If a couple of punks had climbed the fence, he'd scare them off. If they were turneds, he would kill them if he had to.

Nick got on his radio and called Kev. "You seeing what I'm seeing?"

"Yep. Figured I'd wait to hear from you." Kev's voice was youthful and so was he. But he was no less authoritative for being only twenty-three.

"I'm going out. If you don't hear from me in thirty, call for backup."

"Right. Be careful."

Nick grinned. "Yes, Mother."

Kev snorted and Nick disconnected the call. He slung the bow over his shoulder. The razor-sharp arrows were barbed and tipped with liquid nitrogen, capable of taking out humans and turned vampires instantly.

If his visitors were born vampires? Well, Nick was shit out of luck, because as far as Nick knew, they couldn't be killed. Best to be prepared though . . .

Out of habit, Nick counted the arrows.

Six.

That oughta do it. He rarely missed.

Even when he wished he could.

Barrett continued the strenuous climb up Nick's mountain. The trees were short and spindly by now, thinning out or dead. Outcrops of rock appeared in their place. Barrett stopped to rest, stepping to the side of the trail, and nearly lost her footing again. To her left, a hidden canyon sloped down to an unseen spring—it couldn't be a creek, not this high up. She could just hear a faint gurgling and wished she'd thought to bring water.

On she went. The uneasy feeling that she wasn't alone began to bother her.

Barrett turned around several times, seeing nothing and hearing nothing. She was comforted by the weight of the blade strapped to her calf underneath her pants, a blade that had been dipped in liquid nitrogen. Only here, now, she was more afraid a wild animal or redneck human would jump her than she was of vampires. Just in case, she took out the small pistol in the holster under her arm and stuck it into her waistband. Not a regulation carry, but faster to get at in case she needed it.

She checked her smartphone to see how close she was to the mountain's top, frowning. The screen was entirely blank, which was weird. Not so much as the standard No Network Connection message. The usual rows of cute little apps had vanished.

The gurgling grew louder. She wondered if she was closer to the source of the spring and whether it would be safe to drink from it. She was about to step toward the sound when a twig snapped over her right shoulder. Tensing, she turned—

Huge hands, unnaturally strong, encircled her throat

and squeezed. Barrett clawed at them, choking on a foul smell of decay that intensified as the hands squeezed harder. There seemed to be nobody attached to them. The gurgling was loud, wetting her neck, as if an unseen mouth had opened. She felt the brush of something— fangs?—and twisted frantically against the gripping hands. She strained to reach her knife, but got nowhere near it.

The fingers dug in.

A blackness rose inside her brain but she heard a shout before she fell.

Her name . . . someone shouted her name.

She knew that voice . . .

Nick recognized the two individuals instantly. Barrett Miles, a woman he hadn't seen in over a year, and Tim Murphy, a man he knew only from the photographs he'd seen and the file he'd reviewed.

Murphy also happened to be number two on The List, a turned vampire target who had somehow managed to avoid detection . . . until now. He was a stinking, dis-eased mess, suffering the most advanced physical deteri-oration that Nick had seen thus far. That made sense since those on The List were ranked in order of their "expiration date."

Murphy had his beefy hands wrapped around Bar-rett's throat, and even as one question reverberated through his brain—what the hell Barrett was doing here—Nick drew his bow back. He couldn't make the kill by shooting Murphy in the heart, not with Barrett in the way, but he could damn well fire the arrow into Murphy's head. The turned vampire towered over her.

He had to give Barrett a fighting chance. She arched in agony as Murphy's fierce gaze lifted to him. Barrett kicked and jabbed her attacker in the right spots, obviously well trained, but her strength was ebbing fast. Nick aimed, right between the vampire's blazing eyes.

Dead center.

Easy shot.

CHAPTER THREE

Barrett regained consciousness with agonizing slowness. She was lying down. Her head banged like someone was hitting it. Hard. Over and over. She willed the pain down but it didn't go away, interrupting her awareness of the rest of her body and her surroundings. Bit by bit she got it back.

Her wrists were loosely bound. She was alive but she wasn't sure why.

The decaying smell of the unseen creature that had nearly killed her still hovered in the air. It could be near. Watching her. Its captive.

Waiting to kill.

Vaguely she thought of working her hands free and running for her life . . . but . . . she was someplace inside now, no longer surrounded by stunted trees. It seemed to be night. The air coming in through a reinforced window was cool. She forced raw breaths in and out of her swollen throat.

A face swam into view. A man was leaning over her. He smelled nice. Like the outdoors. The sun. Trees.

She took in a few details. The shadowy light in the room didn't help much. Dark brown hair, messed up. There was a leaf in it. He had rugged features that were somehow familiar and a strong jaw. Dark eyes, serious. He was strongly built with broad shoulders, wearing faded jeans and a camo shirt with the sleeves rolled up.

Brawny arms lightly dusted with dark hair reached out to her. He drew back when he saw her flinch.

She blinked, forcing herself to focus. Who was he?

"You got a hell of a knock on the head." He reached out a hand and brushed his fingertips over an aching lump on her temple. The gentleness of his touch made her even more confused.

"Huh?"

He shook his head. "You fell. Do you remember?"

The effort of thinking made her head throb painfully again. Automatically, she tried pulling herself to a sitting position.

"Stay still," he commanded. Something hidden in his other hand gave off a steely glint and Barrett cringed. "I'm not going to hurt you. Let's get these off." He clipped through plastic zip ties, by the sound of it, and released her hands.

She didn't have the strength to hit him.

"Did you—why—?" Barrett was just barely able to think that maybe it was better not to ask.

She had no idea who'd attacked her, but as the man got closer to the light and memory returned, she knew with absolute conviction that it hadn't been him.

She didn't know how and she didn't know from what, but Nick Maltese had saved her. More fleeting memories came back to her. He'd drawn back the mechanism of a crossbow and aimed. The arrow flew. She'd heard it sing. After that, nothing.

"Sorry," he said. "Had to tie you to get you across my shoulders and run back here. It was two miles, uphill."

Barrett blinked, summoning up a memory of stunted trees and scattered rocks. Seemed to her she'd been closer to the top than that. Nick was just as strong as she remembered. Maybe stronger.

"I didn't know when you'd come to or how you'd

react." He sat on the bed—she realized that she was on one—and examined her wrists. Then he let her go.

"You carried me here?"

"Like a little lost lamb."

He'd said that about her once before. During one of their arguments about whether she was suited to military life and working with refugees. He'd never said it again, probably because she'd ripped him a new one and then hadn't spoken to him for over a week.

Despite everything, Barrett managed a weary half smile. "I wasn't lost. And I'm not that little. But thanks." She touched her neck.

"You could have called or texted." He held up her smartphone.

"Yeah, well, you never were reachable unless you wanted to be."

She hadn't meant the words to sound accusatory but they did. Nick stared at her for a second before grinning and handing her the phone. "So shoot me." He reached into a pocket and came up with her gun. She noticed that the holster was lying on the bed next to her sheathed knife.

"Would that get your attention?" she asked, falling into the easy, teasing banter that had come so naturally to them. "I did think about calling you when I was driving up, decided not to at the gate."

A minor lie. She hadn't wanted to give him the chance to tell her to go away, that was all. She'd just wanted to knock on his door and see his face when he opened it.

Hello, Nick. Imagine finding you here all alone.

Stupid fantasy. He didn't seem inclined to pursue the subject.

Barrett's sigh hitched roughly in her throat. "So who or what tried to strangle me?"

"I'm not sure," he said after a fractional pause. "Whoever he was, he was big." His gaze moved to the crossbow he'd left leaning against the wall, then back to her. "I took aim the second before you moved. Threw me off."

"Sorry about that," she murmured. "I was only fighting for my life."

He gave a curt shake of his head. "No shit. Good thing I got there in time."

"Yeah." She cleared her throat. It hurt inside and out.

"Anyway, not a total miss. The arrow took a chunk of his ear. He let you go and ran. I thought it best to stay with you rather than give chase."

"I appreciate that," she said softly.

With more determination this time, she once again tried to sit up, bracing herself on wobbly arms. With an impatient sigh, Nick helped her until her back was braced against the wooden headboard. Other than that, the whole room seemed to be made of stone and furnished in steel. Taking shallow breaths to keep the dizziness at bay, she asked, "Are we in a safe location?"

"For now. I've got satellite tracking. It's how I knew someone was heading up. But I had no idea it was you until the last second."

"Oh."

"I think the video feed from the gate cam broke down or got whacked. Did you park down there?"

"I was looking for a camera. Didn't see one. And yes, I left my car."

"The camera's hidden in the poison ivy. Low maintenance and no one goes near it."

"Kind of low tech for you." Tiredly, she closed her eyes, then jerked them open again when she feared she was dozing off. What had she been talking about? Oh right. His gizmos. "So you're currently doing the type of research and development that requires you live on a mountain?"

"For some projects, yeah."

She watched him carefully. "Projects designed to identify vampires for the FBI?" she asked.

Given Mahone's report to Carly, that was Barrett's best guess at the moment. Why dance around the subject? Granted, she had no idea how he'd react. He might know more about vampires than she did and volunteer nothing. She hoped he would simply tell her the truth.

Rather than appearing confused or denying what she'd said, he narrowed his eyes at her. "So this isn't a social call. And you still haven't learned to stay out of trouble, I see. What happened to going back to your privileged life and taking up drawing again? Wasn't that part of the plan?"

"Maybe in your mind. Never in mine." And he'd effectively avoided her question.

For the next few minutes, the tense silence pulsed between them, but she refused to go any further into their past, what he'd encouraged her to do, and what she'd known immediately upon stepping back onto U.S. soil was never going to happen. She also wasn't going to bring up the mistakes she'd made and would make again if she had to, even knowing it would end the same way. She prayed he wouldn't bring them up, either.

Nick finally sighed, then said, "So I guess you're working for the feds, too."

Thankful he wasn't going where she didn't want him to, she relaxed slightly. So Mahone had been right. Nick knew about vampires and freely admitted he was working with the FBI. And he didn't seem overly surprised by the fact she did, as well. "In a manner of speaking."

He cocked a brow. "Meaning?"

"Like you, I'm an independent contractor. I like my freedom."

"I remember."

Her gaze flew to his. Had that been bitterness in his tone?

He hadn't seemed terribly upset when she'd ended things between them, even if he had protested a little. She'd assumed it was a token effort so he wouldn't hurt her feelings. Yet his next words seemed like another dig. "You never liked following orders, even if they were there for a reason."

So she'd been wrong. He had no intention of letting sleeping dogs lie, but he couldn't force her to talk about it. "Let's not get into all that. It's in the past, Nick."

Clenching his jaw, he stood again. For a moment he seemed to be listening to something outside that she couldn't hear. Then he returned his dark gaze to her. "Okay. Then let's get into something new: Why you're here, how you knew to find me, and whether anyone knew you were coming."

The last part of the question confused her, but only for a second. Then she realized why he was asking it. Her attacker . . .

It hadn't been some random assault by a maniac wandering in the woods. He'd been inhumanly strong. What if he was a vampire who'd been instructed to follow her and kill her? If so, who had sent him? Jane's captors? The FBI? And why had he smelled like a rotting corpse, unlike every other vampire she'd ever met or heard of?

She looked sideways at Nick.

Was it totally crazy to wonder if he'd sent that thing after her? Or to speculate whether he'd only pretended to save her?

She shivered at her thoughts and shook her head. She hated this. Being suspicious of everyone around her, including the man she'd once trusted enough to welcome inside her body. She'd come here for a reason; she had no choice but to trust Nick again. It shouldn't be such a difficult task.

She answered him slowly. "There's a lot I need to fill you in on."

"Including what you know about vampires and what you need from me."

At her slight nod, his mouth twisted. Something disapproving radiated from him and he didn't even bother to hide it.

"What's on your mind?" she asked him. The Nick Maltese she'd known hadn't gone in for displays of emotion. But he was older now. His eyes showed it—and revealed more than he probably wanted to.

"I wish you were here for a whole different reason, Barrett. A personal one. But I wished for a lot of things over the past year that never came true, and something tells me nothing's changed."

Memories were in his eyes and in his voice, forcing her to relive what she'd sought to forget. Again, Nick's hint that their split had wounded him in some way surprised her.

Back then she'd told herself to be practical—their brief affair hadn't been the romantic kind, but one driven by powerful and mutual desire to connect on a purely physical level. Craving intense sensation. The stress of being far from home, picking up the pieces of random wars and trying to put someone else's country back together, was overwhelming without some form of release.

Some drank to blot out the chaos and the violence, some did drugs. They had fucked. A lot.

Nick was skilled and ultra macho but he never rushed it. He knew just when to be tender and he knew exactly how to take her to climax again and again until she screamed his name. Naked in his arms, blissed out underneath his big body or riding him hard, she was a different woman. Too open. Too vulnerable. Needing him way too much.

She didn't want to love him, damn it. Loving someone just opened you to hurt. To loss.

So she'd always planned to end things with Nick before she returned stateside. If not for Jane Small, Barrett hadn't planned on ever seeing him again.

Nonetheless, the fact that he might have truly cared for her and mourned the end of their relationship filled her with a wave of pleasure. One she immediately tamped down.

"Never mind." The bluff command snapped her back to the moment. "So what security clearance do you have?" he asked. "Six-Vee?"

"Six—what?"

He stared at her. "V as in vampire. You contract with the FBI. You mentioned vampires. And given what attacked you—I mean, I assumed you worked in the Bureau's Turning Program before it was shut down. That you'd know the lingo."

Something he'd said bothered her, but she was still foggy, distracted by her memories; she couldn't quite put her finger on what it was so she just shrugged. "I obviously haven't done all my homework. Guess nothing's changed." She shrugged again, trying to make light of the topic even though she could tell by the immediate flare in his eyes that he didn't think it was funny.

"Get up to speed. You nearly fucking died out there, Barrett."

"I remember," she whispered. "Being strangled is not fun." She didn't want to think about what would have happened if he hadn't gotten to her in time.

"So don't joke about this. Ever."

"Okay."

He took advantage of her weak reply. "How about if we don't discuss it, either?"

She cleared her throat. It was still painful. "Won't work. On a need-to-know basis . . . well, I really need to know a few things."

"Is that right." His tone was suddenly wary. He'd

never liked conversations where he wasn't in charge. The words *we have to talk* had always made him pace the room and eye the door. But he stayed where he was. "Fire when ready."

"The thing that attacked me? I'm sort of remembering more now. I'm guessing you've seen something like it before."

"Why is that?"

"You didn't blink when you drew the bow. You didn't seem shocked by what was happening. And you missed."

Nick just stared at her again. "You moved."

She ignored that and persisted. "Was it a vampire? And why the hell did he stink like that?"

"Some do."

It was an answer but it didn't tell her much of anything. He was better than ever at calmly deflecting questions.

"Why did you assume I work for the Turning Program, Nick? And what exactly do you do for the FBI?"

He didn't answer right away. Wondering if she'd gone too far, she almost jumped when he finally did. "You sure have lots of questions for someone who just dropped back into my life with no warning, Barrett. And you haven't told me a thing."

"Maybe I have my reasons. Good ones."

"C'mon," he said coaxingly. "Share. I used to love it when you shared. Your eyes got all misty."

The sarcasm in his tone made the dull ache in Barrett's head began to grow in intensity again. "Go fuck yourself, Nick."

"Can't. I have work to do." He walked over to what she guessed was the security system and stared into a screen. As he fiddled with some buttons, she got the sense that he was trying to regain his control. "Stupid remote feed got fried somehow." He gave it a smack that rattled something inside. "Won't work the way I want it to."

"What's the matter?"

"The satellite tracker and the security system don't sync." Nick scowled. "Goddamn it." His thick dark brows drew together as he stared into the screen and swore under his breath. "Let's try the zoom."

"What are you looking for?" With difficulty, she rose from the bed and went to stand beside him.

"Your vehicle. And—well, shit."

That was putting it mildly, Barrett thought. They both stared at her smashed and burning rental car. Flames licked against cracked glass and bent metal, devouring, destroying. They heard the explosion. The screen went black.

"Guess you parked in someone's spot," he muttered.

"Oh. So you get to joke and I don't. That's really not funny."

He shrugged and tapped other keys until he got the map function again.

Barrett saw several gold dots begin to move randomly at the bottom of the topo map. "What are those?"

"Could be a malfunction."

His tone told Barrett that he wasn't telling her everything. "And if it isn't?"

"Then several someones or somethings are coming up the mountain and that makes us officially outnumbered. Let's go."

"Go where? In what?" Barrett was shaking, and not from weakness.

"Hang on." He pulled out a radio. Pressed a button. "Kev, do you hear me?" Nothing. "Kev." Still nothing. "Shit." He threw down the radio. "I'll try calling him when we're out of here."

"Him who?"

"Guy who works down the mountain. He's got his

hands full dealing with those gold dots." Nick clenched his teeth. "At least I hope that's why he's not answering."

"So it looks to me like we just ran out of options."

He straightened and took her arm. "Plan H. Follow me."

She wondered what had happened to plans A through G, but there wasn't time to ask.

He reached down to grab his crossbow and arrows, then led the way to a door she hadn't noticed. Once through it, he flipped several switches on a panel in an exterior wall. They were in a hangar. Huge panels opened slowly to reveal the sky. Silhouetted in the faint moonlight was a gleaming helicopter.

Barrett gaped at the craft, momentarily at a loss for words. "Where'd you get that?"

"It was here when I moved in," he answered laconically.

Like she was ever going to get a straight answer to a reasonable question out of him. Nick had been famous for procuring outrageously expensive gear at no cost to himself. Whenever he wanted to see what he could get, he had filled out requisition forms one after the other and his commanding officer had signed off on them without even looking.

"As long as you know how to fly it."

"Just get in," he sighed.

She obeyed, putting on the headset with the attached mic she found on the seat.

They were aloft in minutes, taxiing the short distance out of the hangar to a landing pad and rising swiftly when the rotors got up to speed. There was another scanner with a similar screen mounted on the helicopter's instrument panel. Barrett didn't want to look at it but she did. The gold dots moved higher on the map of the mountain, almost to the top. The deafening noise of the rotors didn't drown out another, much more primal sound. And the headsets didn't filter it out entirely.

Ferocious howls rose to the darkening sky as they flew away.

"Sounds like the hounds of hell," Barrett yelled, wincing as her shout and the helicopter noise seemed to stab into her temples like razors.

"Nah. Those are hunting dogs. The gold dots track them, if you really want to know. A breeding operation adjoins my property. The kennels are down there, below the ridge."

"Are they after us?" The question wasn't meant to be serious but it came out that way.

Nick adjusted his headset mic and glanced at the screen. "No. But someone let them out. They shouldn't have been loose, which is why we needed to get out of there. But it's entirely possible the dogs captured him."

She knew whom he meant but not exactly. They'd gotten off the subject of what had attacked her.

He shut off the scanner and concentrated on a bewildering array of instruments and gauges, then looked out at the clear night sky, his mouth set in a grim line. They didn't speak for some time. Barrett looked out through the clear bubble of the windshield as Nick piloted the craft. Her vision had started to tunnel and she blinked to regain focus. Her mouth was dry, her skin clammy. She needed to lie down. She wanted to close her eyes and sleep for eons.

She had no choice but to remain upright and bluff her way through. "Mind if I ask where we're going?" she asked after a while.

He glanced at her, his eyes narrowing as he took her in. "Got enough fuel to get to the Atlanta area."

"Why Atlanta?"

He shrugged. "Big city. Safer."

"If you say so."

Nick kept his gaze on the instrument panel. "Rest. You look like you're about to pass out."

"I don't want to. Let's keep talking."

They hit rough air and her stomach roiled from the turbulence. Nick righted the heli with some effort and flew on.

"Fine," he said. "You want to talk? Tell me why you came to me, Barrett. When the last time I saw you, you swore to never come to me—or for me—ever again."

His voice echoed distinctly inside her headset. Her face heated at his deliberately crude choice of words. Had she said that? She struggled to remember, distracted by the constant thudding of the rotors.

Maybe she had.

What of it? She'd beaten him to the punch, that was all, by being the first to say they should break up. Then added that she didn't have a place for him in her life or in her bed.

Over and out.

And though she'd meant every word, her heart had known her for the cowardly liar she was. It still did, but as always, she pushed beyond that.

"I came for your help, Nick. Not for you. That's a big distinction."

CHAPTER FOUR

Exhaustion—or shock—finally got to her. Nick looked over. Barrett's eyes were closed. He didn't think she was faking sleep. Her soft lips were parted slightly as she drew in shuddering breaths.

What a reunion. Out of nowhere, she'd shown up in the clutches of a turned vampire and he'd done the required rescuing. Once they were in the air and safely away . . . maybe the rapid change in altitude had gotten to him. All of a sudden he'd turned into Mr. Fucking Sensitive, wanting to know why she'd ended things.

Like he hadn't made it happen back then, for the most part. Witnessing the risks she took and how far she would go, he'd schemed to get her out of Europe and safely stateside—without telling her. Barrett didn't play safe. She took way too many chances, using her cool beauty and smarts to get into and out of places where she wasn't welcome, one step ahead of vicious thugs.

She always had a cause and gave it her all. There were reasons why. They'd been over them. The brother she hadn't been able to save at a critical moment was one. But that had happened long ago.

When he got right down to it, Nick had to admit that she took chances because she wanted to. Because she loved living on the edge, in constant danger. Just like him.

He'd known he had no right to try to change that trait in her, but he'd wanted to. Lost cause. One of many.

They'd both pretended to move on, but he'd known the moment he'd seen her they'd been lying to themselves.

He used the heli radio and tried Kev again. This time he answered.

"Kev here."

"What the fuck happened?"

"Something spooked the dogs. Bad. I let them out and let them hunt."

"And?"

"Nothing. You figure out what spooked them?"

"I have a pretty good guess." He told him about seeing Murphy, but left out Barrett's involvement since he still didn't know why she'd tracked him down.

"So why'd you leave?"

Nick looked at Barrett. Her breathing was steady, too soft for him to hear. Her eyes stayed closed. "I had my reasons," he said, knowing that would be enough for Kev. "I'll be back as soon as I can. Call in. Get some men in to help you and scour that mountain. Keep me posted on my cell."

"Roger that."

They disconnected and Nick stared ahead, seeing the darkened landscape below through his faint, distorted reflection in the helicopter's windshield.

He was glad Barrett had conked out. Gave him a chance to think, although he usually saved his analytical skills for machinery. The ratio of effort to results was a hell of a lot more favorable. But even so.

Seeing her again was a huge rush. He'd forgotten how stunning she was and how intensely her nearness could arouse him. The vulnerability in her eyes when she finally opened them and recognized him was overwhelming.

Nick had kept his distance after he'd settled her in his bed, wondering what to do. He would have flown her out if she hadn't regained consciousness. Same deal in the end.

If he hadn't had the helicopter, he would have carried her back down the mountain to civilization, miles past the end of the road where she'd parked. Safe to assume his jeep had been blasted to smithereens, too. He hadn't bothered to check, not with a fueled-up heli on the pad.

When it came to Barrett, he'd forgotten the strength of the protective instincts she triggered in him. It didn't matter how well she could take care of herself. He still wanted to do it for her.

It was something they'd fought about, his constant need to protect her. His comments that she belonged in a different world. A safer one. He'd been pretty good at getting her to open up to him, and he'd get even greater glimpses of the soft woman she hid beneath her tough exterior. All it took was a little tenderness, like the song said. She was a sucker for it.

God knew she needed it. Doing what she did in Eastern Europe—getting around corrupt officials who lived on bribes, dedicating herself to saving refugee women and girls from the feral creeps who tried to prey on them—took a toll on her. Barrett never admitted to it. But Nick had understood.

Barrett stirred in her sleep and muttered something he couldn't hear. Nick's mouth tightened. Maybe she was reading his mind. Oh, he knew that was impossible given they were both human, but with the connection they'd once had and what they'd accomplished under the radar and without official sanction—well, he'd always fancied them sharing that deeper connection.

One case had almost gotten them both killed: those sisters, eight and ten, whom he'd spirited out of the foulest brothel the human mind could imagine, with Barrett covering him from an armored jeep hidden in a slum alley, automatic rifle at the ready. There hadn't been room for her to fly out with the little girls and their mother. But she'd been waiting on the tarmac when he'd come back alone.

They had been in radio contact on his return hop over the Adriatic. He'd teased her, asking what she would do for him after he'd risked so much, what she would say.

He'd climbed out of the beat-up, borrowed jet and saw Barrett running toward him. She had kept it short. Exactly three words, in fact. *Are they safe?*

Like a fool, he'd been expecting something more along the lines of *you're my hero* or even *I love you*. But she didn't think that way.

Barrett on a mission was a force to be reckoned with. Just how she was. Same principle applied in the sack, which was a plus. Love didn't get mentioned when they were going at it hot and heavy. Or any other time, either. If it had ever been on her mind, she kept it hidden.

Whatever. The girls and their mother had been saved. Shortly after, there had been that final argument. He'd gotten his wish. He'd made sure of it after she'd gone off on her own on another dangerous mission, this one so dangerous he'd refused to help her with it. When he'd found out she'd done it anyway, enough had been enough. He'd blown the whistle on her, something he'd never told her. She'd been forced back to the States. Only he hadn't counted on the fact that when she left her post behind, she'd be leaving him, as well. For good.

Fuck it. The past was past. Nobody got do-overs.

Not Barrett, him, or their brothers.

Nick checked the instrument panel before he looked at her again. She'd curled up some, tucking her long legs under her, her arms crossed over her breasts. Kinda reminded him of how she slept in his bed in his private quarters. Never quite letting go.

She hadn't changed much. Maybe more beautiful, if that was possible. And tougher in some indefinable way.

He'd been scared shitless when Murphy had gotten the jump on her, even though one look at her out cold in his bed told him that she was still super fit. Unlike a lot of ex-army, she hadn't slacked off on rigorous physical conditioning. Whatever it was she did for the FBI, she obviously had to be in top shape to do it.

What was that? And why had she climbed his mountain?

Nick made a slow midair turn to look back at it, half expecting to see his lair on fire. He couldn't see it at all. The mountain was a black shape against a dark night, barely visible.

He got the helicopter back on course.

"Barrett."

At the softly spoken word, Barrett, who'd only been half dozing, opened her eyes and straightened in her seat too fast. Her head and throat still hurt, causing her to wince. Nick flashed her an intense, unsmiling look before returning his gaze to what was in front of them. Tall towers spiked into the night sky, dotted with lights that outshone the stars.

Nick nodded toward them. "There's Atlanta."

Barrett had never seen the city from this altitude. The helicopter was flying low, hundreds of feet beneath the few airplanes she'd seen on the way. What was the term? Under the radar. The words applied to Nick Maltese in more ways than one.

"Are you landing at Hartsfield?" She supposed the busy commercial airport allowed some private craft to land on distant runways.

Nick shook his head. "No. Changed my mind. Too

chaotic, too many small planes coming in. I'm thinking New City. Over there. Toward the west."

He altered course, muttering a reply to the air-traffic controller's radioed request for information. The staticy response faded out. Barrett looked ahead to the sprawling small city. Lit-up highways rolled toward it through empty-looking land.

"Kind of amazing when you think that was rural a few years ago," he muttered.

Like Atlanta, it was composed of glass block buildings, but none were as tall as the ones in Georgia's capital. Some were more concrete than glass, with a dusty, unfinished look made worse by the sickly orange glow of futuristic street lamps.

Nick flew even lower, skirting the New City limits, heading for an airfield that seemed relatively quiet. He landed the helicopter and turned off the rotors, waiting for the thumping beat to die down.

"They have some new hotels. We'll get a suite," he said without looking at her. "Two bedrooms, but I don't want you too far . . . For your safety."

He sounded sincere and unswayable. Not that Barrett was going to argue with him. A suite would do just fine. Plus, since she'd taken her ID and smartphone with her but had left the rest in her car, he was going to have to foot the bill, though that had never been a problem for Nick. He was old school and had refused to let her pay for anything, even when she'd been the one to do the inviting. She would have to stop at the gift shop if there was one, buy a few things for the night. And—

"Hey, you need to call about the rental car," he reminded her in a matter-of-fact voice.

She smiled at the way he'd echoed her thoughts. In many ways, they'd always operated on a similar wavelength. In others . . . "What should I say? Vampires playing with matches?"

Nick snorted. "Just say it blew up. They'll figure it was meth heads trying to steal it for a portable lab. Happens all over the country."

"Here? Whatever happened to gracious southern living?"

"Somewhat endangered. But not dead."

Barrett belatedly remembered that his family had lived in North Carolina for generations. Once Nick had joined the army, he'd never looked back.

"You ready?" he asked her. "How are you feeling?"

"Not too bad." Only like hell warmed over, she thought, just as he said, "Only like shit, right?"

She stared at him, then shook her head and laughed. His expression relaxed until he, too, was smiling.

"I could never pull one over on you, could I, Nick?"

His smile disappeared and he lifted a hand as if to touch her face. He dropped it before making contact and turned back to the windshield. "I don't know, Barrett. You tried so many times, I confess I lost count."

What could she say? He was right. She'd never dropped her defenses with him. Not completely. Not even in bed. The fact that he'd let her go so easily both justified that fact and probably explained it, as well.

"We should be safe here. How about I buy you dinner and a drink before we start the heavy talk?"

They were going to be discussing vampires and sex rings and failed promises while carefully avoiding the fact they'd seen each other naked. Saying they were going to have some heavy conversation was putting it mildly. That realization prompted her to say, "You're on."

He grinned, almost as if she'd agreed to go on a date with him. It would be the weirdest damn date she'd ever been on. But then she and Nick had never actually dated. They'd been too hungry for each other. All he had to do was slam the door behind him and they got naked and went wild. They ended by falling asleep in each other's arms, exhausted and spent, until they had to get up and pretend it had never happened.

About twenty minutes later, Nick conferred with the front desk clerk at an anonymous, brand-new luxury hotel while Barrett waited.

"The gift shop's still open," he said, tactfully not looking at her somewhat shredded khakis and sneakers. "Go crazy."

Barrett took the credit card he handed her. "I'll pay you back."

Nick shrugged, hoisting the large duffel he kept stashed in the helicopter. He'd told her that it held several outfits suitable for different events. Everything but a tux, in fact.

She came out of the shop with a bulging bag holding a black maxi skirt and a gauze top in white, plus some costume jewelry that wasn't too gaudy, makeup, brush and toothbrush, and toiletries. And what the hell. A really nice bikini and black wedge flip-flops. The clerk had told them that the pool was on a high terrace adjoining their floor. She might as well take full advantage of it.

She showered and changed, then met Nick in the lobby. He looked every inch the handsome guy waiting for his gal. She resented the approving glances sent his way from a few women who sauntered by. In the improvised outfit that clearly conveyed gift-shop desperation, Barrett herself was more or less invisible.

The restaurant featured secluded tables for diners who preferred privacy. Their orders came quickly, but Barrett only picked at hers until the silent waiter removed their plates and left their wineglasses.

Nick was patient, but the knowledge that his patience

wouldn't last long made her jittery. Despite the fantasy she'd had of spending time with him, and maybe even swimming before they talked, she'd always been a rip-the-bandage-off type of person.

Barrett took a fortifying sip of her wine. Second glass. Maybe she shouldn't have. She felt tears prickle her eyes.

"You came to me," he said quietly. "Trust me enough to tell me why."

"All right. Here goes." Barrett summoned up her nerve. "I made a mistake. A big one."

"That's not like you."

At the clear sarcasm in his voice, Barrett glared at him.

"Sorry. Go on."

"I had a friend," she began. "She came from a rich family."

"Like yours?"

"Not rich enough for my snooty folks," Barrett said dryly. "But we used to play together. Sarah got pregnant in high school. Mr. Wonderful ditched her and their baby six months after the birth. No forwarding address. Private detectives couldn't find him. So there she was, a single teenage mother with a baby daughter."

"Doesn't sound like she had to worry about a roof over her head or paying the bills."

"No. But there were other things. She'd developed lymphoma soon after giving birth, but it went away with chemo. The baby meant everything to her. We were really close when Jane was little. Then . . ."

"Then Noah died. You joined the army. Went abroad."

"Right," she managed. Barrett really didn't want to tell Nick everything. She swallowed hard, taking another sip of wine to refresh her still tender throat. She'd covered up the bruises with makeup and left her hair down.

"Go on."

"The lymphoma came back. I saw Sarah now and then but not often enough. She swore she was going to beat it. It was convenient to believe that. She was tough, but just before I met you . . ."

"How old was her daughter by then?"

"Fourteen. She's seventeen now. Sweet kid. Shy and imaginative. A little too sheltered. But she hung out with guys Sarah didn't know sometimes, scared her mother out of her wits. At least they were age appropriate," Barrett clarified. "The cute boy in the park with a guitar, that type."

"Got it. Sensitive."

"Just like Jane. Which was one more reason for Sarah to hide the fact that she was dying. Jane didn't know and neither did I until the very end."

Barrett stopped. The room swam. She glanced into Nick's eyes and looked away. His dark gaze held a deep kindness she remembered only too well. Thank God he refrained from touching her. He got it. Sometimes being comforted was too fucking much to bear.

"But there was enough time to say good-bye to Sarah. Make sure that everything was in order. She appointed her sister and her husband guardians for Jane. I barely knew them but I trusted her choice—why wouldn't I? And I promised Sarah that I would always look after Jane. She didn't want to impose but I said yes—she wasn't specific about the details."

Then what? He hadn't asked the question. There was no need to. He just listened.

"Sarah died a few months before I met you. I periodically checked in on Jane but . . ." Barrett shrugged.

"You were dealing with your own stuff."

She nodded. "It's no excuse. I should have been more diligent. Called more, at the very least. I—I assumed if she needed me, she'd reach out. Or her relatives would."

"But?"

"But they didn't. She didn't." She paused, composing herself. "She started dating darker guys. Got mixed up with one who was into the vampire life. About a week ago, they both disappeared and the boy was found dead. Two nights ago, a mark we were investigating related to sex trafficking finally showed me his site of choice, Sex-Flash. I'd told him I was interested in a girl, a virgin, that matched Jane's description. He either already knew about her or found her for me. Suddenly there's Jane on live video. The caption said Runaway Virgin. She recognized me. Called me Miley, her nickname for me. But then she was gone."

He didn't bother asking her if she was sure. If she said it, he'd know she was sure of her ID. Nick sat back, visibly affected. "Hell. She could be anywhere."

"That's not all. Whoever shoved her in front of that camera saw me, too." Barrett's voice was drained of emotion. "If they figured out that I was someone Jane knew, they probably got my name out of her. The hard way. For all I know, she could be—she could be—"

Nick shook his head. "No. Don't go there. A seventeen-year-old virgin is a valuable commodity," he said flatly. "She's still alive."

"Probably." Barrett stared at him. "But for how long?"

He didn't look away. "We're going to find her, Barrett. You and me."

"Don't you have work to do? Whatever that is?" She wasn't trying to be snotty.

"Yeah. I mean, realistically, I can't drop everything to help you, but I'll do what I can."

"Okay. I can't ask for more than that."

"But . . ." He hesitated. "You know about vampires. You said you contract for the FBI. And you said 'we' were looking into sex trafficking, not you. So here's the million-dollar question. Who, exactly, is we?"

That *was* the million-dollar question. One she knew she didn't have any choice but to answer. She'd struggled with that decision. Belladonna was designated black ops for a reason, but with or without a green light from Carly and Mahone, she would have to reveal a little about what was going on. It helped, of course, that Nick was also working with the FBI, and knew about vampires and the Turning Program. It also seemed he knew more than she did. He'd asked her if she had level Six-Vee security clearance. And bottom line, he was a techno wizard when it came to computers and locating missing persons. If anyone could help her find Jane, Nick could.

"I work for a black ops team formed by a division of the FBI. It's called Belladonna."

"How did they recruit you?"

"A special agent named Peter Lancaster approached me. Said he needed human women to help him go places where he and his teammates couldn't."

Nick had suddenly stiffened. "And you just decided to trust him?"

She scowled. "No. I checked him out. He was legitimate. As legitimate as a turned vampire working for the FBI could be."

If he'd stiffened before, now Nick seemed to have turned to stone. "He was turned? In the FBI's Turning Program?"

Barrett hesitated. Was she imagining things or had Nick's focus sharpened the second she'd mentioned Peter's name and said he was a turned vampire? She couldn't even begin to guess why that would be the case, but her guard instinctively went up. She needed to trust Nick with certain information in order to get his help. That information did not include the details of Peter's turning—or the fact he, Ty, and Ana had been attacked and forcibly turned. "I don't know how he or the others were turned," Barrett said, feeling the pressure of the lie in her chest but not knowing what else to do. If she evaded, she'd just make Nick more suspicious. "Anyway, Belladonna's mission is to track down Rogue vampires, even if they once worked for the Bureau."

"Right," he said. "The ones selling humans as blood slaves. And, I'm guessing from what you've told me, selling teenage humans as sex slaves," Nick said grimly.

"Yes," she whispered. "I hooked up with a Rogue vampire named Joseph Powell. And he led me to Jane—virtually, anyway. And then I found my way to you."

Nick nodded. He'd been right, of course. Her latest mission, not desire, had brought Barrett back to him. It seemed, however, that she was leaving a lot unsaid. Hell. If she wanted help, she was going to have to be more forthcoming.

"Fill me in on a few facts," he said. He wanted to ask her about her reference to hooking up with Powell and what that meant, but he held back. He was no saint. There were a lot of things he wouldn't tell her and he wasn't going to judge her.

She gave him a mulish look that he remembered all too well. "I've told you the relevant facts. Why isn't that enough?"

"This is the first I've heard of Belladonna," he began.

"Then I guess we're doing something right."

Nick studied her set expression. He might be better off using his intuition instead of trying to coax further information out of her. So her fellow agent Peter Lancaster was a turned vampire—and apparently not the only one given Barrett had referred to "others." That fact alone had his mind racing. The List specifically targeted those turneds who were a threat. It was a safe bet that since Lancaster was working for the FBI, he wasn't one. Even so, Nick knew better than anyone that could change at any moment, and he didn't like the idea of Barrett being around when it did.

"So," she said in a light tone he knew was forced, before he could say anything further. "Are you in?"

Nick didn't reply right away. "Back to Jane? Of course I'll help you, but I can't do it officially. Like I said, I have my own missions to accomplish." Including finding out if Tim Murphy is still on my mountain, Nick thought.

"That's fine with me. My superiors at Belladonna know what I'm doing, but the fewer people who do, the better."

"Well, I'm happy to help, you know that. But I have to think about how to do it and I need a little time."

He could feel her tense and draw back. Didn't take much for Barrett to stop believing. But given that she wasn't necessarily on the side of the angels, he had to cover his ass.

"You mentioned a superior?"

Barrett shrugged, a troubled look in her eyes. "A woman named Carly."

"And this Carly—she's okay with you officially following up on something that personal?"

A flash of anger lit up Barrett's blue eyes. "I don't care if Carly's okay with it or not. I have to find Jane."

He paused, thinking before he spoke. He couldn't tell her that The List was a mandate to assassinate turned vampires. What if he eventually had to take out one of her colleagues? He chose his next words carefully. "Barrett, you know what could happen. In certain situations, emotional involvement can affect your judgment. You could shoot and miss—"

"Like you?"

Nick scowled, his lips compressed in a thin line.

"Yeah," he said finally. "Like me. Which is a good point, because we can't forget that . . . *thing* that attacked you is probably still at large on my mountain."

"You keep calling it a thing, but I can tell you know what it is. Are you going to tell me?"

She didn't miss a trick. Never had. "You tell me only what you think is relevant and I'll do the same," Nick answered. "That's the way you want to play it, isn't it?"

"Maybe I can connect the dots myself."

He blew out a frustrated breath, ignoring the jab.

She winced, seeming to regret her sarcasm. "Sorry. But I would like to know."

"If you need to know, you will. One thing at a time, Barrett."

"I just wish there was a way to—" She broke off, thoughtful again. "Never mind. Maybe I am too close to the case."

No kidding. Emotionally, she was all over the place. "While we're on that subject, do you mind telling me who at Belladonna decides what's a case and what's not?"

"Carly. Sight unseen. She talks to us through an intercom."

"Huh. So she doesn't want to look anyone in the eye. Ever wonder why?"

"Sometimes. I don't know why she does things that way. From what I've been able to piece together, I think she lost someone important to her. Someone named Ben Porter. Maybe she just has to hide her grief. Who knows. But can we stay on track, Nick? We seem to be having two different conversations."

She wasn't wrong about that. She desperately wanted only one thing: a guarantee of his help finding Jane, whereas Nick wanted to know more about Belladonna. Something about the operation didn't seem to add up and he wasn't sure how to ask Barrett for more information.

"Sure. You do the talking, I'll do the listening." He had an uneasy feeling that a trap had been set somewhere, somehow. Not necessarily for him. Maybe not even for Barrett. Fools rush in, he reminded himself silently. And fools fucked up.

"For starters, Peter was no help. They can't pinpoint the website."

Nick absorbed that information. "I might not be able to, either, not right away. URLs for sites like that sometimes change several times a day. They gotta keep ahead of the law."

"When and if the law is looking." She crumpled her napkin and threw it onto the table. "Doesn't sound to me like you really want to take this on."

"I want to help you," Nick insisted in an irritated tone. "But, Barrett, you have to slow down. In a case like this, you have to consider every step you make. Jane could vanish forever if seeing you on the other end of that transmission scared them off. The only way we can narrow this down is by finding out where she is. So you talk to the last people who saw her. And they would be?"

"Her aunt and uncle. The Prescotts. Ginny and Malcolm." Barrett pressed her lips together tightly, her eyes suspiciously wet. "Ginny tracked me down when Jane went missing. She gave me the information about Dante. When and where she last saw Jane. She gave me a current picture of her, which we distributed to law enforcement agencies all across the nation. Nothing so far."

"Well you don't have nothing anymore. You saw who has her. You know it's related to SexFlash. Go back and interview Jane's aunt and uncle. You know him well?"

"Not at all. I've always talked to Ginny when I called." He nodded, but she didn't need him to tell her what was on his mind. Often young females were sexually abused by those closest to them. She needed to check into the uncle. She'd known it before, she just hadn't had the chance to do it yet given her involvement with Powell.

"I need to talk to them. Both of them. Face to face," she confirmed.

"Lucky for them you have such a beautiful one," he said, with no hint of teasing in his voice but a whole lot of memories and regret.

The waiter returned with a leather folder holding the check and a pen, and placed it on the table. Nick opened it and signed using an alias, Josh Howard.

"Am I Mrs. Howard?" she asked, needing to lighten the tension caused by his compliment.

"For the night, yeah. Don't worry. I'm not making any moves." Maybe it was wishful thinking, but her eyes seemed to flash with a hint of disappointment. It made Nick draw a silent breath and reconsider what he'd said. After all, him wanting to make a move on her had never been in question—whether she'd want him to had been.

"I was just thinking that I need some fake IDs myself," she said brightly. "I had a couple in another bag I left in the car. Those have to be reported as destroyed before I can get reissues."

"Why wait? We can stop by the copy shop out by the college. They do good work."

"Gee, thanks for the tip," Barrett said dryly. "Sooner or later, I'm betting I'm going to have to go undercover for this thing."

"Is that step two? Got a location in mind?"

"You tell me, Nick." She took a deep breath. "Maybe I shouldn't have asked you for help when I don't even know how you can."

"But you did," he said calmly. "So let's take it from here. Keeping in mind that I'm not going to always be available. I just can't be. I—I have important work I'm doing. Work I can't tell you about, so please don't ask."

Barrett looked like she wanted to argue with him but stopped herself. "Fine."

"We're going to have to wing it. I haven't done this kind of thing stateside. And we both know that looking for Jane is going to be like looking for a wave in the ocean. You"—he pointed to her—"are going to be doing most of the work for starters. That's how it has to be. Agreed?"

Barrett held her head high. "I don't mind investigating on my own. I will if I have to."

He held up a hand to stop her. "Whoa. I'm not done. I forgot to ask when you're going back to D.C."

She gave him a long look. "Soon. Maybe tomorrow."

"All right. So we have tonight."

"To recover. And regroup. That's all."

So there it was. Nick had been put in his place. Still, he'd achieved his immediate objective: getting her to set her emotions aside and focus on what needed doing. If she needed to give him a little hell, he could handle it.

He didn't argue with her reply, just got up when she did and followed her out of the restaurant. He put a hand on the small of her back to guide her to the elevators.

Barrett didn't seem bothered by the gesture.

In fact, it might have been his imagination again, but he was pretty damn certain she leaned in to his touch.

Nick unlocked the door to their suite and waved her inside. Barrett disappeared into her room and rifled through the big plastic bag from the gift shop. After everything that had been said, everything that had happened, all she wanted was twenty minutes in the pool. Not to swim but to float on her back. Looking up at the stars. Hearing nothing but the lapping of water. Just drifting.

Nick knocked on her door just when she'd slipped the gauze top over the bikini.

"Yes?"

"Hey. It's me. I know you're probably ready to turn in but—"

"I don't think I can sleep, Nick. Not for a while. I was about to check out the pool, if you really want to know."

"Oh." There was a pause. "Mind if I join you? I'd just like to stay close. There's a lot going down and a lot to think about. Your safety, first of all."

Second time he'd mentioned that. Barrett could take care of herself, but under the circumstances, it would be a good idea to have him there. "Okay."

"Meet you there in five, then."

She padded barefoot down the plushly carpeted hall and pushed open the glass door that led to the outdoor area and the infinity pool. Its far edge was aligned with the terrace railing, giving the illusion that one could swim off the building into the air. There was no one else there. Barrett counted three security cameras, slowly panning the terrace. She was probably safe enough. But she was relieved when she saw Nick come through the glass doors.

He walked over to her, looking around. "Spectacular pool. You going in?"

She nodded.

"I can't. No trunks. I'll just take a chaise and watch, if you don't mind."

"Suit yourself." She waited until he turned around to find one, then took off the gauze top, lifting it quickly over her head and dropping it onto the slatted surround.

Barrett went down the low ladder into the shallow end without making a sound. The rippling water enfolded her. She pushed away from the tiled wall, keeping her head high as she stroked out into the middle of the pool.

Then she rolled over onto her back, making tiny motions with her hands to stay more or less where she was, looking up at the dark sky, thinking about nothing at all.

CHAPTER FIVE

High above in the penthouse suite someone else was watching her. Vladimir Ouspensky was mesmerized by the shimmering woman, her pale, slender body stark against the midnight blue of the water. He opened the window and leaned out slightly.

"What are you looking at?" His girlfriend—he disliked the childish American term but he had to call Tamsin something—came over to see for herself.

"Not what. Who. A woman. She is beautiful."

Vladimir adjusted the thick towel wrapped around his loins, too vain to cover up his torso or legs with a robe. He was impressively built for his breed, smooth-skinned and muscular with glossy dyed black hair that reached below his shoulders. Both nipples were pierced with platinum rings. His tongue had been pierced, too, with several studs precisely placed to intensify female pleasure—or pain—depending on his mood.

Tamsin pressed past him, her scantily clad flesh warm with the heat of the bed she'd just left. "Think so? She's a blonde. You don't like blondes."

She turned her cat-shaped face to him, pushing back the tumbling dark waves that framed it. Her sensual moves had been thoroughly practiced. Less than two weeks ago, she'd been crowned queen of a private pageant in Miami. For call girls only. There had been no swimsuit competition, of course. Just world-class naked women, strutting in impossibly high heels in front of rows of well-dressed johns.

There had been quite a bit of bending over and bouncing. The talent show was a lascivious extravaganza, topped off with a girl-on-girl threesome that had the men crazed with lust. Human males were conspicuously lacking in self-control in such an environment. He felt nothing but contempt for them.

His darling Tamsin had stuck to singing and come in fifth. But Vladimir had paid off the judges to boost her points in the most important category, Sexy Bitch, for an overall win and a crystal tiara. Then he'd paid her to fly north with him.

"My interest is purely professional, my dear." Vladimir placed a cigarette between his thin lips and lit it. He blew the smoke out the open window. "That stupid manager has hired too many brunettes for Club Red and the opening is not far away."

When it came to acquiring females for the club, he no longer had Daria and Oksana to rely on. They'd been picked up during some kind of raid on Salvation's Crossing. Whatever bargain they'd struck with the cops and prosecutors, and he was sure they had, he knew they'd be smart enough not to mention him. Even so, since Vladimir could no longer count on them to provide fresh faces for his latest enterprise, he'd had to explore other "headhunters," so to speak. This time, his best recruiter was a man—or to be more precise, a human male turned vampire—and he obviously didn't like blondes. Vladimir had been meaning to have a talk with him about his shortsightedness, but unfortunately he had more pressing concerns to think about—like the fact Club Red had run wildly overbudget.

Even so, it ought to turn a profit soon enough given Vladimir was planning to cater to the überwealthy, human and vampire included.

For humans (or at least those who wanted to pretend they were human), the club's main area was huge, with a vaulted ceiling and three levels for dancers to entertain the patrons. Private rooms were located on the uppermost level, where expensive whores—also paying a cut to the house—could see to clients behind closed doors.

As for his other patrons? The richest vampires of his acquaintance, though they were few in number, could safely indulge their guilty pleasures below the main level, in a hidden palace of vice. Betting on staged blood sports—with a generous cut taken by the house—would rake in hundreds of thousands per event, but the secret auction of teenage girls—Vladimir's idea—would earn much more. The fighting arena was nearly completed and the machinery installed for the cage to be suspended above a pit. The stage for the auction of girl slaves, a separate and more intimate space, had been finished to his satisfaction. Every seat had an unobstructed view of the innocents who would be chained to the block for inspection and sale.

He returned his attention to the woman in the pool, toying with the idea of installing something like it for an indoor swimming revue. Naked girls, their heads underwater, legs spread far apart in synchronized splits—lovely and a guaranteed moneymaker. Coins in the fountain.

"Why are you smirking?" Tamsin asked. "She's probably not even a natural blonde."

Vladimir was not inclined to argue, though he doubted that Tamsin's snippy remark was accurate.

"What could she do that I couldn't do?" Tamsin persisted. "Besides, you don't know a damn thing about her. She's just some chick swimming."

"She has something special."

"I don't see it." Tamsin shivered dramatically. "Ooh, I'm cold. Close the window."

"In a moment. Go sit on the couch."

She seemed about to protest, but obviously the flash of silver in his hooded eyes made her obey with obvious reluctance. For a few moments, she sulked in silence. Vladimir smoked a little longer, thinking that she might need to be turned over his knee and properly disciplined. Perhaps later. She did like it.

"Looking at her, Tamsin, I am reminded that we need a hostess. For the first level."

"Not some stranger, Vladdy. What are you planning to do, swim out there and hand her your business card?"

"No. There are other ways."

"Come on. I could do it," she whined.

"You will be in charge of the VIP rooms and the bottle service. Just think of the money you'll make off rich fools."

"I hope so."

Tamsin settled herself so that Vladimir could see her reflection in the plate glass. She spread her legs and showed off the lacy thong that barely concealed her shaved pubes.

Vladimir ignored the display. He was fascinated by the swimmer.

She seemed to be alone. The reflecting sparkle of the water caught the low-key lighting around the pool and made her look like a ghostly mermaid. He narrowed his gaze, focusing his keen night vision on her drenched breasts, barely covered by the bikini top. She rose and fell slightly with each breath she took, a delicious tiny pool of water in her belly button remaining when the water sluiced off her skin.

Her hips lifted, too. Not much. Her pretty feet kicked gently to keep herself from sinking. Her face was serene, her eyes closed. The water did its magic, turning her hair into a waving crown of silken strands.

Vladimir finished his cigarette and crushed the butt

into the windowsill. Then he looked at Tamsin's reflection. She was being unexpectedly patient. But then her hands were busy between her legs. Stroking and rubbing. Penetrating herself with a small sex toy.

She interested him less and less, but at that moment he found her behavior arousing.

"That's enough," he said in a low voice, turning around.

"I thought you liked to watch," was the petulant reply.

Vladimir gave a shrug. "Not now. Not what you are doing, anyway. Your pleasure is too selfish."

"Sorry." She withdrew the toy and set it aside.

"Hurt yourself for me. That is what I want to see."

Tamsin sighed.

"Show me your nails."

She raised her hands with palms toward him. "I had them done today. They're extremely sharp." The long, perfectly polished fingernails were lined on the inside with crescents of surgical steel that shone like silver.

"Good."

Tamsin lifted her breasts, holding them tightly. She dug the steel crescents into her skin, watching his eyes widen. A few tiny drops of blood appeared. Vladimir moved quickly to pull her hands away and force them behind her back, licking up the red drops, eager for more, leaning over her. She fell back, playing helpless. The performance was reasonably effective. He sat and pulled her onto his lap, stroking her neck until her head fell back, exposing a pulsing vein in her throat.

The towel around his hips loosened and fell off. His long, rapidly stiffening cock was equally exposed—and pulsing harder.

Vladimir's lips drew back. He sank long fangs into the vein, sipping with restraint. One of them had to hold back. Tamsin relished the languor that followed a loss of blood, a little too much. Her soft body pressed against him, writhing with pleasure. His hands slid under her bare bottom, avidly fondling her squirming buttocks as he drank a little deeper. He closed his eyes.

The blonde swimmer in his mind floated away.

Barrett heard a muffled splash. She raised her head to look around, seeing only the disturbed surface of the water. Strong hands grabbed her ankles and forced her legs down. She kicked free, frightened.

Nick's head popped up next to her. He swam in place, smiling. Barrett splashed him until he laughed.

"Sorry. I couldn't stand it another second. You looked like a water goddess."

"I thought you didn't have trunks."

His shoulders and chest were bare and gleaming with water. He splashed her back when she tried to look down.

"You wish, Barrett. Had to keep on the jeans."

She swam away, letting him follow. They circled each other in the water for a minute or so.

"You okay?" he asked softly.

"Yes."

They played around in the water for several minutes, then drifted together. One minute she'd been swimming by herself, and the next Nick was here with her, playing with her, bringing back memories of how good it had felt to be with him, both in bed and out. She really had missed him. So much. "I'm tired," Barrett whispered.

"Put your arms around my shoulders," Nick instructed. "Just ride. Don't help."

She hesitated briefly, knowing she was being weak. Reminding herself that she'd ended things with him for a reason—to protect her heart—and that she'd only come to him so he'd help her find Jane. She sighed. Just thinking Jane's name made her feel small and powerless.

She didn't want to feel that way. For now, she didn't want to think of anything else but her and Nick. Almost defiantly, she reached out and clung to him, feeling the power in his muscled back, keeping her legs free of his strong kicks. It was bliss to let him take over and go in circles in the warm water. When they were nearly at the ladder, he pushed her arms off and rolled so that they were face to face but still floating. He brushed away the wet blond silk from her cheeks and kissed her. Again and again.

Nick pulled back, breathing hard. "I want you, Barrett. I know it's not a good time, but it's been over a year. A whole fucking year of me not having you. Of not being inside you. You don't want this, just tell me now and I'll—"

Barrett pressed her fingers against his mouth, effectively stopping his words. He'd sounded so damn desperate when he'd been talking. Desperate for her. And she felt that same desperation spiraling inside her. In that moment, all her doubts, self-protective thoughts, and worries fled. She let go of her guilt about Noah and Jane and let herself be greedy. She was going to have to leave Nick as abruptly as she'd found him in order to return to D.C. and interview Jane's guardians. Couldn't she take something for herself first?

She couldn't think of anything she wanted more than to take Nick.

"I want you, too, Nick. I've never stopped wanting you."

At her whispered confession, he snagged her wrist and dragged it away from his mouth. He kissed her again, angling his head for maximum positioning, tangling his tongue with hers and pressing her so close that she felt not only desired but safe.

Neither noticed the glowing cigarette behind the darkened glass of the window high above or the man who had returned to the window to smoke it.

He watched them until they left the pool.

Nick opened the door of the VIP lounge near the pool and looked inside. "Empty. Good. Wait here," he told Barrett in a low voice.

He returned in a few seconds, with a luxurious new robe in his hand, draping it over her shoulders. She was grateful. The thick, velvety terry stopped her shivering.

"Who does this belong to?" The folded towels stacked by the pool for guests hadn't been enough to ward off the night's odd chill.

"The hotel. We can give it back later."

They made their way back to his suite. She stayed with him, not going into the adjoining room. She knew what he wanted. She wanted the same thing. Barrett had no intention of playing coy. The floating kisses had taken her to a different place. A place where she was at peace. Opened up again.

But for some reason, she hesitated to take off the robe just yet. It was as if it represented some last vestige of restraint she had left. The only thing that stood between her and falling head-over-heels in love with Nick Maltese all over again.

He took her by the shoulders and turned her toward the bathroom. "We're going to take this slow and easy. Hot shower first, you and me both. To get rid of the chlorine. I don't want to smell anything but sweet woman."

He'd gotten her good and lathered up lots of times.

Barrett caved. She wasn't going to argue. Barrett shrugged and let the heavy robe slip off her shoulders.

Nick caught it before it hit the tiles and slung it backward through the bathroom door onto the bed.

He slid his fingers under each strap of the bikini bra and pulled them down. Stopped. She wasn't any more naked than she had been. But she felt bared to the soul. His dark eyes rested on hers.

Barrett unsnapped the front clasp and freed her breasts. He smiled and cupped them. She pressed her lips together. If he kissed her right now, it would be too damn much.

He did, but not on the lips. His lips brushed her forehead, pressing in for a fraction of a second. A ritual kiss, not passionate. Silently telling her she was his.

For now, yes, Barrett thought. It was nice to think so.

She stepped back and peeled off the wet bottom half of her bikini, wincing when it dragged over her damp skin. Once it was down to her ankles, she kicked it into a corner.

Then she straightened.

Nick stood inches away, stripped and solid. She drank him in. He'd lost none of the ribbed muscle and virility she relished. The purely masculine line of his groin was just as taut.

She couldn't resist tracing a fingertip along it. He tensed but he was smiling. His gorgeous cock instantly came to attention.

Thick shaft, big veins, plum tip. The gorgeous length of it straining upward. Saying hello.

"Wow." She smiled. "I remember that. Fine as ever."

"Thank you," he said. "So are you." His eyes moved slowly, lovingly, over her bare body, lingering on her breasts, which perked up shamelessly under his hot gaze. His cock twitched.

She moved to hold it but he caught her by the wrist. "Not yet."

She sighed, more with anticipation than with regret.

She knew exactly how good that part of him felt in her hand, especially when he was above her, her legs spread wide to receive him. She didn't mind waiting. Some orders were worth following.

"Let's get in," he said. "After you."

She went first, looking up at the fixed main showerhead above. There was a handheld shower below it.

Nick followed her in, doing his best not to crowd her. There was barely enough room for two normal people. Buck naked, he looked even taller. Barrett pressed back against the tiles so he could turn around.

They had just been in each other's arms. Mouth to mouth. Why did she feel so nervous all of a sudden? Because, she told herself, the thin nylon swimwear that had been between them was gone. No armor.

Nick had a way of reading her mind. "You're okay," he said. "Don't think about what happened on the mountain. That's far away. You're here with me."

"I'll keep that in mind."

He reached for the bar of soap and rubbed it between his palms, making foam. "Turn around."

Barrett rotated until her back was to him. He reached around her, sliding the foamy bar over her breasts and nipples and working down to her waist, moving the soap around it in a swift stroke and over her hips, switching the bar from hand to hand. Then he set the soap aside, reaching up to tilt the showerhead and sluice her off.

She closed her eyes. Knowing he was so close was powerfully erotic. She felt a cock bump on the side of her hip and straightened.

"Stand still." The command was almost a growl.

Barrett still felt like obeying. What the hell. She tensed when his balls brushed the small of her back as he reached around to get the handheld shower attachment. Oh yes.

Nick figured out how it worked and got a pulsing stream going, a stronger sensation than the waterfall over her head. He employed the handheld expertly, flicking the pulse button to greater intensity when he got to her breasts. Barrett arched her body to lift them higher.

He knew what she wanted and narrowed the pulse with one twist of the handle. Tiny jets of water hit each nipple in turn. Barrett moaned under her breath.

"Hold 'em high. Play with those beautiful tits."

She could barely stand up. Barrett swayed back against him, cupping her breasts, pushing the tips into the rapid pulses.

The jets of water felt like a licking tongue. His. She couldn't wait for him to suck her wet nipples into tight pink peaks.

Nick had other ideas. He treated her to a few more variations of the pulse setting. Down her belly. Over her pussy. She reached down to open her labia.

He got the point. Her clitoris got the attention. After a glorious minute, she closed her legs tight and pushed his hand away. "I don't want to come too soon."

"If you say so," he muttered, moving the handheld around to her back. The pulsing stream splashed over her behind. Nick seized his chance—and her. With a low laugh, he copped a squeeze. Then another. "Oh yeah. Round and firm." The squeezing turned into an erotic, one-handed massage and intimate rubdown that made her rock her hips back and forth.

"Ooh. Yes. Nick—yes. More. Don't stop."

"Guess you like that."

"You know I do."

Being thorough, he parted her cheeks and kept the handheld in play.

"Not that," she said quickly.

Nick laughed again. "Don't worry. But don't think I've never thought about it. Your ass is beyond cute."

Pulse pulse. Between her cheeks. Splash. Up her back. Down her front. Back. Front. And around again. The constantly moving sensations were almost too much. Barrett turned around and made him drop the thing.

She draped her arms around his shoulders, giving herself a boost when he scooped her up for a kiss.

"We're going to fall!"

"Wouldn't be the first time. Let's get wild. *Rawrrr. Grrr.*" Nick growled into her wet neck, making her laugh, too. She stretched out a hand against the wall to brace herself and him. He turned and set her down outside the shower enclosure and stepped over the low sill.

His magnificent erection was still going strong. Barrett slid a hand over his hip, admiring all that. She had half a mind to drop to her knees and—

"Not yet, girl."

He unfolded a huge towel and wrapped it tightly around her without his hands ever touching her skin. Somehow that seemed more erotic than a caress after a shower like that. And she knew his hands would be all over her naked body in a short while.

"Take a breather. I gotta make some calls."

Disappointment slammed through her at his abrupt about-face. It made her reconsider what she was doing, but only for a split second. After what they'd just done in the shower, she wasn't going to pass up the opportunity for more simply because he had work to attend to. She had, after all, popped in out of nowhere, and their little helo flight hadn't exactly been planned.

Barrett snatched a towel off the rack to make a turban for her dripping hair. She could act as blasé as she needed to and give Nick the time he needed.

She studied her face in the mirror, liking the rosy glow. A good man was better than any makeup.

Wet, her eyelashes looked like she had on mascara. She patted her flushed cheeks. No blusher needed. Barrett hummed to drown out what she could hear of his conversation.

Sounded like business. Not interesting. But she had never been above eavesdropping. Under the circumstances . . .

Barrett gazed into the mirror, seeing the anxiety in her blue eyes. He'd better be talking business.

Too bad that coming back to a former lover meant having to accept who he'd been with since her. New moves. Different rhythm. Clues to someone else's pleasure. Female demands that weren't hers. So far, so good. But Barrett didn't imagine for a second that Nick had been celibate in the year they'd been apart.

She didn't like the thought of an invisible woman getting between them. Correction: women. Plural. Had to have happened. But there was nothing she could do about it. Considering how close she'd gotten to Powell, she couldn't exactly ask Nick a bunch of nosy questions.

Barrett took the hair dryer from the hook by the sink and switched it on, yanking off the towel and running a hand through the worst of the tangles before using the hottest setting to begin to dry her damp locks.

After a while, she switched it off. Her hair didn't have to be perfect. Nick gave a single knock on the not-quite-closed door and came in when she said to, moving behind her, gazing at her in the mirror. He lifted her hair off her neck and let it slide through his fingers.

"Nice," he murmured. "Feels like hot silk. Now where were we . . ."

Barrett said nothing. It was delicious to be treated with such gentleness.

He wrapped some longer locks around his hand and bared the nape of her neck, bending down to kiss it.

His lips moved over the sensitive skin with the skill

she remembered. Barrett stood riveted to the spot, not wanting him to ever stop. When he got to the back of her ear, he took the lobe in his teeth and nipped. The tiny flash of pain made her hiss. With pleasure.

Nick opened his fingers and released her hair. She shook her head and pushed the tumbling strands back into place, more or less. He rested both big hands on her bare shoulders.

"Look at you," he said approvingly.

"Big deal. You can't see a thing what with this towel."

She inspected him from head to toe. Slouchy athletic pants covered him from just below his taut middle to his ankles. The sleek bulge below the low waistband looked beyond tempting. "Why'd you get dressed?"

"Room service. I ordered for both of us. They came while you were blasting that dryer."

"We had dinner."

"Just a little something more. Come on. I'll show you." He guided her out with a hand on the small of her back.

Nick was being a gentleman. His hand stayed where it was, not drifting lower to enjoy the softness of her un-pantied ass beneath the towel. Which was so not like him.

Barrett willed his hand to move. It didn't. She was distracted from her frustration by the sight of the room-service table that had been wheeled into the middle of the suite. Immaculate white damask showed off a silver wine cooler, dewy with icy moisture. It held a bottle of very good champagne, wrapped in a white napkin.

Oh wow, she thought. So that's who he'd been calling. At least, it had been one of the calls he'd made. So he hadn't interrupted their make-out session as easily as she'd thought. He'd been trying to be romantic . . . and man, he'd succeeded.

"For now. Or for later," he clarified. "Whenever you want."

"Thanks." Barrett lifted the domed cover of a small dish and saw huge, chocolate-dipped strawberries. Also chilled, also dewy. "Definitely later for all of this," she said, turning to Nick. "I want you. Now."

The towel dropped. The athletic pants joined it on the floor. She fell backward on the bed and took him down with her.

The foreplay got wild, way wilder than the shower. In a few minutes, he was kneeling over her, pumping the huge cock he was so proud of because he knew she liked to watch him do it.

He had reason to be proud. His cock was more than twice as long as the width of his palm. He had to move his muscular ass back to do a complete stroke, root to tip. Barrett's gaze was soft with desire as she watched intently. She curled forward when he stopped for a second, putting her tongue to the swollen head just inside his encircling fingers.

Nick groaned, holding absolutely still as she licked him. Barrett saw no reason to stop. She lifted a hand to caress his balls while she teased him with her tongue. Once more Nick got her by the wrist.

"Whoa. Please. You gotta stop," he muttered.

She came up, stroking his flat belly and wiping her mouth on the hand that had stroked him between the legs. She'd gotten him way too hot. Nothing hung down. He had to be aching.

Barrett got on her knees and rubbed her body against him, kissing his chest, his small male nipples, and nuzzling his neck while she whispered how much she'd missed him. His touch. His body. His dick—

He knocked her flat. Then stayed over her on all fours and returned the favor, saying things into her ear that had her writhing with anticipation. "I've dreamed about you every night for the past year," he said. "I remember the way you feel. The way you sound. The way you smell and taste. But memories aren't the same. I want to sink into you, Barrett. I want to drown in your beauty. But first . . ."

It took three seconds for the condom conversation. The tests, four seconds. All clear. She was on the pill. He didn't seem to give a good goddamn why.

Barrett positioned his long cock just where she wanted it. And lifted herself to him. But he hesitated. She lowered herself, lifting her knees to cradle his body between them.

"I'm not going to break, Nick. Rock me like you mean it." She sank her fingers into his thick dark hair and pulled his face to hers for a scorching kiss. Tongues tangled as his hands slipped under her ass. The smooth head of his cock paused just outside her pussy.

One hot touch. Teasing her. Opening her. Then he thrust again and again. She almost screamed with joy. He still knew exactly how to drive her wild. She would never get enough. Not if they lived and loved for a thousand years.

Afterward, however, doubts started to intrude. It's how it always was with her.

It's why she'd run from him and why she knew she'd run from him again.

"You're safe with me," he said from where he lay spooned behind her, his arms wrapped around her so one hand cupped her breast and the other her hip.

"Am I?" she whispered, belying the fact she'd felt exactly that when she'd been in his arms. Now she knew there was a distinction to be made.

Here, now, she was physically safe, and she knew Nick would always do everything in his power to keep her that way. While she'd never be emotionally safe with him, she still craved what he was doing. The warm, strong, male hand on her skin took away the lingering taint of Joseph Powell's chilly touch.

Barrett relaxed under Nick's stroking hand. After a while, she fell into a dreamless sleep.

CHAPTER SIX

The soft ringing of the phone in his suite drew Vladimir back into the room. He was dressed now, in a silk robe worn open over flowing pants beneath. Tamsin had been quite thorough about licking him clean after his orgasm. There had been no need for a postcoital shower.

He looked toward the bedroom to make sure she was asleep. Tamsin lay on her side with her back to him, her outline a sweeping curve that narrowed at the waist and flowed up again to her hips. He smiled at the sight of her bare behind, still rosy from the spanking she'd begged for. He was half tempted to tongue her awake and make her come for a third time. But he picked up the receiver.

"Hello."

"Mr. Ouspensky?" The male voice was deferential. Gil Mansfield was a former U.S. soldier and turned vampire who'd decided he had better things to do than take orders from the FBI. A mutual acquaintance, the same one who'd designed the traveling white room that transported Vladimir's girls, had "introduced" them several months ago (the introduction had included breaking Mansfield out of federal custody), and since then, even though Mansfield was subject to the odd fit of rage, he knew better than to direct that rage at Vladimir. Even better, he knew how to follow orders, and he'd been surprisingly enterprising when it came to giving Vladimir what he wanted most.

Little did he know that within a relatively short time, he'd be losing his mind and most of his flesh, all compliments of the experimental drugs given to him by the FBI.

"What is it?" Vlad replied.

"I just wanted to let you know that the merchandise is in transit."

"Have there been any problems?"

The other man laughed. "Nope. None. I monitored her on the webcam all the way down. I can stream it live if you want."

"How interesting. Please do." Vladimir provided the man with the necessary contact information and opened his laptop, settling down on the couch.

In a few minutes, he downloaded a video feed of a white room that rocked with the motion of the highway traveled by the trailer carrying it and the captive girl inside.

He knew she would see only his eyes. But she would clearly hear his voice. It was important to establish control gradually, teach her to depend on him. But without harming her in any way. Delicate goods, this one. He searched his mind for her name. It would be changed, of course.

Jane Small. That was it.

How fitting. She was a slight thing. Her dress had been ripped at some point but there was no mark on her, not so much as a scratch. He touched a key, bringing her sweet face into sharp focus.

Either her complexion was naturally pale or her terror had drained it of color. The delicate sprinkling of freckles across the bridge of her nose emphasized its childlike upturn. Her hair was reddish-gold, long and wavy. Despite her ragged attire, the girl had a refined quality about her, as if she had stepped out of a fairy tale and not into the nightmare Vladimir had planned for her. Her intelligent eyes were a dark hazel, her expression as soft and startled as a fawn discovered in its hiding place. Using her fingers—he could see that her unpolished nails had been bitten to the quick—she rubbed her eyes. With particular enjoyment, Vladimir noticed the traces of the tears she'd shed, still visible on her cheeks.

Such innocence. Such fear. She would fetch a high price.

Vladimir pressed the key for a two-way. "Hello, Jane."

The girl gasped, looking around desperately to see who had spoken. He knew how his deep voice would echo in the smooth-walled room. Suddenly she saw his eyes high above her.

"Who are you?" she whispered.

"We will meet soon enough, my dear."

She fell silent, pulling the torn dress around herself in a charming attempt at modesty. He knew she was still feeling the effects of the drugs she'd been forced to take to keep her quiet. She seemed dazed. Certainly disoriented.

"Why is—why is everything so round and smooth in here?"

The traveling room had no sharp edges and no angles. Previous versions had resulted in minor injuries to its unwilling occupants as they banged on the walls and tried to climb them. Now the molded furniture was part of the seamless walls.

"Just for you, Jane," he replied. "What a pretty girl you are. We would like you to arrive unhurt so we have removed all dangers. It seems that you have threatened to cut yourself from time to time in the past. Or was that only a phase brought on by that wanna-be vampire you were seeing? I was told he tried to save you when you were taken. Quite admirable. In any event, you cutting yourself won't be allowed, you know. You must follow the rules."

Her eyes widened with terror. No doubt she knew who had betrayed her. "Who told you that?"

"Someone who knows you well." Vladimir gave a low laugh. He tapped a key that would plunge the white room into darkness. Gradually, of course. She would have plenty of time to crawl into a molded sleeping alcove.

The temperature of the traveling room was comfortably warm. There were no blankets. Not since a desperate abductee had torn a long strip from one and used it to hang herself. The closet rod intended for longer journeys when girls were stripped of their clothing and inspected en route had since been removed, solving that potential problem. The clandestine transports represented a considerable investment of money and time.

Until the transaction was complete, no one was allowed to damage the merchandise—not the abductors, who sometimes got carried away, and not the girls themselves, some of whom, unfortunately, were rather good at self-harm. Hence the warning to Jane.

Of course, once an auction was over and a large sum of cash had changed hands, the purchaser was welcome to do whatever he wanted with his young victim.

No returns. No exchanges. Every sale was final.

Vladimir watched as she stood unsteadily and took a few steps. The trailer truck went around a curve and forced her to sit down. Jane Small was on her way to a whole new life. For as long as it lasted.

"Good night," he whispered.

CHAPTER SEVEN

Barrett woke up long before Nick did. She made coffee in the in-room coffeemaker, not liking the sour smell. The self-serve packet couldn't be fresh. And there was only powdered creamer.

Welcome to reality, she told herself. She poured a cup anyway and wandered back into the main room of the suite. The champagne bottle was upside down in the silver cooler. They'd finished that after the final round of unbelievable sex. The strawberries, too. There was still a half of one. The top half. No chocolate. She picked it up by its slender green stem and nibbled the sweet, juicy flesh absently.

This was breakfast. She wanted to be out of here before Nick woke up. She peeked in at him. Snoring like a tiger. Legs apart, pillow in his arms instead of under his head.

Dreaming of her, maybe. Dream on, she told herself. He'd had more women than there were pillows in this hotel.

Still, it had been great, a total release for both of them, multiorgasmic satisfaction, and something like oblivion when they were spent and finished. The homicidal creature that had attacked her had stayed out of her dreams. In one night, Nick Maltese had vanquished the incomprehensible loneliness of a year without him. When it came to sexual healing, he had all the moves.

In the cold light of dawn, she knew that she never wanted to need him for that. Needing him, period, was just plain dangerous. If he helped her find Jane, then great. But she wasn't setting herself up for heartbreak ever again.

His eyes opened. He'd always had a sixth sense about being watched.

"Hey, angel. What are you doing?" he asked drowsily.

"Drinking coffee. It's terrible. I gotta go."

"Where?" He patted the wrinkled sheet beside him. "Come back to bed."

"Nope," she said calmly. "Just got a text. There's an early meeting in D.C."

Not quite a lie. Carly did like to get them over with before noon. Nick made no reply.

"Taxi's waiting."

It would be. She could be dressed and downstairs in five minutes if she skipped a real shower and made do with a wet washcloth instead. He buried his face in the tangled sheets and groaned.

"Call me later." She wasn't going to not talk to him.

"Okay." He yawned hugely and rolled over.

Barrett thought he had fallen asleep by the time she had made herself presentable in the adjoining room and collected the few things she was taking back with her. She went past his bedroom without looking in—and stopped short when she turned. He was standing right in front of the suite door.

Naked. No longer sleepy. And morning-handsome, with dark stubble edging his jaw and adorably scruffy hair.

"Good morning," she said crisply, reaching around him to open the door.

He didn't catch her wrist, just stood there. "You look nice." He smiled encouragingly.

"Don't get ideas." She pushed the latch down hard

and pulled at the door, bumping it against his bare butt. Nick didn't budge. He folded his arms across his chest. "And don't get a hard-on. Think about vampires."

"Won't work. You're too close."

Barrett stepped back several inches. "Move, Nick. I have to leave."

They both heard a housekeeping cart rattle down the hall and stop not far away.

"Do you want the maid to see you like this?"

"No."

He unfolded his arms, standing behind the door as he opened it for her. Barrett moved past him in her gift shop outfit, the rest of her things in the plastic bag meant for guest laundry. She stopped on the sill to get in a parting shot. "Bad enough I have to do the walk of shame."

"Hold your head high," he instructed, lightly slapping her on the butt before wrapping his hand around the back of her neck and pulling her in for a kiss.

She'd just started to lose herself in it and in him before he pulled away.

"Be careful, Barrett. And touch base soon."

Hours later, Barrett had taken a cab to the Atlanta airport, caught a flight to Dulles, and made the meeting at Belladonna where she'd updated Carly on the destruction of her rental car and the "thing" that had attacked her. Now she was in yet another rental car heading to western Maryland.

During the meeting at Belladonna, she'd listened to the discussion of what the other agents were working on. Collette had flown to New York after wrangling an invite to a board meeting at a big pharmaceutical company, hoping to spin that into an insider's look into their blood-bank subsidiary. Ty and Ana were doing all right, according to Peter, but weren't ready to appear at the meeting, even though Ana's turning process was nearly completed. Barrett had kept quiet until the end. She had said nothing about the attack on the mountain. Just that she'd talked to Nick about Jane. All preliminary. Nothing to report.

Only Justine had looked hard at Barrett's atypical attire. But she hadn't commented on it. For a former exotic dancer who liked to obsess over clothes and shoes and hair, it was a rare example of tactfulness, for which Barrett had been grateful.

She really hadn't had anything to report that would convince Carly the case was a worthwhile use of Belladonna's resources and time. There still was nothing specific that linked Jane to the original mission: taking down vampires that sexually enslaved underage girls.

But Powell's involvement aside, something had told her from the second she'd stared into Jane's frightened eyes that there was a connection. Her hands tightened on the steering wheel.

Nick hadn't challenged her on that. She knew he wouldn't have offered to help otherwise. He believed in intuition. His own and hers.

He'd listened. Offered some good advice. She couldn't expect him to drop everything and ride to the rescue with banners flying. Even though he'd done it for those two girls and their mother. What had he said at the time? That it was a miracle everything had gone off without a hitch.

One miracle, once in a lifetime. Maybe that was all anyone got.

She reached toward the dashboard console, scanning radio stations for something to listen to. She hummed along with a forgettable song, her mind elsewhere. The western section of the Beltway had much less traffic than the rest of it. But she knew from experience how easy it was to zone out and go in a giant circle, ending up where she'd started, crawling along in the usual jams to I-95 north and south.

She wondered what Nick was up to. He hadn't gotten around to telling her anything more about what he was doing on the mountain or why he had to be so isolated. She supposed that wasn't unusual. As he'd said, he'd tell her what was relevant, and apparently his work wasn't relevant to her or Jane's situation.

He'd been secretive about his work when they were stationed in Eastern Europe, too, sometimes disappearing for a week or more, supposedly at forward operating bases on assignments he refused to discuss.

It was common knowledge that black ops personnel operated under neutral cover identities. He really was a tech wiz. But she'd gotten more than one glimpse of the amazing weaponry he designed and used.

If the evil thing that had attacked her came back, Nick wouldn't miss a second time. Partly because she wouldn't be there to fuck up his aim. Least she could do.

Barrett was less tense than she had expected to be. Which might have to do with her and Nick and crazy sex. What a night. It had been *intense*. As a lover, he was one of a kind.

The only one she'd ever really wanted to keep. Probably just as well she'd been booted out of the service, she thought, even though it had been an honorable discharge. She would have hung around him for too long, wanted more than he seemed to want to give her.

She had other things to think about.

Barrett pulled at her constricting seat belt, not wanting to wrinkle her clothes. The conservative navy blue suit and sky-blue blouse she'd changed into for the trip to see the Prescotts looked kinda FBI.

She wasn't going to tell them she actually worked for the FBI as an agent, however, nor was she going to explain why she hadn't given them warning she was coming.

It wasn't polite to show up unannounced but it had been a deliberate decision. Barrett wanted to catch them off guard.

She was going to get some answers. Especially after reading brief but heartbreaking personal stories on the websites she'd visited while looking for Jane. There were only a handful of happy endings and reunions when it came to abducted girls. Most were the victims of violence. And not all of the missing had loved ones searching for them, or even names.

The unidentified dead were duly recorded and buried after a while. Morgues filled up. New victims arrived.

Barrett changed lanes when a big truck started tailgating her. It zoomed past. She saw her exit and sped toward it.

The Prescott house was a solid brick mansion set in beautifully landscaped grounds. The houses in the new Maryland subdivision had been constructed on two-acre lots to provide maximum privacy for their well-heeled residents, who probably didn't know their neighbors at all.

Barrett stretched out her hand to press the polished brass doorbell. The door swung open before the sound of the chimes died away, revealing a fiftyish man. Barrett noticed that his graying hair was a shade lighter than the charcoal shirt he wore with a dark tie. Dark pants and black wingtips completed what seemed to be a carefully chosen ensemble, on the conservative side. She would have pegged him for a professor even if she hadn't researched him online and read a few of his published articles in psychology journals. He specialized in adolescent dysfunction. "Mr. Prescott? I'm Barrett Miles. A friend of Sarah Small's. I'm sorry to just drop in like this, but I was in town and wanting to see if you've gotten any new information about Jane."

His brow furrowed for several seconds, then cleared. "Of course. Ginny said you'd spoken. Please, you can call me Malcolm. We're almost like family, after all." Somehow the words sounded rehearsed, and his face had become expressionless.

Barrett smiled politely.

"Please come in." He stepped aside to let her enter.

"Thanks."

His gaze stayed on her, but suddenly Malcolm Prescott smiled back, as if he had just remembered he was supposed to. Barrett tried to think nothing of it. The few shrinks she knew personally—though not well—were all a little nutty.

She walked into a double-height foyer. The arched window above it was covered with drawn curtains that made the entrance rather dim.

A slender woman with cropped brown hair rose from a modern beige sofa as they entered the living room. Barrett's first impression of the room was of absolute tidiness.

The space had been decorated in neutral tones, none of which stood out or caught the eye. The four throw pillows on the sofa hadn't been thrown but placed diagonally on their points an equal distance apart. The magazines on the sparkling glass coffee table had been arranged with similar precision and looked unread. Across from the sofa was a glass-doored fireplace stacked with never-to-be-burned birch logs.

The message was Don't Touch. With a postscript: Don't Breathe. The vibe was startlingly similar to her mother's showplace houses. Barrett couldn't imagine Sarah's creative, gentle daughter being happy in this environment. She felt a renewed wave of guilt that made her sick at heart.

"Ginny, I'm Barrett."

"Barrett. Of course. I remember you from the pictures Sarah showed me before she died." She wrung her hands. "Do you have any information on Jane?"

"I'm afraid not. I was hoping you . . ."

Closing her eyes briefly, Ginny shook her head. "Nothing."

Malcolm summoned a housemaid using a bell mounted in the wall and turned to Barrett. "What would you like? A drink? Soda?"

"A cold ginger ale would be very nice. Thanks."

Once seated, they got through the requisite small talk—and nervous apologies on both sides for not being in touch over the years.

Ginny gave Barrett a mournful look. "My poor little half sister," she said in a watery voice. "We were so many years apart and we never lived in the same house. But I did care for her and I wanted to do right by her daughter."

"I'm sure you've done your best for Jane," Barrett said, thinking it was more than she could say about herself.

The older woman composed herself, pulling her navy blue dress down over her knees. "Yes. Of course." She glanced somewhat nervously at her husband.

"Jane has tremendous potential but she also has multiple issues," Malcolm said vaguely. "Unresolved grief for her deceased mother is one, of course. It manifests as inappropriate rage and threats of self-harm, that kind of thing."

He sounded almost bored, as if Jane wasn't his foster daughter, but more like a subject for an article. He confirmed Barrett's take on the situation by looking through the magazines on the table and holding up a professional journal with his photo on the cover.

"As you may know, I'm an expert in the field of adolescent psychology. Jane's case is atypical but her behavior isn't far from the norm. If you'd like to read it, I wrote up her case." He handed the journal to Barrett. "Of course I changed her name and other identifying details."

Big of him. Some expert. More like a pompous ass, Barrett thought. Just listening to him was bringing back unwelcome memories. Her own rebellious streak had been managed, if that was the right word, by her mother's pet shrink, Dr. Agee. He'd echoed every single one of Mrs. Miles's negative opinions of her daughter and prescribed pills that Barrett refused to take.

"Mal, she knew you were talking about her," Ginny said sharply. "That was when she began to withdraw. And she didn't always come home, though that was nothing new."

Years ago, Barrett had heard Sarah say the same thing. "What did you do when that happened?"

"I waited here," Ginny began. "Right by the phone. Waited and waited, just in case—"

Her husband interrupted her. "Jane never called. Simply put, she was developmentally unable to take genuine responsibility for her actions. But I took the time to drive around and look for her—I knew her favorite haunts. She usually would come back with me if I spotted her."

Between him and a ride to the station in a patrol car, Jane evidently hadn't had much of a choice.

"I was able to reason with her when no one else could," Malcolm added. "Her boyfriends didn't want any trouble with the law. She certainly didn't want to be remanded to a youthful-offenders facility. Did I mention that I also consult for the county juvenile justice system?"

Malcolm was a fountain of information, very little of which made him look good.

"No. How interesting," Barrett said. "So you must know everyone from the local cops up to the judges."

"I do, yes."

"But Jane was never in any real trouble, was she?"

"Actually, no," he answered thoughtfully. "She had me to thank for that." Another smug smile. "I kept the boys at bay and I kept her out of jail. Things changed abruptly after she met *Dante*." Despite the fact the boy had been violently murdered, Malcolm's use of his name dripped with disdain.

Barrett mentally added *controlling* and *jealous* to his personality description.

"She always confided in me the most when we were in the car," he rambled on. "Our time together was effective therapy. Sometimes we drove around for hours."

Like that didn't sound super creepy, she thought. But Malcolm Prescott didn't seem aware of how unsavory his boasting sounded. Conscientious therapists didn't see clients in their cars. And a responsible guardian ought to have better things to do than drive around with his young ward for hours.

"Which worried me sick," his wife complained.

"I couldn't interrupt Jane to check in with you, dear. She had so much on her mind. There were things that she would only tell me."

His smug reply grated on Barrett. So Malcolm Prescott went out of his way to force a foster daughter who undoubtedly hated him to spend hours in his company, away from his passive wife. Barrett was beginning to understand more and more what Jane's life had been like. She just hoped she hadn't suffered anything worse at Malcolm's hands.

"Since you spent so much time with her, do you know who she talked to online? Because I can't be sure, but I think I saw her there a few days ago." Barrett had no plans of telling the Prescotts that she'd spotted Jane in a sex-for-sale lineup. If it turned out that she was wrong, had imagined the resemblance in the fleeting seconds of the girl's appearance, the consequences could be devastating.

She had to proceed carefully. In no way could she represent herself as investigating in an official capacity. She was here in Maryland as a friend of the family. Nothing more.

"Was it one of those social media sites?" Ginny asked.

"Not exactly. It was more like a—oh, I can't think of the right term. And it was only for a few seconds. I'd guess you could call it a party site," she ventured. "But it didn't seem like the kind of party a young girl should be attending."

"You mean she was posting photos from one of those raves?"

"Could've been."

"I—I don't know anything about what she did online," Ginny said.

Barrett set aside her slippery glass. The condensation from the iced drink made a puddle on the coaster. Ginny took a white cocktail napkin from a square holder and mopped it up, then crumpled the napkin and held it in her fist. She was thin-skinned. Her knuckles seemed nearly as white.

Malcolm deliberately caught Barrett's eye. She could practically hear what he was thinking. *My wife doesn't have a clue.*

What he said was different. "Ginny and Jane just weren't that close."

Barrett looked at Mrs. Prescott to confirm her reaction. Without looking back at her, the older woman gave the slightest shake of her head. It was impossible to tell if she agreed or disagreed with her husband's cold words.

Malcolm got to his feet, seeming impatient. "Barrett, I'd like to show you where Jane hung out, share some very personal things she said to me—would you mind?"

"Do you mean take a drive?"

"Yes. It might help. I've already done it, several times, but by myself." He slid a contemptuous glance at his wife. "I think a fresh eye might pick up something I missed."

"Maybe." Barrett didn't want to go.

"You're obviously a smart young lady. By the way, I don't believe you mentioned what it is you do." He gave a bland smile that was hard to read.

She was on the spot. In her defense, the subject hadn't come up. But had he deliberately backed her into a corner? There was no way to determine that for certain. So much for not telling them everything. But she could still stall. "I work for the FBI."

Malcolm's gaze narrowed.

"Nothing dangerous. Just systems management," she explained. "You know, data in, data out. Report in triplicate. Someone has to do it."

"Weren't you in the army?" The question came from Ginny.

"Yes. I guess Sarah told you that much."

Ginny's gaze held hers. Barrett had the strong feeling that Jane hadn't been the only one trapped in this house.

"I left after a few years," Barrett said. "Burned out, I guess. And I never had time for my family."

The Prescotts seemed to buy it. At least they stopped asking questions. Barrett thanked Ginny and followed her husband to a side door that evidently led into a garage.

Malcolm gave her the grand tour of the suburban main drag. The development the Prescotts lived in was one of several around the original small town at their center.

The vehicle was new but crammed with papers and food trash. She pushed aside a crumpled, greasy sack with her foot and he looked down.

"Sorry. Not like the house, is it?"

"I don't really care."

"Some of the mess belongs to Jane. I'm not ready to toss it. Not until I know where she is and what's going on."

He seemed different in the car, noticeably so. Somewhat less pompous and more real. But Barrett still didn't trust him.

"Is that the fountain?" There was a boy with a guitar and a girl with a flute, playing together as water jumped behind them in intersecting arcs.

"The one and only. Drowns out the so-called music they play, thank God. Jane went there often. It's kind of a haven for the arty kids."

Barrett had been one herself as a teenager. She never went anywhere without drawing paper and about a thousand colored markers, creating complicated abstract drawings that tied together every sad and funny and wonderful and miserable thing in her life.

She saw other kids that didn't look so arty in the near distance. "Who are they?"

"The punks. They pretty much stick to the other side of the park."

"Do you have any gangs out here?"

"Not that I know of. But these days they're everywhere, or so I hear."

Barrett acknowledged that unfortunate fact with a nod. "Did you ask any of the kids whether they'd seen her?"

"Yes. All of them. She's well known and well liked."

Prescott's jaw tightened. "No one's laid eyes on her for three days. I don't know what else to do but believe them."

He pulled the SUV over and parked it, resting his hands on the wheel.

"Look, I'll be honest with you, Barrett," he said after several moments of silence. "Ginny and I really aren't getting along. I guess you could say we've been drifting apart. Slowly. Excruciatingly slowly. We probably would've filed for divorce if not for Jane. A few months ago Jane found another article, an unpublished one I'd written about a patient she thought was Ginny and confronted me. I tried to explain myself. Big mistake."

Barrett wasn't buying Malcolm Prescott's new, improved story or his sudden honesty. She didn't trust anyone who could switch personalities so easily. Although it wasn't that big of a leap from pompous fuck to self-righteous bastard who thought he owned the rights to other people's lives.

"Anyway, she started acting up awhile ago. It got worse and worse."

"That's unfortunate." Barrett wanted nothing more than to get out of his car and into hers. But she had to hear him out. There was a chance he might give her some useful information. She forced herself to listen to him.

"I did spend a lot of time with her just driving around. But don't get the wrong idea. I just wish I hadn't gotten high with her. Seemed like the thing to do at the time." He slammed his hand punishingly hard against the steering wheel, then winced.

Barrett felt no sympathy whatsoever. She remembered when she was young enough and needy enough to think certain adults were cool because they were willing to share with kids. Their lives, their dope, their need for attention. Impressing a naive teenager wasn't difficult.

Even the smart ones got suckered into mind games like that.

Prescott rubbed his knuckles. "Anyway, you get the idea," he was saying. "Nothing in Merrytown for teenagers to do but hang out and think of new ways to get in trouble. There's the Shop-N-Bell."

Barrett looked out her rolled-down window at a cracked, white plastic sign that showed a shopping cart inside a stylized bell.

"Popularly known as the Cop-N-Hell," he continued. "The police come here for snacks and scatter the kids on their way out. They drift back when the cruisers leave. Jane used to meet her best friend here to split one of those giant slushy drinks."

Barrett had noticed the cup from one crushed into the side compartment with a lot of other paper junk.

"Want anything?" he asked her, pulling into a slot.

"No. Nothing for me."

"I'm going to get a burrito. If that doesn't kill me, nothing will."

"Are you suicidal?" she inquired, not all that politely.

"I wouldn't give Ginny the satisfaction," he replied, back to being himself again. He opened his door and stepped out, going through the doors of the Shop-N-Bell.

Barrett waited until she saw him give the clerk his order and wait for it to be microwaved. She looked down at the clutter in the side pocket, realizing that much of it was probably Jane's. The handwriting on some of the papers was girlish and round, with a lot of curlicues and doodles in the margins. There was probably a unicorn in there somewhere, unless Jane had finally outgrown the damn things.

It bothered her incredibly that she hadn't even written the girl in all this time, thinking that they would connect on Facebook and then never making it happen. Of course, she hadn't exactly wanted to share what she was doing. Jane Small had had enough trouble in her life without looking at the ugly reality of insurgent warfare overseas.

But it turned out the United States had ugly realities of its own. Barrett still visualized Jane as a human sacrifice in the making. The clock was ticking. She still had no idea where Jane might be, although she had an inkling—more than an inkling—why the girl could've felt compelled to run away. And then what? Who had found her, who had sold her?

On impulse, Barrett grabbed a large handful of the disorganized papers, thrusting them into the bottom of her bag without looking at them. Malcolm Prescott had moved to the front of the burrito-eaters line. She stole another large handful and used what was left to conceal the fact that the compartment had been rifled.

He was coming out. With his free hand, he opened the driver-side door and got in, resting the smelly burrito on the dash. "Do you want to go back to the house and speak to Ginny again?" he asked, turning the key in the ignition.

"Some other time."

"I'd offer you a bite but my guess is you don't eat crap like this." Prescott unwrapped the paper and sank his teeth into the limp flour taco and mummified beans. "Mmm."

"Not if I can help it."

He chewed and swallowed. Barrett almost gagged.

"Must be why you look so young," he said, carelessly wrapping up the burrito again but putting it into the cup holder this time before he put the car in gear. Not upright. Leaning like a limp dick. Seemed appropriate for who was driving.

She reminded herself that she still might need Malcolm Prescott. Jane could come home. Or call Ginny.

There might be something in the crumpled papers that she'd have to ask the girl's guardians about.

"I'd like to get home. Please just drive me to my car." Then she'd head back to D.C. And home—an apartment she'd hadn't been inside of in weeks.

CHAPTER EIGHT

Nick brought the helicopter onto the pad and surveyed the bunker from his seat. Even from here, he could see that the slot windows had been broken from the outside. The interior was probably trashed. A lot of vampires, especially turneds experiencing neuron-rage, were like rock stars in hotel rooms—they went all out when they were mad. And nicking Tim Murphy's big, ugly ear had probably made him madder than he'd ever been.

Kevin was nowhere in sight, although he'd called Nick less than an hour ago, confirming that he and a hastily mustered team had combed the mountain from top to bottom. Although they'd found no evidence of Murphy or any other vampire, turned or born, they had isolated several pairs of footprints next to what remained of Barrett's rental car and what appeared to be a set of different tire tracks farther down the mountain. As to the latter, the condition of the prints and surrounding area suggested some kind of fight—the only questions were who had won the fight and who had driven the vehicle off the mountain? Based on Murphy's condition when Nick had seen him, he seriously doubted Murphy could drive—which meant he'd been the one who'd lost the fight and been driven away. But where? And by whom? According to Nick's contact at the FBI, whom Nick had talked to this morning, he wasn't to worry himself about that. Their agents would continue tracking the turneds.

Nick's only job was to kill them once their locations had been confirmed.

Nick had barely stopped himself from snorting and telling the guy to fuck himself. But he hadn't. He also hadn't revealed anything about Barrett's presence or what she'd told him. Until he knew more, he was keeping anything having to do with Barrett close to the vest. And playing nice with his handlers would only serve to keep them in the dark while preserving ties Nick might need at some point in the near future.

Nick got out of the heli and ducked under the still-whirling rotors. He walked around the rough concrete walls of the old bunker to inspect the damage. Not that much. The just-about-bombproof doors hadn't been forced.

It was the slot windows hanging in jagged shards that puzzled him the most. There was almost no glass on the ground. That meant someone had squeezed through one to get in, then gone outside again the same way and broken all the others for spite or for fun.

But Murphy was big and blocky. Whoever had done this had to have been incredibly thin and flexible. Maybe the molecular disintegration of the turneds was accelerating faster than they'd thought.

"Nick, you in there? Saw the heli come over the ridge." A dog also barked in greeting.

"Who said you could bring that dog here?" Nick yelled back, obviously joking.

"Aura, sic his ass!"

They both knew the massive dog with the golden eyes would do no such thing. For one, the command was incorrect. Aura was a stickler for procedure.

She found Nick and thrust her nose into his hand. He let her have a good sniff, then petted her rough, three-color fur, noticing that she'd been thoroughly brushed. Kev took very, very good care of her.

He was still outside, probably taking an al fresco piss. Fine with Nick. He was happy to spend a little extra time with the dog.

Aura was a whole new breed, even though she was a mix, rescued from a shelter by Kevin, who'd been looking for a dog with major smarts and a lot of potential. As it turned out, she had both in spades. But she couldn't be trained to find the missing or the wounded or the dead.

It was the undead she went after. And Nick had been the one to figure it out. Kev, his sometime jogging buddy, had brought her along for a run in the flatlands and she'd singled out an ordinary-looking guy on a park bench that Nick had happened to know was a vampire. Born. Not turned.

Kevin had been ahead by several strides when she stopped and indicated. Nick had almost tripped over her. Her hackles were up and a low growl simmered in her throat. The golden eyes that were now closed had lit up and glowed. It had been the damnedest thing.

He didn't really believe it had happened. After that, Nick and Kev had tested Aura again and again with amazing success.

"Ninety-five percent recognition," he murmured into her ear. He did that rumpling thing to her ears that she loved. The big dog grinned foolishly and let her tongue loll out. Her thick tail banged on the floor. Both men were convinced they'd only scratched the surface of her abilities. And Nick had convinced the FBI that despite the termination of its Turning Program, the Bureau could at least use sniffing vampire dogs as a detection tool. He'd also requested Kev head the program.

Across the country, military dog trainers who knew what to look for had found others like her. The mutation was rare but it kept cropping up and seemed to be linked to the golden eyes.

Kevin was training the new arrivals, young and eager to learn, that'd been flown out to Tennessee a few weeks ago. But Aura was the alpha female and let every other dog know it.

She had recently bred, but only two in the litter were golden eyes. The ones that weren't were considered nearly as valuable. The unique trait of vampire sensing was in their DNA, as well, but recessive. Every one of the dogs was kept to maintain genetic variation.

Nick liked to think of Aura as the mother of them all, even though she wasn't. She had been discovered first—that much was true.

He heard Kev come in the door Nick had left unlocked. "Okay if she stays on my bed?" Nick asked. "There's broken glass on the floor."

Kevin looked around. He nearly reached the ceiling, tall as he was, what with the bristling shock of blond hair buzzed to the scalp everywhere but the top of his head. His broad shoulders and lanky walk marked him for the easygoing country boy he was. Right now he wore secondhand camos. More often than not, it was ripped jeans and an old chambray shirt. He didn't give a hoot in hell about clothes.

"Sure." Kevin gave a signal and Aura leaped high, clearing a military trunk piled high with gear. She made herself comfortable, trampling the comforter into a flat space in the center and settling down in it.

"Good girl," Nick said, then addressed Kevin. "Do you make her sleep on rocks or something?"

The dog's eyes were barely open. Narrow slivers of gold observed them both, then her eyes shut tight.

"Of course not. Nothing but the best for Aura. But she sure likes your bed. This is her second long hike in twenty-four hours," Kev said, then looked at Nick from the corners of his eyes. "So you never told me why you missed Murphy."

Nick scowled. "Maybe I shouldn't have told you that. It happens, that's all. Even to me."

Kev eased off the subject. "Never used a crossbow myself."

"I can teach you."

"Some other time," Kevin said. "I'm kinda beat."

"I don't doubt it. I followed you and the dogs on the screen, but the readout is ridiculous. Just dots. Looked like a freakin' Pong game. Sometimes I wonder what they're thinking with this V-gear."

Nick's supply guy at the FBI had loaded him up with great new equipment and some that had been used to hunt vampires since the program's inception. The latter didn't need to be tested, in Nick's opinion. It needed to be junked.

"These new dogs do better than them machines. Aura almost got the fucker, you know. I saw him, then I didn't. He disappeared, fast. It was like—" Kevin searched for words to describe it. "Like the darkness after blowing out a candle," he said finally. "When you can still see the flame for a second."

"You mean he teleported?"

"He was gone. Just gone."

"Huh." Tim Murphy was turned. As far as Nick knew, he shouldn't have been able to teleport. Unless he had help. Could a born vampire have dragged him along during a vanishing act?

"So what's all this?" Kevin asked.

Nick covered the basics of the gear and gadgets on the trunk. "More stuff. I actually asked for some of it. We need better basic surveillance."

"Yeah? I'll stick with the dogs." At Nick's quizzical look, Kev added, "Hey, request anything you want. Apparently the brass thinks the world of you."

"Yeah?"

"You shoulda seen the team they sent in after I radioed them. SEALs, recon specialists, invisible types from the CIA—you're kind of a big deal, Nicky boy."

"We all have to answer to the NSA now. We're supposed to work together."

"The National Security Agency would like to think so," Kev drawled. "Kind of weird to think of the feds and the army and the rest of 'em mixed up together, spying on everyone and each other."

"I promise not to tell anyone you said that."

Although it had given him an idea. Nick knew people at the NSA. Every bit and byte of computer intelligence in the U.S. or affecting the U.S. went through their data pipes. If he was going to be able to get any information on the whereabouts of Jane Small, that was his best place to start.

"They need to work on coordination," Kev added. "Took them an hour to get here, on ATVs and I don't know what. I kept my head down and Aura close to me until the cavalry came thunderin' up the mountain."

"I wouldn't have ditched you if they hadn't been so close and you didn't have the dogs and your arsenal of liquid nitrogen–coated knives," Nick told him. "But thanks for holding down the fort."

"Gotta roll with things, now more than ever. Hey, almost forgot," Kevin said. "I saw a torched car down by the gate. Who owns that?"

"Some rental company. A friend stopped by before we were so rudely interrupted," Nick said. "She hiked up. The security setup is busted."

"She?" Kevin snapped his fingers. "Aura. Find panties."

The drowsy animal yawned and rolled over, her back to the men.

"Shut the fuck up, Kev. Even the dog thinks you're immature."

"Sorry. It was a lame joke."

"Yeah, you could say that. We were dealing with the nastiest vamp I ever saw in my life, not fooling around."

Nick thought about Murphy or something else like him or worse sneaking up on them. But the dog was relaxed. He told himself to act the same way. She shifted. Dreaming? He hoped so.

"Funny, you didn't mention having company when you called in."

When Nick remained silent, Kev grinned. "So you got her to safety?"

Nick nodded, still not wanting to explain about Barrett. The other man didn't need to know and Nick had never once mentioned her in the whole time he'd known Kevin. He went for a broom and a dustpan and swept up the shattered glass. They dropped the subject by silent mutual agreement and went through the gear piece by piece, dividing it into piles and making a list of what else they might need to stay safe on the isolated mountain.

Refreshed after her nap, Aura jumped off the bed and went into the kitchen.

"She wants water," Kevin said.

"Okay. I'll take care of it." Nick rose and flung an ammo belt in Kev's direction, nodding with approval when the other man caught it single-handedly.

Aura was sitting on the floor, looking fixedly at a shelf above her. Nick realized belatedly that she was indicating something. He looked around, not getting it. But then he didn't quite speak her language.

Every dog of her type, from search-and-rescue to cadaver dogs, was an individual. There were slight variations in terms of how they communicated, their signals interpreted by their own trainers after long months of practice. Dog and handler worked so closely together it was as if they became one being, developing their own signals over time.

Kev was her handler, always would be. Nick wasn't up to speed, although he understood the basics. But not her specific way of communicating her finds. The process was nothing like the sniff-sniff-bingo! people saw on TV. It took time. The best animal wasn't always sure and didn't always get it right. But Aura's outstanding record spoke for itself.

What the hell had she smelled and where was it? The kitchen didn't look any different to him. Nick rinsed out a bowl and filled it with fresh water.

She stayed where she was when he put the bowl in front of her, not lowering her head to take a drink, not moving a muscle, 100 percent focused.

"Kev," he called. "Aura won't move. She's signaling something I can't find."

"Be right there."

Kevin came in and let his gaze follow the straight line of the dog's gaze. Then he frowned. "I think Murphy left you a little present. It's up there."

"Hey, if you're so goddamn tall you can see that high up, you get to bring it down. What is it, anyway?"

"Not sure. Get a ladder. I'm not touching it."

Nick looked around for a plastic bag to cover his hand. He used two, slipping them on after he unfolded a stepladder and climbed high enough to see the shelf.

Murphy had been here. And he'd been well enough and mindful enough not to leave any other evidence of his visit. A portion of the curved outer edge of the vampire's ear remained intact. The rest was ragged flesh crusted with blood. Aura continued to signal, motionless and intent. Nick handled the disgusting thing gingerly, putting it into a glass jar and screwing the lid on tight. Then he looked at Kev. "As soon as it's light, the three of us are going to do another sweep. We're tracking this bastard down."

CHAPTER NINE

Crystal City looked pretty good in the moonlight. Barrett was glad to be coming home after the odd meeting with the Prescotts, and relieved that she didn't have to report to Carly until late tomorrow afternoon.

The airport was less than a mile from her building, one of many tall, anonymous structures that towered over the flat land on the west side of the Potomac River and south of D.C. But the area was sought after for its proximity to the Mall, the Capitol, and other important government buildings on both sides of the river. It was where you rented if you wanted a nice place and some degree of solitude. The tenants were a varied lot. Military and ex-military. The single and divorced. Nobodies who weren't broke and weren't rich.

She qualified for all three categories.

The taxi driver pulled up in front of her building and she paid him, getting out quickly and going into the lobby to pick up her mail. Barrett pulled out several envelopes that looked like bills and stuck them into her shoulder bag, on top of the papers she'd swiped from Malcolm Prescott's car.

Wondering if there was white wine in the refrigerator and if so, what frozen food product could be nuked to accompany it, she waited for an elevator.

Considering she'd bounced around to three different states—Tennessee, Georgia, and Maryland—she didn't feel particularly tired. She was a little worried though. She wondered why she hadn't heard from Nick. She'd called a couple of times and texted once. No answer. Did it mean anything other than he was busy? With his own work or with helping her find Jane?

True, she didn't have anything extraordinary to tell him, but every little detail could count. She knew more about Jane Small than she ever had, despite Malcolm Prescott's self-serving bullshit. The girl was no angel. But Barrett liked her even more for it.

Jane's bad behavior wasn't all that bad. If she wasn't properly grateful to her guardians, it was because she was smart. Ginny seemed like kind of a doormat, but otherwise all right. Malcolm was a lecher and a phony. Still, Barrett had the feeling that Jane had been able to handle him. And she just didn't think he'd put a seventeen-year-old girl in harm's way.

Someone else had done that. But Jane had to be out there somewhere. Barrett would find her. She adjusted the bag over her shoulder, making the papers crammed inside rustle a bit.

Could be a clue or two in all that. Trash told the truth more often than not. She was looking forward to going through it, piece by piece, down to the gum wrappers.

A box of crackers was nearly empty by the time Barrett got everything sorted. There were no gum wrappers, though. Just a gray lump of chewed gum that looked like a miniature brain, wrapped up in a scrap of school-ruled paper. She put it into a small plastic bag for possible DNA collection.

Missing persons cases required every possible means of identification. With no living relatives, Jane could go unidentified if the worst happened and the months dragged on.

There was no telling if Jane or Malcolm had done the chewing, though Barrett's money was on Jane. Into the fridge it went.

There were scribbles about mean teachers, snobbish girls, dumb boys. Even veiled insults about Malcolm's lack of intelligence; it had probably given Jane a kick to leave that type of thing in plain view of the guy. So far, normal enough. But almost too normal. If Jane was missing her mother—a given, since she and Sarah had been very close—she was keeping it well hidden. Maybe Prescott was editing the clutter. Maybe he'd deliberately left her alone to go into the convenience store.

There were school assignments. English, math—Jane got mostly A's. And other miscellaneous stuff. The girl seemed to be in the habit of cleaning out her backpack in the car. Malcolm Prescott's four-wheeled garbage can didn't get emptied out much. Some of the dated items were months old.

He must have done most of the chauffeuring. Unless Jane had her license and was allowed to use his car.

Barrett started a separate pile for Malcolm. There wasn't much. His business cards, a couple of reprints of his articles, and—why was she not surprised—several flyers for gentlemen's clubs.

One offered a discount strip package for groups, Tuesdays only. A white box had been filled in pen: *Prescott, party of four, table* 9. She looked more closely, recognizing the sign in the photo. She'd driven past it. It was a local joint, really sleazy, that had closed last year. He must have come in from Maryland with pals. Lecherous *and* cheap. She felt even more sorry for his wife.

Barrett sat back. Kind of a bust but not a total waste of time. She'd learned a few more things about Jane and Malcolm, but found nothing that might lead her to the girl or cast suspicion on her uncle. She polished off the last of the crackers while looking absently at the piles.

Whoa. She sat up straight and put the empty box aside. There was something. She'd missed it the first time around.

She picked up the flyer on top of the nearest pile, for a luxury club opening in New City. It touted the coming attractions in great big letters. Hot girls. Strip shows. Top-notch bands. She looked more closely at the overall design.

The background was patterned with a distinctive motif of intersecting triangles. Could be just a coincidence, but the motif seemed suggestive of fangs.

A subliminal message to vampires everywhere? Could be.

Club Red. Even the name kinda fit that theory.

She checked the location info and the directions on the other side of the flyer. The club appeared to be somewhere near the hotel she and Nick had stayed at in New City. Barrett felt a tingle of excitement.

She could start there. She had to start somewhere

First she had to get in. She studied the flyer again. *We cater to discerning gentlemen of means and distinction. Ladies welcome. Ask about our private rooms.*

It was true enough that women went to strip clubs intended for male customers. Some were gay. Some were curious. And there were straight women who didn't mind their guys turning into sex monkeys if they got to come along and keep them from spending too much money.

It was a way in. But she wanted to talk to Justine first. This was her area of expertise.

Her colleague didn't seem to mind working after hours. Justine was a night owl, never saying a word in morning meetings unless she'd downed several cups of strong black coffee.

Long dark hair tumbling over her shoulders, she made her entrance in an oversized slouch sweater and narrow jeans. Neither hid the spectacular figure of the exotic dancer she'd been before being recruited for Belladonna.

"Dinner's almost ready," Barrett said.

"Oh good. I'm starving." Justine slid her black leather tote off her shoulder, and sauntered in.

The microwave beeped. Barrett went into the kitchen to take out the plate. She carried it to the table where Justine had zeroed in on the club flyers, an untouched glass of wine in front of her.

"Drink up," Barrett said. "That chardonnay cost big bucks."

"Nine? Ten?"

"Seven and change." Barrett put the plate on a trivet as Justine took a sip of wine and tried not to make a face. The food seemed more to her liking.

"Ooh, fish sticks," Justine cooed. "I always had a thing for that captain in the rain slicker. I like my men wet."

Me, too, Barrett thought, thinking of Nick when they'd been in the pool, out of the pool, in the shower, and out of the shower. She felt a small quiver run through her body and shook it off. The man had so much power over her, whether he was close by or not. She wished he was close. That it was him drinking wine with her instead of Justine.

Which raised the question of where he was and what he was doing. Not a topic she was going to discuss with Justine. Barrett didn't need to be teased.

They nibbled at the quick meal while Justine continued to look through the stuff on the table.

"Are you sure this girl's abduction is connected to the sex-slave ring you were trying to break into?" Justine asked after a while.

"Not positive," she said honestly. "But I have to find

her. I knew her mother, among other reasons." Barrett left the promise she'd failed to keep out of it.

"Got it." Justine rifled through Malcolm's pile of stuff one last time, studying the small photo of him on one of the articles. "Okay. Here's my two cents on this guy."

"Whoa. Don't tell me you met him."

Justine snorted. "I met a thousand guys just like him, put it that way. Middle-aged. Affluent. Looking for one last chance to run wild. The smarter ones keep their horndog bullshit out of their workplace because they're afraid of sexual harassment suits. But they all think strippers are up for anything." She cleared her throat. "Some girls are."

Barrett was willing to let it go at that.

"Not me," Justine said quickly. "I never fooled around with customers."

"I'm not judging you. I just want to know if you think he might've had something to do with her disappearance."

Justine didn't answer right away. When she did her tone was thoughtful. "That's hard to say. But right now, Malcolm Prescott is your only connection to Jane Small."

"That's true." He was also the last person to have seen her alive, Barrett thought. Several days ago.

"Listen, Barrett, there has to be more going on. Once a closet freak gets started, he can't stop. The way you describe him, he sounds like a boring guy who tries to be cool and craves excitement. He can afford it, obviously. What does his wife do?"

"Apparently nothing. I didn't ask."

Justine shook her head. "She probably knows about his extracurricular activities. Wives usually do. Maybe she just doesn't have the bucks or the backbone to dump his sorry ass."

"Jane saw through him."

Justine shrugged. "He's a whole lot older and more experienced at lying. She had him pegged for a jerk, but that doesn't mean she could predict what he could do to her."

"Maybe she wasn't forced." Barrett picked up the sleaziest flyer and waved it at Justine. "Do you think he talked her into something like this? I'm playing devil's advocate here. Maybe she thought she could beat Prescott at his own game. Lie about her age, make a ton of money, and use it to run away. That was the tag on her SexFlash vid."

"The money is real. It's what you have to do to get it that does damage," Justine said bluntly. "Young girls underestimate that part of the life. A lot of them get used up and burned out before they can blink. Or strung out on drugs. Or dead."

Seemed like Justine had said all she wanted to on that subject. Despite her smart mouth, there was pain in her eyes. For friends and acquaintances, Barrett assumed, who hadn't gotten out. Not everyone had Justine's knack for self-preservation.

The two women fell silent. Barrett got up and used the remote to switch on the TV just for background noise, keeping the volume low. Justine stared at a reality show without really seeing it. Another set of housewives in heels, scratching and spitting.

"There's more than one way to sell yourself," Justine said after a while. "Meow, meow," she said, referring to the catfight on the screen." She shut off the TV. "Anything else you wanted to ask me?"

"Yes. But I'm sorry if I pushed it."

"Someone has to. Time is obviously a factor."

Barrett still hesitated but only for a few seconds.

"So. Theoretically speaking, if I had to, ah, infiltrate a place like that, how would I do it?"

Justine finished her wine. "In disguise. Loud getups,

tinted contacts, minky-winky false eyelashes, wigs—maybe red hair for a swinger wife looking for cheap thrills with her husband, platinum for the pole dancer—"

Barrett gulped. "I'm not ready to go that far."

"Whatever you decide, go all out with it. You gotta be convincing. Any crooked club owner has a sixth sense for undercovers. But keep in mind that the girls don't get paid to chitchat at the tables. You're going to need a man to come along unless you want to stand out as single or play gay."

"You have a point. No to both." Barrett automatically thought of Nick.

Now that would be weird. But he might do it.

He was willing to do a lot of things.

For her. To her.

And once again it freaked her out how much she thought of him. How much she wanted him. One night with him had only made her long for more when all of her focus should be on finding Jane.

That was Nick's power over her and always had been. The power to make her forget everything but him.

And no one could have that kind of power over her. No one.

No matter how much she wished otherwise.

CHAPTER TEN

The next morning, Nick, Kev, and Aura went hunting.

Unfortunately, they found no hint of Murphy.

On their way back to the bunker, however, Aura froze and indicated. After visually sweeping the area and finding nothing, Nick knelt down beside her.

He spotted something on the ground beside her and bent down to pick it up.

"What's that?" Kevin asked. "Hope it's not my watch. Couldn't find it when I woke up."

"A lump of something that is definitely not a watch."

"Add it to your rock collection," Kevin said without interest.

"I don't have one." Nick held up the lump. Its pebbled surface gleamed dully as he brushed off the dirt.

Nick took out a pocketknife. He pressed it hard into the lump, making a bright slash. Brighter than the sunlight. "Whaddya know. Gold. Solid. And close to pure, if it's soft enough to cut." Nick held it out for Kevin to look at.

Blond eyebrows went up. "You think Murphy had it? Intended to melt it down and make some jewelry?"

"Don't know," Nick murmured.

"Well you can keep it. I don't want anything that touched his ugly skin."

"Okay." Nick folded the knife and tried to slip it and the lump of gold into a pocket. He picked the wrong one. He took out a thin wallet that was in the way and held it in his hand, half open.

Kev spotted the photo of Barrett before Nick could close the wallet and shove it back into his pocket with the other things.

"Cute. Who is she?"

"You ask too many goddamn questions."

The other man shot him an amused look. "That the friend who visited you yesterday?"

Nick tried to sidestep that line of inquiry. Let Kev fill in a few blanks if he wanted to. "Yeah, she's a friend. We were both stationed in Europe, operated out of the same base," was all he said.

He glanced at the photo. He'd taken it, had it printed, kept it ever since.

Barrett was laughing, her blond hair tucked under a camo cap and her gorgeous body still revealed to advantage in fatigues. They had made love less than an hour before, then shared a field shower when no one was looking and scrambled back into their clothes.

Her blue eyes sparkled and there was high color in her cheeks. Nick had enjoyed making that happen. They hadn't had many chances to be together. Then somehow they'd used up every last one and it was over.

But maybe not. They'd gone at it in the hotel as if they had never said good-bye. He'd made sure to throw in every hot move they'd ever dreamed up together. Done it her way, all the way. One night. He wanted a thousand more. With her.

Kev chuckled.

"What's so funny?"

"A gearhead like you carrying around an honest-to-God actual picture of some gal in your pocket. I don't get it."

"Smartphones get stolen. Laptops get hacked." Nick

glanced at Kev. "Gotta have a girl in your pocket, right? For good luck."

"True love is what I was thinking."

Nick put away the wallet. "Nothing like that."

But the words felt forced. He'd never actually thought he'd been in love with Barrett. Attracted as all get out. Protective certainly. Cared about her without a doubt. But love? To Nick, love had always been a flowery cover-up for chemistry. But when he looked back now, when he thought about how hard it had been to let Barrett walk away from him and how right it had felt when they'd made love in New City—well, fuck, if love was a flowery cover-up, then he was buried in the stuff.

Of course he'd loved her. And he still did. Kev was right. Why else would he have carried her picture around with him? Why else was he chomping at the bit to get off this mountain and get back to her?

Make sure that whoever had sent Murphy after him or even her hadn't gotten to—

Nick frowned, realizing that his subconscious had been working overtime to process all the possibilities. It obviously thought Murphy hadn't been acting on his own, and while there was no real evidence of that, his intuition told him he was on to something. That meant Murphy wasn't the only potential threat to Barrett.

He needed to finish up here, talk to his contacts at the NSA, then get to Barrett.

"Want some lunch?" Nick asked, mainly because he wasn't about to tell Kev he was going to call Barrett.

"Sure."

Nick went back in and slapped cold cuts and bread together on paper plates, grabbing a squeeze bottle of mayonnaise on his way out.

"Here ya go." He handed Kevin the plates. "I'm going to take a piss. Be right back."

He stepped outside, saw the missed calls from Barrett

on his cell, and cursed. Not a surprise, living up here on the mountain, that he sometimes lost cell reception. He'd just never cared all that much before. Anyone on his team could reach him on the radio. He had to walk awhile before he picked up enough bars to call Barrett. He got her voice mail, closing his eyes at how damn good it felt to hear her voice, then left a terse message asking her to call him back.

After lunch, Nick fed the scraps to Aura when she woke up and came over.

Kevin looked out over the shadowed valley below. "Do you know why Murphy was after you?"

The more he'd thought about it, Nick wasn't all that sure that he'd been the actual target, but he still didn't want to explain Barrett. The fewer people who knew that she'd visited him here, the better.

"They have to have obtained a copy of The List. He was on it."

"Who are 'they'?"

Nick shrugged and crunched up the paper plates. "The turned vampires. Maybe they've organized. Would make sense. They put two and two together, come up with the fact that the FBI is now targeting their asses, and decided to stick together. Formulate a plan. Go on the offensive. Murphy wasn't with anyone else?"

"Nope. Nothing like that. Aura woulda let me know. She only seemed to see the one fella."

Nick's spine prickled. He shifted position and saw that Aura had circled around behind him. Her rough coat felt like hay even after she'd been groomed.

"So what's next for you?"

"Ranking on The List is based on level of expected mental and physical deterioration," Nick said. "Murphy was number two and by far in the worst shape of any of the turneds I've seen so far. It's been harder and harder finding the turneds that are farther down on The

List. I'm betting that's because they still have mental acuity. I'm waiting for intel on their whereabouts, though. Until that comes, I'm pretty much a free agent." Except for what he was helping Barrett with, of course. Damn it, where the hell was she and why hadn't she called him back?

"Okay. Guess Aura and I will head back over to the ridge," Kev said.

"Who's in charge at the kennels?"

"Local kid. Eighteen, thinking about enlisting, wants experience with military dogs. He doesn't know anything about the vamp op."

"Keep it that way. Anyone from the team still around down your way?"

"Nope."

That would leave only him on top of the mountain. Whether to stay or go was his call, though. Nick knew that being alone made him an easy target. Kev had responsibilities of his own. The kennels and the breeding program were a top priority. Nick was basically a hired gun.

It was a good thing Barrett hadn't fought him about getting her pretty butt back to D.C. She'd be safer there. He just wanted her to call and confirm it was true.

If she didn't get back to him soon, Nick thought he might fly out later, stash the heli, and catch a plane from somewhere closer than New City. He wanted to check out where she lived and make sure her security setup was adequate. She hadn't known what Murphy was and he hoped she never had to find out.

The FBI wasn't going to tell her, that much was for certain. He hadn't heard about Belladonna and she hadn't heard about The List or the threat posed by some of the turneds. Nothing too suspicious in that. Teams operated independently on different missions all the time, and they often did so without knowledge that the other existed. However, one thing that kept bugging Nick was the fact that Barrett worked with turned vampires, yet no one had bothered to tell her that some turneds went bad and it couldn't be guaranteed that her coworkers wouldn't inevitably do the same. Was it just a matter of the FBI wanting to get as much out of those like Peter Lancaster as possible? Maybe, but Nick didn't like the potential danger keeping such secrets posed to Barrett.

She was brave and she was tough and she was smart, but she was still a woman. His woman. He'd always thought of her like that. He wanted her safe.

Last year he'd let her walk away from him, secretly betraying her in order to keep her safe. Maybe with this second shot, he had to switch things up. Maybe instead of hiding anything further from her, he'd be brutally honest instead. Not just about his feelings for her, but about what he'd done in the past, and what could happen in the future if the turneds she worked with caught neuron-rage.

It would be a lot for her to take in and he had no doubt her first instinct would be to punch him in the nuts and tell him to go to hell.

Which meant he needed to think things through very carefully.

Nick turned to Kev. "Think you could get some of those guys who helped you back for a day or two?"

"Probably," Kevin said. "Why? You going someplace?"

"Yeah. Do I have to tell you where?"

"No." His partner eyed him warily. "But I'm heading out, too, if no one'll come. I don't particularly feel like being alone up on the ridge with just Aura and the other dogs."

Nick gave a curt nod. "Then take them with you."

"I intend to."

CHAPTER ELEVEN

Barrett listened to Nick's message on her smartphone.

It was good to hear his voice. Good to know he was safe. And even as she prepared to call him back, her screen lit up and Nick's number appeared.

"Hey," she said, trying to sound businesslike. "What's up?"

"Are you going to be happy to see me? Because I'm sure as hell not waiting any longer to see you."

Barrett's eyes widened. "Are you in D.C.?"

"Around the corner."

"You could have given me a little warning."

His deep voice was teasing. "Consider yourself warned."

She wasn't going to bother to ask him how he'd gotten her address, either. "How have you been? Any more trouble?"

Silence.

"Nick?"

He seemed to be weighing his next words. "You could say that," he said.

A chill settled over her.

"I'll explain when I see you, Barrett."

"Okay. I'm in 14-B."

"I know," he said with a smile in his voice, and she wondered if there'd ever been a time in the past year that he hadn't known where she was. Maybe it hadn't really been over even when she was alone and missing him. Nice thought. Even if it was probably hogwash.

She went to the door, then walked away from it. Pacing and thinking. Counting the minutes until he got there.

One knock. Barrett was in her bedroom, smoothing the comforter. She didn't want him to see the tangled sheets and get any ideas about how she'd slept—badly.

She finished and went back to open the door. Nick filled the doorway.

There was that grin. Higher on one side than the other. A flash of a dimple to set it off. He seemed really happy to see her. But there was a folder and a laptop under one arm and a tote bag with more papers and some books under the other. He was here on business.

"Hi, Barrett." His dark eyes gleamed as he took her in. She wore ordinary jeans and a loose, unstylish top. But he looked at her like she was coming down a beauty pageant runway.

Her skin responded with a faint blush. What the hell. She hadn't bothered with the powdered kind.

"Hello, Nick."

Her gaze flicked downward. His brawny chest was encased in a dark T-shirt, an item of clothing that he'd always worn, even during his soldier days. He had on old jeans with frayed knees and scuffed work boots. So he hadn't dressed up for her, either. Keeping it real.

She'd seen him in everything from a full-dress army uniform to buck naked. What he was wearing now was probably her favorite. Purely Nick, being himself.

"Come on in," Barrett said. "Would you like anything?"

"I'll take a soda if you have one."

"Be right back."

She could feel his gaze on her behind as she walked away from him into the kitchen. The loose top didn't make any difference. She could be wearing a swirling black chador that covered every inch of her body and he'd still check her out. Front and back. He never had been able to decide which was the best view.

Barrett returned with two ginger ales on ice. Nick was examining the papers on the table.

"What's all this?"

"Stuff from Malcolm Prescott's car. I swiped it and I'm still sorting it out. Grunt work, but you never know. So why are you here, what's in the folder and the bag, and does it have anything to do with the trouble you said you had encountered and were going to tell me about?"

"Two reasons, lots of stuff, and yes, in a way."

"Let's start from the top. You're here for two reasons. And what are they?"

"To fill you in and get filled in, of course."

"And?"

"And this . . ."

Striding up to her, he wrapped his hand around her neck and pulled her in for a kiss.

Barrett didn't fight him. He was too quick for that. Her body arched against his, not because she willed it, but because she'd been expertly positioned by him. Nick knew exactly how to get her off balance and keep her that way. In another few seconds, his hand slid over her thigh and lifted her leg, bending it to get her even closer. His lips smiled against hers before he really kissed her, claiming her mouth with deep thrusts of his tongue, then pulling back to nip at the sensitive cord of her neck. Barrett closed her eyes and tipped her head back, enjoying his sensual play, just rough enough to let her know who was boss.

For the next few minutes, anyway.

He wasn't always this dominant. Which made her wonder what else was on his mind at the moment. For

Nick, sex or the prelude to it had always been easier than talking about what was going on with him. His lips reached her ear, murmuring a few interesting suggestions not suitable for the workplace, and then he got back to kissing her. Even harder.

"Whoa," she said, pulling back. She touched her fingers to her swollen lips, loving the way his darkened eyes followed her movements. "What was that for?"

"That was me being damn grateful you're okay. And celebrating the fact that I am, as well."

"So what's spooked you? Does it have to do with a certain something that tried to strangle me to death a few days ago?"

"Yeah, it does," Nick said. "And it has to do with some of the stuff I brought along. And stuff I need to tell you. Despite the fact I'm not supposed to. Despite the fact you obviously don't have the security clearance to hear it. But you need to know."

So he told Barrett how he'd been hired by the FBI to eliminate vampires. How those vampires were former U.S. soldiers, soldiers who'd voluntarily been turned in the Turning Program but for unknown reasons had started to show signs of neuron-rage and physical deterioration. How those symptoms had progressed until the turneds had become violent. Unpredictable. Dangerous.

And how he was afraid the turneds Barrett worked with might eventually suffer from the same condition.

She was sitting there stunned, not knowing how to respond, when he said, "And that's not all, Barrett."

"Oh, God," she whispered. "What else is there?"

"You know me. You know I wouldn't take this kind of job unless there was a damn good reason. You know I wouldn't just believe what the FBI was telling me."

"You did your own recon," she said flatly. "Online?"

"I accessed whatever I could. Enlisted friends to do

the same. I didn't get much. But I got enough to know that vampires might just be the beginning."

"What the hell are you talking about?"

Nick turned and grabbed the bag. He pulled out reams of paper. "This is research I stashed in various places. Places the Bureau wouldn't think to look. Read the highlighted words." Barrett did and with each word her eyes widened in disbelief. The documents referred to paranormal creatures, vampires just being one kind of them. Rumors. Reports. Speculation. An occasional reported sighting. Her hand shaking so much the paper rattled, she weaved toward a chair and sat down hard. "Are you saying—You think there are other creatures out there? Others, like the vampires, that are born to another species. Not human?"

"If vampires exist, why not more? I haven't seen anything myself. Haven't been able to find proof."

"So why are you telling me this?"

"I'm telling you this because we have no idea what we're dealing with. Even when it comes to vampires. Born vampires, Rogue vampires, turned vampires, turned vampires that are okay, turned vampires that are violent and shouldn't be able to think too logically but still manage to leave me a piece of flesh where I live without leaving any other signs he was there . . ."

Barrett's brow furrowed. "I don't know what to do with this information. You're telling me our world, the world that has already gotten strange enough, might be even stranger. That everything we've believed is a lie. That everything we've fought for, all the good we've tried to do, could have been for nothing."

She heard the hysteria coming into her voice and obviously so did Nick. He took her arms and shook her. "That was always true, Barrett."

"So what now?"

"Now we deal. We bury the information we don't

know what to do with or can't do anything about and we work with the information we can do something with. We help who we can."

"My friends . . ." she whispered, thinking about Ty and Peter. And, God, Ana. The woman who'd just found love after years and years of suffering. Would she and Ty be torn apart by insanity and physical disintegration? It wasn't fair.

"No, Barrett. Don't think about them. Not yet."

She shook her head. "Then who do I think of? Just who do you think we can help right now?"

"Jane."

The single word was like a slap to the face. Her mind had been reeling, but as she stared at Nick and saw the resolution and an odd excitement on his face, her spiraling panic lowered several notches.

"Jane," she repeated.

"Yes, Jane."

"You've found her?"

He shook his head. "No. But I've found something. I've got a lead, and that's something we didn't have before, right?"

She nodded and tried to swallow her disappointment. "Tell me."

He tapped the laptop he'd brought. "The stuff we need to be working on is in here."

"I have a flash drive. Copy it and transfer it to my laptop so I can have a separate record and analyze it if you're not here."

His dark gaze moved quickly to where she pointed. His reply was blunt and immediate. "That thing? No way."

"It's encrypted—" she started to say.

"Barrett, if I didn't personally do the encryption, I don't trust it. And no system on earth is 100 percent safe from attack. Unless you want a blast of malware to shred your hard drive—and some character getting his jollies reading your files—you use a throwaway laptop with a dead-end URL."

"With everything you've told me, I don't need a tech lecture right now."

"I think with everything I've told you, you'd want to focus on any mundane fact you can."

True. She stuck her tongue out at him.

His brows lifted. "Don't tempt me. Not yet. I'd love nothing more than to strip you naked and forget about everything else, but I think you're going to want to hear what else I have to say."

"Okay, fine." She made a wrap-it-up gesture with one hand, not wanting to admit how much she wanted to be in his arms, as well. "So you only trust your laptop. I get it."

"Yep. Only problem is this thing takes a little while to warm up," he informed her.

If he meant to be deliberately annoying, it was working.

His grin told her he knew it was true. It also told her he was trying to keep her calm. Focused. She appreciated that more than he could ever know.

He clicked open the lid of the laptop. It did look like an old one. "The information this contains comes from the NSA. Guaranteed to be true, accurate, and relevant to your investigation. There's nothing I wouldn't do for you."

A huge rush made her heart hammer because she knew he was speaking the truth. It hit her then. This was a man she could trust. She'd known she could trust him with Jane. Hell, with her life. Why couldn't she trust him with her heart? With everything he'd just told her, including the fact that her friends might be—that they might be—

She closed her eyes, refusing to think that way.

The point was, life was crazy. To survive it, she had to grasp on to whatever she could regardless of the risk. That meant when she found a man who made her body sing when he touched her and her heart jump with joy just at the sound of his voice, she should grab him and hold tight rather than letting fear drive her away. "Now, I want you—" he started.

She threw herself at him, causing him to stumble slightly before he caught her. Wrapping her arms around him, she kissed him with a loud smack and hugged him firmly. "Thank you, Nick. Thank you for always being there for me."

The strong hands that encompassed her upper arms held her fast for an unbearable moment. Then his fingers stroked her skin. Barrett wanted to melt. His head bent to hers, his gaze serious and intense.

There were no other words. Just a sensation of nearness that blew her mind. She swayed in his gentle grip, taking a half step forward to balance herself. The move brought her close to his thighs. Nick drew her even closer. His belt buckle—army issue, flat metal, pressed against her middle, bare under the loose top. Everything that rounded out his worn zipper said hello and got hard as she leaned into him.

The denim held the heat. She kicked off her slippers and stood on tiptoe to make the most of that fine erection. Nick pulled her against his chest, looking into her eyes one more time, sweeping her hair back over her shoulders, sliding a hand around the curve of her waist. Shamelessly, Barrett rubbed her breasts against him, her nipples instantly taut with the sensual friction.

Then he kissed her. His soft tongue ran between her lips, then opened them. She tipped her head back, sliding her hands into his thick, dark hair, wild for what only he knew how to do. No one could kiss better than Nick Maltese. Deep, slow thrusts. Pulling back. A nip on the earlobe. Then another. A soothing lick and a tug with just his lips, taking the whole earlobe into his mouth, teasing it.

Then more kissing. She writhed with pleasure. It had only been two days. Not that long. But unbearable without him nonetheless. Barrett gave in completely.

Until Nick stopped all of a sudden. He held her flushed face between his hands, then let her go completely. He was breathing hard.

"I want to, angel. Believe me, I want to, but let me tell you what I found first. I don't want to be right in the middle of things when you remember Jane, okay?" When she didn't answer, he shook her slightly and stared deeply into her eyes. "Okay?"

"Yes," she said quickly. "Of course. I just had to tell you. Had to show you . . ."

She bit her lip, hesitating, and he cupped her cheek.

"I know. Me, too. And I'll tell you more. I'll show you more. As soon as I get you up to date and the moment's right. I promise."

She butted her cheek into his palm one last time and whispered, "Okay," before stepping back. She took a deep breath, pushed back her hair, and said, "Tell me."

The white room was the same, except that it had stopped moving. The rumble of traffic had stopped, too.

Jane felt different. She had slept, she knew that. There was no mirror, but she could feel the puffiness in her face she got when she'd conked out for hours.

The strange dreams she'd had still hovered at the edge of her mind.

Silent women dressed in outfits like maids' uniforms had undressed her, commenting on how skinny she was and how undeveloped.

Malcolm would say she dreamed that because she was

anxious and conflicted about the developmental stages of adolescence. And then assure her that she was perfectly normal, just right in his professional opinion, quote unquote. Keeping that creepy smile on his face until his eyes glazed over.

She wasn't anxious about crap like that. Some girls she knew had been granted their three magic wishes by Mom and Dad and a plastic surgeon: giant boobs and weird little noses and butt-cheek implants to fill out their seven-hundred-dollar jeans.

Jane had only ever wished to be even thinner than she was. So thin she could slip under a door. So she could get away. Where to, she didn't know.

She looked down at what she had on, realizing that the dream had been real enough. Her torn dress was gone. It had been replaced by a chemise made of flimsy plain fabric, almost see-through, trimmed with lace that itched.

Her underwear was gone, too. She wore bras just to keep the nipple maniacs in homeroom from staring at her nearly flat chest. But the lightly padded one she'd had on had been taken away by the women. Her panties were nowhere in sight.

After she and Dante had been separated, she sort of remembered her panties being dragged off and down her thighs. She had tried to fight back. Then one of the women had pressed a cloth over her nose and mouth. So much for that.

They had left her some food. A sandwich cut in quarters, mayonnaisey glop on soft white bread. Ugh.

But she did feel weak. She would eat some. Just to keep up her strength in case a door ever opened in the seamless plastic walls. Jane took a small bite and set the quarter sandwich back on the plate. No cutlery, she noticed.

A vague recollection about getting a lecture on the

subject of not hurting herself came back to her. It wasn't allowed. A man had told her that. He had some kind of accent. She hadn't seen him—well, she had seen his eyes.

On a little screen, high up in the wall. That was gone, too.

Where in the fucking fuck was she? Shit. She was totally fucked.

She never should have gone with Dante at night, never should have told him to follow Malcolm to that crummy club where he drooled over girls half his age wearing nothing but teeny G-strings. Her guardian was even creepier when he was off the chain. She'd snuck in by herself one night and watched from backstage. And he thought no one knew.

Jane had intended to take pictures and post them online, then tell Ginny. The revenge had backfired. Someone had grabbed her. Dante had tried stop it, but others had moved in to take care of him. She'd blacked out and then . . .

Jane crossed her legs just in case some voyeur—she'd found the word in Malcolm's *Encyclopedia of Sexual Dysfunction*—was looking up her chemise. Staying in the sleeping alcove, she leaned back on her palms, troubled by a different memory. Before she'd ended up in this box.

There had been another woman. Not in uniform. In one of those things that jacked up women's boobs super high, with a ton of hair and red fish lips that looked like a gallon of collagen had been pumped into them.

She'd shoved Jane around, pushed her in front of a video camera on a tripod. Told her to say something.

Jane had refused to cooperate. Then something else had happened. She'd seen someone she knew on a screen in back of the camera, but only for a few seconds. She closed her eyes, willing the memory to return. Her mind was a blank.

A collapsing sound made her open her eyes. The floor of an empty alcove was sinking. The surface of the walls changed, opening up into pores that oozed water. It was a bath. Hot and steamy.

She was sore all over from sleeping on a hard surface. She didn't care who might be looking.

Jane stared down into the bubbling water, wondering if it would overflow when she stepped into it. There didn't seem to be a drain.

She peeled off the chemise and tossed it onto the floor, then lifted her hair and tied it in a thick knot. One foot in. Then the other. Jane squatted down.

The foaming, surging water felt amazing. She splashed some over her shoulders, feeling it trickle down her spine and into the water that circulated around her, up to her waist.

The walls of the bath changed shape again, lengthening in one direction and widening in the other. She could actually lie down if she wanted to. Even float.

Cautiously, she extended her legs and sat. Then she lay back. The knot in her hair came loose and her hair floated free, weightless in the water.

She arched her neck, letting the water cover her ears, listening to the bubbles pop. There was a rumbling sound. After a few seconds, she understood that it was a voice and lifted her head out of the water.

"Jane."

It was the same man who'd spoken to her the first time. The one with the angry eyes. She sank down until the words became rumbles again.

Louder this time.

Fuck it. Fuck him. Jane forced her entire body under the surging water, held her breath until the tip of her nose was under it, too. The water covered her eyes. Death spa, she thought, almost cheerfully. It wouldn't be a bad way to go.

The water gurgled, sucked back into the walls almost instantly.

Jane sat up, angry at herself.

There was only the man's voice this time. Not the screen with his eyes. Maybe it was busted.

"You can't drown yourself. You can't hurt yourself in any way."

She said nothing. There had to be a way. She wanted him to burst through these goddamn walls. She needed something to slash them with. Slash herself while she was at it. Blood would be a relief from the glaring white.

"What a little peach you are. We wouldn't want to bruise you."

She stood and grabbed the chemise, using it to dry herself. Then she looked up. The screen was working now. His gaze was frightening. Hard. Intense. Cold.

Jane bit her lip, hard. She was cold but she refused to shiver. She went back to the sleeping alcove and lay down, her back to the eyes.

Somehow, some way, she was going to break free. Another memory, not the one she'd strained to recall, came back. And not the unknown woman.

Her mother.

Weak but alive. Talking to Jane with the last of her strength, trying to reason with her. Unless Jane was hallucinating her voice to drown out the one emanating from the wall.

Jane, listen to me. Please listen. If something bad ever happens, I won't be there to come get you and bring you home. You have to take care of yourself. You'll have Ginny and Malcolm, but—

She had broken off, grabbing an oxygen mask, breathing it in from the tank by her bed. What about them? Jane had asked.

Never mind. Just remember that I love you. Remem-

*ber when life was good. Hold on to that. Hold on to
your memory of me—*

The man's voice broke in. "I don't like being ignored,
Jane. And soon, you won't have any choice but to give
me every ounce of your attention."

The sly menace in his voice sickened her. She refused
to look at his eyes. Prying. Watching. Judging. Let him
watch, then. She didn't have to respond.

A silence fell that echoed off the white walls. Several
minutes passed as she lay there, mute.

When Nick's ancient laptop finally came to life, he sat
down in front of it and proceeded to give her a crash
course in cybersurveillance and real-time hacking. She'd
stared at rapidly scrolling code flashing over the laptop's
screen for at least an hour, not understanding it, while
he talked.

Barrett got the gist. U.S. data on trafficking victims
and sex criminals connected to a global spiderweb of
evil. Drug cartels. Illegal arms trading. Murders and as-
sassinations. The National Security Agency collected
information on all of it through cybersurveillance. Ter-
rorism had well-established links to global crime.

A division—Nick knew the woman who headed it—
had been investigating SexFlash. The code on the screen
had taken them into the site and out again. Now he
wasn't sure where he was.

Suddenly the scrolling stopped.

Blocky pixels got smaller, shifted around. A white
room resolved in high definition on the screen. Within it,
curled up in some sort of nook, was a slight girl with
wet hair. It was hard to tell what color it was. Darkish.
Her back was to the camera providing the live-streamed
feed, barely covered by a damp garment not much bigger than a rag.

"Oh my God. Is that Jane?" Barrett whispered.

"You tell me."

"Nick—I think so! I have to get her to turn around—but where is she? What is that room all about?"

Nick shook his head. "I don't know."

The girl turned. There were tear streaks on her face and a deep bite mark on her lip. It looked like she'd done it to herself. And not long ago. Her eyes rolled wildly.

"Oh, God. That is her! Oh dear God. She's been beaten—or tortured somehow—"

The video shut off abruptly. The screen went black.

She glanced at Nick.

He seemed as stunned as she was.

The hysteria that she'd barely been holding at bay since Nick had arrived swelled out of control. "We have to get her out of there! Now!"

Nick grabbed her arms again. "Calm down, Barrett. We have to find out where she is first. Then we can come up with a plan. Now sit down and put your head between your knees. Breathe deep. Jesus, you look like you're going to pass out."

Barrett obeyed him. It took several minutes before she felt calm enough to raise her head. Her gaze instantly went to the laptop. "There must be a way to pinpoint her location."

"Not instantly."

"How long can you stay?"

"Another couple of hours. Then I have to report in. And I actually have something to report."

Barrett was taken aback. "What do you mean? Report to your superior? But there's no connection between The List and Jane . . ." Her words drifted off at the look on his face.

"There is now," he muttered. "But I wanted to wait to explain everything so I could help you out first. I needed to see how far I could get with the code. I never thought we'd find her so quickly."

"We haven't," she said without thinking. "You didn't go far enough." She knew her words were unfair and she didn't mean to sound so bitchy, but Jane had looked terrified. And Barrett was terrified, not just for Jane but about everything Nick had told her.

He rubbed his eyes. "Barrett, I'm doing what I can."

And he's probably just as freaked out as me. Maybe even more since he probably knew more he hadn't told her. "I know, Nick. I'm sorry. So why do you need to report to your superior?"

"A name came up while I got started on this with my NSA contact. Before I came here. She believes it's the same person who's coordinating the movement of underage girls out of SexFlash and into this setup."

Barrett could guess. But she had to ask. "Who is it? Malcolm Prescott?"

"No. Not anyone you know. Gil Mansfield."

Barrett threw him a puzzled look. "And?"

"Gil Mansfield is on The List. He's number seventeen. And I'm supposed to kill him."

CHAPTER TWELVE

"You can't kill him." Barrett drew in a sharp breath. "Gil Mansfield could be our link to finding Jane."

She kept her tone calm, controlling her inner anguish. Even so, she couldn't erase the vision of Jane's tear-streaked face from her mind.

"Maybe. First I have to find him." Nick adjusted the position of the laptop. "Anyway. About Gil. SexFlash is a big operation and he's not even one of the top guys."

"The NSA wouldn't be tracking him unless he's up to something really bad. They must have given you solid info."

Nick didn't say anything. Barrett prodded him. "You can tell me. You have to tell me."

"I don't. For many reasons."

She wasn't going to let him slide. "I want to know what he looks like and what he's done. Come on, Nick. Photos and physical descriptions, prior arrests if any, last known whereabouts—what do you know?"

Nick finally answered, but reluctantly. "All of the above. I don't have his dossier in my possession, I only read through it. He was being contained in some kind of holding cell at an FBI-run facility along with other turneds. He was kept isolated because he wasn't deteriorating yet; he seemed normal, but that was expected to change any time. One day, he was sent to the labs for testing. During transport, he attacked his guards and drank their blood. All of it," Nick added in a flat tone. "The others couldn't stop him. Anyway, during the break someone on the outside used a remote hack to disable the alarms and open the gates."

Barrett sank her head into her hands and tried to think. "But how could they do that? Unless it was someone working from the inside. Someone within the FBI." She closed her eyes briefly before looking at him. "On a prior mission, one of our agents was told she'd been set up. We weren't sure by whom, but we've had to consider the possibility it was someone in the FBI. This supports that theory, don't you think?"

"It's one theory," he agreed. "With everything we're dealing with, of course it's possible there's a mole in the FBI. Especially when we're talking about the kind of money involved in these types of operations. SexFlash is making major bucks. They sell franchises, believe it or not. Strictly cash. A quarter million buys the right to use the name and setup for online sites, but they have to follow certain rules. Anyone who wants more than that, pays more."

"Sounds like someone is talking," Barrett said. "An informer?"

"I heard it from my NSA contact."

"And who is that again?"

"I never said. She uses the name Adrienne Wong."

Something about the way Nick said her name irked her. "Do I get to meet her?"

"That's not a good idea. She's high level."

"Oh." *And I'm just a little FBI girl*, Barrett thought, annoyed by the tone of his reply. *Selling cookies to raise money for new filing cabinets and get my junior-law-enforcement badge.* Okay, whatever. He wasn't going to volunteer how he knew Ms. Wong? She wasn't going to ask any more questions. It wasn't like she needed to keep tabs on every female Nick knew or worked with.

"And Adrienne's really not supposed to be doing me any favors."

Barrett let that go.

"Apparently SexFlash is laundering about a hundred million a year through different banks. So there has to be infighting. Thugs versus thugs, vampires versus thugs, vampires versus vampires. Gil was taken into custody once other turneds started to deteriorate, but before that, who knew what he was doing. Who he was talking to."

"But you think he was talking to whoever has Jane?"

Nick hesitated, seemed to consider something, then sighed. "Listen up. I wasn't sure so I didn't say anything to you right away. But after a while I had the feeling all that code we were looking at wasn't random. The holes in it were tagged, for one thing. Like detour signs. Danger! Do Not Proceed! Giving me no alternative to do so, if you know what I mean."

"You mean someone wanted you to find the code?"

"I don't think so. I was avoiding the detours. Refusing to fall for them. Then, wham, it was like someone got impatient. That white room appeared. And disappeared." He met Barrett's eyes. "I didn't just stumble on it. That glimpse of Jane was bait. Someone had us on the hook and cut the line."

"That room exists. We didn't hallucinate it." She pushed the laptop back in front of him.

"I can look again but I don't know what we're getting into." Nick leaned forward and tapped at the keyboard. Barrett gasped silently when the screen filled with white. He pulled back using a negative zoom. "See what I mean? That was too easy," he muttered.

The room was empty.

"Now you see her. Now you don't."

Barrett took a couple of deep breaths, collecting herself. She had expected to see Jane. "Maybe she's—outside the frame."

There was not the faintest shadow of movement in the room. The whiteness seemed unreal.

"It has to be a trap," Nick insisted. "We're being tricked into staying connected."

"But we can view the room. Use the zoom again," Barrett said.

"What for?"

"Just do it."

He covered every corner of the empty room in slo-mo. "What are you looking for?"

"Blood." She hunched over the screen, peering at the gleaming white walls and floor. "If Jane got dragged out, she'd fight back. Biting and clawing."

Nick shook his head. "My guess is that she didn't. See anything?"

"Not a drop. Maybe they cleaned it up."

Nick studied the screen. "This could also be an identical room that never had Jane in it."

Interesting. That hadn't occurred to her. Nick had always had a knack for thinking like a bad guy, while never crossing that line himself. *As far as you know,* she amended the thought.

"Like I said, SexFlash is a big operation," he continued. "And while I'm on that subject, she can't be the only girl for sale."

As far as Barrett was concerned, Jane was the only one that mattered right now. That there were others held against their will as sex slaves was a fact that required no confirmation. But they were faceless as yet, not part of the deep claim on her heart and her conscience that Jane evoked.

One rescued victim could open the door to free many more.

He was only being practical, Barrett reminded herself.

She would need him more than ever, if he had access to NSA intel.

"That's true. But she is the one they decided to show us," Barrett pointed out. "So that makes her the most important. And I'm not just saying that because it's personal."

"Okay, so we're up against an intelligent enemy who seems to know a few of our weaknesses."

Nothing had changed when they both looked back at the featureless white of the room and fell silent for several minutes. Until the screen went black again.

Nick took the chance to stretch his fingers. "Over and out. She's gone. They have our attention. I'm not going to tell you not to worry, but my guess is that Jane won't be physically harmed at any point."

"Good." Barrett's tone was iced with cool efficiency. "But I don't care who or what has her hostage. I'm going to hurt them badly."

"Hold on there, Rambo. First, fill me in on the Prescotts and these papers."

She did. She told him everything. And Nick came to the same conclusions about Malcolm Prescott that she and Justine had.

"So the Prescotts reported her missing, right?"

"Yes. And posted a fifty-thousand-dollar reward."

He gave a low whistle. "The Prescotts aren't fooling around."

"They could have used a more recent photo," Barrett said. "She still has braces in the photo they used for her missing poster. And her hair was much shorter then.

"It's from her middle school yearbook. I happen to have it in a frame. Her mother sent it to me." Barrett scowled. "Seriously, why that one? It's the wrong choice. I'm beginning to think that the Prescotts are being purposefully unhelpful."

"Don't read too much into it," Nick said in a low

voice. He shut down the laptop. "I've got to take this back to the NSA and let the experts deconstruct the hard drive. See if they can track down whoever's playing us."

"You can't do that yourself?"

"I could, but the laptop will be safer there and I don't want to risk destroying anything that can lead us to Jane."

"*Safer*." Barrett echoed him. "Not safe." She knew she was obsessing to the point of being irrational. But she didn't want to let the laptop out of her sight.

"Exactly." Nick interrupted her racing thoughts. "Safer. Would I lie to you? I hope they can pull data we can use," he added. "Because I need to check Gil off my list."

"What does that mean? You're going to kill him?"

He had a good grip on the laptop. It wasn't like she could wrestle him to get it back.

Barrett stepped closer to him, jabbing a finger into his chest. "Just keep in mind that a young girl is in mortal danger. Don't kill him before you exhaust all possibilities that he can somehow help us find her."

He scowled. "You don't have to tell me how to do my job, Barrett. I'm here. I got you this far. What else do you want from me?"

"Total commitment."

"Don't you get it yet? What am I if not fucking committed?"

She crossed her arms over her chest. "Nick—"

"I've always been committed to you, Barrett. You were just too fucking scared to trust in me. Well, despite your suspicions, I'm going to do my damn best to find Jane. I just can't make any promises. No one can guarantee anyone's safety, and that's certainly true of me. I tried to guarantee yours and I fucked up. I tried to guarantee my . . ." He hesitated so long she placed her hand on his arm.

"What?"

He stepped back, rejecting her touch. He shook his head. "Never mind that. The point is I'm going to do what I can. I might fail. I hope I succeed. The real question is, whichever conclusion we're left with, when these things with Jane are settled and we've halfway gotten our bearings back, if that's even possible, are you going to run from me again or are you going to finally fucking trust me? Are *you* going to commit to *me*?"

She was so shocked by his words she simply stared at him.

And when she tried to answer, she couldn't. She couldn't say a single word.

"Yeah, that's what I figured," he said with a look of disgust on his face. "So don't talk to me about commitment. This thing between us, whatever it is, it's on the back burner. We're finding your girl. We're figuring out who's playing us. Too bad for the both of us that we have to do it together."

He packed up his things, stalked to the door, and threw it open. Then he looked at her over his shoulder. "Since we have to work together anyway and you clearly don't trust my level of *commitment*, you should probably come to NSA with me. I'll wait in the car."

As he left, he yanked the door shut behind him with an audible thud.

Barrett and Nick passed through several NSA security gates before Nick pulled into a slot relatively near the vast glass block. The parking lot seemed to extend for miles in all directions.

He was about to open his door when she said, "I'll wait for you here." She didn't look at him when she said it, instead focusing on a point just over his shoulder, but she sensed him stiffen anyway.

"Goddamn it, Barrett—"

She shook her head and forced herself to meet his gaze. "I'm sorry. I should never have questioned your commitment. I know you're doing the best you can. So I'll just stay here. It's okay. Honest." She forced a smile.

"Yeah," he said, rolling his eyes. "Like that smile looks believable."

She laughed, but the sound cracked and she had to close her eyes to try and hold back the sudden moisture in her eyes.

"Oh, angel." Nick pulled her in for a hug, and for several seconds she allowed herself the comfort of his embrace. "We'll do our best, I promise."

She nodded, sniffed, then pulled back and stared at her wringing hands. "I know. I—I just keep thinking of Jane. I have to help her. I have to. I wasn't able to save Noah, my own brother, but Jane—"

"You know Noah wasn't your fault."

"I *know* that. But how I *feel* is something else entirely."

He tipped up her chin so she couldn't look away. "It was just his time. It's not Jane's. I feel it. Even though we have no guarantees, you know how accurate my instincts are. Let's choose to focus on that."

She took a deep breath and nodded. "Go."

"You're okay?"

"Yes."

He handed her the key to the ignition. When she reached out for it, he caught her hand and lifted it to his lips, placing a kiss on the palm and curling her fingers as if instructing her to hold the kiss tight. "You should be safe. Can't think of anyplace safer than here, as a matter of fact."

While he was gone, she thought about what had happened and gave it up after a while, her mind as blank as the walls of Jane's white room. Nick came back more quickly than she'd thought.

"That's done," he said, sliding behind the wheel of her car. "And let's get one thing straight before you even ask. You're not spending the night alone."

Not what she wanted, either, but she joked, "I wasn't expecting you to sleep in the helicopter."

Nick's forehead creased in a puzzled frown.

"I forgot to ask how you got here. No whirlybird?"

"It can't get from Tennessee to D.C. without refueling. Besides, it was due for a tune-up. If you really want to know, I thumbed a ride on an army jet."

"Lucky you."

"Like I said, you're not spending the night alone. The way I see it, that's going to make both of us lucky."

He waggled his eyebrows up and down, and unbelievably, despite everything, Barrett laughed and felt better. And she continued to feel better while she was in his arms.

CHAPTER
THIRTEEN

Barrett's bedroom looked invitingly shadowy with the candles she'd lit and placed in front of the dresser mirror. Barrett felt like taking things nice and slow.

The hotel had been all about lust. After what Nick had said, about being fully committed to her? Sure, part of her was scared out of her mind, but the other part of her had instantly clasped his words to her heart and refused to let go. She wanted lust and loving now, and Nick seemed to guess as much. He stood slightly to one side behind her, studying her reflection in the mirror as she took off her earrings.

She held the sparkling drops in her palm for a moment before she poured them into a shell.

"You're beautiful," he murmured, still keeping a little distance as he watched her brush her hair.

She wasn't seeing it. As far as Barrett was concerned, the emotional strain of the investigation already showed on her face, even in the candlelight. "Tell the truth."

"I am," he insisted, taking a step toward her. "I still can't believe that I got my girl back."

My girl. The words and the tender tone in Nick's voice combined to fill her with fear.

She'd been willing to let herself go. To hope, given the earlier fervency in his tone, that they could have a future together. But as soon as he said those two words . . .

The intimacy and the intensity of their lovemaking

was almost too much. She didn't trust it. Sex was easy. Loving him—and keeping it to herself—had always been the hardest part. That wasn't going to change.

It couldn't.

Barrett put the brush down, allowing her gaze to meet his dark eyes in the mirror without turning around. "Well, thanks for the compliment. But I'm not—that."

"How about for just one night?" he asked gently.

He finally was close enough to touch her. Nick raised his hands and placed them on her shoulders. Then he moved them slowly down over her upper arms. Stroking her. Warming her. The sensation was unsettling. What with everything that had happened—and being constantly aware of the long odds against ever finding Jane—Barrett already felt too much like a stray come in from the cold.

She gave a highly indecisive shrug. Nick reached around and undid the first two buttons of her blouse, then drew down her top on one side to bare some skin.

"You're not sure? Let me convince you." He bent his head and pressed soft kisses on the subtle curve where her neck flowed into her shoulder.

"I might change my mind," she breathed, after a few minutes of that.

"I'm going for something a little more definite." He smiled against her cheek, still meeting her gaze in the mirror.

"Such as?" she murmured. "Tell me exactly what I'm getting into."

Nick undid some more buttons, admiring the fragile camisole she was wearing underneath. "Nice. You might as well be wearing nothing." He stepped back and began to unhook her bra.

Barrett couldn't catch his hands. "Nick. Stop for a sec. Answer me."

He didn't stop. "For one night, you swear to be my girl and nothing but my girl."

The bra back was clasped by a single remaining hook. He lifted her shining hair away from the nape of her neck and proceeded to kiss her there. Barrett had to hang on to the dresser.

"I'm not swearing to anything."

His lips moved to her ear again. He kissed it and took a suck of her bare earlobe. Then tickled it with a whisper. "Okay. Want me to stop doing this?"

Barrett didn't hesitate to answer that question. "No. It feels too good."

"All right then. Swear."

"I damn well won't—"

"That was a swear word. That counts," he said with amused satisfaction. He stepped back and took off his shirt, standing tall when Barrett whirled around, wearing nothing but a clean white tee and jeans. Somewhere along the line he'd taken off his shoes.

She put her hands on his chest like she was going to push him away. And then she didn't. The muscles under the thin knit material of the tee were hard, almost hot to the touch after being confined under clothes all day. Her palms rested on small male nipples.

He drew in a breath as she made small circles, teasing them. Then she spread her fingers and dug all ten of her nails into his chest right through the T-shirt. Nick winced with pleasure.

In less than a minute, he'd stripped her and shucked the rest of his clothes.

Then he backed her toward the bed, his hands clasping her waist as if he was thinking of throwing her onto it if she gave him any more guff.

Barrett had no choice but to fall into the peach silk comforter, her arms reaching for him. He rolled her over and pushed aside the fancy thing, getting down to the smooth sheets and down to business.

Nick gave as good as he got. Thrusting into her deeply and repeatedly, but holding himself up so that she could move. And breathe. He paid exquisitely sensual attention to both breasts when she arched up as he bent his head down and suckled her nipples into wet, tender points.

She knew he was close to climax—very close—when he finally slipped his big hands down to hold her ass, squeezing her cheeks with each uninhibited thrust of his thick, raging cock.

Nick moaned as he buried his head in her neck, calling her name with raw urgency. Barrett came once, pulsing so strongly she cried out, and then came again with dizzying speed and intensity as he pumped. Harder and harder.

Then stopped. Dragging in a breath like a low howl. He filled her. Body and soul.

And it was in that moment that Barrett thought: *Maybe*.

Maybe it was time not just to hope.

But to *believe*.

Later, Nick and Barrett sat across from each other with a better bottle of wine than Barrett had offered Justine. He'd dressed again, putting on the clothes he'd been wearing. So had she, just to keep things equal. She didn't have a robe that was big enough for him. He'd actually seemed pleased about that.

"Still my girl?" he asked in a low voice.

"The night's not over." She didn't quite meet his eyes as she popped the lids off the containers from a Chinese take-out place that delivered. "Let's eat."

"Gotta keep my strength up." Nick set out plates and

napkins and cutlery and chopsticks in red paper wrappers. She dished up the food, starting with her favorites, and they both stuffed themselves.

"What is this?" Barrett said, peering at the rubbery thing that dangled from the tips of her chopsticks.

"Looks like part of a Szechuan sandal."

She made a face and put it inside a folded napkin.

"Try the kung pao chicken. It probably won't kill you."

She nibbled at a bite of chicken. "It's okay." She put down her food. "I'm done."

"Yeah? Well I'm not done with you."

He got up, picked her up in his arms, and carried her to the sofa where he dropped with her in his lap. She giggled as he kissed her, but when a masculine hand flicked the steel button of her jeans out of its buttonhole, her fingers encircled his strong wrist.

She rested his arm diagonally on his chest. Nick crossed his other arm over it, closing his eyes. "This is what I'll look like when I'm dead," he intoned. "Because you're killing me."

"You'll survive, dude. We can't just have sex, then eat, then have sex. We've got work to do!"

He raised aggrieved eyes to the ceiling. "Fine. But can I at least have more wine?"

"It just so happens I have another bottle."

She went to retrieve it. And when she returned to the living room, he was sprawled out on the sofa, absently rubbing his hand along his jaw. The dark stubble she'd seen in the morning was getting a tentative start.

She pushed a large pouf next to the sofa and perched on it. A reluctant smile curled one side of his mouth. "Is that thing a tuffet and are you Little Miss Muffet?"

"No to both. I'm just staying out of temptation's way."

"If you're so tempted, why'd you stop me?"

She shook her head. "I have no idea."

"Then get up here and cuddle with me, goddamn it. I promise I won't try anything more and that we'll get right to work."

He slung an arm around her when she rose and joined him, fitting her body against his side, sliding a hand over his chest.

"What's that?"

Nick slid two fingers into his pocket and retrieved a grayish stone, tossing it into the air and catching it again. "A lump of gold." He showed her the cut he'd made in it. "Found it on the mountain after Murphy was there."

The name made her stiffen slightly. "How about that. It will come in handy."

"How? I mean, I know it's valuable, but I'm keeping it for a souvenir."

"Pure gold keeps a vampire from reading your thoughts. Didn't you know that?"

"Nope. The question is how you do?"

She bit her lip and he narrowed his eyes. "I'm sorry," she said. "I can't tell you. Does it really matter how I know?" Barrett rested a hand over his heart to feel the strong beat. "It's not that I don't trust you, Nick. It's not my secret to tell."

He studied her for several seconds, then nodded. "Okay. If you don't feel it's important for me to know how you got that little bit of information, I won't push. But if things change—"

"I'll tell you. I promise. We're a team and I've got your back. Just like you've got mine." She peered at him, hoping he caught the full significance of her words. When he didn't look at her, she said, "Did you hear me, Nick? I know you've got my back. That you've always had my back."

He cursed and rubbed his forehead roughly. What the hell? She hadn't said anything worth cursing about.

"Nick—"

"I'm the reason you got kicked out of the army, Barrett."

Huh? She gave a disbelieving laugh. "No you aren't. I got kicked out because I disobeyed orders. Because I refused to stand back and let a woman and her teenage daughter be victimized by rebel soldiers even though you warned me it was too soon to move."

"Yeah. And when you didn't listen to me, when you put yourself in danger yet again, I reported you to headquarters. Anonymously. I'm the one who blew the whistle on you. Because I was worried about you, yes, but I still betrayed you."

Shock held her immobile. Speechless. But only for a few seconds. She believed him. It actually made total sense, and she'd been an idiot for not considering it before. With a violent lunge, she got to her feet and took several steps away from him.

Wearily, he came to his feet, as well.

"And why are you telling me this now?"

"Because we're at a crossroads, Barrett. You feel it and so do I. Finally, you're starting to let me in—"

She laughed scornfully. "And this is the result. You fuck me over."

He narrowed his eyes at her. "I'm not fucking you over. I made a decision last year. Was it the wrong decision? Maybe. Because it backfired on me and I ended up losing you for over a year."

"You've lost me for more than a year, you bastard. You've lost me forever."

"No, I haven't," he said calmly.

"What?"

"I said I haven't lost you forever. Right now, you're pissed and that's completely understandable. But you're also so angry that you're missing the fact I was honest with you. I told you what I did, Barrett, because I don't want any more secrets between us. I want to deserve that trust you were giving me. I want to acknowledge our past but move beyond it into a future, and if you care about me, if you love me the way I think you do, you'll see that and you'll forgive me."

She felt like he was landing one blow after another. "I *never* said I love you."

"No," he agreed. "But you do. Just like I love you."

"You love me? Since *when*? We only saw each other again less than a week ago."

"Since when have I loved you? For a long time, Barrett. I loved you back when I was scared you were going to get yourself killed and I did something stupid as a result. I've loved you the entire time I've carried your picture around with me in my wallet."

"What?"

Nick reached into his pocket, pulled out his wallet, opened it, then retrieved a photo so she could see it.

"Are you kidding me?" She vaguely remembered him taking it. She still had that camo hat on the top shelf of her closet. But she'd never seen the photo. It was hard to believe he'd been carrying it around for all this time.

Nick let her look her fill. Then he turned the photo around so the back was to Barrett and studied it himself. "Gorgeous girl. Beautiful. And fearless. But she scared the shit out of me. Because I didn't want to lose her." He lifted his gaze to hers. "That's why I did what I did, Barrett. But I lost you anyway. I don't want to lose you again."

She didn't know what to say. Felt her anger dissolving into nothingness. And it scared her how much power this man had over her. She believed him. He did love her. And he had been trying to protect her.

And she loved him.

But she couldn't tell him. Not yet. Maybe never.

When she said nothing, a shadow crossed his face and he slid the photo back into the wallet and tried to flip it shut. Wanting to say something to make things right between them, at least until she gathered the courage to say what she really needed to say, Barrett grabbed for his wallet. "I want to see what else you have in there." She was trying to defuse the tension in the air. To be playful. It didn't work.

Nick snatched the wallet so fast Barrett gasped. Then he cursed. Then he shook his head. "God, you really want to kick me where it counts. Why not," he said. "Why not get everything out in one fell swoop. Here." He held the wallet out to her. "Take it."

She shook her head. "No, I'm sorry, Nick, I—"

"No. You wanted to see it, here it is. I've put myself out there about everything else, why not this, too."

Nick—"

"Take the fucking wallet, Barrett."

She took it. She opened it. With shaking fingers, she explored a hidden, smaller pocket behind the ID. It was another photo. Barrett took it out.

She paused before she spoke. Her confusion was obvious in her voice. Why had he reacted so strongly about her seeing this?

"It's your brother, Gary, right?" Nick had mentioned him in passing, but that was years ago. "You resemble each other." The man in the photo had the same dark hair and ruggedness but seemed weaker somehow. She didn't see a trace of Nick's inner strength in his face. "Is he younger than you? I forgot."

Nick nodded. His troubled gaze bothered her. Barrett had a sickening feeling that she'd gone too far without knowing why. "What's going on, Nick?"

"He's dead, Barrett."

Oh shit.

Oh no.

Nick hadn't talked of Gary often, but when he had, it had been obvious he'd adored his brother.

It had to have happened after they'd both returned to the U.S. She put the photo back in its secret place, searching for the right words to make up for her blunder. "I'm so sorry. So so sorry. But you know how I feel, Nick. You know about Noah—"

"It's not the same. Not at all."

Barrett felt even worse. She should have kept her mouth shut and not offered those meaningless words as comfort. She had endured similar comments from well-meaning relatives and friends when Noah died.

I understand exactly how you feel.

No one had. No one could.

I was just like you. I cried a river—surviving doesn't always make you feel lucky, does it? Especially under the circumstances, with you right there and nothing you could do to save him.

A shake of the head. A pat on the hand and an offered tissue.

But I stopped crying. Like you will. Life goes on, Barrett.

Yes and no. Nothing was like anything else when you lost a beloved brother. Noah wasn't replaceable.

"He was five years younger, to answer your question," Nick said in a controlled voice.

"That's right. But—but what were you talking about before? Why didn't you want me to see his picture?"

"Because I killed him."

She inhaled a soundless breath.

"I killed him," Nick repeated. "He begged me to."

Barrett went numb.

"Gary had been turned. He'd seen action before me. He'd suffered injuries to his back and PTSD. When the

FBI went looking for volunteers for its turning program, he was one of the first in line."

Oh, God. Oh no.

The List.

She thought of Murphy, the turned vampire that had attacked her, and the way he'd smelled. Rotting flesh. Nick's brother, Gary.

"I didn't even know about it. I'd been overseas, of course. He didn't tell me. But when the FBI approached me, it wasn't just so I'd kill a bunch of turned vampires. Gary said it was what he wanted. He'd talked about me. He told people that he—that he loved—"

Nick's voice broke and Barrett started to move toward him.

His hand shot out, holding her back. "No," he shook his head. "No! Don't you see, Barrett? Gary was on The List. You think you're to blame for Noah's death. Bullshit. But me? I drove an arrow into my brother's heart and killed him."

Nick stopped. The silence seemed endless.

She didn't want to, but her mind immediately went there, picturing what the scene must have looked like. Nick, reeling from the news that his brother had not only been turned but was going insane. Suffering. His brother needing to be put out of his misery. Wanting Nick to do it.

Oh, God. Oh, God.

Nick.

"Jesus." Her mind was reeling.

He looked up at her, and her eyes were riveted on Nick's dark gaze. It glistened with unshed tears.

"Baby," she whispered. "Did your parents—did you tell them?"

"They died in a car crash a few months earlier. If they'd been alive . . ." The tears fell now, all the more poignant because he immediately tried to swipe them away. Only more followed. "I don't think I could have done it. But I had to. I had to. I had to. He was suffering. I had to. If you could only have seen him. I had to."

She couldn't take it any longer. She took him into her arms.

His body shook with his low moans of despair.

She rocked him. She kissed his tears away. Tears she knew he hated her seeing.

Finally, she gave her heart to him, this man who loved so much, who wanted only to protect those he loved from harm.

"Nick," she said. "Of course you had to. You did what you thought was right. You did."

It took a long time, but eventually he quieted. She continued to hold him in silence.

Then she said, "You loved him, Nick. You did what you had to for him. Just like—just like you love me. I'd want you to do it for me if it came to that, and you would. I'd do the same for you. I'd want to die myself, I might even try to make it happen, but I'd do it. I would."

He raised his face. Looked at her as if he didn't quite believe her. Then he closed his eyes and leaned his forehead against hers.

Later that night, after they'd fallen asleep in each other's arms, Barrett thought about everything they'd said to each other that day. It was almost too much to process, but she had no choice.

Nick Maltese had killed his younger brother. And she'd chosen him to help her find a vulnerable girl.

Something should have been radically wrong with that picture.

But nothing was. She'd do it again in a heartbeat.

Nick had been Gary's only salvation because only he

could have done such a difficult thing. A man that strong was someone Barrett could rely on to protect her.

To protect her and Jane.

When she finally went to sleep, she had no doubts about her feelings for Nick or her trust in him. Dreams, however, plagued her. And when she woke, her heart thumping and sweat covering her body, suspicion was the first thing she felt. Suspicion that both she and Nick were being lied to.

Barrett shook Nick awake.

"What is it?"

"Nick, I know you're tired, but I have to talk to you."

He stared at her with sleepy eyes before his expression turned to dread.

She immediately shook her head. "No. Nothing's changed, Nick. I didn't suddenly decide that you're a monster because you did what you did for Gary."

"Then what?"

"I've been dreaming . . . and thinking . . . about Murphy. The possible mole in the FBI. About Gary."

"So tell me."

"First, I need you to answer some questions about Murphy."

"What do you want to know?"

"Do you think Murphy had anything to do with the SexFlash operation?"

"I have no reason to think so. I can't tell you anything for sure except he was halfway to dead—you got a whiff of him."

"So he was like Gary?"

"Gary was nowhere near that far gone. Nor were the others that I killed."

"So obviously the turneds you're hunting are getting worse with time."

"I'd say that. Gary still had moments of lucidity. He could still ask. Beg." He closed his eyes, obviously fighting off bad memories, before determinedly continuing. "Murphy seemed much farther gone. And batshit crazy. Full neuron-rage."

"Nothing we've heard suggests born vampires have experienced anything like this."

"It's a result of the turning."

"But not all turneds. My friends Peter, Ty, and Ana, they're perfectly fine."

She saw his expression close up. "For now. Doesn't mean it's not coming, Barrett."

"I know that, but you're assuming it will. Why?"

"I don't understand."

"You assumed it was coming because you trusted the FBI. Now we know there's probably an FBI mole. If that's the case, what if the turneds they've targeted are different from others? What if the FBI took their experimenting one step further, and gave a select group of them something to see if their powers could be enhanced?"

He seemed to be considering the possibility.

"Something that poisoned them," she continued. "They'd need to get rid of the evidence, the same way they formed Belladonna to get rid of the evidence that Rogues are engaged in criminal activity so they could keep the Turning Program going."

Nick stiffened. "What?" he whispered. "The Turning Program has been shut down."

Barrett frowned. "Not according to what I know."

"Then you don't know shit."

"Nick—"

"You're wrong," Nick said abruptly. "About the Turning Program still being in effect and about the FBI poisoning Gary. You're grasping for straws because you don't want to acknowledge the possibility that your friends are in danger."

"That's one concern, yes, but—"

"Damn it, Barrett," he roared, "it's the only possibility. Or else I've been working for the same assholes who did that to my brother. Assholes who are continuing to turn humans into vampires, knowing the irrevocable damage they're inflicting."

"But you already knew that they'd done it to Gary. How is it different if they went a step further?"

"Because he volunteered for it. And the FBI admitted to it. If what you're saying is true, they lied to me. They fucking fooled me and I've been doing their dirty work for them. No. It's not true."

He got up and swept into the bathroom, shutting the door behind him. Barrett went to follow him when her phone rang.

She picked up her cell, barely able to see the screen. The number swam. "Hello?" Barrett said.

"Barrett? It's me, Ginny Prescott."

Barrett immediately tensed. "Hi, Ginny. What's going on?"

"I don't really want to tell you over the phone. Can we meet somewhere?"

She looked at the closed bathroom door. "Sure. When and where?"

She memorized Ginny's suggestion: two days from now in the park along the Potomac. The walkway through it ran for miles and there were plenty of places to stop and sit down.

Barrett walked into the kitchen to conclude the conversation. She endured Ginny's nervous chatter for as long as she could. The woman talked a lot for someone who essentially had nothing to say at the moment.

Ginny's voice was tinged with fear and she hesitated often, stumbling over ordinary words. But she made it clear that she had something important to communicate. Polite reassurances from Barrett weren't enough to get Ginny to reveal them over the phone.

They got through awkward good-byes and Barrett hung up.

When she reentered the bedroom, she realized Nick had left and she hadn't heard him.

And he'd left not just the bathroom, but her apartment entirely.

She hated reminding him of his brother's death and his part in it. Yet what she'd said was valid—it was entirely possible the FBI had experimented with a select number of turneds, including Gary. Given that, Nick's reaction to her supposition had seemed a bit over the top. Moreover, while he'd obviously been torn up about Gary's death, the fact remained that he'd *killed his own brother* and had been able to go on with his life. It had been less than a year. A year after Noah had died, Barrett had still been tormented by his death and her limited part in it. Sometimes she still had nightmares about it. If Nick could so easily get over killing his own brother, whom he'd clearly loved, it must have been easy as pie for him to get over Barrett's sudden departure from his life. Maybe all the affection and care he'd shown her in the past few days wasn't so much about truly lingering feelings but about convenience.

She shook her head to stop her runaway thoughts. What the hell was she doing, trying to analyze the depth of Nick's feelings for her? Nick was helping her find Jane. That was all that mattered.

No matter how well adjusted he seemed now, she knew killing his brother had been difficult for him.

But he'd done it. And she had no doubt in her mind that if he had to kill Ty and Ana and Peter, all vampires that Barrett cared about, he'd do that, too.

CHAPTER
FOURTEEN

Club Red
New City, Georgia

Vladimir swung first, catching the beefy contractor off guard. The other man crumpled to the cement floor without a sound. A few hard kicks to the head with a polished, custom-made black boot finished him off.

Tamsin, who had been watching the fight from the shadows, came forward, stepping carefully around the fresh pooling blood. Her stiletto heels clicked against the raw concrete until she reached her lover's side. She looked up adoringly.

"You still have what it takes," she purred.

"I would rather not do such things."

She slipped a hand through the crook of his elbow, smoothing the clingy material of her low-cut scarlet dress with the other. "What did he do anyway?"

"He talked too much."

"In here?" Tamsin gestured around the small underground arena, which was empty except for them. The space echoed with construction noise from the much larger floor above. "Who would even notice?"

"All it took was one word, my dear. He said yes to an interview with a big Atlanta newspaper. I don't want our building plans splashed all over the front page."

"Who cares?"

Vladimir scowled at the offhand question. "I do."

Tamsin did not have to know about the hidden floor beneath this one—or who was concealed there, though the subterranean cells were mostly empty, except for a wayward girl. And a restless monster. The contractor might have happened upon both, if he had gone beyond the Keep Out sign and somehow made his way through the locked door of the immense, climate-controlled vault where Vladimir stored living things who were apt to be noisy from time to time.

"Oh. Well, what is that saying? Any publicity is good publicity?"

"Dead men never are. And I understand that someone from the paper is still in the parking lot, waiting for this one"—Vladimir used the toe of his boot to push the man's limp arm against his body—"to show up."

He put a hand to the earpiece he wore and spoke softly to someone outside. "Get rid of the reporter. No, don't kill him. Just tell him our construction supervisor is busy. Yes, all day. And give him a guest pass to our grand opening. The elite pass, idiot. We want him in our pocket, do we not? A private skybox plus two whores is something to look forward to."

Tamsin leaned over a little to get a better look. The contractor's sightless eyes stared upward, as if he were gauging the strength of the steel beams crisscrossing the space far above a square pit sunk deep into the floor. Then his head slowly tipped to the side as the muscles of his thick neck stretched with its weight.

Vladimir laughed. "He seems to be looking up your dress. Rigor mortis has not set in."

She gave a ladylike shudder. "Eww. That's so creepy. All I have on under this is a thong."

"Since when are you modest? But if it bothers you—" Vladimir looked around and spotted a dirty canvas tarp. "Then cover him up."

Tamsin sighed but she obeyed, dragging the tarp by a corner and throwing it over the corpse. She could have been making a bed. Badly.

She bent over several times to spread out the tarp, just to give Vladimir an eyeful, hoping that would net her a few good-girl points.

"Is it the thong I left in the drawer for you? With the hole in front?"

She tried to remember. She had an extensive collection of tiny G-strings and thongs. "Um—yes."

Her answer was a little slow for his liking.

"Don't lie to me." Vladimir took command of her when she straightened and walked the short distance back to him, away from the draped body.

"I didn't lie, Vladdy. I just had to think for a sec."

"Stand still."

He shoved a hand up inside her dress, feeling for the thong, then probing roughly, penetrating her with one finger. Then two. His dark eyes glittered, fixed on her lovely, bored face as he hand-fucked her. Hard and fast. He entwined his fingers in her tumbling hair, holding her in place.

Tamsin stepped her feet wide apart and let him have his fun, not into it herself. He satisfied himself as to the complete truth of her reply by lifting her dress and exposing her to his hot gaze. Her bare pussy was no longer covered by the gossamer thong, which Vladimir had pulled down.

"You sounded uncertain. You know better, Tamsin. Or do you need a taste of punishment to remind you to obey me in every way?" He withdrew his slick fingers and pushed them into her mouth.

"Yes. I do. You know how much I like it when you make me behave."

"Hmm. Well, then. Lick."

Dutifully, Tamsin licked his fingers clean, her pink

tongue darting and swirling until Vladimir smiled faintly. He released her and undid his fly, forcing her to kneel in front of it.

He reached down to pull her breasts out of her dress. Propped up, they were spectacular, the dark red nipples standing out against her ivory skin. Vladimir had never understood the popularity of tanning salons. He preferred his women as pale as moonlight.

Staying on her knees, she bounced a bit to make her luscious tits jiggle as she did what she did best: suck him off. Her hard nipples, chilled by the cold air underground, touched his thighs. The friction of the expensive material of his suit seemed to excite her somewhat. Tamsin put more effort into pleasing him.

There was the off chance someone might see. She had once told him she liked the element of surprise.

No one appeared. He came explosively in her mouth. Tamsin was skilled. Not one drop of come spilled out as she swallowed several times.

His semen was as cool as his blood. Vladimir had found over the centuries that very few women gagged on it for that reason. He flattered himself that the taste was superior, as well.

He gave her a hand up as they both adjusted their clothes. She bent forward to brush grit from her knees and, when that was done, stood up and settled her breasts back inside the bra underneath her dress, glancing once in the direction of the dead man.

"You're not just going to leave that there, are you?"

"No." The blue-lit receiver in Vlad's ear flickered as he listened to whoever had just called. He turned away from Tamsin, who took the opportunity to check her makeup in a compact. Perfect, she thought, except for the smudged foundation around her mouth. She moved away to a worktable and set down her purse. Time for a touch-up and never mind the sawdust. She knew better than to leave Vlad when he hadn't told her she could.

"Send someone at once," he instructed the caller. "I want the body to go into the framework of the rear staircase. The concrete is ready."

Controlled by remote, a huge pipe coated with gray slurry moved to where Vlad was looking. The unseen being who was maneuvering it positioned the dripping mouth of the pipe between temporary plywood walls braced with rebar.

Tamsin observed the action discreetly in her compact mirror. An open stare would earn her a vicious slap from Vlad. He considered it disrespectful, and had even told her once that it was a sign of aggression among his people.

She was *so* not looking forward to their upcoming clan gathering. She just wasn't all about family, not after growing up in foster care until distant relatives had taken her in. Left to the mercy of her nasty boy cousins, Tamsin got an early education in rough sex.

But at least they didn't drink blood. The vampires might just decide that she was the goddamn first course. She had only ever allowed Vlad to drink from her. The unusual sensation intensified her natural inclination toward submission, something she hadn't explored much until Vladimir had introduced her to its pleasures. He did the thinking. She could just drift and enjoy herself. The way he handled her was seldom gentle once he was aroused—it helped her really let go. She was perfectly willing to get spanked, tied up, whatever he wanted to do.

He had hinted at other, stronger pleasures in her future. Tamsin was eager, in her lazy way. Vlad was older than she was—he never said exactly how much older—but he had a rock star body and a long, gorgeous cock to match.

And if she satisfied him properly, he could be quite generous. There was a lot in it for her in this relationship if she behaved herself. The occasional dead body underfoot was no big deal to Tamsin.

One of Vlad's underlings was crossing the unfinished arena toward them, keeping his head down so as not to look at her.

That was something else Vladimir Ouspensky didn't allow. She snapped the compact shut when she felt his dark gaze sweep toward her. Tamsin turned to him, totally focused on his face. He stepped in front of her, running a hand through her hair, stroking her cheek in a possessive way.

She couldn't see the murdered man being rolled into the tarp. But she heard the dragging sound of canvas over concrete as Vlad's terse orders were carried out. They had left the arena by the time the pipe disgorged a flood of cement and embedded the shrouded body forever.

Vlad guided her past the elevator to a private staircase tucked behind closed doors to which only he had the access code. He indulged himself once more in the pleasure of sliding his hand up her skirt, fondling her intimately as she mounted the stairs, staying in front of him. The high heels she wore made her hips sway temptingly under the filmy dress that clung to her bare behind.

He withdrew his hand to tap a code into a keypad and exit with her to the main level. He stopped and let her go on, wanting to experience what ordinary customers would see. A runway bracketed with footlights split the space in two, with front-row seats for the big spenders and cocktail tables for others. The strippers and the dancers would work the runway in timed shows. Above it were two balcony levels; with the second, higher level cantilevered over the first so that no one would miss a second of the constant action. Each level was glassed in, so that clubbers could see and be seen. Access was restricted to the attractive ones who made it past the velvet rope, of course.

All of that was for humans. The far more exclusive group of born vampires with wealth, his personal A-list, would not care to mingle with them. Vlad had built the underground level for his own kind, where no disturbing ray of sunlight could penetrate. Dark deeds could be carried out within its shrouded spaces and no one above would ever be the wiser.

"Looks super great," Tamsin enthused, looking around like she was seeing it all for the first time. Vlad barely heard her.

They did need publicity. He hoped the media coverage of the preopening party would be favorable. He wanted to outclass every club in Atlanta, put Club Red on the map in a big way from day one. To do that, he'd spent a fortune to host a press junket, including dozens of plane tickets and deluxe rooms at the hotel and a charter bus to herd them all back and forth. And then there were the swag bags. Reporters and bloggers who posted glowing reviews would find ten thousand dollars cash tucked into theirs. They all gossiped. The critics would sing a different tune the second they found out about Vladimir Ouspensky's generosity.

He had planned it all.

CHAPTER FIFTEEN

Barrett strolled beside Ginny along the river, sidestepping an occasional jogger and rejoining the older woman at a wider part of the walkway.

Ginny kept looking around, as if someone were following them. Barrett didn't push, knowing whatever it was Ginny had to tell her, she had to do it in her own time.

Finally, the other woman fumbled with the strap of the large tote over her shoulder and checked inside. Barrett glimpsed a file folder stuffed with what looked like legal documents and a closed paper bag.

The older woman looked up again, down the path to a stone bench in a secluded nook. "Let's sit there. I—I found some papers in the attic that I wanted to discuss with you. That's why I couldn't meet with you at home."

A few minutes later, Barrett was reading them quickly as Ginny's nervous gaze darted up and down the path. No one seemed to notice them. The slowly flowing river, a dull gray-green, carried a few kayakers downstream.

Barrett turned to Ginny, her stomach churning with disgust. "These are dated a year before Sarah's death."

"That's correct."

"He wanted Sarah to die. Because he knew you'd get custody of Jane. Because he liked looking at her."

"Because he wanted to do more than look at her," Ginny whispered. It was as if the older woman had no rage left, only sadness. Her worn face seemed defeated. Yet she had come here to try and make things right.

"He was so controlling with her. I thought he was trying to be a good father figure. Not . . ." She pressed her lips together.

"You need to get these back into his files. And you need to pretend you never found it. Not yet, Ginny. Not until we have a better idea of what's going on with Jane. If it turns out he had something to do with her disappearance, we don't want to tip our hand."

"I can fake like nothing's wrong. I've had a lot of practice at it." Ginny's terse reply had the ring of truth. "Those are copies. You can keep them. A friend of mine has a second set. The originals are back in his study."

The women exchanged a look of mutual understanding. Barrett knew she had an ally in Ginny.

"I stayed with Malcolm partly so that Jane would have a home until she was at least eighteen. Now? I hate that I didn't see him for what he was. That he posed such a threat to Jane. But at least now I have no choice but to leave him, something I should have done long ago."

The older woman reached into her tote and took out a new paper bag folded over several times at the top. She met Barrett's curious look. "No, this isn't evidence. Even though I saw on TV that they collect it this way."

"Oh. What is it?"

Ginny handed the bag to Barrett. "Jane's sleep shirt and sleep socks. They were under her pillow. In case you need them—" She broke off.

Her meaning was clear enough. Sooner or later in abduction cases, trained dogs were used to help find victims.

* * *

Barrett took care of other business once she had returned to her apartment. The folder of Malcolm's documents she stashed in a desk drawer, not wanting to look at it again for a little while. Pedophilia was nothing new to her, but she needed time to get her anger under control. Then she'd analyze the document more closely for hidden clues to his relationship with the girl. She might be able to find some hint in there of a plan—his—to abduct Jane someday. For her own good—or so he seemed to think. Men like Malcolm Prescott were capable of fooling everyone.

Her cell rang from inside her purse, muffled. She dug around, not finding it, and picked up on the last ring.

"Hey. It's Nick."

Barrett stiffened. "Hello." She hadn't called him since he'd left without saying good-bye. She hadn't known what to say.

"You were right, Barrett. The Turning Program hasn't been shut down. My handler—Director Rick Hallifax—has been lying to me."

"Hallifax," she whispered. "I know that name."

"You should. Apparently he's the person in charge of Belladonna. Fuck, no wonder he never told me about it. Told me about you. Your whole mission is to contain vampire criminals so the Turning Program *doesn't* get shut down."

"How did you find all this out?"

"I went searching. And once I went searching with certain names at my disposal—Peter Lancaster, being one of them—it wasn't hard for me to come up with the name of Kyle Mahone."

She sucked in her breath on a hiss. "You *talked* to him?"

"I did."

"And?"

"And I ran your theory by him. The one about the FBI

experimenting with a select few turneds. Then recruiting me to get rid of them when the experiments backfired. We don't know if it's true, we might never know, but it's on his radar now. So, unfortunately, am I." He took an audible breath. "Barrett, listen—I owe you an explanation."

"You don't owe me—"

"I do. And I'm sorry, angel. I know you were just saying what you had to say."

"And *I* know why you reacted the way you did," she said quietly. "And why you wouldn't want to believe it. But it doesn't change anything, Nick. You did what you had to. You saved your brother needless suffering."

"Maybe. Or maybe if the FBI poisoned him, it had the means to reverse that poison. Or it might . . . in time."

Oh, God. She hadn't thought of that. "Nick—"

He barked with bitter laughter. "God, we're a pair, aren't we. How could we possibly be together? Our combined guilt and baggage doesn't leave room for much else."

Was he trying to tell her something? Like he'd changed his mind about how committed he was to her? When he said nothing else, she asked, "So that's where you've been all this time? Tracking down Mahone. Because I was hoping you'd call me eventually."

There. It wasn't exactly a declaration of love, but he'd have to know what she'd meant. What *he* meant to her.

"Of course I was going to call you, Barrett."

Of course, he said. Because of Jane?

Or because of them?

He'd told her he loved her. And she hadn't said it back, even though she felt the same way. Even now she was relying on his intuition to guess how she felt. Was she really that much of a coward? Maybe at one time.

Nick had accused her of running before. Running

away from him. From the certainty that loving him would hurt.

But for the past two days, not knowing where he was or if he'd actually get in touch with her again? That had hurt more than anything she'd ever experienced.

So she wasn't running again.

She *was* fully committed. Enough for both of them, if need be.

"Anyway," he said, his voice tight, and the sound of it made her heart clench. "I just wanted to apologize, fill you in on what I learned from Mahone, and let you know what the NSA techs found on the laptop's hard drive."

There it was again, that sharp bite of jealousy. By now she knew it was unwarranted, but she couldn't resist needling him a little. "Hmm. Let me guess. You talked to Ms. Wong again?"

He paused, then spoke, his tone far lighter than it had been. "That's right. I had to sleep with her and her identical twin sister before she'd talk. Twenty times in all. Together. Apart. Whew. They wore me out."

Bastard, she thought with more humor than heat. It was no use sticking out her tongue when he couldn't see her. "I'm sure you did your best, stud. Did the NSA find anything usable on your computer?"

Nick sighed, finally accepting that Barrett had truly accepted his apology. "Easy hacks, apparently. There is no such thing as privacy in cyberspace."

"So why were we lured into it? Who saw us looking?"

"Whoever wanted us on the hook. For whatever reason."

"I take it there was no way to identify that person or persons."

"Correct. The URL wasn't registered to an individual." She heard the rustle of paper. Nick sounded like he was looking at notes he'd made. "Let me double-check my hard copies. Okay. Long story short, all of the Sex-Flash websites are traceable to one hub. Just one. You would think with that much money at stake that they would be more careful, but no."

She stuck to the subject. "Where is the hub?"

"New City."

"What about the portal to the video feed from the white room?"

"That came from somewhere very close to a place that hasn't opened yet, also in New City. Ultra luxury, for the discerning man about town, according to their online ads. Multilevel space, not completed. It's going to be called Club Red."

"Seriously? I found a Club Red flyer in Malcolm Prescott's car trash. It's opening in a few days. There's an open call for auditions. Dancers. Strippers."

"How the fuck about that."

They were both kind of stunned. She spoke first. "Anything else, Nick?"

"Yeah. The owner has an unusual name—hang on, I have it on my phone." He paused to tap into a different screen. "Vladimir Ouspensky. Russian national, papers in order, no expired visas, hasn't done anything bad. Shacks up with a Miss Silicone at the same hotel we stayed at."

"I wonder if I saw him," she whispered. "Or her."

"I'm looking at her photo right now. I know I didn't. I would have remembered her." She knew he hadn't meant that in a good way.

"The FBI's official task force on trafficking confirmed an influx of several hundred women and girls to the area in the last year. Strip clubs, exotic dance revues, you name it. Club Red is muscling in on the action. And this is interesting. There's a nice new blood bank in town. I'm thinking their clients might include vampires who can pay top dollar for scary smoothies."

"Riiight," Barrett said. "God, of course. So simple. But has Belladonna checked around at any local blood banks? No. Too obvious and a waste of our super spy time."

"No one can think of everything at once," he said.

Nice of him not to slam the competition, if her agency actually was any competition for him.

"Let me back up, Nick. Collette is investigating the most important blood businesses in the U.S. We need to get on this."

"Don't be too hard on yourself. I've got skills," he said.

"You do, Nick," she said softly. "The best."

Had he thought she was being sarcastic? Not anymore. A silence stretched out until he cleared his throat. When he spoke, it was only to say, "Getting back to the flyer and the ads—there has to be a connection between Club Red and Jane."

"So what am I going to do?"

"You mean, what are *we* going to do? Because one thing's for sure. I'm not a hired gun for the FBI anymore. Not given what I've found. I'm just not going to tell them that yet."

"Okay. So what are *we* going to do?"

"First, aerial surveillance of the club."

"You have the chopper."

"Yeah. But seeing as how my bunker's no longer safe, both me and the chopper have been holed up at the base just outside of New City."

"Right," she said, rubbing her temple.

"You okay?"

"Sometimes I still struggle to process all this, you know?"

"Yeah," he whispered. "I know." He cleared his throat. "So, how about you? I'm going to be flying. What are you going to be working on?" he asked.

He was going to get a look at Club Red from the air. It only made sense that she try to do so from the ground. But something stopped her from telling him that. Maybe it was the fact things were already so tense between them. Or that she didn't want him to try and stop her because he wanted to protect her again. Whatever it was, it guided her answer.

"I'm going to check in with Belladonna. Make sure Ty and Peter and Ana are doing okay. You know, no signs of neuron-rage." She was also going to call Justine and enlist her help to get inside Club Red.

He didn't respond, as if he was weighing whether she was being truthful or not.

"Keep me posted," she finally said.

"Same with you, angel," he replied. He hesitated for a fraction, as if he wanted to say something else.

But he didn't. So she did, blurting it out before she lost her nerve. "I love you, Nick. I always have."

Before he could respond, she hung up.

CHAPTER SIXTEEN

Nick did another flyover of New City. He didn't swoop down or do any wild moves that would attract attention, keeping an eye on the feed from the gyrocam and following its grid, which matched the street layout, except where it ended in sprawl.

Even so, his heart was pumping and his adrenaline was rushing.

He wished he was inside a jet, conducting high-G maneuvers: rolls, climbs, loops, barrels, and turns. He wanted to pump his fists and scream like a madman.

Because Barrett loved him. And she'd actually said it.

And fuck-fuck-fuck, if he wasn't already up in the air, he'd still feel like he was flying.

Grinning, he shook his head and told himself for the thousandth time to settle down. She'd said it. She'd meant it. The next time she said it, he was going to make sure he was inside her and she had her legs wrapped around him. Until then he had to keep his shit together and focus on the mission at hand—finding and saving Jane. Then there was the fact that the FBI had lied to him, that Barrett had turned vampires for friends and that they might pose a problem in the very near future, and a hundred and one other concerns to deal with.

But right now, Barrett loved him and he was holding that close.

A minute later, he was over Club Red.

It had been built on the outskirts of the city, standing alone in a lot of raw land. Green turf had been laid around the building, and the parking lot spaces marked off.

He used a remote cam to take dozens of photos. You never knew what was going to be important. Visibility was excellent, for what it was worth.

The ground-penetrating radar didn't show tunnels running into the club, just plumbing. No supersize pipes. If underage girls were being secretly shipped in for private sale, the physical transfer was probably relatively straightforward.

Meaning, Nick thought, that they would need to rely on humans and not just gizmos to find out more. The abducted girls didn't just stroll in. There were witnesses. The trick was finding one who was willing to talk.

He'd gotten a rough idea of the structure's height, which would be easy to confirm at the city department that issued the building permit. Just like everywhere, exact dimensions were on file, available to the public. He made a rough mental estimate as to the structure's square footage, using a car parked next to it for a unit of measurement.

Club Red was big, somewhere around nine thousand to ten thousand square feet. But that was only a guess.

He increased his altitude. Most of the city was so new that planted trees were few and far between. They looked like matchsticks dabbed with green. Nothing aboveground was concealed.

The radio crackled. "That you up there?" Kevin's southern accent softened the static a little.

"Yeah. Where are you?"

"At the base. Inside the lookout tower. They just tracked a heli. Looked like yours."

"Not yet, but I'm on my way. What have you been doing?"

"Teaching Aura some new tricks. And letting her teach me."

Nick smiled. "Smartest dog I know. See you soon, Kev."

Nick swooped away to the west, toward the base.

There was nothing out of the ordinary about the landing and the runway crews were busy elsewhere. Nick was cool with that. Being more or less invisible fit his MO. He shut down the bird and leaned back, waiting for the rotors to stop spinning. He felt safe on base. The army, he knew. The FBI? Obviously, not so much.

It still pissed him off that he'd been lied to. Every time he thought about it, he wanted to rip someone apart. But again, he had to keep his mind in the current game, including what the hell Barrett was about to get herself into.

Because she'd sounded weird on the phone when he'd asked her what her plans were and he knew Barrett well enough to know what that meant.

She was planning something dangerous.

So what was he going to do about it?

After he settled in, Nick compared the images he'd snapped to hundreds more he'd downloaded from drone archives, taken with cameras that could focus on a milk carton from sixty thousand feet. The drone photos were backdated for months, enabling him to compare large vehicles parked in and around Club Red and other newly developed sites.

A semi was the most likely bet to conceal and transport a cell the size of Jane's. And there had been several pulled up to the club that sometimes didn't move for days. As far as human activity around the big trucks, there was very little. If trafficked girls were being moved in, the process wasn't visible from the air.

Following procedure, he requested information from a classified database with automated entry—for those who had the right code, and Nick did—on one semi in particular. Unmarked from what he could tell, it showed up several times in the more recent images, parked away from the club's front entrance. It was big. More than one transport cell—he'd made an informed guess as to its dimensions after studying the screen grab—could fit inside.

Definitely worth a look from on the ground.

It was past midnight, but he reached for his smartphone and called Kevin, who had taken over a disused barracks at the edge of the tarmac for himself and the dogs. Nick had obtained the necessary clearances.

"Hey. Let's go jogging."

"Ha-ha. Very funny." Kevin yawned. "Fuck you."

"Not now. When the sun comes up." There was a short silence. Nick waited.

Kevin cursed again. "That's at oh-six-hundred hours, you son of a bitch. It's oh-one-hundred now."

"That's right. We need to do surveillance on the ground. Dress like a jock. Ball cap, sunglasses, track suit, sneakers."

"I don't have any of that stuff," Kevin complained.

"I'll loan you some of mine. Bring Aura and another dog."

"So we're supposed to be ordinary guys exercising our dogs. Where?"

"The Club Red parking lot. It's huge. We can do laps, stretches, cooldowns, whatever, so we can take pictures on the sly and let the dogs sniff around, see if they pick up any vampire tracks."

"What if we get run off? Or picked up for trespassing?"

"I don't think their security is up to speed. They don't even have a perimeter fence."

"Okay. See you at dawn." Kevin ended the call.

Nick set down his smartphone. In another minute, it buzzed, signaling an incoming text.

Barrett.

Sublet a condo in New City.

His eyes narrowed. Was it just him or did she not want to give him the exact address?

Driving down from DC w. Justine.

Her colleague from Belladonna.

The one she'd mentioned used to be a stripper.

And everything fell together.

She was going in undercover. Going to get inside Club Red. And she hadn't wanted to give Nick warning because she'd been afraid he'd stop her.

It was his first instinct, of course, but one he restrained.

He'd learned his lesson.

Barrett loved him. The only way he was ever going to *keep* Barrett was to let her go. To believe that her experiences and her training and her sheer fortitude and courage would guide her out of dangerous situations and back to him. The way the world was shaking down, it was the only way she'd survive. She had to be able to take care of herself.

But he'd always be there to help if at all possible.

He just had to make sure she knew he didn't want to get in her way, just have her back.

He messaged her: *Kev and I doing ground recon 2mrw. Do not enter club until u review info & exterior photos.*

He hoped he got his point across.

When she texted back a smiley face and the address to the condo, he knew he had.

Then he started putting together a file of material for her to read. If she didn't have her laptop with her, she could read it little by little on her smartphone. There was plenty to send from the drone archives. And there would be more when he and Kevin got done.

He figured it would go smoothly. There had been no employees in the aerial shots time-tagged before 11 a.m. and not a single car. Just that semi.

The dawn surveillance would provide crucial information that she wouldn't necessarily be able to get. Barrett in athletic wear in a mostly empty parking lot? Please. She would stand out way too much, with her curves on display and a long blond ponytail bouncing against her back. Might even be followed by some creep.

He and Kevin would look too ordinary to notice. The dogs would get more attention, especially Aura in all her furry glory, with those mesmerizing golden eyes.

When Barrett got into the club and stayed there, he had to have a plan in place to rescue her if things went wrong or their cover was blown. The aerials didn't show everything. He wanted to memorize every door and window and back alley and service entrance in advance, get it pinpointed on a mental map that couldn't be taken away by an officious guard or beaten out of him if he infiltrated the club and got caught.

Barrett walked into the condo first, dropping the heavy box of miscellaneous stuff she'd stashed in the trunk onto the floor. Then she texted Nick.

Got anything now?

Yeah. Not that recent but useful. Aerial photos. Sending now.

She responded. *Okay.*

Then she hesitated, wondering if she should repeat the declaration of love she'd made earlier. Or at least end the conversation with an XOXO. After all, he hadn't commented on what she'd said, either via phone or text. Granted, he'd been busy, but . . .

"Grrr!" Barrett blew several strands of hair out of her face and told herself to stop. She was worse than a schoolgirl with a crush on the quarterback. Nick loved her. She loved him. The world wasn't going to implode now that they'd admitted it. But neither was a happily-ever-after going to drop out of the sky for them or Jane. They had to get to that happy ending on their own, and that meant she needed to stop obsessing about why Nick hadn't written or texted her a love letter in the past twenty-four hours.

Barrett looked up as the partly open door to the condo banged against an inside wall and Justine came in, dragging two wheeled suitcases. She kicked the door shut and looked around.

There wasn't much furniture. Just a ratty sofa and a matching armchair in the living room and a dinette set in the narrow kitchen. Through an interior hall, two twin beds, made up with faded coverlets, were visible.

"Kind of a dump," Justine sighed. "I hope we don't have to stay here very long."

"Me, too." Barrett didn't want to say her reasons why out loud. If they didn't find Jane within a week, the odds would be against them ever finding her at all. "Who owns this place again?"

"A friend of Moira's. At least it's close to Club Red."

Moira Finn was a former colleague of Justine's who now ran a talent agency, Tail Feathers, supplying dancers to clubs from Boston to Miami. According to Justine, she repped most of the girls who would be showing up at the publicized public auditions at Club Red. Whether the agency was on the up-and-up was none of Barrett's business. She was grateful for a place to stay, no questions asked.

Justine headed for the bedroom, dragging one of the suitcases. "That was a *long* goddamn drive. Ten hours from D.C. to Atlanta. Sheesh, I need a nap."

"Go ahead and sleep. I'm waiting for visuals from Nick on the club."

"Okay," Justine said cheerfully. "Then you won't care if I snore."

Barrett kicked her shoes off and sat down on the couch. The phone stayed silent. If he was sending a large file, it could take awhile. She looked around, not seeing a magazine or any other reading material. She got up again and dragged the box she'd brought in next to the couch.

The highlighted papers Nick had brought to her apartment were inside, along with the paper bag Ginny had given her that held Jane's sleepwear. She realized she hadn't told Nick everything Ginny had told her.

She picked up Jane's clothes.

Closed her eyes.

Hell, if vampires existed, why not other things she'd given up hope on?

Resolved, she did something she hadn't done since Noah died.

She prayed.

CHAPTER
SEVENTEEN

At 5:30 a.m. sharp, Nick reached the barracks and pounded on the ground-level windows. The frames, not the glass. Made more noise and nothing broke. After a minute, Kevin yanked open the door and peered at him.

"You're early."

"Rise and shine, soldier." Nick handed him a bundle of clothes. "Get your dress-ups on. Time to go play with vampires."

Kevin swore, but he took the clothes and disappeared, coming back in the same T-shirt he'd slept in, wearing the sweatpants over his boxers. "Too short. My ankles show."

"That was intentional. I love your ankles, Kevin."

The taller man flipped him the finger and sat down to put on the sneakers. Aura padded into the sparely furnished room and watched with interest.

"Walkies," Kevin told her.

She went back to wherever she'd come from and returned with another somewhat smaller dog, a male that resembled her. Son of Aura, Nick thought.

Kevin confirmed his guess. "That's her pup. Goes by Ray. When he listens."

Nick rumpled their ears and smoothed their fur as Kevin finished tying the laces and went to grab their leashes from a hook.

Both dogs could be canine geniuses but they still got

that look of stupid bliss when they were petted right. "Okay. At ease," Nick said, straightening and turning to the pile of clothes.

He handed Kevin a ball cap. Then sunglasses. And an athletic jacket. Kevin jammed the cap onto his head and hung the sunglasses from one arm by hooking it into the knit collar of the T-shirt, before slipping on the jacket. Then he got his first good look at Nick, who had turned to open the door.

"Dude, what is the gray thing hanging down your back?"

"That's my aging-hipster ponytail. It's a clip-on. I rubbed a little zinc oxide into my stubble to match it."

Kevin looked disgusted. "This is embarrassing. We look like the Dork Patrol." He flipped up his collar and pulled the zipper of his jacket to its limit, right under his unshaven chin.

"Doesn't matter." Nick smirked. "It's still dark out. Let's go."

Kevin issued a command to the dogs and they heeled instantly.

It took them about fifteen minutes to drive to Club Red. They parked on a side street with no houses, just empty lots with temporary electricity hookups, and got the dogs out.

Canine business completed, they headed to the club's vast parking lot. Nick noticed right away that the semi was gone. And that there were no cars. The light of dawn turned the expanse of asphalt blackish-pink.

"Let's just walk them," Kevin suggested. "If Aura senses anything of interest, she'll let us know. Ray's new to the game. Don't expect much from him."

Nick took the younger dog's leash and started jogging around the parking lot. Kevin stuck to the area closest to the building. From a distance, Nick saw Aura stop several times. Kevin nodded to Nick without calling to him.

They lost sight of each other and reunited around the other side of the club.

Kevin had Aura short-leashed. Her eyes were glowing and her back fur was up higher than usual. She gave Nick a brief sniff and moved on to her pup, slapping a maternal tongue across Ray's greasy snout.

"He found a dead cheeseburger," Nick explained.

"Aura was all excited," Kevin said, lengthening the leash. He nodded toward the parking spaces next to the building entrance. "Those VIP spots over there? She just went nuts. That must be where the big vampire puts his wheels."

"Makes sense. Lots of big black cars in and out of there in the aerial shots. Anything else?"

"Nothing you could take a picture of. But I wish I could read her mind. She was picking up all kinds of information."

"Speaking of that, let's walk the perimeter and get some photos of the exits and entrances."

Kevin held his ground at a yank from Aura. "Maybe we'd better jog. She needs to work off some excess energy."

The two men and the leashed dogs started off at a slow lope, with Nick pressing the button for the camera hidden in the chest pocket of his fleece jacket. The lens was positioned right through the logo.

They went around twice.

"How 'bout we go get breakfast?" Kevin asked. He was breathing hard. Aura pulled the leash taut, straining toward a town car that had just swung into the parking lot.

It stopped, rocking back on its wheels.

"Check out the tinted windows. I can't even see the driver clearly. So why'd they stop?" Nick muttered.

"Your scary ponytail," Kevin said.

"Shut up."

Without looking at the car, they moved along casually. Kevin stopped to rub his calf, getting one last surreptitious look at the car when it rolled forward slowly again. "Vanity plates. And guess what they say."

"Keep going."

"RED SPELL." Kevin straightened up, holding tight to Aura's leash.

"Clever. Don't look back."

But Aura did, disobeying Kevin's command. He just about had to drag her.

Vladimir rubbed his temple. A flash of pain had hit him hard. Even from a distance, the large dog's golden gaze had captured his. He had not been able to look away until it had.

"Who were those men?" he demanded.

The driver shook his head. "Dunno, boss. Sometimes people walk their dogs in the lot. You don't usually get in this early."

"They could have been undercover cops."

"Nah. Not with mutts like that. Did you see how the big dog pulled? Obedience class dropout, for damn sure."

Vladimir let him think so. The driver pulled into the VIP spot and waited for instructions. "You can go ahead and open the door," he told the man, handing the keys to the building over the back of the front seat.

"Yes sir."

Vladimir wanted a minute more to calm his racing thoughts. The joggers had no way of knowing that their badly behaved dog had the infamous golden eyes of the giant, six-legged taiga wolves, but resembled them in no other way. Nor did it display the intelligence of the breed. The ancient taigas were extinct, thanks to the old-world vampires they had once preyed upon, who had returned the favor by hunting down and slaughtering every one. A long-ago vampire king had decided that they must be eradicated from the earth.

But that one, by some hideous coincidence, showed a trace of their vanished blood. He was sure of it. There might be others, given the indiscriminate sexual habits of dogs.

Why him? And why now?

There was no telling. But there was no mistaking those eyes, which had bored through his skull, radiating instinctive awareness of what he was. It had not been safe to order the driver to go closer to the men and insist that they leave.

Though the dog was only a dog. Four legs and two ears. Not even much like ordinary taiga wolves, he reminded himself.

He would have been doomed if it was otherwise. Only a true giant taiga could read the minds of vampires. Blessedly, the long-vanished animals had had no way of communicating with humans beyond crude physical signals.

The pain of the dog's steady gaze stayed with him after the men walking the accursed animals had gone. Vladimir swore. He had no time to research an antidote, and pills for humans had alarming side effects.

The first audition for Club Red dancers was scheduled for today. Gil would have to oversee it. The pounding music might make his own head explode. Vladimir winced at the sound of the passenger door opening.

"Sir?" The driver poked his head in. "Are you okay?"

"Yes, thank you." Vladimir gritted out the lie. "Is the door open?"

"You bet. Want me to carry your briefcase?"

Bootlicker. But at the moment Vlad was secretly grateful for the man's obsequiousness. "If you would. Please go ahead."

He had to use the car door to lift himself out. Vladimir made a mental note to look at the security footage of the parking lot. If the men were nobodies, he would have the dogs poisoned somehow, if they returned. But it was possible they hadn't been joggers at all. He had rivals at other crime syndicates just as steeped in blood.

A vision assailed him. A thin trickle of blood widened into a river that engulfed him. He stood, bracing himself against the car, until the vision faded away.

There was only the building. And his driver, holding the door open with a smile.

CHAPTER
EIGHTEEN

Barrett blinked the sleep from her eyes, wondering why Nick, who was wearing athletic wear for some reason, had decided to stop by her condo at an indecently early hour. Then, after taking in his obvious "Joe Shmoe" disguise, which did nothing to detract from how sexy he looked to her, she immediately hoped it was because he wanted to do something "indecent" to her. But apparently not . . .

"We did the perimeter check on Club Red and I just downloaded the photos."

When she just continued to blink at him, he smiled, bent down, and kissed her on the forehead. He was freshly shaved and had splashed on something with a hint of spice.

"You look nice," he added. "Sweet and sleepy." His gaze moved over her wrinkled, army-issue T-shirt. Her cherry-print pajama shorts didn't go too well with it. But he seemed more interested in her bare legs.

"I remember how you always used to get up before me, Barrett. And how you'd always let me take you back to bed and make love to you one more time before I had to get up. Those were the days."

She smiled at the warm memories his words evoked. "Yeah. Land mines and valentines."

He chucked her under the chin. "You're funny. Got any coffee?"

That was it? Their first face-to-face after she'd told him she loved him and he kissed her forehead, chucked her on the chin, and asked if she had coffee? She scowled. "No."

"Are you alone?"

"Yes. But I don't know for how long," she added reluctantly. She didn't know where Justine was this early in the morning, but she was betting her temporary roommate would be waltzing back in at any moment with the coffee they were sorely lacking. Well, there was something else she'd been sorely lacking.

Him. In her arms. On her tongue. In her body.

If he wasn't going to make the first move . . .

She leaned toward him and his eyes heated as he obviously read her mind. Stepping inside, he kicked the door shut and pulled her against him. Covering his mouth with hers, she took the taste of him she'd been wanting. Then he pulled back, rested his forehead against hers, and gave her what she'd been wanting even more. "I've been thinking of you ever since you told me you loved me. And thinking of ways—*good* ways—to punish you for hanging up on me right after you did it."

"Good ways for you or for me?"

"That's right," he agreed.

She laughed, rested her cheek on his shoulder, and wrapped her arms even tighter around him.

"I've missed you," she said. "I'm glad you came, even if it is far too early."

"Ditto, angel."

They gave themselves a few minutes in each other's arms before separating. "Okay," he said. "We've got things to do. Things to go over. I put everything on this for you. Here." He handed her a flash drive.

She yawned and ran her hands through her hair, not missing the way his gaze latched on to her breasts as she stretched. Smiling, she held up the flash drive and waved it even as she shimmied her hips. "I have a feeling I'm about to be buried in recon data."

"That's right. Aerial photos and data extrapolation, to be exact."

"From drones?"

"Yes. And satellites."

"And I used to think angels watched over us all."

"Not these days."

"Thanks, Nick." Unable to resist, she went on tiptoe and pressed her lips against his. He wrapped his arms around her waist again just as a clattering sound broke the silence.

Justine opened the front door with a bang. "Fucking elevator," she muttered to no one. "Pushed the fucking button ten fucking times and the fucking door jams. Just what I need with this fucking bag about to split—"

Then she saw them.

"Oh. Hello. I'm Justine. You must be Nick. And hey, you're in luck."

"I am?" Nick asked as she breezed past him. Though he stepped back, he kept one arm around Barrett's waist, something Justine saw, causing her to wiggle her brows at Barrett.

"Barrett, I couldn't remember how you do your brew, so I actually got two extra coffees, one cream, one skim. Take whichever you like. Nick can have the other." She entered the condo and plunked down a disintegrating paper bag splashed with coffee. She grabbed paper towels from a roll and started mopping up the mess.

"There's plenty for all," Justine continued. "But the leaky one with the foam and cinnamon is mine. You know something, guys? If I had a boyfriend, this would be a brunch double date."

None too subtle. There was no use telling Justine that Nick wasn't her boyfriend. With his arm around her, that was clearly what he was communicating. It was a new thing for them—PDA. Barrett leaned into his side, finding that she really liked it.

About a half hour later, the impromptu breakfast for three was over and Justine was heading to the door. "See you guys later. I expect to be fully briefed after you get through."

Nick waved at Barrett's friend. She seemed to approve of him, which he took to heart. He hadn't missed how in one moment Barrett seemed to relish the small signs he gave of being her lover—the occasional brush of his hand against her shoulder or kiss on the neck—and how in the next moment she seemed to be uncomfortable with his PDA. He supposed it was natural given how new this was for both of them—a couple of declarations of love did not a completely comfortable relationship make. But he'd been determined not to lose the ground they'd made. So each time she'd shied away from his affection, he'd simply amped it up all the more, something that had made Justine laugh out loud.

Barrett rose from the table to see Justine out and returned with her laptop.

Not meeting his eyes, she plugged the flash drive into the USB port. "While you're here, let's go over this together."

Tilting his head, he looked at her, then sighed. Because they needed to do some work, he'd give her space for now. But not long enough to build a wall between them again.

Reviewing all the photos and the additional intel he'd garnered from various sources took almost two hours. When they were done, she sat back. "This isn't going to be easy."

"Nope."

Barrett sat up straight. "Shoot. I almost forgot. Ginny

Prescott gave me some clothes of Jane's that hadn't been washed. Is it possible that one of the dogs could work with them?"

Nick hesitated, thinking it over. "Tracking dogs are specialists. Aura doesn't find missing people. But I'll talk to Kev. He knows other handlers and maybe one of them can help. He and I were spotted in the club parking lot. In disguise, but even so."

"Who spotted you?"

"I don't know. Couldn't see through the tinted windows, but the car looked expensive, so my guess would be that it wasn't the janitor arriving early."

Barrett found the bag with the sleep T-shirt and socks. She held it up without opening it. "This is Jane's stuff. I'll keep it here for now."

Nick nodded. "Okay. It could be useful. I just can't say for sure and we can't be too conspicuous."

"Meaning the Club Red parking lot can't turn into the New City dog run all of a sudden."

"Exactly."

"Moving on." Barrett adopted a crisp tone. "We need to formulate several escape plans if we go in. And decide on a method of keeping in touch. And signaling for help."

"I have a few ideas. On this." He took another flash drive out of his pocket. "The photo files ate up the memory on the first one. So swap and we can take it from there."

"Okay. Thanks, Nick. I'll try to gather whatever intel I can at tonight's auditions." This time her voice was far from crisp. She tried to hide it, but she was nervous. In a way, that was good. Fear kept you on your toes. But she had to know that he'd die before he let anything happen to her.

"Tonight you're just like anyone else auditioning for a job. And once you're in? Don't forget I got my start as an infiltration and extraction specialist. If something goes really wrong, I will get you out of there, Barrett."

"Jane comes first."

He looked at her, not surprised in the least by what she said. But he obviously surprised *her* when he suddenly stood, grabbed her hand, and yanked her toward him. Cupping her chin and tilting her face up, he stared into her eyes. "I hear you. But I'm not leaving you behind. Now, can we stop pretending to play it cool and let me do what I've been wanting to do since I got here?"

She swallowed hard. "What's that?"

He simply lifted his brows and continued to stare at her.

Laughing, she wrapped her arms around his neck and swung her legs up, confident that he'd catch them, which he did.

As he cradled her to his chest, she cupped the back of his head and pulled his face close. "All right, soldier," she whispered with her lips pressed against his. "Let's make this quick."

Only he didn't.

He took things slow.

And he made sure that this time, when she said she loved him, she said it the way he'd been wanting. With him inside her and her legs wrapped around him.

And he said the words back to her.

Praying that sometime soon, she'd actually believe and trust in them.

CHAPTER
NINETEEN

"**Now refresh my memory,**" Justine said hours later after Nick had left and the two had commenced Operation Shopping. "Why are things moving so slowly? Why can't we just call in some help and move in on Club Red? Like you, I'm learning more and more with every day that passes, but I'm still not as up on all this secret agent whoop-de-doo as you are."

At least Justine was straight about what she did and didn't know. Bottom line, Justine knew the world that Barrett was about to enter in a way you couldn't learn from books.

"Because we have no evidence that Jane's actually here. We only know that she was taken." Barrett looked at Justine over the clothes racks to make sure she understood.

"Can't the local cops just close Club Red down and look for her? I want to be sure on the fine points. One of these days I'll be a real agent just like you," she said drolly, playing down the badass abilities she had and that Barrett had seen for herself.

Barrett shook her head. "Not without a warrant and without cause. We'd have to go in front of a judge and we have no solid evidence right now. And I'm very grateful you came with me for backup. You are a real agent."

Justine screwed up her face in a comical smile. "While we're on that subject, I guess Sheriff Lester and Deputy

Jim Bob don't have the manpower or the brains to conduct an investigation on their own, right?"

"Right. Which makes New City a desirable location for strip clubs and prostitution for that reason, among others. Out in the boonies but near enough to the main East Coast highways to get its share of the action."

"That's about what Moira said—oops, I mean, I understand. Let's get you a disguise so you won't get killed."

Justine pulled out a skimpy dress that wasn't much bigger than the tag attached to it. "Now that's cute. Matches your eyes. Celery blue."

"I think you mean cerulean blue."

"Whatever. It's a pretty color."

"It is." Barrett shook her head again. "But it's way too short and looks too tight."

"Short and tight is what club attire is all about," Justine said, rolling her eyes. "So where do you usually shop?"

"Preppy places. You know, like Jay Canoe or Van Sailor."

"I went into one of those stores once," Justine said. "Rubber-soled flats in brown or navy. Stripes on everything. The sales associates didn't look too happy to see me." Justine slung the blue dress back onto the rack.

"My turn to pick your brain," Barrett murmured, frowning at an even skimpier dress. "What's a strip club audition like?"

"They refer to them as cattle calls for a reason. Some of the girls—well. Don't be surprised if they push and shove. The competition is fierce."

"I bet. I'm not dancing."

"You don't have to. It's not the only job on offer. But whatever the boss is looking for, it is about how you look and the way you move. You gotta be a little shameless and super sexy. For you, that would be sexy in a classy way."

"Sounds doable. What are you going to pretend you're applying for?"

"Anything behind the scenes. Sometimes they hire older chicks to keep an eye on the brats. Cuts down on the hair-pulling in the dressing room."

"You think I could do that?"

"No. They need someone loud and tough to be in charge backstage. That's my guess, anyway. You have that haughty look, though. But it's not enough."

"Haughty?"

"A little. Look, you asked and I answered," Justine said in response to Barrett's expression of indignation. "Remember that you're going to be mixing with girls who didn't have all your advantages. And listen, some of them are really nice and work hard—college girls trying to pay tuition, single moms whose baby daddies don't pay child support, girls who never had two nickels to rub together—"

"I get the idea." Maybe that sounded more snippy than she intended. But Barrett already knew she was likely to be regarded with suspicion by nearly all of them.

Justine shoved several hangers together, inspecting another relatively modest dress before moving on. "There will be plenty of girls who are tougher than you can probably imagine."

"I don't doubt it."

"Girls like that—just don't judge them, because they'll know. But watch your back."

"I didn't come here to judge anyone," she muttered.

Justine quickly changed the subject. "You'll be surprised by how young some of them look. Maybe you know the type? Fresh-faced teen temptress? I worked that angle until I was in my late twenties."

"I never had a baby face."

"I'm sure you didn't. Not with those cheekbones. You look rich, Barrett. Like you could give a man a whack with your gem-encrusted riding crop. Make him beg for—um—whatever he wants," Justine said brightly.

"I don't own one. And a real riding crop is plain saddle leather."

"Well, that would work, too," Justine said cheerfully. "Anyway, you practically scream class. Club Red isn't going to put a gum-chomping bimbo at the front station."

"So you think I should go for the hostess job?"

"Easier to get. You're not a dancer. And hostesses don't handle cash. They just have to look good, keep track of time, and be able to tell the riffraff from the real deal."

"I'll keep that in mind. Guess I better invent a résumé."

Justine laughed. "Hell no. Don't. Believe me, they're not looking to hire Ivy League grads. So shut up about that. And by the way, change your last name at least."

"How about Klein? Sounds real."

"And it's nice and short. Go get a fake ID," Justine added.

That had been on her list since she and Nick had checked into that hotel.

"I've already got my cover in place from when I met Powell. If they run a background check—"

"Well, they will." Justine gave Barrett a friendly slap on the butt. "On this. It's all about your appearance, honey."

Barrett thrust all the dresses on hangers over her arm back onto a rack. Haphazardly. She straightened them out and smoothed the tags into place. Then she picked up the two dresses that had fallen under the rack, not wanting to make extra work for some sales associate.

She was a compulsively good girl. And she was not looking forward to the audition.

"Here we go," Justine whispered. The surging crowd of women in front of the low stage formed a human wall.

"We need a battering ram," Barrett muttered.

"Just ease through. Or stay put. You'll get noticed no matter what."

Barrett looked down at her feet, which were already hurting from standing for so long. Her plain, high-heeled pumps in ivory had cost more than the conservative evening suit they matched. The cut was classic except for the neckline that plunged between her firm breasts. No camisole. Justine had insisted that she show a little skin.

She smiled at a supertough-looking dancer who pushed past her, glancing at the tattoos swarming all over her arms and the tarnished stud decorating her nose. The woman trod heavily on her toes in reply.

Barrett winced.

"Not the girl-next-door type," Justine said without moving her lips.

"No kidding."

The tattooed dancer's forward march through the crowd produced howls and shoves. The bouncers escorted her to the door as soon as she reached the stage.

"She's a natural for a biker bar." Justine wasn't being catty, just putting in her two cents. "A luxury club like this would never hire a girl with that much ink," she added. "The bouncers know the ropes."

There were several up there. Massive men with thick necks and bald heads and sharkskin suits with no lapels. Plus fists decked out with rings big enough to serve as brass knuckles.

If her mom could see her now.

Barrett concentrated on memorizing details Nick would be sure to ask her about. She tried to relax. She was inside. If she got picked, she would have a chance to explore the inside of the club whenever she was free. If she didn't get picked, she'd sneak in. Fortunately, according to Moira Finn, who offered insider information every time Justine called her to gab, there was a media junket scheduled before the club's grand opening.

Apparently every girl in a G-string between New City and Atlanta was hoping to be interviewed by a national reporter and get a taste of fame. The club would be crowded with all kinds of people coming and going at odd hours, which was to their advantage.

There were over a hundred applicants vying to be noticed. A lanky man in a suit that didn't fit him too well strolled onstage.

"Gil!" His name got screamed over and over, like he was a rock star instead of a sleazebag pimp.

So this was Gil Mansfield, turned vamp and suspected child abductor.

If only she had a way to alert Nick right now. But a cell call could be overheard, even intercepted and recorded. They had no way of knowing if electronic surveillance was operative inside the club. Nick had emphasized the danger. They'd agreed to call only when it seemed safe to do so. And even then they would be taking a risk unless they were several miles away from the club.

Mansfield ran a hand over his slick hair and adjusted his tie, blatantly preening for the girls.

Barrett's eyes narrowed, memorizing his face and the way he walked, in case she ever had to figure out who he was in some dark alley.

She almost missed the entrance of the man who owned Club Red.

Tall, magnificently built, and expensively dressed,

Vladimir Ouspensky radiated sinister confidence. He had a quelling effect on the overexcited girls. They went quiet as he strode across the stage.

A pouty brunette with a beauty-pageant body joined him, draping her slender arm across his broad shoulders. She was the one Nick had pegged as Miss Silicone, Barrett realized. She seemed to be advertising her status as Vladimir's girlfriend, in case the dancers didn't get it.

His long black hair fell over his shoulders as he leaned forward, studying each girl in turn with remarkable concentration.

Then he made his choice, pointing only to the ones he liked. The bouncers began to escort the rejects out. Many were chattering like magpies again, not exactly heartbroken. The pouty brunette skittered off the stage to talk to a girl she seemed to know.

Barrett remembered the other clubs she'd glimpsed from the outside when she and Justine had driven through New City to the condo. Most would probably find work.

An uneasy feeling came over her as she glanced around at the rapidly thinning crowd. Justine, who was standing right by her, elbowed her hard.

"He's staring at you, Barrett," she said under her breath. "I told you you'd get noticed."

Barrett looked up quickly at the man on the stage. She was immediately riveted by his dark eyes. It wasn't a cliché to say they looked like burning coals, because they actually did. The irises were black with a spark of incandescent red.

Despite the heat in his gaze, she shivered. His mouth had a cruel sensuality, with lips that curved but never smiled.

Definitely a force to be reckoned with, she thought, trying to ignore the uneasy feeling that kept growing.

His gaze lifted as he half turned to speak to a woman

who'd just joined him. Her plump figure was encased in tight fuchsia knit, with hennaed, spiky-short hair.

Barrett strained to hear Vladimir Ouspensky's murmured words and the woman's soft response.

Only one word came across clearly. *Stripped.*

She turned to Justine, who had heard it, too.

"No need to go that far. You don't have to do this," Justine whispered out of the side of her mouth. "I'll walk out with you. Come on."

Barrett shook her head. She was inside the club. He wanted her. She was staying.

Sure enough, Vladimir had wanted Barrett to strip, but not in the way she'd assumed. Yolanda, the woman in fuchsia, had been ordered to remove the natural color from Barrett's hair and do a white-silver rinse with polymer finish. The result was stunning and wildly sophisticated in an otherworldly way.

She barely recognized herself, though Vladimir, watching, had insisted that her long hair not be shortened, but only trimmed. The precision-cut result was a masterpiece of geometry.

Standing behind her, he had let her pure white locks run through his fingers over and over again. Each time they fell into the same perfectly straight horizontal line at the end.

He never touched her skin. Just her hair. The air moving against the nape of her neck was an infinitely subtle sensation. She would have called it erotic if Nick had been the one doing it.

When Vladimir Ouspensky did it, it was sexual. She was disturbed by her instinctive reaction to him, dismissing it as only physical. But it was something more than that. She sat in silence as he stepped back, feeling ashamed of the answer that came to mind. It was a thrill.

Being so close to such a powerful and evil man was an undeniable thrill.

Barrett corrected herself. Not a man. A vampire. Barrett was certain that's what he was.

Profoundly evil.

He met her eyes in the mirror she was facing. She crossed one wrist over the other, as if she were protecting her body from him. The warmth of the heavy gold bracelet reminded her that he could not read her mind.

Thank God for that.

He murmured his thanks to Yolanda, who stood to the side, her hands on her hips, critically surveying her handiwork. Then he spoke to Barrett.

"Welcome to Club Red. I think you will make a most elegant hostess."

Justine had been right. No one had asked to see a résumé. It really was all about the way you looked. She'd offered a few vague lines about having worked in a New York nightclub and given it an imaginary name. He'd waved the explanation away, and as far as the club's made-up name, hadn't seemed to care. Clubs opened and closed with blinding speed in any big city anyway, trendy one minute and passé the next.

"Thank you for the opportunity," Barrett said. "I was wondering, though—what do you want me to do until the grand opening?"

"Various things." He gazed approvingly at her in the mirror. "Feel free to move about the club in order to completely familiarize yourself with the layout. Even I lose my way from time to time."

She nodded, not believing that for a second. Club Red seemed like an extension of him. Overwhelming. Complicated.

"You are expected to arrive before the girls do, and supervise their signing in and so forth. Learn to use the software. Although if you've worked in a nightclub I suppose it will be familiar to you."

"Of course." She gave him a confident smile. Justine could probably download the program—or Nick could—and tutor her at the condo. She was going to have to learn fast.

They were interrupted by a low whistle.

"Look at that fantastic hair. Girl, it don't get no whiter. And blown straight as a ruler."

The woman who spoke to Barrett was African American, tall and stunningly beautiful, with dark doe eyes outlined in smoky pencil and breathtakingly long legs. Jeans and tee and platform sandals made the most of a feline figure that didn't quit.

Vladimir nodded to the woman, a hint of a smile playing about his lips. Then he spoke to Barrett. "I must go. I will allow this lady to introduce herself."

"Oh—okay. And thanks," Barrett said to her. "I like the look. It just takes a little getting used to."

Barrett wasn't lying. She stared into the mirror, feeling somewhat unsettled by Vladimir's abrupt departure. Her sudden self-consciousness compelled her to tame the waterfall of white—or maybe just brush away the strange feelings her transformation had evoked.

A few more long strokes and she was done, setting the brush down.

"Yolanda did it after my interview," she finally replied, wondering who the woman was and whether she was being criticized or admired. "Mr. Ouspensky was pretty specific about what he wanted."

She felt really different with her hair stripped and bleached to no color at all, as if she'd acquired an alternate persona: cold and unapproachable. Which wasn't what she would need to successfully infiltrate Club Red.

"Yeah, he's like that," the woman said knowingly. "I heard Yolanda's supposed to do hair and makeup only for the important girls now." She snapped her fingers and pointed at Barrett. "You must be the new hostess."

"As a matter of fact, I am. But I don't think that makes me particularly important. Justine recommended me for the job." Barrett left out the chain of events. If you had to lie, keep it simple. One of Nick's mottoes.

"Never heard of her. But I know Vladimir likes white," the other woman said. "Don't ask me what I'm doing in his brand-new club," she joked.

"Did you just get hired, too? By the way, I'm Barrett Klein." Barrett extended a hand, the fake last name flowing smoothly from her lips.

"Sammy Privett. You can call me Sam. Pleased to meet you." She confirmed that with a warm handshake. "And don't get me wrong, I love the platinum princess look. Can't rock it quite like you do myself, but so what. And to answer your question, me and Vlad go way back. I've worked for him before and I've got a lot of connections he finds invaluable. Sure hope they finish fixing up the club before the grand opening."

"Me, too." Barrett twisted her gold bracelet and noticed how Sam's gaze tracked the movement.

"Be sure you keep track of your bling. Or just wear the fake stuff. That's what I do." Sam grinned. "Want to see the dressing room? Some of the dancers are already steaming up the mirrors."

Barrett was taken aback. "Doing what?"

"Generating hot air, honey. Between their damn blow-dryers and the way they gossip, it's probably about a hundred degrees in there already."

"Oh. Got it."

"Come on. We can listen in. Nothing but lies. Better than TV any day of the week."

Sam motioned to Barrett to follow her as she swung open the door to a backstage corridor. There were bare bulbs in wire cages strung from a long rod fastened to the ceiling.

Barrett trotted after her, noticing that the fixtures just barely cleared Sam's high hairdo, she was so tall. Despite her long strides, there was a sensual swing to her walk that Barrett envied.

"What is it you do, Sam?" she asked, catching up to her.

"I used to strip but that game got old. So I switched to warming up the audiences before the shows. That's what Vlad wants me to do here. With a side hustle," she added. "I'm a costume consultant."

"Great. Can you help me out?"

Sam turned and eyed Barrett's conservative suit. "Sure. Burn that and start over."

"Thanks a lot," she laughed.

"I wasn't insulting you. You just need to find yourself something sharp to match that hair."

Barrett stopped at the door to the dressing room when Sam did, peeking inside over the other woman's shoulder.

"Ladies, this is Barrett Klein. She's our new hostess, so show respect, because she'll be checking your time sheets if you dance and bottle sales if you're serving."

Dead silence. Which did not bode well.

Sam forged on. "She comes highly recommended by a lady called Justine—excuse me. What are you all staring at?"

"Her."

The terse reply said it all. The unknown name got Barrett nothing but suspicious stares. Blue eyes, brown eyes, green eyes, and one pair of brilliant purple eyes—tinted contacts, she realized—fixed on her face. No one smiled.

"Justine is Moira Finn's friend, if you're trying to figure out the connection," Barrett said quickly. "I understand that a lot of you are represented by Moira?"

"Yeah, okay."

"My agent."

"Really? Hey, can you give me her business card?"

"Fuck off."

The ice was broken. Most of them seemed to know Moira or her agency or they acted like they did. Barrett was welcomed into the dressing room and then more or less ignored in a friendly way as the strippers went back to what they had been doing: putting on makeup and fixing their hair and talking a mile a minute. About their boyfriends and husbands, mostly. They moved on to which clubs didn't pay their dancers promptly or docked them for little infractions. They were hoping for better from Ouspensky.

Sam gave her a nudge. "Had enough of these heffas?"

"What did you call us?" a girl asked, more amused than annoyed.

"You heard me. Let's go, Barrett."

She stopped on her way out, her attention captured by music blasting from a closed room. Someone cranked it up even louder. Barrett was almost deafened.

Pounding feet jumped in and kept the beat. Stampeding cattle would have stepped more lightly. Was the show choreographer putting a chorus line through their paces? It certainly sounded like it.

Barrett looked around, realizing that she was alone for the first time. With the blasting music as a cover, she ought to do some snooping for as long as she could get away with it.

She walked quickly away, turning left into a corridor that also looked empty, glancing into rooms with open doors and grimacing at the new but tacky loveseats and other suggestive furniture. No doubt there for striking a pose, novelty chairs shaped like giant stiletto heels had been placed in each room. Ugh.

So Nick wouldn't give her hell, she quietly turned the doorknobs of rooms that were closed. All locked. Her instincts told her that Jane wouldn't be held on this level or the ones above it. She was looking for stairs that went down.

A heavy door, almost vaultlike, stood shut at the end of the corridor. There was no exit sign above it and no clue as to what it was for. But there was a keypad next to it with a tiny, blinking red light. No way to tell if that meant it was open, or shut and alarmed.

Barrett stopped for a second, uneasy. Had she heard footsteps? The music wasn't as loud here but it still didn't seem possible.

A man appeared near the heavy door. Not one she'd seen. By her guess, a guard. Bald and ugly, with a thick neck. His dark suit and dark glasses creeped her out.

"Looking for something?" he called.

"Ah—the rehearsal."

He pointed in the general direction of the way she'd come.

"In back of you."

"Thanks so much." Barrett turned around and walked away with measured steps. She could feel the guard's eyes burning into her back.

Seemed like a good idea to follow through on where she supposedly wanted to be. By the time she reached the source of the loud music, the door was open. The dancing part seemed to be over. She stopped in her tracks again, transfixed by the sight of strippers showing off their latest routines.

The pole-dancing class at her upscale gym was *nothing* like this.

Nearly naked bodies shone with glitter and sweat. Their heavily made-up eyes had a feral shine. Barrett

had never seen anything like what they were doing. Un-
dulations and rolls so sexy any man's mind would be
permanently blown. Back bends with their heads
through their legs. Lifts with silk straps into lascivious,
spread-legged positions that left absolutely nothing to
the imagination. Solo girls in pin-up poses. Several girls,
entangled.

Barrett stared with wide eyes until someone all in
black, not definitively male or female, came to the door,
threw her an annoyed look, and slammed it shut.

Time to go.

CHAPTER
TWENTY

The auditions over, Vladimir headed back to his office, the secure one that was below the main floor of the club. He frowned when he saw who was lounging on the chaise in the hall outside the office door. Gil Mansfield had his eyes closed as he listened to music that Vladimir could hear playing faintly in his earbuds. The toes of his stretch-sided narrow boots were scuffed. No doubt from keeping the beat, as Gil was doing now, to the abominable tunes he preferred.

For a former soldier, he was slack-bodied and going to seed, and that was even before the physical deterioration caused by the FBI's drug had started. You got what you paid for with a turned vampire, Vladimir thought angrily. Apparently, the FBI's experimental programs could use rigorous oversight in more ways than one. He ought to offer himself as a consultant, if only to increase his chances of poaching the better ones. As it was, however, he already had a contact inside. One who kept him one step ahead of the feds. One who'd led him to Gil.

And one who'd led Gil to Murphy, through the tracking chip planted inside all turned vampires. Gil and his men had tracked down Murphy on some godforsaken mountain and he'd soon be one of Vlad's guests.

Then he'd be Vlad's gladiator, competing against another turned vampire in the cage.

Real blood would be spilled. Physical limbs ripped off. It would be quite thrilling to watch.

Mansfield yawned suddenly, bringing Vlad's attention back to him. Vladimir scowled with disgust, wondering how Mansfield had ever survived the U.S. military. The fellow had betrayed every principle he had sworn to uphold, had aided the enemy time and again. How unwise of the army to have given up on executing traitors.

"Get up," Vladimir snapped, yanking the earbud out of Gil's ear. "Why are you here?"

The lanky man scrambled to his feet.

"That girl we just brought in? She's kind of spooky. Those big eyes of hers get on my nerves, the way she stares. She keeps banging on the walls. We gotta stick her in a soundproofed cell somewhere else."

"Do it after I talk to her."

"First I have to do a walk-through of the dressing rooms," Gil said. "You know, keep an eye on the regular girls."

"Look, but don't touch," Vladimir advised him. "Do you think you can remember that this time?"

"Yeah, sure. Sam is always hanging around there anyway. She's so tall she sees everything. I can't cop a feel."

Vladimir made no comment. Gil sauntered out, sticking the earbuds back in before he was over the threshold.

"Wait," Vladimir said loudly. "Murphy."

Gil turned around. "What?"

"Tim Murphy. When does he arrive?"

"Oh, him. He's supposed to get here this afternoon."

"Notify me as soon as the truck comes in," Vladimir said. "Now bring me the girl."

"What do you think?"

Jane had been studying the art on her captor's office

walls when he spoke. She jerked at the sound of his voice, but couldn't take her eyes off the gleaming white plastic panels that were essentially three-dimensional molds of girls.

The panels were different in some ways and the same in others. Each girl was unique but each was slender and short like her. And about her age.

"What are those things?" she asked, still staring at the panels.

"The series is called *Runaways*. Do you like it?"

Jane gave another start when she felt his breath against her face. She hadn't realized that he was so close to her.

"No. But I get it," she muttered.

"Very clever of you, Jane. You might have guessed that is now your official designation. Certified by your guardians. Including the one who gave you to us. I believe his name is Malcolm. Can't blame him really. Knowing you were a virgin. He actually wanted you for himself, but given how much we'd pay for you . . . How could he resist?"

Malcolm Prescott.

Jane's stomach roiled at the thought of him.

He'd known how she felt about staying a virgin until she was married. He'd pretended to respect her decision even as he'd used it as a bargaining tool to sell her for the highest price possible. Just like he'd pretended to respect her relationship with Dante—

Jane closed her eyes for a moment as grief for her friend overwhelmed her. Dante had been dark. Troubled. She'd known that. And sometimes how dark he was, how he liked to bite her, scared her. But he'd been smart. And despite being into all that was vampire, he'd been kind. She'd known they'd never last for the long haul, but she'd cared about him. He'd tried to help her when this guy's goons had grabbed her, but . . .

Jane nodded toward the molded art. "So these are a warning or something?"

"Everyone has their own interpretation. That is the purpose of fine art. To make us think."

Christ. He was more pompous than Malcolm.

"Who are they?"

He only shrugged. "They don't have names anymore. They were street girls, not like you."

Jane turned around and met his unreadable dark gaze. "You killed them."

He smiled thinly. "They were immortalized at the moment of their last breath. I would rather not explain how. I assure you that they felt no pain. And now they will live forever." He gestured to a chair. "Sit down."

Jane glanced back toward the door they'd entered by. A silent man with a scarred face stood just outside it, his thick hands clasped in front of him. He held rope and manacles.

Vladimir went to the door and shut it with a nod to him. She wondered what had happened to the other guard.

"I have no wish to force you to do anything, Jane." His tone held chilly courtesy. "And if you are imagining that I will, think again. You are a valuable commodity as long as your virginity can be verified. After that— well, your buyer will determine what happens to you."

She moved toward the chair and sat, forcing her thighs together until the muscles hurt.

"You're going to sell me?"

He remained standing, looming over her. A long lock of roughly combed black hair fell over his chiseled jaw, shadowing his eyes. He was much too big for her to attack. She was puny by comparison, a stray kitten facing a vicious monster superior to her in every way. Including intelligence.

"To be precise, you will be auctioned off. Your purchaser will determine your ultimate worth. Connoisseurs are flying in from all over."

She hesitated, then asked an audacious question.

"Why don't you keep me for yourself?"

He looked at her with curiosity. "Are you bargaining with me, Jane?"

Why not? She had never been as innocent as a lot of people seemed to think and she couldn't help it if she had a baby face. Though she really was a virgin. Maybe that was why she had hung on to that useless bit of flesh. Just to keep herself to herself as long as possible.

But time was running out.

This guy was like no criminal she'd ever imagined or seen on TV. Well groomed. Cultivated. And cruel in a sophisticated way.

He'd mocked her helplessness.

Yet when the journey here was over and Vladimir had come to get her, she'd stayed in a corner of the cell, numb and silent and staring at the door when he opened it. At that moment, she'd actually felt grateful. Which was so weird she didn't want to think about it.

She'd kept her emotions on lockdown and stayed in survival mode. Better the devil you knew than the one you didn't. For some reason, he seemed to be intrigued by her.

If she could find a phone or use a laptop—there was one on his desk—she had a chance. Slim, but still a chance. She'd caught a few glimpses of a suburban-type development with spindly trees during her transfer from one cell to another. She had made eye contact with a few of the furtive women who'd bathed her and dressed her. If they were captives, too, maybe she could persuade one or two to escape with her. They hadn't been shackled.

There had to be a way out. She'd always been good at finding one.

How long had the girls in those panels been allowed to live?

"Did any of them sit in this chair and look at you?" Jane bit her lip. "Never mind. It's not like you're going to tell me the truth."

"But I will." Vladimir followed her gaze to the art. "And no, to answer your question. It was clear from the beginning of their captivity that they were unsuitable for auction." He looked at her again. "We prefer docile girls. It would be best if you cooperate."

She said nothing.

"Unbutton the top of your dress, Jane. This will be only a visual inspection," he added calmly.

She hesitated but did as he asked. So what. Let him look at her tits. But he didn't.

"Now spread your legs," he said firmly.

His dark eyes bored into hers. Compelled by the aggressive intensity in their depths—and suddenly afraid—she obeyed.

"Wider." His tone was cool and professional.

Again she obeyed, inwardly amazed that he never looked down. His eyes held hers. Jane realized that he probably got off on humiliation more than anything else.

"Thank you. I have no need to perform a physical examination," he said. "I merely wanted to see if you would do as you were told."

"Oh. Then may I—" She rested her hands on her bared thighs, playing along, loathing him. If she didn't escape, she would find a way to kill Vladimir Ouspensky.

He smiled benevolently. "Very good. I see that you comprehend the fact that you must ask permission for everything. Your modesty only makes you more desirable, you know. You may close your legs and fasten your dress."

Jane looked down so he wouldn't see the burning hatred in her eyes, tugging at the hem of the short dress as she brought her knees together, buttoning herself up but awkwardly.

"Keep in mind, Jane, that you will be required to expose yourself completely upon the auction block."

No dress. No nothing. She could survive that. She knew how to retreat inside her mind and stay there.

"Can you imagine it?" he asked in a silky voice. "You cannot hide. Every man present will see you naked. Some will request additional views and poses, of course. Our female attendants will help you display yourself. But no one will be permitted to touch you intimately. Only to look as often and as closely as they wish until the bidding begins. Your air of innocence ought to fetch a high price."

Jane fought to subdue the fury that seethed inside her. If she tried to physically fight with him or anyone else, she would be damaged goods. And God only knew what would happen to her then.

She had to stay calm. To do that she would have to accept that she was fucking terrified. The shell around her soul was cracking into a thousand places.

"You don't have to sit there," he said after a while. "Feel free to walk around."

Jane waited for a few seconds. Something in her screamed at her not to jump up to do his bidding. And she suspected that he liked a bit of fight in his victims.

But if she got up, she could look around and see more. She rose slowly. Her gaze strayed to the panels on the walls, drawn inexorably to the frozen girls.

Vladimir smiled. "Get a closer look, Jane. The detail is remarkable."

He took a step to her and reached out a hand. Jane pretended not to see it. Vladimir shrugged, moving her toward the panels by the simple expedient of coming even closer. She had to go toward them to avoid his touching her.

She stared at them.

Each face was different. Most had closed eyes. Two had met their death with their eyes wide open. What had they seen at that moment? The man beside her? Other men? How had they died? They seemed unharmed.

He was right about the detail. The tender curve of their cheeks, the soft lips—everything about them conveyed their vulnerability. Down to the delicate eyelashes, the girls looked almost alive. Now that Jane was this close, she realized that at least two had been younger than she was.

All were barefoot. One wore an ankle bracelet, the tiny links of the chain barely visible.

Their short dresses were unbuttoned, as hers had just been, the light material perfectly captured by the mold-making process, the folds pulled halfway up over their thighs.

Vladimir was right behind her again. His arm reached past her, touching the flowing hair of the youngest girl. It was then that Jane noticed another similarity.

Their heads were at different angles but all were tipped slightly back, revealing their necks.

Vladimir's hand traced downward—and stopped at two small indentations in the hard plastic skin, riveting Jane's gaze on them. Scars? Wounds? Some of her friends were into cutting. She'd threatened to do it once, just to see Malcolm's reaction. But it wasn't her thing.

She looked at the other molds more closely. They were puncture wounds. Deep ones, that didn't look self-inflicted. Aligned with a barely perceptible vein.

Jane shrank back . . . and stumbled.

Vladimir caught her, his embrace without warmth. "Now do you understand?" he murmured.

He turned her around.

She looked up as he stretched his mouth open in a ghastly imitation of a smile. Revealing fangs as polished and white as the walls of her transport call. As white as the faces of the girls he had probably murdered one by one.

His hand rose to her neck, nearly encircling it with his exceptionally long fingers.

"I am a vampire, Jane. And I have a taste for virgin blood. The flavor is exquisite."

Jane managed to draw breath despite the tightening grasp of his hand. He was stroking her hair with the other.

"If only I could turn you without dying," he murmured. "Then you could taste it yourself someday and experience its intoxicating effects. We could even share a girl to drink from."

Some self-preserving instinct made her return the caress in an attempt to distract him. She ran her fingertips lightly over the masculine hand that could very well choke her.

Vladimir relaxed his hold fractionally. "What are you doing?"

"Let me go. I bruise easily."

He chuckled. "Thank you for the reminder. We do want you in prime condition for the auction. And— getting back to your question—I don't think it would be a good idea to keep you. For one thing, I doubt that you are strong enough to be turned, no matter who does the honors."

"What does that mean, anyway?"

"Humans can be turned into vampires. Sometimes the process is forced." He smiled without letting go. "Some call it vein rape. I would never do such a thing."

As if he could be trusted. Jane was afraid all over again.

And even more determined to survive. She had to. And if she could, she would avenge those girls who'd entered this nightmare and never left it.

They'd had names and someone knew who they were. Their families had never found out whether they were dead or alive, or who was responsible. Back at home, Ginny Prescott had to be waiting to find out what had happened to her. For very different reasons, so was Malcolm.

Jane vowed not to go down without a fight.

"You can fight all you want, girl. It won't do you any good."

Jane jerked, finally understanding how powerful her captor was.

He smiled. "I suppose I should not toy with you," Vladimir sighed. "I haven't held an auction since I started building Club Red and I do need the money. Cash flow is a constant problem."

His hand dropped but he stayed where he was, looming over her.

"Virgins are my business. The supply is relatively limited, at least in this country, and there is plenty of demand."

"Oh."

"Especially for you, I should think." His gaze held an unhealthy glitter as he surveyed her from top to toe. "There is something different about you, Jane, though I cannot define it precisely. But I suspect you would be interesting in bed."

Suddenly her fear was gone. Or at least she was willing to talk past it. He could read her mind anyway, so why even bother to control her mouth. "Try me." Just don't leave anything sharp where I can get it, Jane thought. Knowing who he was and what he'd done—she'd cut his throat before she'd cut herself. But would that be enough to kill a vampire?

He studied her for a long moment, his assessing gaze moving over her face. "No."

With a deft move, he pulled her right arm behind her back hard enough to hurt. If she fought back, she was likely to dislocate it. He marched her to the door, opening it. The guard stationed there hadn't moved a muscle.

"Take her back to room 5 until we have a cell ready for her," Vladimir commanded him. "And make sure that she is watched at all times. Be very careful. This one thinks for herself. Always a dangerous quality in a female."

"Yes, sir." The guard restrained her and took her away as Vladimir watched in silence.

CHAPTER
TWENTY-ONE

"Guess who I saw at Club Red?" Barrett said into her cell phone. She'd just pulled into an empty slot at the condo.

"Just tell me." Nick's voice sounded distracted and distant.

"Gil Mansfield."

There was a momentary pause. "What did he look like and what was he doing?"

"He looked like his mug shot. Maybe a little sleazier. He was wowing the girls at the audition for dancers. I think he may be the second in command."

"Good work for your first day."

"I didn't find him. He just appeared on stage, like I said."

"I'm giving you full credit, Barrett. But I gotta get inside and do my own recon. First, however, can I come over? I need to know what else you saw inside Club Red."

She got out of the car and slammed the door. "At the condo. And yes. But I warn you, I look really different."

"Why?"

"You'll see."

"Interesting. I think I like it." Nick studied her hair, walking around Barrett as if she were suddenly untouchable.

"It was Vlad's idea. He had the club's hairdresser do it right then and there."

"Worth it if he wants you as the hostess. But what did you have to do to convince him to hire you?"

"Nothing, smartass. According to Justine, I was a shoo-in for the job. Meaning tall and classy and not into chewing gum."

Nick grinned, his hands on his jeans-clad hips. "Yeah. My kind of woman."

"Oh shut up." Barrett ran her fingers through her newly white locks, purposely messing up the severe geometry of the cut. "Yikes. I just can't get used to this. At least I can dye it back to my natural color when this is over."

"Whatever you want." He reached for the laptop he'd brought with him and propped it up on his knees when he sank down into the couch. "So break it down for me. What does the place look like from the inside?"

"Chaotic. It's overwhelming. I barely know where to start. It's totally fabulous and really trashy at the same time."

"Specifics, please. But wait." He held up a hand. "Before we start, was there any sign of Jane or other girls who didn't seem to belong there?"

"No."

She knew that his quick question was anything but casual and that there would be more. Her answers, no matter how trivial, would be fitted into a mental grid to help him plan strategy. For anything that involved kids or innocent victims, he put his whole heart into it. If his mission was to take out a bad guy, there were no emotions involved whatsoever.

Unless, she thought, that so-called "bad" guy happened to be his brother.

He frowned, his expression soberly thoughtful as he looked at her. "Barrett, what is it?"

She jerked. "I'm sorry. I—I lost my train of thought. Where was I?" Barrett asked.

He hesitated before saying, "You were about to describe the interior of Club Red."

"Right. The main space is big. There's a runway right down the middle. Lots of seats and little tables. The strippers and dancers are above all that, I guess."

"They have to be. There's always some bozo who tries to grab a girl by the ankles," Nick commented.

"Always? And how do you know that?"

"Believe it or not, I have been to more than one strip club." He glanced up at her. "Don't give me that look. I'm a guy. We do a lot of things women don't like."

She gave him that look anyway.

"Please continue, Miss Miles."

Despite the exasperating smirk on his face, she did. "There are wraparound balconies with glass walls for the party people who want to watch from on high."

"How many?"

"Two. The top one is bigger. It kinda juts out over the bottom one."

Nick typed. "So when exactly does the club open? I looked online. It still didn't say. What the hell are they waiting for?"

"Rave reviews. Big buzz."

"Don't they need customers first?"

"No. They need bloggers, reporters, scene makers, columnists, and trendsetters. A reliable source—Justine's pal, if you want to make a note, her name is Moira Finn—says that Vladimir bankrolled a press junket. It's happening tomorrow."

"A junket? What is that exactly?"

"They vary. Could be for a movie, a big event, a publicity campaign. Media types ask bullshit questions and get phony answers and try to scoop the competition. Besides the free plane ticket and hotel room, there are the swag bags. At Club Red, there's also the, uh, entertainment."

"Who's doing the entertaining?"

"Could be the strippers. I happened to see them rehearsing when I was wandering around."

"What exactly did you see?"

"Like I would answer that."

He shook his head. "I meant when you were wandering around."

"Oh. Rooms with tacky sex furniture. Locked rooms. Before the rehearsal, I walked around some and went down a long corridor. There was a door at the end of it with a keypad."

"How close did you get to that?"

"Not very. A guard appeared out of nowhere, asked me what I was looking for."

"Do you think you could find that door again?"

"Of course."

Clickety-click. Click click click. The faint blue glow of the laptop gave his dark eyes an odd, distant look. He sure was focused. Barrett couldn't remember him getting his head stuck in a laptop to this extent back when they were overseas.

"Hey, almost forgot to ask about your roommate," he said, still staring into the screen. "Did she get hired? It would be great if there were two of you inside before I get there."

"The answer is no. Justine's going to be our outside contact and liaison to Belladonna—but wait a sec. How are you going to get in? I haven't had a chance to figure that one out."

Barrett hoped he got her point. Actually, she had two points to make. He needed to work with her. And she didn't work for him.

"I'm mulling it over." The keys clicked as Nick kept on. "Getting back to the original topic, a crowd of random people on the loose will drive the security staff crazy and provide cover for us."

"Or totally get in our way." He didn't answer. Her logical comment must not fit in his mental grid.

"Do you happen to know where the media mob is staying?"

"At the same hotel we stayed at. On Vladimir's dime, most likely."

He nodded. "I'll pay my own way."

"Excuse me?"

He finished taking notes and shut the laptop. "I'm going to the hotel after I pick up some stuff. I'm thinking canvas jacket with big pockets, netbook, black-frame glasses. If I get the same clerk, he won't remember me."

Nick had been the one who'd gone up to the front desk. He was just being careful. But she wasn't so sure that he should infiltrate the media bash. Barrett covered up her uncertainty with a vague reply. "Whatever."

"It's a start. Look, we don't have a warrant to search the club, and if Vlad or Mansfield get suspicious, they'll get Jane out fast."

Or kill her. Barrett knew it could happen. No matter how much money Jane was worth, there was always the chance they'd decide she was more trouble than she was worth and go looking for another girl.

Nick seemed to take her silence for agreement.

"I need a way to get in and now I have it. Let's not waste time."

"Nick, I'm not done discussing this."

He didn't seem to think that was particularly important. "This media thing dropped in our lap, so let's take advantage of it. Reporters are supposed to ask questions. I can wander around with a drink and spy right out in the open."

He could have asked if that was okay with her. Nick may have been to a few strip clubs, but he knew zip about the behind-the-scenes reality of this one. She didn't mind him having her back, but she really didn't want him taking over the hunt for Jane.

Why was that, she asked herself suddenly?

"Okay," he said as he stood. "I gotta get started." He set aside the laptop and rose from the couch to stretch, but not for long. He gathered up his things briskly, effectively keeping her at a distance. It almost made her panic.

"Nick, is everything—"

"We're done for tonight, right?" His tone was cool. Abrupt.

Instinctively, she slammed down a mental door between them. What other choice did she have? This morning, he'd been all over her, showering her with affection in front of Justine. Now he was all about business. And distance.

Confusing her.

And pissing her off.

"Yeah," she said. "We're done. I won't keep you."

His mouth twisted. "No one can."

That seemed to be a joke but his timing stunk.

"I'll call you a little later," was his parting shot.

After he left, Barrett picked up her cell phone and paced with it in her hand. She looked out the window. Nothing to see. His car had to be long gone. Ultimately, Barrett decided against programming the phone to send him to auto-answer hell.

It wasn't that late and she wasn't sleepy. Barrett couldn't go back to Club Red to hang around or someone would get suspicious. She had to think and she might as well do it right here. Alone.

The first deep breath she took to clear her mind was

ineffective. She drew in another and blew out all thoughts of him with it. Then she calmed down.

There had to have been a clue right in front of her during her brief foray into different parts of the club, something much less obvious than the heavy door with the keypad lock. That was how it always worked. She'd missed some tiny thing that would lead her to Jane. Her visual memory had a way of unfolding when she wasn't distracted or half nuts.

It was a part of herself that she barely used anymore. Once it had meant so much. Art had seemed like a refuge, a world she could escape into and make beautiful.

She thought of trying to draw what she'd seen without analyzing it. When she was in a state of flow, she was sometimes surprised by what appeared on paper.

Barrett unzipped the large pocket on the outside of her suitcase and took out the pad of sketch paper and inexpensive colored pencils she'd purchased at a highway stop.

She put it all on the kitchen table and poured herself a glass of white wine. In another few minutes, she was absorbed in a drawing that seemed to have a life of its own.

Slowly, the dancers she'd glimpsed in the rehearsal studio got set down on the paper, caught in sinuous lines. She left out the dirty details, sketching fast. Flowing hair. Hands reaching out, legs kicking high, bodies as supple as cats.

The faces were only a suggestion, and not because she didn't remember each one. All were young and pretty even without makeup. But there had been an unmistakable hardness in their eyes. They weren't dancing out of joy. Their critical gazes at themselves in the mirror said it all. They were on view. They had to be physically perfect. And there were hundreds more waiting to take their place on the stripper runway.

Barrett filled several more pages, doing careful re-creations of the rooms and hallways, forcing herself to concentrate with her mind's eye. Nothing clicked. If there was a clue, she had missed it. After a while, she literally drew a blank. And stopped.

She selected dark colors—black for the outline and brown for the eyes—and drew Nick. The finished sketch lacked an indefinable something that would make it a good portrait. Barrett frowned. The lines were too light and too fine. Nick was all about being big and bold. He could be captured, but to get his ruggedness right, she would need a thick-tip marker and paper she could slash at.

Some other time. She quickly removed the drawing from the pad, leaving a jagged edge along one side.

She turned to a fresh page and switched to graphite pencils, sketching Jane's face from memory, doing the outline first in hard pencil, and shading in the skin tones with a soft one in light gray. When she finished, she studied the drawing for a long time. It was a mix of the innocent girl she'd once known and the frightened teenager who'd appeared on SexFlash.

It was a good likeness, much better than the dated photo on the have-you-seen-her poster. Barrett detached the drawing, being very careful not to tear it, and set it aside. It seemed like a talisman, something of Jane that she could always keep.

But it wasn't as if she could show it or a photo around the club or ask questions. While she was at it, she removed the drawings of the sex rooms that she'd hoped would jog her memory. The dancers, she left in. They might come in handy to break the ice, get the girls to talk to her.

If they had that much time.

For a moment, she wondered if she would even recognize the real Jane if they found her. When, she told herself. Not if. But it was a possibility that the abductors might have forced her to change her appearance in some drastic way. The girl's ordeal was far from over.

Thinking of Nick, she knew theirs wasn't, either.

CHAPTER
TWENTY-TWO

One day after getting hired, Barrett was wandering Club Red, thankful that the hostess station had been overrun by Vlad's publicity people. The preparations for the junket were under way, with party planners running around in teams, handling everything from banners to swag bags. Guys were unrolling the inevitable red carpet for photo ops.

Vladimir had gone all out.

The club's top dancers shoved past her in the hallway, even though only a few media people had arrived. Barrett looked back at them with annoyance and brushed glitter off her sleeve. It was a sure thing that the glammed-up girls intended to preen for the cameras and starstruck male reporters.

She headed upstairs and into the dressing room, not surprised to find it mostly empty.

Two girls were over by the corner mirror, basking in the brilliant illumination of the bulbs surrounding it. Only one looked like she belonged there. Barrett was pretty sure she'd been at the rehearsal.

Her fresh complexion, which she was slathering with makeup, and her round eyes made her look way too young to be a stripper. But it was hard to tell. She supposed it was possible she was over twenty-one.

The girl with her seemed out of place. Her clothes were shabby and she was thin, with hollow cheeks and a pinched mouth. She let the dancer, who was now brushing on eye shadow, do most of the talking, answering in monosyllables. Barrett didn't want to seem like she was listening.

She got busy. The bleaching compound used to turn her hair pure white would also make it brittle and dry. Barrett reached into her bag, searching for the shine goo Yolanda had given her, taking out her drawing pad and markers, her phone, and some other personal stuff before she found the unlabeled jar and the scoop that went with it.

The goo was cool in her palm. Barrett dabbed her fingertips into it and applied it evenly to her hair. No split ends yet.

The conversation in the corner seemed to be ending. The dancer got up and adjusted her skimpy outfit. Still, Barrett thought, it was a lot more than she would wear onstage.

"You look great," the thin girl told her.

The dancer made a kissy-face at herself in the mirror. "I want my picture in the paper."

"What if your mom sees?" the thin girl asked.

"I don't care." She grabbed a tiny evening bag from the cluttered counter under the mirror.

Her careless reply was still a reminder that these girls had mothers. And that none of them were as tough as they pretended to be. The dancer pulled out a smartphone and stretched out her arm, tilting her head and arching her back so her breasts rose high.

"Gotta get a selfie," she told her friend. Another kissy-face, a couple of taps on the screen, and the photo was posted online.

Barrett stared straight ahead at her own reflection. The dancer sauntered past her, freshly dolled up and ready to prowl, the thin girl tagging after.

She was alone again. When Barrett was done with her

hair, she thought about calling Ginny. That would have to be later. She felt bad that there was no information she could share, though obviously there was none on Ginny's side, either. There were no new messages on her phone.

Not since Nick had texted her before she'd left the condo this morning.

She picked up the phone and scrolled through the stored messages for something to do. There was his.

In hotel. To club by 10 tonite. OXOXO. Clark Kent.

Right. The black-framed glasses. He would be easy to spot. Too bad he wasn't easy to understand. His flirty email, complete with hugs and kisses, confused the hell out of her after last night's freeze-out. She didn't know what to think of Nick's erratic behavior, but one thing was for sure—she didn't need it distracting her. Barrett tucked the phone into a pocket of her bag and flipped back the cover of the drawing pad, leaning on the counter and looking through what she'd done.

Barrett took a hairbrush out of its holder and replaced it with a handful of markers.

She started several pages in, doodling intersecting shapes and filling them in with different colored markers, then lifted the page and used the bits of color and line that had bled through to start another drawing. A half hour went by.

"That's really nice."

Startled, Barrett looked up into the mirror. The thin girl was standing behind her, watching her draw. "Oh—thanks."

"Can I look at it closer?"

Barrett thought before replying, not seeing any harm in the request. The girl reached out a hand.

"Why not." Barrett handed her the drawing pad.

The girl sat down in the chair next to her, starting at the beginning. She looked at the sketches of the dancers with something like awe. "You're so lucky that you can do this," she said softly. "I always wished I could draw."

"I wish I had more time to do it. But you know how it is. Work, work, work."

"Yeah." The girl flipped through the drawings again and stopped, idly touching the jagged edges of torn paper stuck in the spine. "You ripped out some."

"Sometimes I do. I don't like looking at my mistakes."

The girl smiled slightly. She lifted the pad and tipped it toward the brilliant illumination coming from the mirror.

An impression of the drawing of Jane was clearly visible. Barrett almost gasped. She must have been pressing down harder than she'd thought with the pencil.

"That doesn't look like a mistake," the girl said thoughtfully. She tipped the pad this way and that, peering at the page.

"No. It wasn't. I took that one out to—to give it away." Barrett held her breath. There was an outside chance someone had seen Jane. Could it have been this odd girl?

"Who is she?"

An invisible sigh of disappointment escaped Barrett's lips. "Just someone I know."

"Would you draw one of me?" The girl handed back the pad.

The sudden request surprised Barrett. But it was her way out of a very awkward moment. She sat up and got to work.

The thin girl had gone off with several portraits in pencil, carefully removing them from the pad, including the ones Barrett thought weren't that good.

Looked like she'd made a friend. It was too bad that the girl didn't work for the club and wasn't supposed to be there, about the only fact Barrett had gleaned while she was drawing her. For some reason, the girl had never mentioned her name and Barrett had been too preoccupied to ask.

Someone had just come up to tell her to get ready and deal with the arriving reporters. She was mostly done and her gown, borrowed finery from the Club Red wardrobe, looked good and fit perfectly.

In a few minutes, the stage bell sounded and they decamped in a clatter of high heels and a swirling cloud of scented body mist, leaving her coughing.

Barrett looked in her bag for a throat drop, finding one that had come unwrapped and was fuzzy with lint. She popped it into her mouth anyway and instantly regretted it. A movement in the doorway behind her made her turn around.

The thin girl was back. Not in the room. Outside it. Waiting. In the dark. Someone had switched off the dangling lights in the corridor.

Her eyes shone, reflecting the light in the mirror Barrett was facing.

"Hi," Barrett said. She found a tissue and took the throat drop out of her mouth, wrapping it up. "What's up?"

"Can I talk to you?"

Barrett scooped up the markers and pencils and the pad, and put it all hurriedly into her bag. "Of course."

"Not here. In the parking lot? Around midnight?"

"Of course. But what's going on? Can't we talk now?" The girl shook her head and backed away. Barrett wanted to stop her. Shake her. Ask her if she knew anything about Jane. Instead, she let the girl go, not wanting to risk scaring her off.

*　　*　　*

She got to the hostess station just as Vlad walked by, giving him a fluttery wave and a breathless smile. He stopped to admire her borrowed finery, gave her a thin smile, and kept on. His second in command, Gil Mansfield, followed, barking out orders when he wasn't shaking hands with media guests.

Barrett hid her bag on the shelf inside the hostess station and scanned the screen with the guest list. She recognized several names.

Thatcher Clapp from the *Atlanta Newshound* show. Melanie Khan from the *WeWatchTheWeb* blog. The one and only Vincent Hurok from the *Times-Tribune*.

There were more names she didn't know, from social online sites devoted to the latest and trendiest. Barrett snorted. From what she'd heard, those reporters got paid next to nothing and would jump at the chance for a free minivacation. By the length of the list, they had arrived in droves. Behaving badly was the idea.

Club Red was angling to compete with the decadent luxury of the hottest clubs in Atlanta and the rest of the U.S. Justine had explained that the business wasn't that local once a club took off. Rich execs really did fly in from around the country. Famous athletes showed up, trolling for new additions to their harems.

The media bash was meant to get the ball rolling.

She could hear Sam warming up the first arrivals with naughty jokes and then a song. Her rich contralto voice rolled out to where Barrett was standing.

It was a couple of hours before she could leave her station and go in for a peek. By then Barrett had missed most of the show. No big deal. She'd seen it in rehearsals, however briefly.

Several more girls came down the runway, wearing just about nothing, doing some of the same moves. They were greeted with lusty roars from men on the verge of drunkenness and some well past it.

The atmosphere in the main room was hazy and suffocating, thick with expensive scent and sweat. Dozens of onlookers, tanked up on comped drinks, had abandoned the small tables to get up and writhe to house music that was so loud Barrett could almost see it pulsing in the air. The bottle-service girls were working the crowd, squeezing between knots of people to deliver free champagne and pricey booze. All the flesh on display made male eyes glaze over and male hands wander, copping a squeeze or a feel until the girl in question managed to wriggle free.

Barrett had been to a male strip club once. The women who paid a premium for front-row seats so they could grab at the guys just seemed pathetic. She'd left with a friend, feeling sorry for the performers.

The gender mix of this crowd was about fifty-fifty, but the men seemed to be a lot older than the watching women, who looked bored. Some seemed to be already posting, tapping on their tablet screens to send a live report from the scene.

What she wouldn't give to take a peek at a scathing blog review or two. But that wasn't possible. Barrett swept her gaze around the main level, searching for Nick without seeing him. She looked up. The top balcony was as empty as if it had been sealed off. The glass walls of the balcony below it revealed lots more guests milling around, many dancing to the deafening music or getting wild with attractive strangers or some office hottie they'd been lusting after.

Then she spotted him, right above her. His back was turned to her, smashed against the glass. She knew that stance and those big shoulders, although his hair was different, streaked a color between blond and brown. Some reporter had her press pass draped over Nick's shoulder and her leg wound around his as she slid up and down.

Barrett headed for the stairs, scooping up the folds of her long evening gown to go faster. What he was doing was not part of the plan, even though they'd never nailed down the details, and did not qualify as winging it.

What he was doing was pure horndog freestyle humping while *her* back was turned.

She pushed open the door to the first balcony, banging it so hard against the wall that the bouncer stationed near it jumped.

Barrett calmed herself, nodding to the startled man before she located Nick a second time. Whoever the reporter was, she was glued to him and giving him sloppy kisses that landed randomly all over his face.

She strode over and planted herself directly in back of Nick's new friend. Barrett's hands fisted on her hips. Nick's eyes widened as he peeled the reporter's hands off his body and turned his face away from her sucking mouth.

"Hey. Stop it," he told her.

"No," she complained. "Ish fun."

Nick dragged her press pass over his shoulder and looked at the name. "Mary Nesbit, I think you've had enough." He opened the lanyard into a circle and hung the pass around her neck.

Barrett gave the high sign to the bouncer, who made his way through the crowd to gently lead the reporter away, probably to the ladies' lounge, where someone else would see to her before she puked.

Nick followed Barrett to a circular glass table for two and sank into a chair. She took the one next to him, so he could hear her and no one else would.

"What the hell do you think you're doing?" Barrett hissed at Nick.

"I'm working," he said, defending himself.

"Oh really." Her contemptuous glance took him in from head to toe. The outfit, she had expected. It was the bad dye job and the cheap shoes that were awful. The black-framed glasses did make him look like Clark Kent. "Under what name? Dare I ask?"

"Does it matter? I'm not going to do this again."

"I guess I should be grateful."

He folded his brawny arms across his chest, rumpling the canvas jacket. The big pockets held a lot of gear, including a camera and a tablet.

"I got bodycam pictures of that door you saw, Barrett. And two other doors that look just like it on the other side of the club."

"Which door do we want?"

"Good question—and by the way, the exterior recon didn't show them."

She knew how good he was at remembering things like that. Barrett let him talk, even though she was still pissed as hell.

"That means they don't lead out but in, and probably down to another level. I hid micro electronic-pulse readers by the keypad. The next time those numbers get punched in we receive a readout."

Barrett nodded. You could always trust Nick on the tech stuff. But not necessarily everything else.

"Did Mary Nesbit go with you?" One last jab. He deserved it.

"No. I just met her when I came up here to get an inside aerial view, so to speak. And don't accuse me of getting her sloshed. She was sloshed to begin with. That's the idea. We're all supposed to be having a great time and enjoying the show."

"So I noticed. I just wish you—" Barrett fell silent as a cocktail waitress she didn't know came over.

"Can I get you anything?" she asked cheerily, bending over to display breathtaking cleavage for Nick's benefit.

"Two Shirley Temples. Charge it to the house. I'm Barrett Klein."

The waitress straightened up immediately. She might not know Barrett's name, but she understood that tone of voice. Barrett knew the waitress would ask who she was the second her darling little tray with the boob-print napkins slammed down on the bar.

"Yes, ma'am."

Being *ma'am-ed* grated on her nerves even more than Nick's outrageous behavior. Barrett rested a hand on the glass table and looked down through it. It was obvious that he had a hard-on, even though it wasn't as stiff as it had been five minutes ago. She pulled her gaze away, really riled now.

"One more thing," Nick said. "The area of the parking lot where Aura did the most indicating is where Vlad parks his car. It has vanity plates that said red spell. I think we have ourselves a vampire."

She'd suspected as much herself, but she said, "That's not quite concrete proof."

Nick leaned back in his chair and stretched out his long legs. His cock was definitely getting smaller. "Guess you're not done frosting my shorts."

"No," she replied, her tone honey sweet.

"So finish what you were saying before the cocktail waitress came by. You just wish I . . . what?"

"Nothing."

She rose and started to walk away, then practically hissed when Nick's fingers clamped around her wrist.

"Don't fucking touch me," she ordered even as she smiled and turned back toward him, a hostess dealing with an unruly customer.

"What the hell's wrong with you?"

She shrugged and pulled away from him, banking on the fact that he wouldn't make a scene. She was right. He immediately released her. "I was going to ask you the same thing last night when you were acting all cold and distant."

His expression closed up.

"That was a question by the way. I know we don't have a lot of time here, but I'd appreciate a quick explanation."

"You want quick? I was worried about you all day, Barrett. I don't like worrying about you. I'm trying not to repeat the past and go all overprotective on you, but I'm sorry if me struggling with all that was a downer for you."

She just stared at him openmouthed. "Jesus," he said, running a hand through his hair. Then he threw himself back in his seat. "Yes, I was an asshole, but I wasn't trying to be. I just haven't got the hang of all this quite yet—loving you, knowing you love me, and still letting you be your own woman. I don't want to fuck up and lose you again, Barrett, and my way of ensuring that was to go quiet. It's just my way."

And it was probably the same reason why he never talked about Gary. Not because he wasn't hurting. But because when he hurt or struggled, he got quiet.

Jesus, she was an idiot.

She rubbed her arms and looked around to make sure the bouncer hadn't come back yet.

"You could've just told me that," she said, knowing she sounded childish.

"I just did," he said wearily.

She bit her lip, not liking that tone in his voice. Not liking that she'd been the cause of it.

He sighed. "So what now? You gonna leave me to do what I need to do, or you gonna keep on punishing me for a crime I didn't commit? I can take it. I might even deserve it."

Barrett thought about it, then brightened slightly. "Thanks for the invitation. Would you like me to tell you in advance what your punishment is?"

He gave her a wary look. "Go ahead."

She put her palms on the table and leaned over to whisper in his ear. "First of all, you learn a few tricks working in a joint like this. When women get naked, men get stupid."

"That's true. Your point? My punishment?"

"I'm going to tease you until you can't stand it. Starting with a private strip, just for you." She glanced down. His cock was responding. She raised the stakes. "But you'll be tied to a chair. And all you'll be able to do is watch while I take off my clothes."

"Uh-huh." His dark eyes glowed. He didn't mind the game so far.

"Remember, you can't move. I'm down to nothing but superhigh heels and a sparkly G-string."

"I can see it. So far, this is not torture."

Barrett cleared her throat and went on whispering. "Then I turn around. I wiggle my ass and spank myself until my cheeks are rosy red. Begging to be kissed."

Nick didn't respond. But she could see a faint flush rising over his strong cheekbones.

"You want me. But you can't have me because I'm standing and you're sitting in a chair. And you can't touch me because your hands are tied. Now close your eyes."

He obeyed. Barrett stroked his face with utmost gentleness. "That's right. How do you like it so far?"

She could see for herself that talking dirty was getting amazing results. His cock was straining against the material of his pants. No one could see. Just her.

"Stay with the fantasy. Think about it. Think hard." She stroked and patted.

"I am." His voice was so low it was almost inaudible.

"Now you have a big, throbbing erection. And I bet your balls ache."

"Good guess," he muttered hoarsely.

"There's nothing you can do about it. You have to save the hurt for me."

"Fuck. But okay. Sign me up."

Barrett gave him a final, much harder pat that was pretty close to a slap.

"What was that for?" he asked, opening his eyes.

She nodded toward the approaching cocktail waitress. "We have company."

Nick crossed his legs and winced. Then he frowned and stood. "Shit. It's Vlad."

Seconds after he spotted Vlad behind the approaching cocktail waitress, Nick left by the opposite door. Barrett was alone by the time the club owner appeared at her table.

"Barrett. Are you enjoying yourself?" He glanced at the two Shirley Temples the cocktail waitress placed on the table.

She rose to greet him. "Yes. I was just grabbing a few drinks. I get thirsty at my station."

"I will escort you back."

So he had come to find her instead of sending an underling. That seemed strange. And courteous. In a creepy way.

She disliked the feel of his hand touching her elbow. There was a forcefulness to the way he guided her that was very different from the subtle way he'd played with her hair after it had been cut. He seemed to enjoy the admiring looks other men gave her as they walked together.

When they got to the hostess station, he slipped a piece of paper from his inside jacket pocket and handed it to her. "This is the club's updated schedule, which you're going to need. We only have a few more things to deal with before the opening. The first is some repairs to the upper tier. Construction workers will be coming in the day after tomorrow to take care of them. That evening, I'm also hosting a special VIP event. I'd like you to be there if possible."

"Of course," she said with a smile.

He studied her for a moment, then said, "You're doing a wonderful job, Barrett. Keep it up."

Barrett smiled until she thought her teeth were going to crack, relieved when he finally wandered off. Her "wonderful" job for the next couple of hours basically amounted to telling guests where the restrooms were.

The dancer from the dressing room strolled by, on the arm of Thatcher Clapp, whose bow tie was askew. Barrett made no comment as the pair headed in the direction of the staircase to the private rooms on the second floor. But she quickly checked the time on the monitor in front of her.

Almost midnight. She was supposed to meet the other girl, the thin one she'd sketched. Barrett looked around.

She wasn't going to ask permission. She grabbed her bag and left.

The girl was nowhere in sight when she got outside. Barrett put the bag over her shoulder and started walking around. In ten minutes, she'd gone around the whole building. Since it seemed she'd been stood up, getting a better look at the outside and making a mental comparison with Nick's thorough recon and surveillance was worthwhile. But she couldn't stay out indefinitely.

She was almost at the front door again when the heavy sound of approaching footsteps crunching over gravel made Barrett whirl around. It was one of the bouncers.

"Joe—you scared me."

"Sorry, Miss Barrett. I just wanted to make sure you were all right. We've had prowlers around this side of the club. The guy on the morning shift showed up early and I decided to come check on you."

"I'm fine. I was just—" Barrett looked over her shoulder. There was no one there. But she couldn't quite escape the feeling that someone, maybe the thin girl, was watching.

"Just, you know, sneaking out for a smoke," she covered. "I take a few puffs and that's it. I keep telling myself it counts as quitting. Which is crazy."

"No, it isn't. I do the same thing myself."

She walked back inside with him.

CHAPTER
TWENTY-THREE

An hour after the media circus was over and Club Red was once again quiet, Vlad looked for Tamsin. She was not to be found in her usual haunts. He had covered most of the club in long strides, walking faster as his impatience increased. The dressing room, normally abuzz with the chatter and gossip of the dancers, was empty and quiet. Most had left for the night.

Vladimir pricked up his ears, hearing a faint moan echoing from somewhere. His sensitive nose smelled woman—his woman. Was Tamsin pleasuring herself again?

She was constantly hungering for sex, greedy for his company. The self-control exhibited by the much younger Jane was far more to his taste. In part, he silently admitted, because breaking Jane would be much more challenging.

Tamsin thought it was just another game, begged to be badly treated if it didn't mess up her makeup. She couldn't get enough of his careful cruelty and liked to urge him on. But she had ceased to interest him, outside of the fresh blood she was eager to provide.

He heard the moaning voice again. Slightly louder. He must be getting warm. A metaphor that was all wrong for a vampire—until Vladimir checked the thought as he turned the corner into one of the skyboxes and saw Tamsin standing inside by the plate glass window.

There was a crack in it near the corner. No wonder he had been able to hear her.

Her skirt was hiked up to her waist and her legs were apart. Her eyes were closed. Her head rolled back and forth against the wall behind her.

Between her legs kneeled a vampire, a stud who'd been hired as a backup dancer, his shirt tossed aside to reveal a heavily muscled back that tapered to his jeans-clad buttocks. Talking dirty—and, inevitably, giving the young fool pointers—Tamsin threw a leg over his shoulder and balanced on the other, none too steady. She sank her fingernails into his thick blond hair, forcing his head against her pussy. Excited, she dragged the heel of her stiletto up and down his spine, leaving welts.

The vamp didn't seem to mind. He clutched her bare thighs as his blond head stayed firmly in place. Tamsin added tiny shrieks to her vocal repertoire as Vladimir listened and watched, aroused to some degree but furious with her.

He didn't have long to wait.

She climaxed, noisily. Then she opened her eyes and looked down at her lover. "Nice," she purred. Then she yawned. "But I'm done with you for now." The young vamp hauled himself up from his kneeling position, about to demand a kiss, but she pushed his face away. Her eyes widened when she saw Vladimir. Who said nothing.

He strode to the other vampire and grabbed him by the hair, smashing his head repeatedly into the wall, leaving his rival slumped and bleeding. Not dead. They did need a male dancer and the blond man had the moves. Vladimir might let him live.

"Don't—don't kill him," she pleaded. "Don't hurt me."

"It won't hurt at all. Come here, Tamsin," Vladimir said quietly.

* * *

The panel was quickly completed and left in his office for him to view, propped against the wall. The artist had done an excellent job. Tamsin seemed more lifelike than the others. But her frozen expression lacked the innocence of the younger girls. The difference would ruin the symmetry. Vladimir decided against installing the artwork. He dragged the thing across the carpet and shoved it into a closet.

CHAPTER
TWENTY-FOUR

The day after the media junket, Barrett had barely gotten a few hours' sleep before she was back at the club again. Setting up the work shifts for all the dancers—most of whom were headstrong to a fault and foulmouthed to boot—took Barrett and Sam until the evening. Throughout the day, she thought of Nick and how he'd confessed to struggling against his protectiveness of her. Knowing he was still protective of her felt safe. Knowing he cared enough to give her the free rein she needed made her feel loved. However, other than a quick text exchange between them that morning—one that had included a wry statement that he was still feeling his "punishment" from the night before—she didn't hear from him.

She hadn't had a second to snoop around the club again. Lunch had been delivered for her and Sam, along with a take-out vat of coffee and gooey cupcakes to sweeten up the girls. Hadn't worked.

The last in line had arrived fashionably late and decided to negotiate her fee. She'd been a headliner at a major Atlanta club and knew what she was worth.

Barrett watched Jewell walk away, sashaying down the corridor in impossibly tight leggings and a shredded T-shirt that said Electrick Beetch on the front and back, an enormous designer handbag over her shoulder.

She turned to Sam. "Hope she doesn't tell the others she's getting paid more."

"Girl, please. You and I both know that's the first thing Jewell's going to do." Sam checked the chunky faux-diamond timepiece on her wrist. "It's five minutes to catfight by my watch."

Barrett cleared away the lipstick-smeared cups of take-out coffee, shoveling them all into a wastebasket and folding up the chairs.

"I never knew running a club was this much work," she said impatiently.

"Hope those media people got what they came for," Sam said. "Club Red is going to be the biggest place I ever worked in. But let me tell you, some things never change. The dancers are the most trouble. This new bunch better hustle the hell out of the customers once we open. We got goals to reach. Vlad is gonna track every penny we take in."

"Who spends the most?" Barrett asked.

"The Triple M's, honey."

Barrett raised a quizzical eyebrow.

Sam spelled it out. "Middle-aged, married, and money to burn. I feel sorry for the wives. Most'a these bitches are out for what they can get."

An argument was kicking up down the hall. Sam grinned. "Right on time. What did I tell you?"

Barrett groaned. She really, really wanted to leave. "Should we interfere?"

"Not unless you want your beautiful white hair pulled right out of your head and a few scratches on your face to go with it."

Barrett rolled her eyes. "Nope."

Sam took a compact out of her bag and fixed her makeup. "Vladimir won't approve fat paychecks for the new hires just 'cause Jewell's got a big mouth on her. The others will just have to shake it harder if they want to earn more." She flipped a phenomenally long ponytail over her shoulder. "That's what I used to do. Paid for my hair extensions back then."

"And now?"

"Yolanda does 'em for free," Sam said. "Hey, leave all that trash for the cleaning crew. Can we get out of here? I have a date. How about you?"

She thought of Nick. Thought of punishing him again, this time for making her crave him without even trying to. She quickly shook her head. "No."

"Hmm. For a second there your eyes got misty."

"Allergies. The club ventilation system couldn't handle the atmosphere last night."

"Really? I didn't notice that. And I was on stage and you were out front." Sam tossed the compact and lipstick back into her bag and swung it over her arm. "See you tomorrow if you don't want to go just yet. But get some sleep if you're sleeping alone. You look tired."

"Yeah, I am. But it's interesting work." She was stalling just a little. Barrett preferred to leave by herself.

"Glad you think so. As far as I'm concerned, the thrill is *long* gone. Done this shit for too many years. Heard it all, seen even more." Sam turned the knob and cautiously eased the door open again, peering up and down the corridor. The argument was getting louder.

"All clear," she said to Barrett. "But I strongly suggest you leave now."

Instantly persuaded, she gathered up her things.

"Okay. I really don't want to be trapped in here with a bunch of pissed-off strippers."

Barrett trotted out with Sam, laughing. They turned a corner just before a different door banged open and the clicking sound of high heels reached them.

They ran down the stairs as quietly as they could and went through the first-floor fire exit without setting off the alarm. Barrett walked Sam to the parking lot and said good night, turning just as Sam reached her car several spaces away.

Sam popped the trunk, throwing things around as she looked for something, muttering to herself. "Fucking heels are killin' me. Now where's those damn sneakers?"

"Hey, Sam." The female voice was almost too low to hear. It was the thin girl. Barrett looked in her direction. The girl was under a tree at the outer perimeter of the Club Red property.

"Xecala, baby. You feeling okay?"

"Yeah, Sam. I wanted to talk to Barrett about something."

Sam frowned. "Barrett, huh?" She looked at Barrett, her eyes assessing. "Xecala's my friend. Like the daughter I'll never have," she said. "I don't want her getting into trouble."

Warning and implied threat noted, Barrett thought.

"I'm no threat to her," Barrett said. "I don't even know why she wants to talk to me."

Sam nodded then said, "All the same . . . don't make me sorry I've trusted you, Barrett." With that, Sam got behind the wheel, roaring away with a manicured wave out the window.

Xecala shuffled over the grass to Barrett.

She seemed almost spectral. Her pale skin glowed faintly in the evening shadows and, once she'd gotten close enough, Barrett saw the violet shadows under her eyes.

"Sorry I bailed on you last night," the girl said timidly. Her voice was weary.

"I came out and looked for you. Thanks for coming back." She heard someone else coming before she saw the person. "Hang on a sec."

It was another bouncer. "Hi, Lewis."

He was a rangy guy, older than the one from last

night, but still built. He could have been a middleweight boxer once, with a long reach that hadn't been long enough to keep his nose from being broken a few times.

Lewis looked over her shoulder at the girl, who shrank back. "Xecala. You know you can't come around here. We have our orders."

"Miss Barrett wanted to see me."

Miss Barrett. The term sounded so polite and so southern that Barrett almost smiled. But the name certainly wasn't southern. There was no telling where the sad girl came from.

"Mr. Ouspensky told our guys to keep an eye out for you, Xe. I don't want no trouble. My boss will give me hell."

"What's the matter?" Barrett took a take-charge tone. "She's not lying. I really did ask to see her."

Might as well be honest. Lewis would probably scribble some kind of report for his boss, who might or might not send it to Vladimir. The bouncer didn't look like the superconscientious type. Just mean in a petty way.

Lewis kept an eye on the girl, who didn't seem particularly afraid of him, and drew Barrett aside.

"She's a junkie."

That explained the scrawny body under the loose clothes.

"Been in and out of rehab, but nothing ever worked. Tried to kill herself a couple of times, couldn't manage that, either. She's a bad influence," Lewis finished up. "Mr. Ouspensky doesn't want her near the other girls. Especially the new ones. Like I said, we got our orders."

"I understand. But she's not inside the club. And we're just going to talk for a few minutes. I—ah—I know her sister. Her family wants her to come back. Look, here's something for you." She held up a fifty. "Your boss doesn't even have to know."

Lewis didn't exactly hesitate. "I'm coming out again

in five minutes. Talk fast." He pocketed the bill and left them alone.

"Did you take that top piece of paper?" Barrett whispered urgently. The girl nodded. "Why?"

Xecala wavered. "I wanted to look at it more."

"I gave you the drawings I did of you. That one wasn't yours to take."

"I know. But . . ."

"Xe, you have to tell me."

The girl turned away, racked by a cough. Barrett was shocked by the way her shoulder blades protruded through the fabric of her dress. Xecala was wiping sweat from her face with her sleeve when she straightened and faced Barrett again.

"I kinda thought it might be—this girl I saw coming into the club."

"You mean Jane?" Barrett breathed the question.

"Is that her name? Yeah. It was her. They brought her in at night."

"When? Where is she now?" Barrett stared at the girl. She was heartbreakingly young to look so haggard. But she wasn't the one Barrett had to help. "Do you want money or something? I have to know."

"I need a fix, that's all. Need it bad."

Barrett swore under her breath. Handing out cash was one thing. Heroin was another. "I don't have anything like that."

The girl stepped back. "Not asking you for it. I hid some." She turned and looked over her shoulder.

"In the tree?" Barrett was almost angry. The girl was drifting in more ways than one. She didn't have time for this.

"No. By that bench." She nodded toward a bench with a high back not too far from the building's outer wall. "I sit behind it. Sometimes I sleep under it. I'm homeless."

Guilt slammed into Barrett. She was asking a lot of someone who had nothing to give.

"I don't care anymore." Xe coughed again. She walked to the bench and Barrett followed. She didn't want to watch. But she didn't want to lose the girl before she found out where Jane was.

Without saying a word, Xe found the drug paraphernalia she'd stashed and got to work. Her hands trembled when she cooked up a nickel bag and slipped off her shirt to tie off, tapping her skin, looking for a blood vessel that hadn't collapsed.

Lewis had told the truth. Xecala's arms were scarred with ugly tracks. Barrett felt sick. There was no way to help this girl.

Xe positioned the needle and looked up at her. Her voice had an odd clarity. "I saw Jane, like I told you. They took her from a truck into the club through a hidden entrance." She shook her head. "They didn't hide it too good. No one saw me when I followed."

"Through the same entrance?"

"No. I went in through a side door, a different one, when the guards weren't looking. I figured out the keypad code before that."

Xe paused, getting her breath. Barrett waited.

"One of Vlad's guys . . . he took me down there . . . wanted privacy. He thought I was too stoned to see. But that's just what I wanted him to believe."

Deftly, she pierced the skin of her inner elbow with the needle tip, going into a threadlike vein. Then she stopped. Xecala rocked a little, smiling in a weird way, as if she were anticipating the rush to come.

"Want the code?"

"No. I can go in through the front. But—"

Xe held a thumb over the plunger of the syringe.

"Stop that. Please," Barrett begged her.

The girl shook her head. "Maybe you saw the three doors on the inside that don't open out."

She knew what she was talking about. Barrett had to find out more. "I saw one. I heard about the others. Do they all go to the same place?"

"Dunno. But I got those codes, too." She gave a low laugh. "I know you have a pencil and paper."

Barrett grabbed both from her bag, writing frantically as Xecala told her the codes: 447574373, 85234647, 5355748. If the microsensors Nick had hidden by the doors were found before the keypads were used, they had something to go on. She prayed the numbers weren't changed every day.

"Which one would get me to Jane?"

Xecala shrugged, frowning when the needle tip moved. A bluish spot of blood pooled under her skin. "Maybe all three. I heard someone say to take her to the little room."

Barrett didn't bother to ask why Xecala hadn't helped. The girl would have been overpowered instantly. As a witness, her life was worth nothing.

"I couldn't do nothing. Then I sorta forgot about her. And then there she was. Like a ghost on the page that you drew."

"Do you have any idea where the little room is?"

"Underneath the pit. I heard that, too. I guess that's where they take the kidnapped girls in this club."

A horrifying understanding came to Barrett. "Were you one, Xecala?"

"Almost," she said, her voice ragged. "At the other place, before it burned down. I didn't make the cut. For some reason, Vladimir just let me go. I figured he forgot about me. But I still don't know why the others didn't kill me."

"You doing a damn good job of that all by yourself."

Barrett whirled around. "Sam?"

"I dropped my house keys when I got in the car." The other woman bit out the words. They didn't sound like a lie. "Came back to get 'em and saw you here with Xe."

Sam hadn't made the slightest sound when she approached the bench. She could have flown there on silent wings, for all Barrett knew. She had no time to wonder why. Xecala moaned when the needle went in.

You couldn't just jerk it out. Barrett thought she'd heard that or read that somewhere. The syringe was empty, the plunger down. Xecala's veins glowed blue from whatever it was she'd injected. "Oh, God. What is that?"

Sam crouched by Xecala, helping the girl rest against the bench for support. Sam's voice dropped to a whisper. "A strung-out bitch at the other club got her hooked. Wasn't long before she started to wander between this world and the next. That shit she uses is different. Real strong. Can't buy it on the street." Xecala moaned, the color draining from her face.

"Jesus, she looks like she's going to die! Sam, we can't just—"

"Let her be." With considerable strength, Sam forced Barrett to move back, then kneeled by the girl. "Let her go easy. That's all we can do."

"No—how—"

"Sam . . ." Xecala's voice. So faint the word could be her last.

Sam stroked the girl's tangled hair.

"Just wanted you to know . . ." Xe murmured. "Wanted to . . . do one right thing before . . ."

"Shh." Sam tried to soothe her. "You did, baby girl. You did right."

A supernatural glow emanated from Xecala's eyes. Then they closed. Her lips turned blue but she smiled. To herself. She saw only the hallucinations in her mind.

Barrett was speechless. She could see them, too, as if the girl's skull was made of glass. Visible under her translucent skin, the lethal drug coursed through her veins, spreading in a delicate tracery of death.

Xecala took her last breath.

They both stared at the girl for several minutes before Sam turned to Barrett. "No one can know she's dead. Especially not Vlad. Help me get her in my car."

They put Xecala in the backseat of Sam's car before she drove them away, pulling into an isolated parking garage about five blocks from Club Red. Leaving the girl where she was, Sam got out of the car and Barrett followed. "You'll have to walk back to the club. I'll stay with her. Take care of her."

"Why can't Vlad know she's dead?" Barrett asked yet again.

This time, Sam answered her.

"I've worked with Vlad a long time. He trusts me more than most, partially because he knows I love Xecala. He likes the people I know, the favors I can bring him, and by promising to leave Xecala alone, he knew I'd give them to him. If he knows she's dead, he'll know he no longer has his hooks in me. Not in the same way. He won't trust me the way he's trusted me. And that won't be good for me. Or you."

Exhausted, Barrett leaned against the outside of the car. She couldn't stop herself from looking at Xecala. "How much did you hear of what I said to Xecala?"

"Enough to figure out that you're hunting for someone hidden here. Probably one of Vladimir's auction girls."

"So you know about them?" Barrett wanted to scream, to accuse, but if Sam knew anything at all about Jane, going ballistic wouldn't get her more information.

"That's right."

Barrett cast her a sideways look. Sam's beautiful face was stony. Maybe she had been auctioned, too. The more Barrett found out, the uglier it got. But she couldn't hold back the next question. "Have you seen the little room? The one under the club?"

Sam frowned slightly and shook her head. "No. Don't know nothing about that. There is a fight pit, wasn't on the grand tour for the media. Vlad's got something in the works there, but I couldn't say exactly what. Xe was s'posed to go on the block at the other club. But she didn't make the cut, not after she started using again. Vlad was going to kill her, but I bargained with him for her life. What little life she had left. Someone smuggled in nickel bags for her but she never got enough. Sold herself for more. Then she started using the other stuff."

Barrett felt sickened all over again. What if the same thing happened to Jane? She could have been injected with a lower dose of the strange drug to keep her under control.

"She started wasting away, got to where we could practically see through her."

"How come the bouncers let her hang around Club Red?"

"She kept 'em supplied at the other club. A couple of them use, too. I ain't gonna name no names. And so do some of the girls. Smack for sex."

Barrett closed her eyes. Said nothing.

"You all right, Barrett?"

"No," she whispered. "That girl just died. And I didn't—I couldn't save her." Just like Noah. Maybe like Jane.

"She didn't want to be saved. There's no cure for what she was putting into her veins. Xe never caught a break in all her life. She's in a better place now."

"How do you know?"

Sam took a deep breath and jammed her hands into her pockets. "Because I want to believe it," she said in a soft voice. "You gotta believe in something. This business makes it hard. Wish I could get out. But I have a reason to stay."

Nothing to lose. Barrett went for it. "Can I ask what it is?"

"I hate Vlad's fucking guts. Hate what he does. But he's had me by the balls." Sam rubbed her eyes. "These damn contacts gotta come out. You can't cry and be beautiful, right?" She lifted an eyelid and pinched the soft plastic lens, flicking it on the ground. Then she did the other eye. "Disposables."

Barrett figured as much.

"So I'm biding my time, acting nice, like I'm going for Employee of the Week. Hoping I can find a way to take Vlad out and not get sent up for life or killed. But now you and me are on the same side. You some kind of undercover agent, ain't you? Yeah. Thought so. Wait until the bastard figures that out."

She turned to look at Barrett. Sam's beautiful eyes were black with silver pupils.

Barrett gasped. "You're a vampire."

"Yeah. I'm a born vampire."

Barrett stared at her.

Sam shrugged. "There was a human or two or four in the mix somewhere. Another reason I haven't moved against Vlad. My powers are weak compared to his."

So they'd been right, Barrett thought. About Vlad. About Jane. Now what were they going to do?

"You might as well keep on asking me questions," Sam said. "I know you will. If I don't want to answer, I'll tell you."

Barrett was baffled for a moment. But she knew better than to waste time. "Okay. The heroin Xecala used. What was that?"

Sam looked off into the near distance, her silver eyes shimmering. "It's something new. Vamp Smack Prime is what they call it. VSP for short. Potent shit and not easy to come by. You have to have the right connection."

"Meaning a vampire."

"Yeah."

A drug that enslaved and ultimately killed had to be a Rogue product. Barrett made a note to run it by Collette. If VSP hit the streets anywhere, there would be a wave of deaths far higher than the average.

"Is there anything else I should know?"

"What the hell." She clasped her hands, not in a casual way. "That I was on to you from the beginning. You didn't look like no nightclub hostess to me. Then one day, you didn't know I was there, but you were in the dressing room and your bracelet snagged on something. You took it off and—"

"You read my mind."

"I sure did."

Barrett hadn't noticed it. She had experienced the probing sensation once or twice, long before she got to Club Red. But never since she'd been there. Sam had to be awfully good at subtle mental exploration. Having a human ancestor probably helped her follow the pathways of human thought. And being female had to as well.

"I'm not," Sam said.

"Beg your pardon?"

"Either put on your bling or get used to having me inside your head." Sam sighed. "When I said Vlad had me by the balls, I meant that literally. I'm not a biological woman. And that's the last thing you can't tell anyone. Everybody doesn't have to know everything, and the club girls gossip."

"I don't. Your secret is safe with me."

"Good."

Barrett thought that she should have known that Sam was trans. But she really hadn't. No big deal these days. It was just a strange time to find out.

"So . . . Sam isn't short for Samantha?"

"Nope. My birth certificate says Samuel."

Barrett looked out into the growing darkness. She didn't say anything for a while or even think anything. The other woman had brought her clasped hands up to her forehead, her body bowed.

Barrett offered a silent prayer for Xecala, sure that Sam was doing the same, hoping that her soul found the peace that life had denied her.

Xe had tried to help a lost girl she didn't know. Barrett was infinitely grateful.

She was going to see that Xe wasn't forgotten, either.

Barrett walked back to the club, got into her car, drove a few blocks away, then parked and took out her phone. She tapped the screen, then switched to her messages.

There was a text from Justine asking for an update. Barrett responded. *New developments. Text you later. Where are you?*

Didn't take a minute for a reply. *Fancy bar. Nice-looking man. Possible not-so-nice association with Club Red.*

Be careful, Barrett typed with a fingernail.

I always am.

Barrett sent another text to Collette, asking if they could connect tomorrow. No answer. She knew the former police officer would get back to her as soon as possible.

Now for Nick.

Meet me at the condo, she texted. Then, with tears stinging her eyes, she started driving again.

Ten minutes later, he met her in the parking lot. He'd

washed the ugly streaks out of his dark hair and ditched the rest of the disguise. She was relieved that he looked like himself again.

"What's going on?" he asked right away.

"A lot." She looked around to see if anyone was watching, feeling even more paranoid than usual. "Let's go inside."

She practically pushed him through the door.

He turned around and studied her businesslike demeanor. "You look serious. Guess I have to take a rain check on the kinky sex you were threatening me with."

"What?" Barrett blinked at him, not even remembering that for a few seconds. Then it clicked. "Oh. Not now. Jesus." She proceeded to tell him everything she'd found out from Sam. Barrett told him about the vampire, describing her at length but leaving out the part about her being transgender, since Barrett had sworn to keep that secret and it wasn't really relevant.

"Have you gotten feedback from the microsensors?" She went to get the pad of paper.

"Yeah. I have the codes for all three keypads and I know how often they were entered in the last twenty-four hours." He moved to the table and got his laptop booted up.

She came back, thinking that everything in the hard drive was duplicated in his brain, including the little spinning wheel that signified *wait for it*. So she waited.

Nick pulled up a frequency graph, separated into three columns marked by numbers:

447574373. 85234647. 5355748.

Barrett slapped down the pad once she'd checked the codes Xecala had given her. "Okay. They're the same." She took several jerky breaths.

Nick laid a comforting hand on her shoulder.

She looked up at him. "Xecala probably wasn't much older than Jane," she said, her voice quavering.

His eyes darkened. "I'm so sorry, angel." He reached out to give her a hug, not letting go when she instinctively tried to brush him off. Giving in, she allowed herself the brief comfort of his arms as she blinked back tears.

With a sniff, she drew back, took a slow breath, and nodded, indicating she was calm enough to continue. "I've texted Collette, need to see if VSP heroin has hit the streets yet and what the FBI is going to do about it if it has. But she hasn't gotten back to me yet."

He studied the frequency graph as she spoke briefly to Collette, then moved to the stored data on the club structure, which he'd stitched into a rotating 3-D display.

It seemed solid. But there was no telling what was down there.

Barrett wrapped it up with Collette and ended the call. "She's on it. No buzz yet on VSP."

"Doesn't surprise me if it's a vampire thing." Nick blew out a breath. "So we're dealing with not just a turned vampire in Gil Mansfield, but at least one born vampire. Maybe more. I hate the idea of you going back in there, Barrett."

"Then don't think about it. And don't go all quiet on me, either. Please. Me being inside has been fruitful. Not just because of Xecala and Sam, but because Vlad trusts me. He told me there's two events scheduled tomorrow. Construction work and a VIP event. We've got to get in there, Nick. Get you beyond those doors."

He nodded, then directed her attention to the graph. "Look at how the dots cluster. Those two doors are used relatively often. The third, hardly ever."

"Okay. Then that's the one to use."

"That's what I was thinking." He paused, looking up

at her. "You do know we're outgunned here. We don't know shit about born vampires, in particular how to kill them. Do you think you're tight enough with Sam that she'll tell us?"

"I don't know. Maybe. If she trusts that we're going after Vlad, I think so. She hates him. Wants to be free of him."

"She's not the only one," he said.

"You think we're facing impossible odds, don't you?"

His mouth twisted. "Impossible, improbable." He shrugged. "Either way you look at it, we're definitely the underdog."

"You can't bring in someone to cover you? Not even Kevin?"

Nick shook his head. "I can't ask him to risk his neck. Besides, the fewer people who try to go in in a situation like this, the fewer chances there are of being caught. We're balls to the wall, Barrett. Just like we were when we rescued those sisters, remember?"

She reached out and took his hand. "You're taking a huge risk," she said. "I—I can't thank you enough."

"You don't have to thank me. Just keep loving me, Barrett. Even when I mess up. Even when I get quiet and you get insecure. Love me. Believe in me."

"I do," she said. "More than you can ever know."

"Then that's enough."

TWENTY-FIVE

Inside his office, Vladimir took care of some last-minute details in preparation for the club's VIP event. The VIPs would be both human and vampires, with the humans dancing to loud music and making enough noise on the club's main level to drown out the festivities below, where vampires would be secretly enjoying the auctioning off of Jane Small.

The human girl had remained strangely composed in his presence, even after he had told her he was a vampire and made the fate that awaited her perfectly clear. He found her to be . . . unsettling.

He could not shake the feeling that the girl might be able to outmaneuver him if she had the chance. His usual victims were apt to be emotional, to snivel and beg for their lives and be disgustingly grateful when they were shipped off to their eventual purchasers, thinking that they would be free. In most cases, they were headed for basement dungeons and never-ending rape.

Jane watched him so carefully, as if she was assessing his every move and predicting what the consequences might be.

He wondered if she had been taught to play chess. If so, she was a smart little pawn. And he would have to be careful not to be trapped in a corner and checkmated.

Annoyed by how distracted he'd become thinking of the girl again, Vladimir tried to imagine how his first cage-fighting event would go down once the time was right. By then, he'd have brought in another girl to auction. He had to in order to give the audience the full experience. Sex and death. The ancient Romans—one of his ancestors among them—had done the same. It would be a double bill. An innocent girl for the sex, and turned vampire Tim Murphy chained in the largest cell under the pit to deal out death. If for some reason Murphy didn't do what he was supposed to, Vlad would move on to plan B—put Gil Mansfield in the cage with a human.

Maybe he'd even play the wretched music Gil liked during the fight to inspire him.

As for the surrounding ambience? The gritty floors and raw walls would pass as an authentic part of the ultimate cage-fighting experience. For the vicious battle to the death that he had in mind, a raw setting was suitable. But unpainted concrete was apt to soak up spilled blood that a paying crowd of Rogues would be avid to see.

The freakiest among them might go so far as to catch the blood in glasses if they were drunk enough and seated close to the arena. The huge cage was designed to swing, to throw the fighters off balance and into each other's arms. It had been custom welded to take every shock and withstand the ferocity of the combatants, hanging above a pit that Vladimir had intended to be white.

He growled deep in his throat. He was losing patience with these damned details and they were hemorrhaging money by the minute.

They could drape the pit with damask, he supposed. No. The material was far too elegant and the dripping blood would only splotch.

He wanted a vivid contrast. Running rivers of scarlet against gleaming, impermeable white. This was theater—

the theater of pain and unbridled violence. Each ticket sold for five thousand dollars. Ringside seats would go for even more. There would be no time-outs and no corner men and no technical victories. The fight began when the bell rang and it was over when one combatant was dead. Both might die if they were valorous. Vladimir hoped so.

The phone rang and Vladimir picked up the receiver.

"Hey, boss," Gil said.

"What is it?"

"Murphy's here."

TWENTY-SIX

Back at the condo, Nick, Barrett, and Justine huddled around the dining table. Nick had set up a triple-encrypted connection and patched in four laptops perched on different objects. One screen showed the fat blue logo of Skype, on hold for a conference chat with Belladonna. Two displayed various parts of the investigation so far. Recon, exterior and interior. Schematics derived from photos. Precise measurements of hallway length and door placement, down to the number of steps it took to move between them all. And one was his, positioned in front of him.

"This is only the main level, correct?" Justine asked, looking into one showing intel.

"That's right. About ten thousand square feet, not including the interior balconies. I don't have anything on what's below it."

"And you're sure there is a level below it?" Justine asked.

"I'd like to find out for sure, put it that way. But, yeah. There may be more than one underground level," he added.

"Pass the potato chips."

He lobbed the open bag at her and it landed upright in her lap.

"Nice throw. Where'd you learn how to do that?"

"I pitch for a weekend softball league. When I have the time."

Justine stuck her hand into the bag and munched on the chip she extracted. "So how are you going in?"

"This time, as a contractor." He nodded to Barrett. "She gets to help me with that." He returned his attention to his laptop. "Whoa. This just in from Kevin. Looks like the team on the mountain made some interesting discoveries."

"Share." That from Justine, along with an avid look.

"Apparently some of the diseased turneds are hiding out in caverns. Tennessee has more of them than any other state. There's a natural tunnel from one that runs under my mountain. That could be how Tim Murphy got there. And went berserk when he came up into the light."

"So he was on your mountain by coincidence? I suppose it's possible," Justine said thoughtfully.

Barrett heard her cell phone chime. "Let me see who that is." She looked at the screen. "Ginny. Be right back."

It was a text. Barrett felt a stab of guilt for not reconnecting with her sooner. But there had been nothing to report.

Any news? Nothing here. Malcolm left. He didn't tell me why, but I can guess. He won't answer his phone. I'm dealing with the police now. No leads. Will keep you posted.

Dogged. Unemotional. But Ginny was trying. If Barrett saw Malcolm, she'd be highly tempted to run him over. But that might affect his ability to confess to the part he'd played in Jane's disappearance. He had to have had something to do with it.

She texted back. *So sorry I didn't check in. No news here, either, just a few leads. But we won't give up. Will get back to you soon. My best. Barrett.*

By the time she'd returned to the table, Justine was studying the recon images again and Nick was absorbed in something new, judging by the frown line between his eyes as he concentrated on the screen of his laptop.

Barrett set a hand on his shoulder. "What's up?"

He tilted the screen so she could see. "Request for information on my original mission. I haven't touched base for a while."

"What do they want?"

"Mansfield. The FBI finally traced him to New City."

"Is that the turned vamp who's on your kill list?" Justine looked up.

"Yeah."

"You want my two cents?" She hesitated for only a fraction of a second. "Blow his head off. May he rot in hell."

"It's not that easy to kill a turned," Nick said quietly. "But I hear you."

The rest of the meeting was routine enough. Barrett caught up with the other agents at Belladonna via Skype, motioning Nick out of camera range when Carly said hello. They knew he was with her and Justine. There just didn't seem to be a reason to bring him in for an agency discussion.

They wrapped it up around midnight. Justine went for her purse and a light jacket as Nick shut down the laptops.

"Where are you going?" Barrett asked.

"Just out. For a drive." Justine winked at her.

Nick pretended he didn't see or hear.

Okay. So she was leaving them alone. Barrett was glad.

The charged mood in the condo was a deeply poignant reminder of how it had been overseas, during the hours before a scheduled raid or an incursion or one of Nick's secret assignments.

The communication and breakdown of intel so that everyone got it. The guarded references to the heavy stuff. The occasional joke to lighten up.

Those who could paired off afterward and found privacy. She and Nick had been no exception to that unwritten rule. The sex could be tender or almost rough. It didn't matter, as long as they reached release in each other's arms.

You never knew if you would come back in one piece. Or if you would come back at all. Lovers in war zones gave it everything they had.

He stood to open the door for Justine. Then he took Barrett in his arms and kissed her.

CHAPTER
TWENTY-SEVEN

Try or die.

Jane jerked violently against her handcuffs. The guard who had chained them behind her back to his metal belt staggered slightly but nothing more. "Knock it off," he clipped out. "Or I'll—"

"You'll do nothing unless I give you permission first."

Both she and the guard jerked at the sound of the man's voice. Jane kept her gaze averted until Gil Mansfield stood right in front of her and forced her chin up so she had no choice but to look at him. "What do you think, Jane? Shall I give him permission to do what he wants to you?"

She spat in his face.

He wiped it off with his free hand and smeared her saliva on her cheek. "That's not nice." Before she could blink, he grabbed her by the hair and said to the guard, "Return to the club. I'll take care of her." When the guard left, Gil returned his attention to Jane.

"You got upgraded to a suite, didn't you?" Gil smirked. "So let's get going." He pulled her in the right direction, still using her hair for leverage. Jane wanted to howl but she wouldn't give him the satisfaction. She gritted her teeth and endured the pain.

He dumped her in front of a closed door, finding shackles for her ankles and a Y chain in a wall cabinet, securing the cuffs to both. Then he shoved her inside. It was a plain cell, with an unpadded bunk and an open toilet, like something in a prison. Like the rest of Club Red, the walls smelled new and raw. Gil closed the heavy door behind him and pushed her down onto the bunk.

"Now let's talk."

Jane blew her tangled hair out of her mouth. "You can talk without chaining me up."

Gil wagged a finger. "Don't be such a smartass. Just thought you should know that Malcolm Prescott wanted to say hi. But he can't. I decided he was a loose end I no longer wanted to leave loose. He's dead. You should be happy."

As creepy as Malcolm had been, some part of her still felt sorry for him. "Screw you."

"Hey, that was what he wanted to do to you, little girl. Just like that guard did." He leaned closer. "Just like I do."

His gaze dropped. She knew her flimsy dress was torn and she didn't care.

"Too bad it would cost Vlad so much money if I fucked you. I can see why old Malcolm was interested."

"I'm so glad Vlad scares you then," she said snottily.

Gil just shrugged. "For now. Someday I'm gonna put him out of business. I know too much about him. And he doesn't treat us turneds with a whole lot of respect. Then again, at least he's not trying to kill us, not like the bastards in the FBI. Some of them have been trying to find you." He smirked. "I'm not only hoping they will, I'm counting on it. Especially the bastard who lives on that fucking mountain and the woman who came to see him. Too bad my friend didn't take care of her when he had the chance."

Another vampire friend, he probably meant.

She frowned as memory returned. She' been so out of it, but now she remembered she'd seen Barrett Miles on that computer screen. She'd been in the army. Was it possible she was working for the FBI and trying to find her? If so, did she realize she was being set up?

Thinking of the woman who'd once been such a good friend to Jane's mother but who'd made little time for Jane since her death made her angry at first. But, God, she'd forgive her, if only she'd come and save her. She sucked back the pain with a breath so deep her ribs had to be showing under the thin dress. "How do you know her? Miley?"

"Like I'd tell you. Let's just say we have . . . *friends* . . . in common. You might even get to meet one before too long. Or should I say, you will meet him in very painful ways unless you play nice with me." He smiled and leaned closer. "You want to get on my good side by doing something for me? *To* me? Now's your chance."

"You're supposed to guard my virginity, remember?"

"Like a hawk. But there's other things we could do besides fuck. Open up."

He put his hand on his fly and bent down like he was going to put his mouth on hers, for starters. Jane head-butted him. She got some satisfaction out of seeing him stagger back just before they heard someone calling his name from outside.

The door to her cell opened and the reserve guard stuck his head in.

Just in time, Jane thought, since Gil Mansfield looked ready to kill her with his bare hands. He jerked her closer to him and whispered into her ear.

"Payback is coming, you little bitch," he whispered.

"I'll die first," she whispered back.

But she couldn't deny the fear that flooded her, weakening her knees when he said, "You'll wish for death. But I won't give it to you. Not for a long, *long* time."

TWENTY-EIGHT

Vladimir Oupensky was pissed because the construction crew was late. As it was, they barely had time to get in, do their work, and get out before the guests for the VIP event showed up. Barrett had been freaking out herself, pacing and keeping an eye out for Nick, who she knew wouldn't arrive until he could meld with the rest of the construction crew. But several construction workers had arrived twenty minutes ago, so where—

Barrett looked up the second a familiar, broad-shouldered man pushed through the glass front doors of Club Red, a heavy tool chest in his work-gloved hand. Nick wore a hard hat with a bandanna under it tied around his hair, and a canvas jacket over a tank top, plus loose jeans and dusty work boots that weren't laced up all the way. He looked hot, actually. Like she wasn't nervous enough already. She told herself not to stare at his hunky getup. It didn't work. She told herself to think of the Village People. That helped some.

"Miss? Could I leave this with you?" He held up a paper bag with a tightly rolled top and slid it across the top of the hostess station. "It's a sandwich." He grinned at her. "My buddy's dinner, actually. I took it by mistake. He's gonna stop by and pick it up."

"Oh—okay. Not a problem." She took the paper bag from him. The contents weren't any heavier than a sandwich. She knew it was a gun and that it was for her. He probably had a small arsenal of weapons with him.

"Where do I sign in?" Nick set down the diamond-patterned metal tool chest he was lugging.

"You don't have to. The crew boss already did for all of you guys." She was faking him in, speaking more loudly than normal. It didn't matter if what she said actually made sense. No one seemed to be listening.

"Great. Thank you, ma'am."

That was a downgrade from miss. She mouthed the words *fuck you*. Nick grinned. It did break the tension to some degree. Obviously she felt it more than he did.

"Okay, let me make you a badge and you can join them on the third tier." She consulted a list, again speaking loudly and rather vaguely. "Say, looks like Gil Mansfield is up there now. He wanted to make sure everyone's on the same page." She turned the hostess-station monitor around and pointed to the screen. "There he is. Just so you recognize him."

Nick looked at the screen. *Good work, Miss Barrett.* He had to say it with his eyes. She'd hacked into the security cam feed on her own.

He couldn't resist a single word of praise. "Cool."

She turned the screen back so it was facing her with a touch of her finger and pulled out a self-stick badge. He watched her write a name she just made up, because they'd forgotten to agree on one, then hand him the badge.

Freddy George.

"That's me," he confirmed cheerfully, peeling off the backing and slapping it onto his canvas jacket. "Thanks."

No one was paying the slightest attention. Even at this early afternoon hour, the activity in and around the club was the best camouflage they could have. Barrett nod-

ded to him and briskly turned toward two men in khakis and striped polo shirts.

"We have a private event tonight. We're not open for
business until tomorrow. But please come back. And
just so you know, there is a dress code."

Hidden at the top tier behind the nosebleed seats, Nick
got set up. The work crew Barrett had mentioned was
all the way on the other side of the main area. Good. He
needed a little time to locate the wiring for the security
system and the feed from this level. The system was
nothing special. The wires could probably be reached in
back of the electrical outlet nearest the camera.

There was no way to turn off the juice. He had to pick
the connection apart with something really low-tech: a
bamboo barbecue skewer. Barrett would laugh if she
knew.

He took off an outlet cover and got to work. First try,
the security camera stopped moving. Its blinking red
light went off.

Done. He opened the tool chest and made sure everything was where he would need it. He lifted out an inside tray. Under it were the light clothes Barrett had
given him in case Jane needed them, tightly folded into
a small square, and a rolled pair of thin flats. There was
a ball cap for him. The jacket reversed to a different
color and, without the bandanna and hard hat, he
wouldn't look like the guy who'd walked in with the
tool chest. Add in sports glasses that fit his face and he'd
really look different.

He located another outlet and plugged a heavy-duty
power cord into it. The nail gun was capable of banging
roofing nails through six-by-six beams—or a turned
vampire's head—using compressed air. The clip looked

like something off an AK-47. Every nail in the lethal row had been dipped in liquid nitrogen.

Gil had won the lottery from hell without knowing it, so he would be taken care of first. The question was how to lure him over. Vladimir's second in command was on the other side of the main area, now on a different level.

Besides the nail gun, Nick had a pistol. The impact of a fired bullet would knock him back long enough for Nick to go for the nail gun.

It'd be nice if the construction crew would start hammering on things or busting up Sheetrock. A nail gun made a pretty big bang. He didn't want to attract attention to himself, not when he had to rescue Jane from the lower level with no fucking backup. Once he iced Gil, he was heading for the stairs to the doors with keypads.

Nick attached the long stub of a silencer to his gun and smacked the ammo clip into place with his palm. He could admit it to himself now. Killing some of the vamps on The List hadn't been easy for him. Easier than killing Gary, sure, but before each kill he'd been plagued by an inner voice reminding him the turned vampires had once been human soldiers. But here and now? Well, putting a bullet into a child-porn-selling vampire freak wasn't going to make him lose any sleep.

He heard footsteps. Gil was on his level, walking toward him around a curve without seeing him yet. In another minute, they'd be face to face.

Nick waited. Then he called in a low voice when Gil was closer, "Hey, where's the work outlet up here? Mr. Ouspensky asked me to check. Said it was sparking."

Gil came closer, looking annoyed. "He doesn't know what he's talking about. Who are you?"

"Freddy George. I'm with the electrician's crew."

CHAPTER
TWENTY-NINE

Barrett grabbed the arm of a dancer passing by, not one of the airheads, and asked her to cover the station for fifteen minutes. The dancer was happy to oblige. Maybe she wanted the position. Barrett didn't look back as she walked into the main room.

Lewis, the bouncer who'd tried to get rid of Xecala, was pacing on the empty runway. Now and then he talked into a mike clipped to his shoulder. She walked in his direction. The long, white-silver gown she'd chosen fell in swishing folds from her hips. It was skintight everywhere else.

The folds now concealed a pocket in the seam into which she'd slipped the small, flat gun Nick had left with her. She'd run into a bathroom stall with her evening bag, which held a tiny sewing kit and manicure scissors as well as her newly issued club ID and basic makeup. It had taken her only five minutes to pick open a seam and cut the pocket out of her bag, stitching it into the seam. Only about an hour was left until the VIPs started arriving.

Seeing Sam, Barrett raised her hand, waved, then hurried to meet her. Her superlong fake ponytail had been replaced by a sleek cropped wig. Enormous gold hoops and a lot of eyeliner kept all the attention on her face. The rest of her clothes were casual.

"Hey, Sam. I love the short hair. What are you going to wear?"

Good thing Nick knew plenty about wiring, because Gil Mansfield didn't. As Nick kept up a steady stream of chatter, Mansfield looked confused but determined not to confess his ignorance. The gun and silencer stayed behind Nick's back. He gestured a lot with the other hand.

He should fan out a deck of cards for this fuck and tell him to pick one, then shoot. Pistol to drop him, nail gun to kill him.

Nick kept talking.

"Haven't decided," Sam told Barrett. "But you stick with that white dress, girl. That is a stunning look. Do you believe we still have work crews coming in up here? Now whose big idea was that? I can guess. It's going to screw up tonight's event." She didn't sound like that would bother her in the least.

"The guests are going to be here soon," she confirmed. She wondered where Nick was, not wanting to be obvious about scanning the tiers. Then she glimpsed him, standing behind a balcony wall at the very top of the huge main room. He shook his head at her and ducked down.

She was glad he was there. Barrett forced herself to look elsewhere. Sam had already turned to help a bottle girl tug down her microscopic dress.

"Do you think it's too short?" the girl asked.

"I can see your lace panties," Sam replied mischievously. "But that's good. The men have to know where to put the money."

Barrett heard a dull pop from high above and checked

her watch. Nine minutes had passed. If she guessed right, Gil Mansfield was dead. She knew what a silenced shot sounded like. The quiet club reverberated almost noiselessly for a few seconds longer.

Nick kneeled beside Gil's twitching body to finish the job. The nail gun had a contact trigger and the poisoned nails had to be fired straight into his heart.

He paused, looking into Gil's clouded eyes. If there was a trace of humanity in them, he didn't see it. His brother . . . that had been different. Very different. Now, Nick felt nothing.

He fired once. Then stood and packed up. Except for the pistol, a lock-pick set, and the items for Jane, he had to leave everything behind. There was nothing in the tool chest that was traceable to him. He reversed the jacket to the dark side, then stashed the hard hat and whipped off the bandanna, sticking it into an inner pocket. The folded clothes got stuffed into one patch pocket, and the thin flat shoes went into the other. Ball cap. Sports glasses.

And presto. He was someone else. The door on the main level was his next stop.

Nick looked at the crumpled form of the man by his feet, knowing that the numbness he worked so hard to maintain never lasted that long. He'd taken a life. More than anything he wanted this to be the last time he had to do that.

But the hunt wasn't over. He wasn't free of this shit yet.

He searched his mind for a reasonable rationale. There were a few.

Another one could be checked off The List. The worst of them all, considering what Gil was doing on the side. The fact that Gil was turned, and the FBI had ordered him taken out, was almost beside the point. There was such a thing as a deserved death. And now there was one less obstacle in the way of Nick's finding Jane.

He hunkered down by the body and closed the staring eyes, resting his hand over them for a little while until they stayed closed. Then he dragged the body into a corner, out of sight.

Barrett had heard the bang of the gun and, more recently, the fainter echo of the nail gun as Nick finished the job. No one else seemed to have noticed either. Sam and the dancer in the short dress had already left the room. She went back to the hostess station.

"Thanks so much," she said to the girl who'd stood in for her.

"Anytime."

Barrett adjusted the position of the monitor and pulled up the hacked-into security feed for all of Club Red again, minimizing it into a corner. The feed from the top level where Nick had been was a blank gray box. She clicked out, moving to the camera covering one of the keypad doors. No telling which one he'd try first, but she would cycle through all three doors until he turned up. What would happen next was a lot less predictable. If there were cameras on the lowest, hidden level, she hadn't been able to access them. Could be a completely separate system.

Which brought up the question of who besides her would be watching Nick if there was one.

Obsessively, she checked the doors one after the other, still minimizing the feed in a view window she could instantly shut down. She might be able to guess which one he'd come back through if she knew which one he would take to go down.

Then she saw him. Door two. The one used least

often. Nick punched in the keypad numbers so swiftly his hand was a blur on the video feed. In another second he was through it and closing it behind him. She hadn't even glimpsed his face.

Barrett stiffened her spine. Even with his back to her, even blurred on the security system camera, the way he moved was resolute and swift. Still, she would have liked to see his face . . . one last time. She told herself not to think that way.

"You okay?"

One of the bouncers.

"Oh—yes. I was just thinking about—you know." She flipped her hair back over her shoulder and gave him a flirty look. "About tonight. After this is all over."

He winked at her. Go ahead and fill in the goddamn blank any way you like, Barrett thought.

"Hot date, huh? That's cool. I don't need to know more."

She forced a smile.

CHAPTER THIRTY

Nick went down a set of stairs with concrete walls and came out in darkness, outside of the circle of light that surrounded a deep, square pit. Above that hung a wire cage big enough for two combatants.

Had to be for mixed martial arts. Looked like Ouspensky was staging illegal fights when he wasn't selling underage girls. Nick didn't see an auction block. Maybe the victims got paraded past the customers as bids were placed.

There were tables surrounding the pit. Red velvet chairs encircled them and red velvet armchairs had been set closest to the pit. A setup crew was bringing in tables, rolling them on their edges like giant toys as a banquet manager directed their placement. Wait staff stood ready with plates and glasses and cutlery on trays.

There were a lot of them. Standing in the light the way they were, they didn't seem to see him. Nick edged through the darkened perimeter, looking for a doorway or a niche to hide in for a bit. The cells couldn't be on this level. His quick visual assessment told him that the basic dimensions of the main room above and this differently constructed arena below matched.

The banquet staff chatted and joked as they worked. Then he saw a guard lumber forward, coming up out of a narrow staircase that didn't connect to the one he'd used. A second guard followed.

The burly men grinned at each other and one gestured toward several young waitresses. It didn't take long for them to stroll over, thumbs in their belt loops, their gear clanking. Handcuffs, short length of coiled rope, billy club, mace, walkie-talkie, and a holstered gun.

Nick was infinitely grateful they didn't have dogs.

There could be another guard below. He would have to take that chance. When the two men started chatting up the young waitresses, he made his move.

Down. And gone. He didn't look back.

A wire door made out of the same stuff as the fight cage had been shut at the bottom of the narrow staircase. Nick looked through it, listening intently for signs of life.

The lowest level was eerily quiet.

He tried the doorknob. Locked. It wouldn't have been if there was nothing down here. Good thing there was no keypad. He took out an all-purpose pick and got it open, closing the wire door behind him without making a sound.

A long corridor extended in either direction. Dim overhead bulbs flickered on and off—motion sensitive, he realized. Cheap ones that didn't work too well. But that was to his advantage. The place reminded him of a low-rent storage facility.

There were the cells. Which one held Jane?

A low growl came from the first. Nick saw massive hands curled around the bars. Then he heard a faint noise.

Sniffing. Something in that cell was trying to figure out what he was. It growled.

Fuck. He would have to get past it to look into the other cells and it didn't sound too friendly. Nick waited, checking his watch, tracking the seconds, then the minutes. In a little while, the hands uncurled and the creature moved back into the shadows of its cell.

There was a scrape of metal on concrete and Nick heard guzzling, as if the thing had stuck its face into its water dish for a drink.

He went quickly past the cell, getting the impression of something hulking in the corner. Nick stopped at each empty cell and looked in. They looked clean and unused. Jane had to be the first victim for sale in the new club.

The last cell was by itself, separated from the others by a storage closet. If Jane was here, she was in it.

This far down the corridor he couldn't hear the creature sniffing and grumbling. But he did hear a soft breathing. Nick stopped and looked through the bars of the last cell just as the bulb overhead flickered off. A slender hand shot out and tried to claw his face.

He dodged it, swearing silently, grateful he had on the sports glasses, and stepped back.

"Jane."

"Fuck off."

"There's not much time. I came to get you." He would swear the creature in the first cell had pricked up its ears. He'd done one too damn many undercover operations not to be aware when someone—or in this case, something—was listening.

For someone who was terrified, she was tough.

"Who are you?" The whispering voice was female and young. She had stepped back into the shadows of her cell.

"I'm with the FBI. Barrett sent me."

There was a pause. He heard her sharp inward breath. "She was my mother's friend."

The young girl inside the cell moved into the dim light where Nick could see her. She wore a thin, short dress that barely covered her body and her feet were bare. Barrett's guess had been a good one. It wasn't the same outfit Jane had been wearing in the transport cell but it was just as skimpy.

"Here." He handed the folded clothes and slipperlike shoes through the bars. "Change into these while I pick the lock."

She hesitated, an expression of fear in her wide eyes.

"I won't look. Step back where you were before." He kneeled and started working on the lock, inserting different picks until he found the one that worked. Good thing the cells weren't electronically locked, either. Keeping girls penned up wasn't that hard. That didn't apply to the creature. Maybe it was too stupid to escape.

Nick listened for the barely audible sounds of the lock's inner mechanism. There it was. A little more fiddling and he had it.

He swung the cell door open but Jane hesitated. She almost stumbled as she crossed the threshold. Even brief captivity changed people, making them fearful and uncertain. Then she met his gaze. Nick was surprised by the fierce look in her eyes that made her seem a lot older than seventeen.

"You have to follow me," he said quietly. "Not too close. We're going to walk up the stairs and wait until I give you the sign to go. They're setting up tables around the arena. We have to move fast. Once we're on the main level, we're going to walk out as if we own the place. Don't look around too much and try not to stop."

"Okay. I sort of know the way. But you can go first."

There was the sound of heavy flesh hitting the floor or slamming against the walls, as if the creature inside the first cell had sprawled out or was upright, scratching its back like a bear.

"What is that thing?" Nick asked in a low voice.

"It doesn't talk. Just groans sometimes. And gnashes its teeth. I heard someone refer to it as Murphy."

Fuck. Tim Murphy. He'd been taken from Nick's

mountain and brought here. By the looks of his swollen hands and the noises he made, it seemed Murphy's deterioration had progressed significantly. For a split second, Nick thought about putting the poor bastard out of his misery and checking another turned off his list, but he didn't have time. He had to get Jane and Barrett to safety.

By the time Barrett had left the hostess station at Vlad's request, the nearest spaces to the front doors were filled with luxury vehicles and SUVs. Tinted glass was everywhere and so were dark glasses. For sure, a club affectation, worn after sundown to look cool—and for a vampire, to conceal silver pupils.

She had no idea who was human and who wasn't. The sleek suits had a devil-may-care expensiveness to them. No women. No need, given the strippers that would be performing on the main level and the fact Jane—barely a woman—was about to go on the block somewhere close.

Nick had keys to both cars. They were parked in different places, with Justine at the wheel of one. Whichever car he and Jane reached first would be their getaway vehicle.

"An excellent turnout." Vladimir shouted to be heard above the music that had started to blare about five minutes earlier. Lights flashed. Dancers began to gyrate. "I want to introduce you to some people. Come."

Reluctantly, Barrett accompanied Vladimir as he introduced her to one guest after another. It was almost twenty minutes before Barrett could get back to the hostess station and check on the hacked feed. To her dismay, there was still no sign of Nick. She was about to close the view window when she saw him. The ball cap was pulled down over his forehead, preventing her from seeing his face. But his clothes were different.

Barrett almost gasped out loud when she saw Jane, wearing the clothes Barrett had sent with Nick. She was right behind him. She glanced nervously from side to side but she kept moving.

Barrett minimized the window, sensing without seeing him that Vladimir was somewhere nearby and heading her way. Her senses were on high alert. Nick knew enough about the club's layout to choose among several possible escape routes, but none were hidden.

She saw her boss in the near distance, absorbed in whatever he was looking at on the screen of the smartphone in his hand.

She risked another peek at the view window. Nick and Jane were heading down the corridor where the rehearsal studio was. They seemed to be alone, thank God. And walking like they belonged there.

Just about every great escape happened the same way.

But a lot depended on who might see them. The banquet staff that had been hired for the private event had no idea who was supposed to be in the club and who wasn't. Tonight, with the junket over, the boisterous media crowd gone, and a much smaller group of well-heeled patrons coming in, Nick might stand out. One of the guards or bouncers could pick up on an unfamiliar guy and girl walking around.

Somehow he had dodged the guards on the lowest level.

The construction-worker disguise had served its purpose to get through the main area. She wondered where he'd stashed the hard hat and the tool chest. At least Jane could pass for a dancer in street clothes.

He wouldn't go out through the front doors. She would have to ignore him if he did.

Vlad went by the hostess station with only a nod to

her, greeted by a tall male dressed all in black. The two of them exchanged murmured conversation that seemed to be about nothing in particular, and moved away.

For several minutes, Barrett stayed where she was, being decorative. Then she gave in to temptation and checked on Nick. He and Jane had reached a curve in the corner that blocked the security camera's view.

Barrett switched to another camera. There was Vlad and his friend. The boss of Club Red had his smartphone out again. She tapped a key to zoom in on the screen, realizing with horror that he was looking at the same feed she had, transmitted wirelessly to the phone, able to switch to different locations at a touch.

She swore under her breath. If she could see Jane and Nick, so could Vlad. By her guess, he hadn't yet. His casual demeanor told her that he was simply strolling with his friend, maybe heading for the rehearsal studio to hook him up with a hot dancer.

Barrett abandoned the monitor and walked fast until she was out of sight of the people milling around in the front of the club. Then she ran.

She might not get to Nick in time. The long, swirling dress tangled around her ankles.

A wrong turn cost her precious seconds, but she finally got close to Jane, gasping when the girl whirled around, alerted by the sound of running footsteps.

"Barrett?"

Nick turned, too—just as Vladimir Ouspensky nearly slammed into them both. A red exit sign glowed dully at the end of an isolated corridor. The tall male in black was beside him. He narrowed his eyes, and a crimson glint flashed in their depths.

Nick whipped around, his body tense and obviously in fight mode, but Vladimir's fist plowed into his ribs and lifted him up in the air, sending him crashing against a wall.

Vladimir gave Barrett a pleasant smile. He wasn't even breathing hard. "Aren't you supposed to be up front?"

"I—I had to go—" She struggled to respond, half thinking this wasn't happening.

In another second, Vlad had her by the throat. "So. You know Jane." He turned to the girl, who tried to bite the long-fingered, repulsively white hand clamped over her mouth as she kicked against the leg that restrained her in an obscene position.

Vladimir shook his head. "Little bitch. I knew she was hiding something from me. But not how. She wore no gold. Unlike you."

With a hard jerk, he ripped Barrett's ever-present bracelet off. Then he began to probe her mind and rape her memory, learning everything that he had not known. Bit by bit, the secrets she'd kept were ripped out of her brain. His deep, agonizingly thorough mind reading was excruciatingly painful. Barrett fought it to no avail. She floated in and out of consciousness.

Jane was watching, she knew that. Until the tall vampire covered the girl's frightened eyes with a black blindfold and tied it, getting her hair caught in the knot, and slapping her viciously when she cried out.

Barrett moaned. Nick heard her and tried to crawl up the wall and stand.

She heard herself screaming as she watched Vladimir and the other vampire kick him senseless. Vlad's thugs moved in when those two stepped aside.

Nick screamed.

She blacked out.

CHAPTER
THIRTY-ONE

Nick regained consciousness in a cage.

The cage. The one he knew was even now swinging above the pit in Vladimir's underground fighting arena.

He was bound with shackles around his wrists and ankles, helpless prey. His chest was bare and slick with sweat and blood. He was barefoot.

Tim Murphy was on the other side of the cage, his massive hands, which had once been wrapped around Barrett's throat, clutching the heavy black wire. He looked barely human anymore, with rotting flesh distorting his features. Thank God, Nick thought. Thank God Gary never suffered through this.

Murphy spit at Nick.

He used his shoulder to wipe the foul slime off his face.

Murphy bent his scabbed knees. Again and again. He was making the cage swing over the pit.

Huge torches set in basins supported by pillars threw flames high into the underground arena. Their red light seemed to bathe the arena in living blood.

"If I may have your attention." Vladimir's voice boomed and echoed. There were not enough guests to fill the underground space. But they looked eager for the show to begin.

"One of tonight's combatants has been forced to cancel. But we have found a worthy opponent for Tim Murphy! Let us call him the Man of Iron." The sarcastic edge in his voice got scattered laughter. "Those of you who joined me in subduing him earlier know how strong he is. Let's test that strength, shall we?"

Applause. Restrained but enthusiastic.

Hundreds of black and silver eyes peered up at Nick, their cold shimmer communicating evil intent. The monster didn't seem half as bad as they were.

Nick looked down through the wire, queasy from the swinging motion and the beating he'd undergone. Where were Barrett and Jane? Vladimir answered that question soon enough.

"The auction is postponed until after the fight. Of course," he said with a smirk, "if the Man of Iron wins, he and the women will go free!"

That surprised Nick. He'd suspect it was a lie, only he knew vampires were biologically incapable of uttering falsehoods. Which meant, of course, that Vladimir was damn certain Nick wasn't going to win. In truth, he didn't believe it, either.

A roving spotlight picked out Barrett and Jane, tied to chairs and to each other. Both were gagged.

A door on the cage's side unlatched, dragged up by a rope from high above. The cage tilted. Nick was dumped out onto a stage set.

A woman who looked like the "Sam" Barrett had described came strolling down the runway, her long dress whispering against her silken legs. The metallic fabric caught the light and reflected it out into the crowd when the roving spotlight hit her. She turned and struck a pose, extending one leg and displaying a garter, which she slid up and down her toned thigh to the cheers of the crowd. Then she started to sing, getting louder and louder, making them beg for an encore. She obliged with a classic show tune, putting a fresh spin on the lyrics.

"My heart belongs to Vladdy! Oh yes it does!"

She walked on to where Nick had been dumped, teasing him, working the crowd, which roared with laughter. She dragged him up with the strength of a man, Nick thought groggily.

Sam's long fingers moved over his fly, cupping and squeezing. She splayed her hand, digging her red fingernails into the material of his pants.

"Should I?" she purred. The small crowd howled a collective yes. She slid the button out of the buttonhole at the top of his fly. Then she plucked at the zipper tab.

She wasn't the stripper. *He* was. Or the strippee. He couldn't think. The beating he'd taken from Vlad and his goons was clouding his mind again.

Little by little, she pulled the zipper down, then slid her hand inside his pants, curving her fingers around the front of his briefs and pulling out the heavy flesh of his still-hidden cock and balls. She rested them on the vee of his open fly.

"Don't they say the low-hangin' fruit tastes best?" Her sultry voice was so resonant it reached the back rows. "And don't those hang nice?"

Dazed, he wondered where she'd learned to make herself heard without a mike. A church choir, maybe. The lady could sing. It made sense in a weird way. Nothing else did. Nick heard catcalls and jeers inside waves of noise. It was hard for him to tell how many were watching.

Sam kept toying with him. Then she pressed her face to his as if she wanted to kiss him. Her slick lips never touched his skin. Jesus. Of course not. His mind began to focus.

This was an act, even if she was making it up as she went along, and she wasn't going to mess up her flawless makeup as she sent him to his doom. Barrett thought of Sam as an ally. Was she playing Vlad or had she been playing them? Fucking bitch. If it weren't for the metal cuffs biting into his ankles and wrists, he'd send her sailing.

Sam flirted with the audience, giving them what they'd come to see. She slid her body against his, up and down, nearly squatting on her high-heeled platform shoes and slithering up again. She pressed against him, regaining eye contact. She was more than tall enough. Her body heat was bringing him back to a semblance of life.

Spectacular rack, he thought dazedly. Strangely firm.

Her hips ground against his. Hard and fast. Nick suddenly realized what else Sam had beneath that dress.

She was trans. Pre-op trans with a fully functional cock. Had Barrett known?

"Take what I'm giving you, white boy!

The audience laughed raucously and echoed her. *"Take it!"*

Sam's lips reached his ear. She breathed into it. Licked the outer rim. Pushed his hair back and thrust the tip of her tongue into it so the appreciative onlookers could see.

Her hands were just as busy.

Nick tuned out his awareness of her grabs and rough caresses. It was all he could do. Then he realized that Sam was talking to him while her tongue was moving. In a much lower register.

"Listen to me and listen good," she muttered. "You gonna need this in the cage."

Her hand slid down inside his briefs, rubbing him up and down with her palm flat to his skin. Nick felt smooth metal press against his groin and the unmistakable edge of some kind of blade. Placed just within reach of his bound hands.

Sam moved her lips to his other ear, undulating against him and keeping up the show while talking to him in the same low voice.

"That's my lucky shiv. It's covered in liquid nitrogen and it's also sharper than fuck. You need to cut out Vlad's heart and burn it."

Nick's body jerked. Sam was indeed an ally. She'd just told Nick how to kill a born vampire. It reeked of not so much trust as desperation. She hadn't told Barrett how it was done but now that Nick had been captured . . .

"Thank you," he muttered.

"You can thank me by killing Vlad. But fight standing or you'll cut off your dick. And that would be a crying shame. It's a real nice dick."

Grinning, Sam withdrew her hand and waved at her fans, ostentatiously licking her glossy lips.

"He's giving me something I can *feel*!" she shouted. "The boy is *blessed*!" She held her index fingers far apart to indicate exactly how blessed Nick was. "Wish I could rip off his clothes right now!"

Roars of laughter.

Sam strutted around him, fondling whatever she could reach.

"Should I keep on?" she asked the onlookers. "Or should I quit? I just don't know. Tell me, people. Make some *noise*!"

Incoherent responses, for and against.

"Guess I have to stop," Sam declared loudly, fluttering her fake eyelashes with mock regret. She stuffed his junk back into his jeans and zipped them up. "If I make him come right here and right now, he won't have no fight left in him."

She patted Nick's face, stroking the stubble, pressing her lips to his. "One last kiss," she purred. "It could be the last one you ever get."

He didn't even flinch away from her kiss. Fuck his pride. He'd kiss Sam all over again once he was outta here if he needed to. Nick bit his lip until the blood flowed down his chin, willing himself to not pass out, searching for Barrett and Jane. They were out of the spotlight now, behind Vladimir, still bound and gagged.

He couldn't lie down and die. He would fight for them. Losing was not an option.

Some flunky shoved Nick down onto the stage. To his surprise, he felt the handcuffs and shackles being unlocked. Wincing, he rubbed his wrists and sat up. Then he stood up. The cage lowered. Before it touched the stage he reached up and hauled himself into it.

The fight was on.

Murphy swung the cage. Nick tried to stand and fell on his knees. Whoever had control of the rope that closed the door forgot about it. The open door swung and banged.

An unearthly roar hurt his ears. Murphy staggered toward him.

Nick pressed his hands against his groin like he was wiping off sweat. He felt the hidden shiv. Blood seeped through the material where the sharp edge had cut him.

Murphy lunged at Nick, arms open. Nick balanced—barely. He got closer. The shiv fit into his palm, dangerously slick from his blood. His fingers gripped it and he thrust the shiv through the slack, rotten-feeling skin of Murphy's chest and into his heart, then drew the blade completely out again. Murphy's scabby knees buckled and he fell against the wire cage, making it swing again.

Nick kept his balance and swayed with it. Still gripping the blade, he watched Murphy take his last breath. That left Vladimir.

Nick bent his knees and made the cage swing again.

The audience was stunned into silence. A few vampires were heading for the exits. Most stayed, looking at Vladimir, loyal to their own kind.

Nick was past caring. Pure adrenaline had burned off

the last of his grogginess and the visceral triumph of his win drove him on. He no longer felt pain.

Vladimir seemed to grow larger and taller as he watched Nick. He didn't rush at him. Just waited. Sizing up his opponent and calculating his advantage.

Nick tumbled out, scrambling to his feet and heading straight for Vladimir.

He slammed into him with bone-crunching force but the vampire grabbed his wrist, stopping the blade from plunging into his chest. It was Nick who got hurt. He'd tried to tackle the living embodiment of evil, concentrated power. Vladimir was still as a statue. Only his eyes moved, boring into Nick's with the precision of a retina scanner.

Nick felt something stir in his skull. The vampire was reading his mind. He didn't need to guess at Nick's strategy when his brain was an open book.

Vladimir smiled when Nick dropped the blade, clutched his head, and fell to his knees, swallowing a scream. There was a burst of noise and pain. The mind probe stopped.

Nick could see again. Barely. Barrett had somehow gotten a hand free. She held a gun and fired again. And again.

The first bullet crept out from Vladimir's forehead, falling at his feet. Another exited his shoulder. Blood spurted uncontrollably as the second bullet reappeared. Strong as he was, the vampire had taken a hit.

The shiv. Nick felt for it. If he could slash through to the heart . . . tear it out bodily . . . and burn it while it was beating . . . He stood.

His hand hid the blade as he struck out with the last of his strength. The vampire's fine white shirt gushed blood in torrents. Another bullet crawled out of his flesh.

Vladimir staggered back. The wall behind him prevented his escape. Nick reached into the jagged wound and searched for the heart.

For a second he wondered if the vampire had one. Then his big hand closed around a throbbing knot of smooth muscle. He squeezed it and Vladimir moaned. With a supreme effort, Nick yanked it from the blood vessels that moored it in the vampire's chest. By chance the roving spotlight hit the heart as Nick held it high.

Vladimir's comrades in blood were riveted by the sight, too appalled to seize the murderer of one of their own. Several more rose from their seats and backed away into the darkness.

Nick was taking no chances with this heart. He didn't see Vladimir collapse as he ran toward the nearest torch. In it went.

The scorching black smoke released by the fireball and explosion had the rest of the vampires on the run. Chaos. Pandemonium. None of it bothered Nick. He prayed the drifting smoke wouldn't harm Barrett and Jane.

He had won. He didn't care. All he could think about was them.

Barrett was kneeling by the girl when he ran back, chopping at her wrists and then at her ankles with the dropped shiv.

How in hell had she gotten free—Nick looked around. He knew. Sam was nowhere to be seen. He hoped she'd escaped. She had to have escaped.

The crumpled body of the dead vampire lay motionless in a spreading pool of dark blood.

His heart was likely black and shriveled.

Nick ran to the woman that held *his* heart.

Barrett.

CHAPTER
THIRTY-TWO

It was early morning before the scene was even close to processed. Both army personnel and members of the FBI, including Special Agent Kyle Mahone, arrived first, containing the area and ordering some hard-core EMTs in masked biohazard suits to see to Nick.

According to Mahone, Director Rick Hallifax wanted to see both Nick and Barrett, who was also being seen by the EMTs, in his office the next day. Nick told Mahone what he thought of that idea in precise terms. Mahone just smiled and said he'd pass the message along, but that when said meeting *did* take place, Mahone planned on being there. It was time, he said, to start putting pressure on Hallifax so they could figure out just how many individual vampire-related operations he had going on.

As for now, the cleanup of Club Red was continuing. There were two disinfectant-drenched body bags awaiting transport on gurneys. Ambulances came and went. FBI town cars pulled up and took off.

Nick refused to go to a hospital. Some joker pointed out that no hospital would want him. For now, Nick lay on an uncomfortable cot, covered in a space blanket, and stared up at the clouds drifting across the dawn sky.

He thought of everything that had happened.

He thought of Gary.

And as much as that still hurt, it felt pretty good to be alive.

But he wanted Barrett.

Barrett sat on a makeshift bench with Jane folded in her arms, noting that the girl hadn't cried, not once. She was strong, maybe too strong, and Barrett wondered if the death of her mother had forever taken away her ability to experience the lighter side of life. Was that why she'd been drawn to that fang banger Dante? Had she sought that darkness out, and would she continue to do so now given everything she'd been through?

She caught a glimpse of Nick sitting on a cot, talking to an older man in fatigues and aviator sunglasses. High rank, by his stance. The man looked over Nick's shoulder in Barrett's direction.

A catastrophe had been averted. The aftermath was a letdown. The clipboard people showed up and took over. Barrett was exhausted, too, but she'd stay with Jane as long as she was needed.

Someone had provided Jane fresh clothes, including a belt to hold up pants that were too baggy for her. Which was what the kids were wearing anyway, Barrett thought with a flicker of weary amusement. She'd been given a set of clean scrubs after someone took her gown away for microscopic examination of the bloodstains and DNA sampling.

Jane shifted, lifting her head from Barrett's shoulder and pushing back her hair.

"You okay?" Barrett asked.

Jane hesitated then nodded. "I think I will be."

"Do you—do you want to talk about Dante? About what happened to him?"

Her expression went blank. "He's dead, isn't he?"

"Yes."

"Then that's all I need to know." She looked away. Looked back at Barrett. "He fought the guys who grabbed me. Even though he was . . . you know . . . he was a good guy."

Barrett nodded. "I'm glad you knew him. He died doing a noble thing."

"People judged him because he was into vampires."

"Yes," she said.

"I—I don't want to be like that, but . . . there are more vampires, aren't there? More . . . like *him*."

"Like him, yes. But also some that aren't. I'm friends with a few."

Jane's eyes rounded. "Friends?"

"Monsters come in all shapes and forms and races. And sometimes they aren't always monsters. That's what makes spotting the true monsters so difficult." She squeezed Jane's hand. "That's why when we have people who care about us, we need to stick together."

Jane's mouth tightened and she withdrew her hand. "You didn't stick by me. You disappeared and I—I needed you." The tears Jane had refused to shed now dampened her eyes and Barrett felt her own tears welling.

"I'm sorry, Jane. I know it's no excuse, but I had my own stuff I was dealing with. My brother died. Then your mom. Then I was in the army . . . But you're right. I shouldn't have lost touch with you. If you give me another chance, I promise I won't lose touch again. Do you think you can give me that?"

Again, that slight hesitation. This time Barrett held her breath. She released it when Jane nodded. "I think I can. After all, you saved me. You saw me on that camera and you came after me. You brought Nick. And I don't think you would have stopped until you found me."

"I wouldn't have," Barrett confirmed.

Jane swiped at her eyes, clearly embarrassed by her

show of emotion, "So now what? Are you heading back to D.C.? Nick told me you live there."

"Yes, eventually. But we need to decide about you. I know you've had problems with your uncle—"

"He's—he's dead," Jane said quickly.

Barrett's eyes rounded in shock. "What? But who . . ." She paused. Thought about it. "Mansfield?"

Jane nodded. "That's what he claimed anyway. And I don't even know if I want it to be true. All I know is . . . I want Ginny."

"I already had someone call her. I was told she was on her way."

Jane's shoulders relaxed slightly. "Good. That's good."

"You'll talk to someone? About everything that's happened? It doesn't have to be me but . . ."

Jane nodded. "I'll talk to someone. And if I need to . . . if I want to . . . can I call you?"

"Anytime. I hope you'll call me often."

For the first time since they'd seen each other again, Jane smiled, and her smile was beautiful, just as her mother's had been.

They sat in comfortable silence for a few minutes before Jane looked suddenly alert. "There's Ginny." She got up, waving to the older woman at the wheel of an approaching car. Ginny's drawn face brightened when she saw Jane. She parked her car, got out, and spoke to an FBI agent. Jane turned to Barrett. "I want to see you again, sometime soon. I know you and my mother were really good friends."

"We were. I'm very grateful I had her in my life—I just wish we'd had more time. But you don't always get what you wish for."

"I did. I'm free."

"Yes. Stay safe. And I would really like to stay in touch. Let me know when you're ready."

"I will." Jane gave her another smile and hugged Barrett tightly before walking away. Kevin had brought Aura to the parking lot. Barrett watched the wild-haired dog sniff at the cars and indicate vampire scent on several.

A tow truck rumbled through.

Aura's pup, Ray, was making the rounds, too, with a handler Barrett didn't know. He sat and indicated a police cruiser, wagging his tail.

Barrett smiled when she saw Nick, also smiling, walking toward her. "He's a rookie," he called. "But he's getting the hang of it."

He took Aura's leash from Kevin and the two of them trotted over to the bench. "You look like you need to hug a dog," Nick said. "Got a good one for you."

Aura gave Barrett a golden-eyed stare, then peered over her shoulder at Kevin, anxious to get back to work. Nick let go of her leash and the dog ran back to him.

"It's okay. I'd rather have a hug from a good man. An amazingly good man."

"You left out the part about me being a fighter and a lover."

"That, too." Barrett nestled into his shoulder as Nick wrapped an arm around her. "Just tell me that it's really over. I sort of don't believe it."

"It's over. Try not to think about it too much right now. I got you." He held her for a long time.

EPILOGUE

Several months later . . .

"Get up, angel." A strong hand caressed Barrett's hip, swooping down over her waist and up against her ribs. Which Nick tickled.

"Stop it." She burrowed back into the pillows and blankets, kicking backward at him. The masculine body curled around hers didn't budge.

"No. I want some coffee, Barrett. You owe me. I saved your life."

"Doesn't mean I have to get up right here and now."

"Yes you do," he insisted. "I set up the filter and filled it with fresh ground coffee last night. So all you have to do is get up and press the button on the coffeemaker. Just once."

"No deal," she said into her pillow, laughing. "Not even once."

"Okay. Then how about you press the button for, oh, the next seventy years. That would be twenty-five thousand nine hundred and fifteen times or so."

"You figured that out before you said it. Way before. Why?"

"I like doing multiplication in the morning."

That wasn't all he liked doing in the morning. Barrett grinned secretly at the feel of the delicious hardness bumping against the small of her back.

"Really." She turned her head to look at him. He tousled her messy hair even worse. "Just what the—"

"Don't say that word. Unless you want me to make your dreams come true." His hand slipped down between her thighs.

She grabbed it and shoved it away, turning her back to him again. He captured her hand by the wrist.

"All it takes is one finger to push a button," he whispered in her ear. "I choose this one."

Barrett felt something warm and round slide over her fourth finger, left hand. A marquise diamond in a plain platinum setting blazed with morning light when she sat bolt upright to stare at it.

"Nick? Are you serious?"

"Yes. I love you. So say yes, goddamn it."

She rolled over on top of him, kissing his face, his neck, his chest . . . it got better. The two of them had always known how.

After a while they were one. Coming together. That was the best. *Then* she said yes. Several times.

ACKNOWLEDGMENTS

Thank you to my friends and family who boost me up not only in my writing journey but in life. Most of all, thank you to my fans, including Crystal Blood, who is always such a huge support. Thank you also to Miranda Grissom for all your help. You rock! As always, much love to my boys, Craig, Joshua, Ethan, and Zachary. A film deal someday would be great, but I have everything I need in all of you. Love you bunches!

Find out more about the Belladonna Agency in Virna DePaul's first book in the series

TURNED

Seattle, Washington
A few weeks later . . .

Back in the Bronx, Eliana Maria Garcia's weapons of choice had been a smart mouth, the occasional threat of a knife, and her fists. Now, standing with her back pressed against the brick wall behind Monk's Café, Ana Martin had something even better—a gun. One she was hoping she wouldn't have to use.

Confronting the man who'd been following her, however, was unavoidable. She'd noticed him at the bank yesterday, then the market. But last night she'd seen him outside her house. And moments before? Across the street.

That was one coincidence too many. She'd left Primos Sangre over seven years ago, but if there was one thing the gang had taught her, it was that survival meant confronting danger head-on rather than running from it. Since she didn't trust the cops—didn't trust anyone—her only choice was to handle this herself. Her way.

If only she wasn't so scared. But she'd put her old life behind her, and even though she wasn't happy—could never be happy without her sister—she was often content. Sometimes when she looked in the mirror she even managed to like the person she saw looking back at her.

The thought of losing that scared her more than any threat of physical harm ever could. And it scared her enough that she was willing to fight to make sure it didn't happen.

The sun had set long ago. Now and then a stab of light from a passing car pierced the shadows of the alley where Ana was hiding, forcing her to dodge back. Invisible, shrouded in darkness, she waited. When she heard footsteps, she knew it was him.

Forcing her near-numb fingers to tighten their grip on the gun, she watched as he walked past her, then made her move, coming at him from behind, pressing the barrel of her gun against the back of his head.

He didn't even jerk.

From the back, he looked big. Broad. Muscles rippling. Dangerous.

But from the front? Even from a distance, he'd looked more than dangerous. He'd looked deadly. Beyond handsome. Midnight hair and eyes just as dark. Savage and sophisticated at the same time. She'd never seen his equal. Certainly never met anyone that came close.

Part of her knew she'd gotten the drop on him a bit too easily. That perhaps she was doing exactly what he'd been expecting. Hoping.

But it was too late to go back now.

"Hands where I can see them," she managed to get out.

Slowly, he raised his hands in surrender. Only she still wasn't buying it. Her nerves screamed at her to run, but logic kept her feet planted firmly on the ground. Somehow, she knew if she ran, he'd only come after her.

"Why are you following me?"

No answer. No surprise.

With her free hand, she patted him down, the way she'd learned to do in the gang. By the time she'd frisked him from the back, she was the one who was sweating. And not from exertion.

Nothing about him was small. He was tall and buff, more than big enough to overpower her slight frame. Sangre-style paranoia set in, and it occurred to her that this guy might be undercover. She instantly recalled the run-ins she'd had with cops as a teenager. The way they'd often pulled her long dark ponytail, hard enough to make her back arch and breasts lift. The way they'd sometimes copped a feel or implied they'd leave her in peace if she made it worth their while. She'd never given them that satisfaction.

But no, she decided. This guy's vibe was just too different. Not so much cop as outlaw.

His entire body was contoured with interesting ridges and bulges and planes. This close she could smell him, a subtle spicy scent that managed to convey unabashed maleness and warmth despite what seemed to be a rather low body temperature. The man held himself in control. Unlike her. Gritting her teeth, she ignored the rush of heat to her cheeks and moved faster to disguise the telltale trembling of her hands.

"Turn around," she commanded.

Slowly, he did.

Despite the heat in his gaze, his mouth was tipped into a mocking smile, as if he knew how affected she was by touching him. What he didn't know—*couldn't* know—was how confused she was by her reaction. He made her feel . . . restless. Edgy. Vulnerable.

She hated it.

As such, she hated *him*.

Methodically, she frisked him from the front, delving between his denim-clad legs to make sure he wasn't packing more than nature had provided.

He grunted slightly and said, "Keep that up and you might find more than you want, princess."

His accent was clipped and tidy—upper-crust British. Despite herself, her gaze shot to his.

"Don't call me that," she said automatically, just before she found the gun tucked into a sleek holster concealed inside his waistband.

She pulled it out, and the sight of the Luger didn't surprise her. The well-made weapon suited him. Swiftly, she slipped it out of his holster and into the front of her own waistband.

The only other time she'd seen a Luger was when she'd delivered a package to Pablo, the leader of Devil's Crew, another street gang, and he'd insisted on inspecting the contents before he paid. He'd told her the guns had been stolen from some Richie Rich who liked fancy cars as well as fancy guns. When he'd asked her what kind of car she drove, she'd told him the truth. None. She'd only been fourteen at the time.

Even so, her youth hadn't stopped her from fighting the gang leader when he'd decided to inspect more than the package she'd delivered. All she'd gotten for her trouble was a beating and the ugly scar on her face.

To her, big and male was synonymous with power and violence.

"I'm not going to hurt you," the man in front of her said softly, as if he'd read her mind. "If you'll listen to me, I can help you, Ana."

The fact he knew her name shocked her . . . and scared her even more. "Fuck you," she snapped without meaning to. Swearing was an old habit, one she'd fought hard to break, but sometimes it came out. When she was angry . . . when she felt threatened . . . the tough girl inside her lost control, cursing and spitting and speaking Spanish in an effort to protect herself despite the fact it merely revealed how vulnerable she really was.

How weak.

She bit her lip, furious that he'd sensed her fear. Furious that his offer of help made her easily long for things she couldn't possibly have.

She'd gotten soft. Too soft. And once again she was paying the price. The only question was how high the price would be this time.

"Move." She gestured with her gun. "Face the wall." He had her so rattled she was second-guessing herself. She needed to frisk him again. Make sure she hadn't missed anything the first time.

He merely stared silently at her, and she forced herself to snap, "Now."

Unbelievably, he practically rolled his eyes just before he obeyed, cursing when she suddenly shoved him face-first against the brick; Eliana Garcia, gang member, was quickly chipping away at the civilized, respectable woman Ana had been trying to become.

But instead of retaliating, he waited while she frisked him yet again. When she was done, when he failed to make a move on her, she relaxed slightly. "Face me."

As he did, she saw the slight trickle of blood now dripping from a cut on his forehead. She felt a momentary pang of guilt. Along with it came the strange temptation to wipe the blood away and kiss the wound better. To kiss *all* his hurt away. Hurt she somehow sensed was there.

Which was beyond ridiculous. Like one of those tear-jerker movies where the love of a good woman saved some useless son of a bitch.

He didn't need her to wash his freakin' pain away. He needed to know who was boss. Besides, she didn't take care of anyone but herself anymore. It was better that way. Safer.

Instinctively, she gripped her gun tighter while he leaned back against the wall and crossed his arms over his chest, no longer smiling but watching her with an intensity that made her shiver.

"You've been trailing me since yesterday," she said, "and not just because you like my coffee. *¿Porqué?*"

At her lapse into Spanish and the thickening of her accent, Ana clenched her teeth, then deliberately modulated her voice so it was once again white-bread Americana. "Why are you following me?"

He smiled again, as if her speaking Spanish had amused him.

Embarrassment washed over her and she wavered, accidentally lowering the gun. "Answer me, *bastardo*—"

In a blur of movement, he grabbed her wrist, wrenched the gun from her hand, flipped her to the ground, and covered her body with his much larger one.

Reflexively, she struck out, striking him in the face before he pinned her arms and his body simply weighed her down. Damn it, she'd known it had been too easy. He'd set her up. And the way he'd moved . . . Faster than anything she'd ever seen before.

But oddly enough, he had his body braced so his full weight wasn't on her. As if he wanted her pinned but not hurt.

As if he was taking care of her.

Breathing hard, she stared into his mesmerizing face. His scent would be all over her, she thought absently. When he shifted, rubbing his lower body against her, she blinked at the unexpected warmth that flooded her. He was cold, yet he made her feel so good. So hot. Literally. For another crazy second, she wanted to grab either side of his face, pull him closer, and kiss him.

Ah Dios. She was losing it.

He tsked. "It was your f-bomb that finally got to me, you know. Normally, you hold back. You don't have to. Your cursing. Your use of Spanish. I like it. I *more* than like it. I just had to see if you felt as good as you look. As you sound."

Again, that dazzling smile. The British perfection in

the way he modulated his words. Those cold eyes. Danger emanated from him like a flashing red light, while charm oozed from him like honey.

He leaned closer and whispered. "Lucky me. You feel even better than I'd anticipated." When she failed to respond, he raised a brow. "What? I've rendered you speechless? Or are you just holding back again? I told you I'm here to help. That starts with offering you a job."

Now *that* she hadn't been expecting. She snorted and shifted underneath him, working to twist her way out from under his weight. The intoxicating feel of her limbs rubbing against his made her want to move slower. To relish the contact.

Instantly, she ceased her attempts to get away from him.

"I'm not stupid or gullible—" she began.

"No. In fact, Téa believes you're extremely smart. One of the smartest she's ever worked with."

Ana went rigid with hurt. Téa—a woman she'd thought was the closest thing she had to a friend—had sent him here with no warning? "Please get off me," she whispered when what she really wanted to do was scream. Cuss. In Spanish *and* English.

He kept his gaze locked on hers for several seconds, then said, "As you wish." Pushing himself to standing, he held out a hand to help her up.

She ignored him and scrambled to her feet, immediately backing several steps away. "How do you know Téa? Why did she—"

"Ana!"

Ana jerked when she heard Paul, one of her employees at the coffee shop, call her name, but she didn't take her eyes off the man. "I'll be right there," she shouted back.

The man in front of her didn't bat an eye.

She shook her head. "Téa misled you. I don't want anything from you."

"Not even information about your sister?"

Her heart stopped beating and for a moment the world around her blurred. She fought against the wooziness, focusing on the man's face. Excitement tickled the back of her throat and sent a buzzing up her spine.

Ana hadn't seen her sister, Gloria, for seven years, not since Ana had tried to jump them both out of Primos Sangre. Gloria had only joined the gang after returning from living with her grandparents. Ana had barely recognized her. Gloria had been angry. Distant. Wanting her sister's company one minute and hating it the next. After the shooting, she'd written Ana in prison, making it abundantly clear she blamed Ana for her injury and never wanted to see her again.

Had Gloria changed her mind? Had she sent this man to tell her that? A wash of excitement shot through her. Buoyed her. Maybe the stranger that had returned from living with her grandparents had finally turned back into the loving sister Ana remembered. Without even realizing what she was doing, she stepped closer. "You know Gloria?"

"I know about her."

"But did Gloria send you to find me?" she asked, hope reducing her voice to a whisper.

"No."

Disappointment. Suspicion. Dismissal. All cut through the excitement and hope, scattering them to the wind.

Nothing had changed. As such, this man had nothing she needed.

As if he could read her mind he said, "I told you, I'm here to offer you a job."

"I'm not interested in anything you're offering." Slowly, her eyes never leaving him, she retrieved her gun, tucked it into her waistband right next to his, covered them with her sweater, and started walking backward toward the cafe entrance.

"I'm quite fond of my gun, you know," he called out.

"It's mine now."

"It's also a violation of your parole for you to carry a firearm."

That made her freeze, but only for a second. She turned and walked to the coffeehouse door, her steps slow and lethargic. Over her shoulder, she muttered, "So tell my parole officer. Téa always knows where to find me."

Ty sighed as Ana walked back into her coffeehouse. She moved fast and loose, as if tackling a guy in an alley and pointing a gun at him was par for the course. He supposed given her background, it was like riding a bike—you never forgot how, not when your very survival was at stake. But that didn't mean she hadn't been shaken up by their encounter.

She seemed to fit in well with the college crowd she served. In fact, in her uniform of short tees and tight jeans, she could have been a student herself. She worked. She went home. She kept to herself.

But she wasn't happy with her life. Far from it. She'd simply convinced herself she couldn't have more. Sometimes, however, her true nature came through despite her best attempts to hide it.

Soon after he'd arrived in Seattle, Ana had ceased to be a fuck fantasy. The hot ex-gang member with the checkered past turned out to be a woman to admire. She kept her distance, but she was hardworking and good to her employees. He'd also been right about her smile. She didn't use it often, but when she did, her hotness ratcheted into heart-stopping beauty.

His surveillance had also alleviated any lingering con-

cerns he'd had about her refusing to do what they
wanted. Because as hard as she tried to keep herself
apart from others, she clearly longed for the type of connections she didn't allow herself.

He'd seen how she'd stared longingly at the couple
playing footsie in the corner of her coffee shop. How
she'd stared at two women at the grocery store, arm in
arm, obviously loving sisters. And how she'd helped a
frail young man with MS across the street; she had
watched him walk down the block until he turned the
corner and disappeared from view.

Over the past few weeks, his protective instincts had
kicked in. So many times, he'd wanted to go to her.
Wrap his arms around her. Comfort her. But of course
he hadn't. Because she would have fought him, yes, but
also because his hunger had grown almost unbearable.

When she'd confronted and challenged him, he'd
managed to hang on to his control, but just barely.
He'd known she was waiting for him in the alley and
he'd been prepared for her to touch him, even if it was
simply to disarm him. Although he'd allowed himself to
touch her back, he'd done so with ruthless restraint.
He'd led Ana to believe he was just a strong human
rather than a hungry vampire lusting after her blood
and her body. His sheathed fangs ached the way his dick
did, longing to penetrate and take everything from her:
her sweet blood and her complete surrender.

Once again he reminded himself it wasn't going to
happen. No matter how he admired her, and no matter
how she made him feel, she was a job and that was all
she could ever be.

He took out his cell and punched in Carly's number.

"You found her?" Carly's voice was husky. Feminine.
It was flat-out sexy—deliberately so—and he couldn't
help compare it to the gravelly, clipped speech that Ana
had used, her occasional melodic slip into Spanish aside.

Despite the sentiment behind her words, the flow of them combined with the touch of her body had made him hard, harder than the brick wall he'd been pressed against. The intensity of his desire as well as his decision not to push her too far—yet—had been the only reasons he'd remained against that wall. Despite carrying an illegal gun, Ana had turned her life around. He didn't want to take that away from her. And she had no reason to hurt him unless he gave her one. Besides, it wasn't as if one of her bullets could kill him anyway.

As far as he knew, nothing could.

"She's not going to be as easy as the others," he said in response to Carly's question.

"I wouldn't say the others have been easy."

"She's good. Even managed to get my gun."

"Right," Carly answered, her tone laced with the knowledge that if Ana had gotten Ty's gun, it was because he'd let her do it. Just like he'd let her spot him watching her in the first place. "Did she shoot you?"

"No, she did not shoot me. She cursed me, though. In Spanish. Something that seemed to bother her." It had certainly bothered him, but only because he'd liked it. Too much.

He closed his eyes and replayed her words, enjoying the way it made him think of heat and skin and sweaty, slippery silk sheets. With her golden skin, cinnamon eyes, and dark hair, he could easily picture her spread beneath him, begging him for release as he crooned back to her in her native tongue:

Todavía no. Not yet.

Un poco más largo. A little longer.

Dé a mí. Give to me.

He bit back a groan.

Give to me.

Even now his dick twitched, ready to get busy, ready to immerse itself in Ana's warmth.

He couldn't have her. Not sexually. Not in ways that might involve her heart as well as her body. And that made him angry.

It fucking made him want to kill someone.

Thankfully, Carly seemed oblivious to his internal struggle. "Excellent," she said. "You're right about that, she hates it when she speaks Spanish. She's trying to deny who she is—who she was—but even after all these years she can't. She's still the tough little girl from the Bronx."

"Yes. The little girl packs quite a punch, too." Raising a hand, Ty rubbed at his mouth, grinning when he saw the blood. She might not be able to kill him, but she sure as shit could make him bleed.

"Was that before or after she got your gun? Pity. I know how fond you are of it."

His silence just seemed to amuse her. True to form, she pounced on it.

"Oh my. Are you saying you can't handle this one?" she purred.

God, he hated Carly sometimes. Hated her bitch-on-steroids act. Hated the necessity to partner with her at all. But she hadn't always been like this. Years ago, as a fellow newbie agent with the FBI, she'd been good at her job but she'd had a gentle side, too. That part of her had long been quashed. And now? Sure, she'd helped Ty and Peter when they'd needed her most, but her assistance had been more about using them than saving them. Carly was doing what she needed to adjust to her new life, part of a team but very much alone. Just like him.

Ty glanced in the direction Ana had disappeared. "No," he said, this time letting a trace of humor leak into his voice. "I can handle her. I'll just have to be a little more direct, that's all."

"You don't have authority to reveal what you are, Ty," Carly snapped. "Not yet. We have one month until the leaders of Salvation's Crossing attend the Hispanic Community Alliance fund-raiser, and we need Ana fully invested before we show our hand."

"I have no plans to tell her I'm a vampire right now. But she still has my gun, and I have no intention of letting her think she can take anything from me and just walk away."